THE JOURNAL

OF

ALBION

MOONLIGHT

BY KENNETH PATCHEN

COLLECTED POEMS
DOUBLEHEADER
IN QUEST OF CANDLELIGHTERS
SELECTED POEMS
THE JOURNAL OF ALBION MOONLIGHT
WONDERINGS

The JOURNAL OF ALBION MOONLIGHT

KENNETH PATCHEN

THIS BOOK
IS
FOR
MIRIAM

The
Journal
OF
Albion
Moonlight

MAY 2 The angel lay in a little thicket. It had no need of love; there was nothing anywhere in the world could startle it—we can lie here with the angel if we like; it couldn't have hurt much when they slit its throat.

The evening slowly turns to black stone and the hammer of God chips at the sky, making stars. A child stands on the road watching us; upon her forehead is the yellow brand of this plague-summer. She waves to us and her hand, like a withered, white

1

claw, falls to the ground; the fingers unclench once, then relax—I stuff the hand into my pocket, and we hurry on.

Very well. We knew we had no other course but to get away with all attainable speed. A light rain had fallen in the night, and morning brought the drizzle to storm proportions. Our coats were wet through as we sogged out of New York on the first leg of our trip. That a great distance separated us from our goal we knew; that we were in danger of destruction at any hour of the day and night we knew; what we did not know was how near madness we would be; how alone; how defenseless: how beset we were with what we had heard, with what we had been taught—this, especially, we did not know.

My idea was to travel along rivers whenever it was feasible to do so. Notwithstanding this intention, we saw no water today. We camped for the night in a little clearing about fifty yards from the highway, near a filling-station. About three in the morning, Jetter, who is my friend more than any of the others, complained of a pain in the back of his head. I managed to transfer the revolver from his pack to my own.

MAY 4 🚶 Yesterday we were set upon by great, ugly-tempered dogs. Two we shot, scattering the rest. In the evening we held conference on the best manner by which to defend ourselves against these surly brutes, for the forest we were entering was known to abound with them. Shooting seemed the only practical method of defense, yet we knew it unwise to have guns in our hands. We decided, at last, to arm ourselves with clubs, which were easy come-by in the thickets of birch and pine. Thus protected we advanced, expecting momently to be attacked; but the dogs did not show themselves, though we heard their vicious threats on all sides. The hours passed without unique incident.

Then today we knew a different hazard, more terrible, more difficult of solution. This I cannot speak of directly now. We must run our natural chances with this thing.

He was the Word that spake it;
He took the bread and brake it;
And what the Word did make it,
I do believe and take it.

MAY 5 🚶 All are agreed that our progress has been good.

A boy of twelve has joined us. He is large, with big, loose hands which are steady on arms made heavy by hard work. His shoes are in fair condition, though his clothing is little better than rags. I asked him about himself; he was silent—not out of suspicion, I think—silence was his way of showing dignity. Poor kid, he has little else left. His shoes are stiff with sweat; his feet have obviously done many miles in them. But he was unwilling to say where his home had been. Jetter began by calling him Jack, and, since we know no other name for him, Jack it will be.

The forest was very beautiful in the morning. Birds of innumerable varieties gladdened our hearts with their song.

We stopped to eat at mid-day under an enormous oak. I was seized with an impulse to laugh and wave my arms about. It was a moment sharp with inner expressions. I shared my cheese with Billy Delian, whom I distrust and despise. He took the food in his fingers eagerly enough, but instead of eating it at once as I expected, rammed the whole piece into the pocket of his filthy coat.

The knowledge that we are being followed is like a stick with which we are forced to beat each other. We have a cancerous fear of our own species.

At nightfall we heard the dogs again. Why do they restrain themselves? They do not fear us. Is there something nearby that causes them to hold back? We *feel* it, too.

MAY 6 🚶 There was a low rumble ahead of us as we set out today. Guns?

MAY 7 🚶 Just as I got started on my journal last night, Carol came into my tent and seemed reluctant to leave. Why am I self-conscious about writing of Carol?

We sat together (odd that together is to get her) for what seemed a long time in the dim light from the candle and finally she said, "Do you remember the first time we met?"

I told her that I did.

"Do you regret any of it?"

"All of it."

"I'm sorry," she said quietly, trying to keep the hardness out of her voice.

"Yes. I regret all of it. I regret that it is gone; that we can't have any of it again. I regret that we ..."

"We have tonight."

"What can we do tonight?"

"We can sleep together," she said.

"But we can't sleep with the people we were when we first met," I told her, and I had no desire then.

The flap opened and Jetter entered, his face vague and somehow withdrawn.

"I shot Jack," he said.

I didn't ask why, I went out into the night and walked across the clearing to the fire where the others were gathered around the body and all the time I was saying, "Poor Jetter. The poor damn fool."

Jack was lying on his side, his mouth open as though to speak but no words would come and the front of his shirt had a dollar of blood on it.

"He won't live," Thomas Honey said.

I said he would and, kneeling, unlaced his shoes and took them off. His feet were bare and covered with sores. The shoes were of good leather.

Having done what I could for him, I went back to the tent and found Jetter reading *King Lear* to Carol.

MAY 8 🏃 The boy seems to be dying ...

4

MAY 9 🏃 There is talk of abandoning Jack. Three words he repeats over and over in his delirium: log, money, and hot.

The rumbling in the distance has ceased.

I am positive now that we are being watched.

It will be good to leave the forest.

I have not been able to determine where Jetter got the gun to shoot Jack: all deny knowledge of it. Jetter will say nothing, of course. He is not to blame for guns: I cannot condemn him.

━━

MAY 10 🏃 The lad is much improved today. Perhaps we can continue on our way tomorrow. I am terribly anxious to reach Galen, the town where we will meet Roivas. Is it possible that . . . but no, I controlled myself sufficiently to remain silent concerning the other thing. We are aware of the danger. Thank God there is this kind of hope.

I found a baby rabbit asleep in a thicket. What a delightful little creature!

What has become of the dogs? It is almost ghostly still in the woods. A pawing, outrageous quiet.

I saw Jack for a few minutes alone this afternoon. Billy Delian has been in almost constant attendance on him since his injury. Jack smiled when I told him I was sorry.

"Jetter had to shoot me," he said.

He has learned very quickly with us. Yet I could not bring myself to tell about Roivas. My description of the rabbit pleased him immensely.

We should be able to move on tomorrow.

━━

MAY 11 🏃 Jack is still not well enough for travel. Besides, Jetter has disappeared from the camp, and our loudest shouts served only to acquaint us with a troubling fact: the dogs have not given us up. Our din brought them barking to the very fringe of the clearing. How will Jetter manage to get back through that snarling pack?

5

MAY 12 ⚭ I have been lying here on my back in the sun. It is late afternoon and shadows pass and repass over this page with its brave scrawl. How naked I feel under the sky. What is there to say about any of this that can be said clearly and simply? Above all I want to be understood. They have said that I am an assassin . . . Carol is coming across the clearing to me, running— perhaps she has news. I shall write again later.

Carol says that the others have learned of my journal. She thinks that I am in danger from them. Poor devils, they do not realize with what effort of will I am trying to save them. But I must be quiet within myself.

(What is a 'thing'? All is movement, a flowing. How stupid it is to speak of the 'mind.' There is body; there is mind: they are mixed up together. Shakespeare with a hole in his sock will not write the sonnet of a Shakespeare with socks intact.

Who has bettered the statement of Francis Bacon?

"It is certain that all bodies whatsoever, though they have no sense, yet they have perception: for when one body is applied to another, there is a kind of election to embrace that which is agreeable, and to exclude or expel that which is ingrate; and whether the body be alterant or altered, evermore a perception precedeth operation; for else all bodies would be alike one to another."

"When one body is applied to another." How many creative spirits have lost themselves through application to the body of 'English Literature.')

Have you counted your toes this morning, little genius? The sea wind says you have nine. You can buy blue soap in the grocery on the corner of 8th Street and 4th Avenue. I am angry today. Carol insists on reading Anthony Trollope to Jack, and at that rate he will never get well.

I have thought it over, Jetter—what you told me tonight of your ideas about poetry. Why the large, messy rebellion against *form?* What do you care? What difference does it make? What does it matter that you don't like this sort of whistling in the dark? The whole thing is somehow silly anyway. But to get ex-

6

cited about it . . . Don't be a poet; be a prime minister, a garbage collector. The point is, I think, how many lays do you get? do your shoes fit well? These things are important. Don't show your bare ass about philosophy either. Leave that to the professional smart lads. Think enough and you won't know anything.

We moved on today.

MAY 15 🏃 Billy Delian has a nose all right. The dog, beating us to the punch with Jack. Him a nurse! It appears that our little "Jack" is a girl. But he hasn't gone along much with her, though she does seem to like him. Jetter must have known before any of us, since he shot her. Now we have Jackeen, a maiden lovely as the sun. She is the fountain that would mingle with the river, the maiden born to sweet delight; the one for whom the wind moves silently, invisibly; the human object so strange and high that two perfect loves reside in her heaven; Jackeen, ah, Jackeen! had we but world enough, and another time; thou art so sweet an enemy, coming into my courtship pure as my prayer; how can I be chaste except I ravish thee? Let me then to the book of thy body where death's fattened dialogue shall never be heard; enter these, my arms, for since thou thought it best not to dream all my dream, we can pretend the world away until tomorrow bang on the doors of us. What did we do until we met? You look nice in those old slacks, but in the raw you are Beauty herself. Christ, that you were in my arms, and the war over and done!

Our supply of tobacco is on the wane. We should be out of the forest by tomorrow. I saw a woodlark this evening, his wings sharp against the sky as a silver radiator cap. My stomach has not been good for the past days: this time Carol has had a go at reading Hemingway to Jack(een). Writes somewhat as I suppose a bull would—big chest and spindly legs.

MAY 16 🏃 We are not yet out of the wood, but a wonderful little river flows now along the road we have taken. The blood-mottled

7

trumpets of yellow monkey-musk seem to be making a music which is for our ears alone. How beautiful are these river flowers—the scarlet water-poppy, the blue cornflowers, the orange marigold, and the heart-breakingly lovely water-lilies—God! it is good to see them—magnolias floating serenely here like tiny swans. The hum of dragonflies . . . a huge old pike sunning himself under the branch of an overhanging willow.

About mid-day we decided to take advantage of the opportunity for a swim. Thomas Honey, once champion heavyweight boxer of the world, was first in the water. His roars of delight caused the trees to stand straighter. I watched Jackeen undress. Her breasts are like two little half-melons waiting for the bite of teeth that their sweetness may be released. The curve of her belly is enchanting; her shoulders . . . but Christ it's all of her, every softness, every curve, every dimple, her hair, her thighs . . . I am mad with the joy of wanting her. Carol's naked body is fine, too. She is queenly as she steps into the warm water. Jetter's eyes never leave her. It was surely only my imagination which caused me to think that Jackeen looked with something more than casual interest at the spectacular maleness of Thomas Honey.

People don't want to be healed. They want a nice juicy wound that will show well when they put neon lights around it.

Jetter paid me a visit in the evening and I asked him how he managed to get back to camp through the dogs. He refused to speak about this, though he did say that an old woman in the hills had warned him of great danger to our expedition.

Suddenly he said: "See that that young girl is kept out of my way."

"Why?" But I already knew.

"Because if I get the chance I'll kill her," he answered.

"Would that make things easier for you?"

"Not the way you mean."

"Then why must you kill her?"

He thought for a moment. "Do you know how many men are

8

being blown to bits in Europe every hour of the day, every hour of the night? . . ." His face was twisted, tortured.

"Yes, Jetter, I know. But I don't see . . ."

"God damn it! you don't see—you don't see—what do I care whether you see or not! How will my killing someone change all that killing—that's what you don't see. Well, it does change it— it blots it out for me. I lie awake at night and think—now, just this minute, hundreds of men, no, not men, kids, kids just out of school, kids with girls, kids with the the first fuzz of hair on their cheeks—you blind fool, you dirty blind fool! don't you see now?" Sobs shake him. His hands tremble.

"I'm sorry. Better get some sleep . . ."

"You're sorry! Get some sleep! Sure, we're all sorry. We walk around, we get up in the morning, we go to bed at night, we eat, we make love, we go ahead with all of it—we don't want to see that other thing, we don't have the guts to want to know about that—then later we'll wave flags, we'll shout, we'll sweat up a big hate—but I can't—I can't! I tell you, I can't shut it out—it's worse not seeing it, not seeing them actually die, to hear their screams, to have the blood run over your hands—that's the real hell—I wish to God I could grab up a rifle and run along beside other men with rifles—to feel their terror, to share it with them, to have someone to share mine—but something won't let me— maybe I can't hate enough, maybe I'm too strong to take that way out—the only escape from war is to become a soldier, to lose all touch with your own identity, to become part of one huge, quivering mass of fear and horror—but to face it alone, to have principles, to believe—that's what I'm trying to say, *to believe*, to have even one belief left—no! it can't be done, no one could stand up under that . . ." I see that his nails are biting into his hands.

"But everything you say . . . I mean . . ."

"You mean why should I want to kill someone."

"Well, not only that . . ."

"Yes, only that. You think I've lost my mind, that I've cracked up, that I'm obsessed."

9

"No, Jetter, you seem more sane than any of us, but . . ."

"Of course, 'but' . . . you say I'm sane, but you don't mean that. You're warning me. Well, it's too late for your warnings, *because I am sane*. How can I shut out the war? How can I save myself from putting a gun to my head? You'd like to know! You want the secret! Well, here it is: *take the murder out of your head.* How? It's so damn simple. When I kill Jackeen, I'll do it in the bloodiest, most horrible way I can devise—for one intense, glorious moment I won't think murder—I'll have it right in my hands —it won't be in my head! God! I hope she screams in absolute torment—she must die in agony—I can handle that. Then at night I'll be able to think about it; I can say: 'I willed that. It was my doing. I stood alone above her poor bleeding body.' O God! they won't be able to enact all their murders before my eyes then . . . how I see the young kids crawling along holding in their guts . . . and their eyes looking at me, pleading, begging me to help them . . ."

At this moment Carol entered the tent.

"Someone just shot at Jackeen," she said. Jetter's face contorted in rage.

"Who? Who did?" he demanded.

"The shot was fired from the woods. It was not done by any of us," Carol said quietly.

"And Jackeen . . . ?" Jetter shouted.

"She was not hurt."

I sat staring into the night after they had gone.

The question is not: do we believe in God? but rather: does God believe in us? And the answer is: only an unbeliever could have created our image of God; and only a false God could be satisfied with it.

MAY 17 🏃 All last night our camp was in an uproar; shortly after the final lantern was darkened, a single bark issued from the forest, then another, and another, until the whole devil's chorus was upon us. There was no moon. Why should the dogs follow with such persistence?

Joe Gambetta was drowned yesterday. His body was found caught in snags by the riverside. There was an ugly bruise on his right temple.

We buried him beneath the shipwreck of a great oak, and on a piece of cardboard printed: Thou who art in Heaven, accept this, Thy servant, Joseph Gambetta, who has thus been given his day, and whose debts were never forgiven; whose heart never saw evidence that Thy will would be done on earth. What a sorry kingdom was his.

MAY 18 🦌 The first communication from Roivas! After informing us that he would be unable to appear in Galen during the period set for our meeting, he gave warning of an exact, definable danger in the following terms: Be on guard at all times for the appearance of one who will indicate himself in many disguises; he is known variously as Alpheus Williams, Lysander Butler, Hiram Cutler, John R. Berdan, Benjamin Hazard, Frederick McPherson, Birdsall Steele, Daniel Ferry, Orris Butterfield, Darius Howe, Fitz Roy Porter, Nelson Barlow, Francis Steele, Christopher Grant, John Bellrope Hull, Kenton Alston, Eppa Rust, Braxton Cockrell, Robert Early, Jubal Ranson, Clayton Barfield, Jefferson Baze, Macon Chance, Benajah Boyles, Noah Prosser, Mercer Groat, Isaac Chapman, Jaspar Wifelove, Zara Bull, Lemuel Stone, Albert Coffin, Castlemoor May, Oliver Crewe, Cyrus Spermilk, Reuben Kellog, Barr Kinsman, Bradford Plimpton, Norton Meadow, Carndon Newpurse—but you may discover him by this (which he cannot change): the little finger of his right hand is missing.

MAY 19 🦌 I have forgotten my mask, and my face was in it.

11

We have come at last to a huge hotel where we may rest and refresh ourselves. Its windows front the river on one side; on the other, stretching away as far as eye can see, lies a great open space pitted by what would seem to be great shell craters. The proprietor tells us that within memory of the oldest resident no human has ever walked across this strange plain.

Provisions are brought down the river by canoe from Galen. We plan to remain here for a time.

By great good fortune my room adjoins that of Jackeen, and we are separated by only a latch which cannot be fastened. I did not learn this until a few hours ago. Silently, holding a small candle, I presented myself at her bed. She was asleep. Her breath came even and untroubled. Quietly I pulled down the covers and gazed in rapture at her body in its child's nightgown; presently I lifted the garment and I could see the way her thigh flowed in exact grandeur into the pocket of her side. I put my hand on her and she opened her eyes and smiled at me. I begged her to let me but she said not now not now maybe another time but not tonight and I kissed her on the mouth and left her.

Returning to my room I found Carol. We went to bed and it was good and later her head on my arm breath coming hard running near sleep not caring about the world much and the strangeness of our position adding interest rather than terror after our long wandering in the wood she asked me if I had ever lied to her and I said no and I opened my eyes in the dark very wide and winked fondling the stump where my finger had been.

In snowy couples the swans sleep.

There is something horrible.

There is something to turn us mad.

The water comes up around us. But it is not water. It is feeling your hand but you won't say I have a hand because you cannot believe it. I know this because there is a habit in me. My habit is love.

Suppose for a moment you are a dog looking at me. I will not kick you. Don't slink away. You see, we are all on the water but there is no need to build a boat because it would be burnt in an instant. I know history. There are many names in history but none of these names talks because of the water which fills them.

A man walks across the fields beneath my window. The left side of his face is bright yellow.

My mother took me into the country. I saw a tiny horse asleep under a willow. We did not take him home.

The hand of someone moves over my throat. I have no fear. My sex is quiet. A whale with a sad smile swims past me. The waves are red as blood. The human race has bled to death here. A great steel coffin churns through the water. There are buildings falling. I am cold. Put your arms around me.

‖‖

JUNE 5 ▸ Hitler hurled 700,000 men in a drive on Paris at dawn today. In direct frontal attack, 45 German divisions, supported by 1,000 dive bombers, 2,250 tanks and 15,000 motorized vehicles, struck at French positions on a 110-mile front stretching across northern France from the English Channel to Laon.

‖‖

JUNE 6 ▸ I have been waiting in the shadow for you.
A bus passes.
The pavement is wet.
You are an hour late already.

Yes, this is mud. I hold my rifle like a club in my hands. Just over the hill they are waiting. Their uniforms are old and tattered. A light rain is falling. No star shines in all the sky. Suddenly I feel something warm and thick moving down my cheek. Through the head—a good aim, I must admit. The wind blows through the hole. Then I understand: they have left me in the field for I was useless to them. They have no work for me now. A tiny mouse begins to gnaw at my hand.

"Do you believe that man can triumph?" asks Joseph Gambetta.

"The question is not clear," I reply.

"Is there hope for the world?"

Now I have a question indeed. I answer gravely, in a quiet, unhurried way:

"Yes, Joseph, there is hope."

"Do you see that small rabbit there?" he demands.

"Yes, certainly I see it."

"Have you seen it before, Albion?"

"Yes."

"Where?"

"It is the same rabbit I saw in the thicket outside of Galen—in the forest." By God!

"Does this surprise you?" Joseph Gambetta is grinning in the fashion of phantoms when they are pleased.

"No . . . I can't say it does," I answer, trying to bring the matter to some conclusion.

"What are you doing now?" he persists.

"Why . . . I . . ."

"You won't tell me you didn't know she was here?" he says, laughing.

"I have been here all the time," Jackeen murmurs. "You should not come to my bed—the others will find out."

"Let them, darling," I say, stroking her hair which falls like a brown cloud on the pillow.

"But there is no time to be wasted," she murmurs. "Roivas may already be waiting at the meeting place."

"I have seen Roivas," I say.

She beats me with her fists. "You disgusting liar . . . !"

"But wait . . . I have seen him. He was walking through the dogs with the ease of a ship through water."

"Could you see his face?"

"No."

"Then how do you know it was he?"

"Because the birds were pecking at his eyes."

14

"What makes you think anyone will understand that?" Joseph asks.

"I don't worry about that."

"You are playing high and mighty."

"I am telling the truth. Man has been corrupted by his symbols. Language has killed his animal."

"And you are resurrecting it?"

"No. It has never had an opportunity to live."

"What will you do about it?"

"I shall continue to ask How."

"How to what?"

"To the strange, unborn thing which is in all men."

"You'll be easy picking for the scoffers."

"I have no interest in that. I see men engaged in activities that would shame a grub under a rock. Their codes and ambitions leave me sick with disgust."

"You'd like to try your hand at being God."

"I'd like to try my hand at *being*."

I have armed myself against their weapons. To be so indolent that the flies will bury their dead on my eyelids. To sit on a beach and let the waves comb all thought of endeavor out of me. To live in such manner that I never make a single, blood-rotten dollar. To study history in order only to have it to forget. Books— all those big, fat-bottomed ashcans where men empty their lives.

I like the leopard. I don't like Benj. Franklin.

The great man fell asleep with open mouth in a room full of flies. From that day his work took a gloomy turn. The man was Marcel Proust and the flies were Tommy and Winnie and Little Meg: all dead now.

⸻

JUNE 7 ⚜ The feeling of love for all beings! The days pass without blemish of any kind. How true it is that every man has his own level, his own geography. I am content to drink at my own lake, to walk on my own hills. How little I wish ill to anyone; yet, and this thought is never far from my mind, what frauds we practice on our neighbors—we permit no one into the web of flesh where we have our home—"There was never a better friend," we say, and we mean: "He never bothered me, nor I him." With every passing hour we retreat more deeply into ourselves; with each advancing moment the 'self' retreats from us—we are cemeteries where lie sleeping the millions of men who bear our name.

Spent the morning on my essay, 'A Pact With Eternity.' The idea of a split-soul has always attracted me. There is no fixed star in the firmament of the spirit.

What are values? Is what happens in a grasshopper's head a 'value'?

Today I went into the hills. The sun was shining. I sat down beside a stream and a cow approached to drink. She had a good look in her eyes and I felt lonely.

"What is it like to be a cow?" I asked.

"Why should I tell you?" she answered politely, dripping water from her spongy lips.

"I'm writing a book and I'd like to record your point of view."

"In that case," she said, "I'll tell you. Do you know the story of the wren and the mole?"

I was compelled to admit that I did not.

"Then the story of the grasshopper who fell in love with a water-lily—surely you know that?"

Again, no.

"Do you know why the little men in the grass are unable to eat barley?"

I shook my head.

"I can't explain anything to you," she said, and walked quickly back to a tree which mounted her after the fashion of husbands.

An amazing thing has happened; we cannot leave the inn. We cannot leave the inn! Today Jetter and I walked to the edge of

16

the river across from which is the great plain. I dipped my fingers in the water: a numbing shock threw me to the ground.

The river is charged!

Back we ran, yelling wildly. God's mercy—on the other three sides around, the dogs! In hundreds, thousands—sitting on their haunches looking at us—hot tongues snaking in and out of their mouths. We are trapped.

|||||||||||||||||||||||||||||||||||||||||||||||||||||||||||||||||||||||||||||||||||||||||||||||||||||||||||||||||||||||||||||||||

JUNE 14 ⚙ What are we to do? How will we get to Roivas? *We were not running away.* That must be understood. It was essential that we bring our message to the people who had lost hope in the world. It was our duty to go into the villages and cities—can't you understand! Our message was this: we live, we love you. Our religion was life. Flowers, brooks, trees . . . Now we are held here and the world will perish because no one is saying we love you, we believe in you.

WE BELIEVE IN YOU. THERE IS NO DANGER. IT IS NOT GETTING DARK. WE LOVE YOU.

We are prisoners from the world, we who wanted only to go into the world with our arms open to all of you.

There is food enough to last us a few days. After that . . .

|||||||||||||||||||||||||||||||||||||||||||||||||||||||||||||||||||||||||||||||||||||||||||||||||||||||||||||||||||||||||||||||||

JUNE 15 ⚙ What horror can be greater than an army of monstrous dogs—*led by a human intelligence.*

They do not bark now. They do not fight each other; there is no mating. They watch us. Their eyes light up the fields at night.

|||||||||||||||||||||||||||||||||||||||||||||||||||||||||||||||||||||||||||||||||||||||||||||||||||||||||||||||||||||||||||||||||

JUNE 16 ⚙ This morning the world ended; a miracle happened. Carol screamed, "Look! Across the river!"

We were all gathered at breakfast in the banquet room whose windows overlook the plain.

It came about as we watched. A great city moved into the plain.

17

It seemed to flow in like a river. How else can I describe it? There is the city. We can hear it. We can see the people moving about in the street and in their rooms. We who would go to the world: the world has come to us.

I look into a room in the slums. A man is beating a woman. Now he kisses her, and she returns his kiss. Children play in a little park. A city.

Literature is what you write when you think you should be saying something. Writing begins when you'd rather be doing anything else: and you've just done it.

||||||||||||||||||||||||||||||||||||||||||||||||||||||||||||||||||||||||||||||||||||||||||||||||||||||||||||||||||||||||||||||||||||||||||||||||||||||||||||||||||

JUNE 17 ⚔ FRANCE SURRENDERS.

The dogs watch us.

How easy it is to lose sight of one's objective. There was the three-cornered hat in the forest near Philadelphia. I made no mention of it in my journal that day because Carol wanted to wear it and I would not give her permission. My reason was excellent enough: the hat had once belonged to my grandfather who was a coal miner and I did not wish it profaned by any of us. Why should the trivial incident of the finding of this reminder of other times seem more important than all other events on our journey? Believe that my grandfather is standing at the pit-head ready to be lowered to the workings far under the earth. It is dawn and the year is 1862. A butterfly alights on the carbon lamp which is attached to his cap. The man makes an impatient gesture with his hand—away flutters the beautiful insect and grandfather enters the lift.

I am beginning to feel proud. Yesterday I was poring over some old papers in the attic and after a little time the hackles on the back of my neck went up—God! he made me happy, that nuzzly little buffalo holding out his hand through his eyes. I threw my arms around his neck and the wonderful cornmeal smell of him made me jump around the room in a new dance. Anything that pleases a man that much is really good. I don't mean your baby-ass snuffling over truth and beauty either. How much better the world would be without 'Art.' I can't expect you to understand this: are you an artist?

I took Mohammed upstairs and just as I got him in the room where the others were, he let all the water out of him. That's the way a buffalo meets people. He doesn't forget who he is—making buffalo water for all he's worth. Another thing I like about Mohammed is that when he looked out of the window and saw the armies fighting on the plain, he saw just that—no allegory for him—he looked out of the window and the cold lightning of the swords pleased his sense of reality. He had just that, a sense of what is *real*.

||||||||||||||||||||||||||||||||||||||||||||||||||||||||||||||||||||||||||||||||||||||||||||||||||||||||||||||||||||||||||||||||||||

JUNE 18 In response to a protest from Carol, I deleted all entries I had made for June 11, 12, and 13.

She objected to my explanation for Jackeen's motive in stabbing the innkeeper. (We have been unable to find his body.)

Jetter and Thomas Honey are wrestling on the bank of the river. Honey is stronger but his opponent is wiry and courageous. Carol, Billy Delian, and I are seated at a little distance watching a hill thronged with ants in combat—red ants and black. The generals stand importantly by as their armies tear legs and arms off one another. Presently, the larger red ants succeed in putting to rout their smaller, more numerous adversaries. My hand steals across to Carol's knee and we smile our happiness at being together. The wind blows up a rain and we seek shelter. Carol and I find an old hollow log where we can lie in peace away from the storm. My arms are around her; I press her body to me. She is soft and full and warm.

19

"Do you love me, Albion?" she whispers.

"Yes," I say, caressing her.

"Do you think people will understand your journal? Have you explained enough?"

"Can you think of anything I've omitted, Carol?"

"You haven't described our visit to heaven."

I feel a little stirring of anger but answer calmly enough: "What is there to tell?"

"You could tell of the war between the bearded and the unbearded angels. It was so funny to see them flapping their wings and rushing at each other." She laughs with pleasure.

"I am surprised that you saw any of it," I tell her, angry clear through now.

"Why . . . what can you mean, Albion?"

"You know damn well what I mean. Making your play for that big, overgrown boob of an angel before we were half in the place . . ."

"I did not! I only felt sorry for him—he seemed so lonely standing off by himself." She draws away as much as the log will allow.

"He certainly wasn't lonely once you got your peepers going on him."

"Oh, shut up. You make me sick." She scrambles out and runs back to the inn.

━━

JUNE 19 ⬛ Yesterday we walked across a large public park. I was in high spirits, humming an old song under my breath. At the drinking fountain, which was situated near an old, fire-trap pavilion, we met a small man who limped very badly. Later, after scouring the entire neighborhood, we discovered his daughter, a girl of seventeen. She was soliciting openly in the street. A sailor looked her over critically, then sauntered on, chewing gum. Tears came to my eyes. I called after her:

"Leah! Leah!" but she did not hear.

Walking back, Jackeen recited:

From the hag and hungry goblin
That into rags would rend ye,
 All the spirits that stand
 By the naked man
In the book of moons, defend ye,

That of your five sound senses
You never be forsaken,
 Nor wander from
 Yourselves with Tom
Abroad to beg your bacon.

With a thought I took for Maudlin,
And a cruse of cockle pottage,
 With a thing thus tall,
 Sky bless you all,
I befell into this dotage.

I slept not since the Conquest,
Till then I never waked,
 Till the roguish boy
 Of love where I lay
Me found and stript me naked.

The moon's my constant mistress,
And the lonely owl my marrow;
 The flaming drake
 And the night-crow make
Me music to my sorrow.

I know more than Apollo,
For oft, when he lies sleeping,
 I see the stars
 At mortal wars
In the wounded welkin weeping,

The moon embrace her shepherd,
And the queen of love her warrior,
While the first doth horn
The star of morn,
And the next the heavenly farrier.

With an host of furious fancies,
Whereof I am commander,
With a burning spear
And a horse of air
To the wilderness I wander;

By a knight of ghosts and shadows
I summoned am to tourney
Ten leagues beyond
The wide world's end—
Methinks it is no journey.

What matters now is to have time. The white lily grows black in the sun on the seventh day. This book cannot be written in the workshop—I wait for that one terrible hour when it shall burst into flames, all of it, my good and my evil, cleansed together, as my hand begins to write, and the heavens open and we enter together, you and I. But now the water moves over our heads—the hour is not yet at hand. A sleeper tosses in the next room. It is two-thirty in the morning. These are the first words I have set down in more than a week. Perhaps tonight I shall open. I cannot know what lies waiting in me; I am asking a stranger to speak. Come out! I say. Do not leave me alone in the shadow: I ask myself to come into this book, to walk upright as a god—I have closed no door; I have not failed to tear out any page which had anything foreign to my purpose on it. My purpose? it is nothing remarkable: I wish to speak to you.

I have such scorn of my wisdom. But something in me is wise. It knows when I labor to make people talk in my journal—the complete fraud of this: it is I who speak; out of no other mouth do the words come—I tell you that I shall be judged. I have brought into being people of my own size: Jetter, the careless murderer; Billy Delian, in whose useless heart treachery and betrayal lie; Thomas Honey, the physical man who has no endeavor worthy of his strength; Carol, the woman like any other; Jackeen, the visible body of man's desire on earth; Chrystle, the pure child who is in all of us—and I did this thing because I was afraid; I had to perform for you; I had to distract you from my failure— my failure to tell you what all of us are waiting so faithfully to hear. Because we do believe in God, you and I—I mean we believe in each other. Yes, the Son of Man—my son, and yours, not God's; because we made God and we are God.

I am not a voice crying in the wilderness. There is no winter here. No dark. No despair. The lights are going on in my house.

I shall not allow the President of the United States to enter here.

What dies in the nations, here shall find life. What shall have birth in your heart, kicks now in this womb.

My tree is a green tree. My father's ghost sings in its branches.

I was troubled, thinking: they will not trust me because I grew weary and told lies; they will not really listen because at times I became afraid and tried to clothe my spirit in Art; but I was a fool to think this—they can *feel* me coming out at them. They will understand that I must guard against total communication. I have no desire to go mad. You have no wish to learn things: you wish to know.

What a lonely thing it is, to write—and to spend the whole night writing (which is the plan in me) is a form of torture. My eyes will have burnt skin on them tomorrow; my hand will shake; my stomach will refuse to empty. Dogs with broken legs are shot; men with broken souls write through the night.

I have no telephone in the house now. Once I called a stranger in the early morning; I took the first number that fell under my eye in the phonebook. A young woman answered. I said: Do not be afraid. Keep your appetite—and I hung up. I am telling you that now.

Go to the devil! Drunks passing in the street, braying 'God bless America.' Indeed, you bastards, I'll bless you.

I never learned to cry properly as a child. I want to cry now. We are all so apart from each other. We never touch. I was never taught to touch another human being. No college in this big land has such a course: to *touch*, to place your hands on someone. How astonished men look urinating! they have it in their hands—an American cock, what is to be done about that! It may blow up on them! The mother of the African native shows him what is to be done, and the matter is ended; but the American male never quite understands what is expected of him. Cultures are lost for less than that. Certainly our literature, from Hawthorne down, demands a new approach to water-letting—Christ had little use for his whining, self-important maw—keep the mothers, both male and female, in the kitchen, is one of my orders. I'll be hungry later on—your eye on the soup! I'll try not to spoil my brew.

I smoke too much. I light a cigarette every time I want to touch someone. People do not want hands on them. They are afraid of the touch of their own hands. Some of you will hate my book, for I insist on touching you. Walt Whitman did not want to touch people; he wanted to paw over them. A man has a privacy and a woman has another privacy. He did not know this because he always wrote as though he stood in a public room, a sort of bath house where fat men massaged slim youths. He spent his time putting soap on the backs of schoolboys, but he never rubbed them clean. I do not say that he was a homo-sexual: no, he was a homeless-sexual. Americans run to this sin. They slap women on the back and offer cigars all around. And she—guileless female— is forever lifting her dress at the wrong time: be patient, not now, that can wait until we are alone in a room with the requisite bed —we are, you know, not monkeys in a zoo, conducting all our affairs with our pants down.

I do not walk in the slums of the city. Dostoievsky loved to walk

24

among the poor. He loved beggars. They made books for him. I hate the poor. Once again: I hate the poor. Oh yes, the kingdom of heaven—through the eye of the needle; but I have no use for their heaven, I could invent fifty better ones in a single day. I was born of the poor. I never had enough to eat. I never had decent clothes. I couldn't stomach it. I said: I won't be poor. I go hungry often enough now, but I am not 'of the poor.' I am richer than the richest banker. Because: I hate the poor *out of my love for them*. Until all men unite in hating the poor, there can be no new society. Stalin loves the poor—without them he could not exist. The revolutions of the future must be directed not against the rich but against the poor. To be poor means to be blind, demoralized, debased. The poor have been the slop-pails of capitalism, repositories for all the filth and brutality of a filthy, brutal world. Do not liberate the poor: destroy them—and with them all the jackal-Stalins that feast on their hideous, shrunken bodies. How the Church and the false revolutionaries draw together: love the poor—for they are humble. I say hate the poor for the humility which keeps their faces pressed into the mud. The poor are the product of a false and cruel society; but they are also the corner-stone of that society. Lift them to the stars; tell them to walk proudly on this earth: the cathedrals and broad roads were made by the labor of their hands; it is the duty of all true revolutionists not only to restore these things into their hands but also—and this is the key—to put them into their heads. Empty stomachs, empty heads: fill both with good food. Don't shove Peter the Great back into their throats.

Are you heavy laden? Throw off your load. Do you understand this? Your backs are bent under the junk of property, which you came by because of your fear. You were afraid to possess your soul, so you went by the wayside and acquired property. It has been said that property is theft: I say that property is murder. The hands of dying children reach up through your bread. You beat me with your stick. You made the war. Even now you take the side of murder: no one must have your money. Your dollars

25

become rifles: you will protect with the last drop of somebody else's blood what was never yours. You walk over my face. I am the poor. I am the one in whose house you live. It is my food you eat.

You leave
nobody else
without a bed

You make
everybody else
thoroughly at home
I'm
the only one
hanged
in your
halter

You've driven
nobody else mad
but me

I walked into a field. Snow was falling on the river. The black water took the white flakes in its mouth. I saw a paper cross floating there. Presently, while I stood in the cold, a woman approached and spoke to me. She said that I would die under angry hands, my last gaze on earth directed into the face of a strangler. She smiled then. But you will kill too, she said. We walked up a hill together. At the top, hidden by trees, stood a small house. We entered a dark room. A miserable little fire sputtered on the grate. I spent my last hour here, she said. For the first time I saw that her face was fleshless, eaten away. She advanced to my side and her fingers closed on my throat. I threw her off—dry bones clattering to the floor. Quickly I lighted a candle and looked about me. Three men sat in a corner away from the fire. A rusty machine

26

gun lay on the table before them. They were grinning as though a huge joke had been made. But their eyes were hard, watchful; and they were staring at something behind me. Swinging round, I saw a man entering at the door. He walked rapidly upon me— I felt his breath entering my mouth—for one moment I felt great pain, then I stood alone. He stirred inside me: I had a double brain and two hearts. A great light filled my eyes. Now you can utter the word that all men are waiting to hear, he whispered. I started to speak. The three men were no longer smiling. They were watching me as a bird watches a cat. I told them that I was seeking God. I said that I was God. I said that a beautiful fool had drawn a picture of God in a cave—in the cave known as Chartres. But that is a false God, I said—that is a God of murder and darkness. I told them that they were God. God . . . now what is *God?* You are God. I destroy that other God. I put all of us in His place. I am a revolutionist. I want this fraud to end. I am calling you to arms. I want no false Gods before me. I am the one Hitler cannot silence. I am Hitler's defeat and death. God is talking to you. God orders that Hitler die, that his bones be scattered in the field, that his eyes be pecked out by birds. And you are Hitler. You have allowed a murderous God before me. You have slunk through the darkness with the skull of a monster in your hands. I tell you now: I will have no more talk of Christ and Joseph and Mary. They are images in a vicious tale which gluts on the animal blood of our race. Perhaps we shall have to learn to speak again in a new way. Our images are fat with the grease of old caves where madmen sit thinking out new horrors—our art, religion, society . . . where is the sunlight! where is the power and the glory! not on the cross with that mewling milk-sop who knew only to turn the other cheek—to whom, You Idiot! Thought you were pretty sly . . . of course, of course, turn the other cheek! That's your Christianity —that's all of it—Father, why hast Thou forsaken me! We have forsaken you because you were a weakling who ran out on your own people. We'll have no more such Christs. I am a revolutionist. I believe in my own people. I tell them to strike before even their

27

first cheek can be shattered. Down, Christ! back into the cave . . . gnaw the bones of your martyrs—the dirty sonsofbitches, putting shit all over themselves in your name—I'll have no more of that! I demand that the body of no one be degraded. It's into the sun with us! We'll learn to talk joyously; we'll smash all those hideous, befouled images . . . God, huh? That's all done and over with: kapoot.

I'll make myself some coffee now. Will you have some?

I am completely without fever. I am cold, hard. I am burning like fire in a block of ice. I know the meaning of pain, but I do not use my pain to protect myself: it is necessary for me to rule this body—to burn away the pig. Nothing else in me is accident: my touch, the way my eyes see in and out—only the body might have been another's. I am an event among men. *I can be absolutely rational.* I can refuse all your institutions. I can move away just out of range. I can perfect targets that laugh at your guns. I am outside the law. I will have my revenge. I am cooked by my anger . . . at The Last Supper, see! it's my body they bring in—but nobody can get this fist down them—they aren't able to stuff themselves on my flesh. Help! Jesus . . . I am sinking into the water. I am afraid! I am bleeding! Snow is falling on the river. It is getting dark. I have squandered my talents. I have blown out my lanterns one by one. I have been proud . . . sick of my pride . . . treacherous . . . a lame child . . . a blind bug dying in the flame. Poor devil, beat your breast; call down insults on your fathers; kiss your own quivering ass; swing your balls like cow bells above your head; expose yourself in the marketplace; spew up your guts for the inspection of the least passer-by; vanish like water—like snow falling on a dark river . . .

Albion . . .

What! Who spoke!

Be quiet. Don't be afraid.

Who are you?

That doesn't matter.

What do you want of me?

I want to warn you.

Warn me? Against what?

Against yourself. You must not ask forgiveness.

I don't understand.

You must instead forgive them.

Forgive them . . . ? the dirt . . . the filth . . . the murder . . . ?

Yes, all those things—and one other. You must forgive them for enduring you.

For enduring me . . . ?

Yes, Albion. It is their duty to kill you.

Who are you?

I am the one you call Roivas.

Roivas!

Do not pretend. You knew me at once. You are playing for time, trying to deceive me as you have deceived the others.

Why should I wish to deceive you?

Because I am aware of what you are trying to do.

What am I trying to do?

You would invent a new crime against the human spirit.

But I don't understand . . .

That's why they should kill you.

Are you on their side then?

No. I am not.

On mine?

You have no side. You are out beyond the last shore-light . . . unknown black water stretches all around you.

Should I go back?

Do not sneer. You cannot go back.

I am shaking with laughter, Roivas.

You are shaking with fear.

What do I fear?

You fear them.

Should I not fear them? You said that they must kill me.

They cannot. You have managed cleverly to remain hidden.

That's a damn lie. I have concealed nothing.

[A silence.]

What is Galen?

Galen is Paradise.

Who is Jetter?

He is the crippled gunman.

What do you mean by that?

Jetter is modern man—the killer demanded by the State.

Why crippled?

Because before the State can get him to do its murder, the State must first kill his soul.

How is this done?

My journal will tell you.

Billy Delian is Judas, I suppose?

Bosh! Billy Delian is Hitler.

That's a pretty idea.

Thank you, kind sir.

And Carol? Not Beatrice, is she?

No, not Beatrice; she is Dante's wife—his good bedfellow.

Why not Bach's?

Because I don't like Bach.

Joseph Gambetta puzzles me. What do you mean by calling him a 'phantom'?

Just that. He is a phantom.

Am I right in thinking that Jackeen is the Blessed Virgin?

I don't like paradoxes. Jackeen is every woman that every man has ever wanted—and couldn't have.

Thomas Honey is a strange character.

He is the easiest of all. Thomas Honey is Beethoven.

Ah, I can see that.

You can see anything once you've been told it's there to see.

There is one thing I can't see.

Yes . . . ?

Who are you?

I am Albion Moonlight.

Yes, I know that . . .

Then you know who I am. All this rot about who is what! Why must you look for bed-time story significances in everything? . . . Take what I give you . . . Billy Delian is no more Hitler than you are . . . Beethoven was Beethoven and Thomas Honey is Thomas Honey . . . my people have meaning in themselves; why try to lard over that meaning by imagining that they are somebody else? When Hitler comes into this record he will come as Hitler. I want that understood: things are what I say they are. If any footnotes are needed, I shall be the one to supply them.

You haven't said what I am . . .

Don't you know who you are?

You imply that I am God.

Well, are You?

I am indeed the voice of God.

[Somewhere a disemboweled horse screams like a woman in labor.]

And I denounce you, Albion Moonlight!

Then you are not God.

I want to go to sleep now but this must not be lost. I am tired. My back aches and a numbness creeps up my legs. I am sorry for the men who are dying tonight—Germans, English . . . *Sorry.* I cannot believe that this slaughter is going on. I see men walking about the streets. Their shoes hit the pavement exactly as they always do. They look at the trees and passing automobiles. They are not made of wood! And women . . . dresses all fitting blue and red and snug around their breasts, beautiful things—looking into store windows, hitching up their stockings. They ask people questions in America. Democracy, Gallup polls. Do you support the war? *Do you support the war!* It is not possible.

No one anywhere ever said anything worth a twopenny damn. No one ever painted a picture. No one ever made a symphony. No one in all the world ever wrote a poem. *Support the war!* That is the question people are asking themselves! I want to take a club and go into the houses and knock them down. I want to tear them to pieces with my bare hands. I want to spit in their faces. But the three men are standing up now. They move to the door. They are grinning. Wait! Wait! you've forgotten your machine gun. We didn't forget it, they call over their shoulders. Then I feel something warm and sticky on my shirt. I put up my hand and feel. My chest is a red sieve through which the blood pumps. I sink to the floor. My hand touches the pile of dry bones. I know what science is. Science cuts up little pigs in order that men may be free of disease. Science points expensive instruments at the stars. What are they cutting me up for? Why did they invent things which could be pointed at me? Murderers . . . getting money for making things to blow their fellows to hell. Make a dollar. *Make a dollar.* I have said that you are not to kill anyone. Tear up all those blueprints, you bastards. Submarines. Think of a submarine! War tanks! What sort of monsters conceived these? What in the name of God are men capable of doing! These slim, well-dressed young men sitting at desks and drawing things on paper, what are they making! Are these designs for bridges and houses? Are they scheming to make me happier? These men are respected. They take their money and buy tomatoes and meat and wine . . . they laugh, they dance with lovely women—but their hands! their hands are covered with blood! Planning machines that tear schoolboys into a million pieces. Make an honest dollar. Well, you will say, Da Vinci did—he thought up most of these things first; and I answer: *he was a murderer too.* He tried to make murder an art; but murder is murder. See how deep this goes . . . We must learn to live *for the first time.* Murder has been in the heart of everyone who has ever lived. It must be taken out. Our images must be destroyed. The Church of Christ . . . more men have died in the name of Jesus Christ than will ever die for Adolf Hitler, and there is not one iota of difference in the butchery . . . tales of death and destruction . . . weed it all out . . . accounts of war and conquest . . . dusty helmets in the hands of school children . . . all of it must go . . . *we have no use for that kind of history* . . . tell me how the birds build their nests . . . tell me what the farmer sings at his plow . . . I refuse to hear how some besotted madman set whole nations at each other's throats . . . I won't listen to a word of it!

A leaf falls to the ground.

The eye of a rabbit has seen it.

Make me such a design!

I walked through the city. I had no wish to speak to anyone. I met William Blake in front of a little hatshop. I like the blue one with the leather sweat-band, he said. A man could walk under the sky with such a hat on his head. I patted the tiger which tenderly followed him.

L——, a noted poet, visited me in my house. He sat near the window and the light fell on his face. I saw that a mistake had been made. He was not a poet at all. We watched each other for a time. Presently he stood up to go. I remained in my chair. I would never read a poem of his again.

So it is with governments. You can sense the fraud.

‖‖‖

JUNE 19 ⟩⟩⟨ They invented the printing press out on the plain this morning; Constantinople fell in the afternoon. I suppose they'll discover America tomorrow. What a lot of running around they do. I saw Charles VIII of France (invasion of Italy led by: 1494) picking his nose with one hand and adjusting his wig with the other. Jetter pointed out that this particular period ended with the diet of Worms.

I found my little buffalo with his throat slit open. All right, God, that's the way you want to play it.

‖‖‖

JUNE 20 ⟩⟩⟨ What a splendid order in everything! Day follows night; the seasons never vary in their sequence; the plant always pushes upward from the earth. I approve of this. I love the way a woman's back is like nothing else under heaven.

An entichahoosh managed to get through with another message from H. Roivas. He thinks that it would be very prejudicial to the emperor's dignity and holiness to touch the ground with his feet; for this reason, when he intends to go anywhere, he must be carried there on men's shoulders (*History of Japan*, Kaempfer). Much less will they suffer that he should expose his sacred person to the open air, and the sun is not thought worthy to shine on his head. There is such a holiness ascribed to all parts of his body that he dares to cut off neither his hair, nor his beard, nor his nails. However, lest he should grow too filthy, they may clean him in the night when he is asleep; because they say that what is taken from his body at that time, hath been stolen from him, and that such a theft does not prejudice his holiness or dignity. In very ancient times, he was obliged to sit on the throne for some hours every morning, with the imperial crown on his head; but to sit altogether like a statue without stirring either hands or feet, head or eyes, or indeed any part of his body, because by this means it was thought that he could preserve peace and tranquillity in his empire; for if, unfortunately, he turned himself on one side or another, or if he looked a good while towards any part of his dominion, it was apprehended that war, famine, fire, or some other great misfortune was near at hand to desolate the country.

(An entichahoosh is a small, invisible animal.)

Billy Delian is whittling a calf from the wood of the olive tree. It is an extremely difficult job.

If you were to become Jesus Christ, what would become of Him? Christ was too proud to live in Christ, you understand; otherwise He would not have asked to dwell in mankind. Religion is always a process of muscling-in by those desirous of changing station: the comedy occurs when men bleed themselves dry in an effort to live in a God Whose sole aim is to live in them.

On the site of the destroyed city, where flames still eat at the biggest timbers, a woman's hand makes sacrifice. I hear the clover-drenched voices of peaceful farmers as my great boat moves over this battlefield; a bird tugs at a worm on the edge of a shell crater—the Lord is my shepherd, baa! baa! How the rifles slap the sky's ass, leaving tiny welts of fire on its blue. Only the mutilated bodies of boy-soldiers have the proper, sacramental attitude; all else is in error, fundamentally. We then, who are incapable of committing murder, pushed to the world's entrail-smeared wall, alone, without leaders, without faith whatever, buried under the pig-snouted statues, apart from one another, inarticulate, *afraid*—I cast you a fleeting glance just before the executioner's cloth is slipped over our terror-wide, glazed, and bulging eyes. "They've fallen asleep," the angels will whisper.

||||||||||||||||||||||||||||||||||||||||||||||||||||||||||||||||||||||||||||||||||||||||||||||||||||||||||||||||||

JUNE 21 ⚜ Everyone is saying: where can we hide when the war comes? No one at all is saying: where can we hide the war?

I keep forgetting to tell you that the dwarf was attired quite smartly in a night-shirt which extended to his knees. What had happened was this: someone was weeping in an uncontrolled manner in a thicket near a ration-tent. The woman whose duty it was to service eight hundred soldiers and twelve officers developed a nosebleed on the seventh day; this astonishing display of shrewdness was rewarded by a free-for-all lashing in which the assembled company demonstrated a ferocity quite without precedent in military annals. The dwarf, who was overlooked altogether in the general excitement, wandered off to a meadow-land where he established a harbor into which cruised destroyers bearingly wonderfully shapely maidens with brightly tinted nipples. But what of today's events in the trenches? I know that I tread on dangerous territory now: there have been so many worthwhile chronicles of War—to tell the truth, regular guys wrote some of them. Why don't they let all the soldiers drive ambulances—just put all the damn armies in hospital-wagons equipped with radios and fat nurses. Move the blue pin, Albert, we just captured Ticonderoga.

The 4th ice age. What a picture that calls up! Galileo Galilei! that's what we have to remember, that big, stoopshouldered, low-browed bastard, the Neanderthal Man.

Saturn is 734 times bigger than the earth, and 800,000,000 miles away. Well, as the principal of my school used to say, exquisite, holy, the days go on, clinging to the hem of God's chemise. The wheeling systems keep to their ancient courses. How wide the ox is to the fly; how wanton Mary is to you who are without sex among us. Should you think to put you down the sea, Carol, be-lieve me ever at your side. The same storm shall pilot us, and when the keel clangs home my lips on your lips and the spray in our hair—O darling, my hands cupping the chalice of your two breasts as we look at the blue and pure sky where the white chariots of the Greeks go by. You lead this man around by your apron string. Echoes and echoes of echoes. Somnambulistic fig-ures hoisting pigeons through marble arches; this is the ballet of the startled housetop and the fog whistle—no one else will ever leave a footmark here. I sit behind the darkness and watch you. Your room is warm, filled with the cries of nursing children and the scent of seaweed. A fishnet hangs from one of the rafters. An old man bends over his daughter and says, "Father, father, don't point your gun at me," rubbing together hands which creak like saddle leather. Even now the forever-man moves his blue, flesh-less lips. The house is in flames. A monkey with a shrunken penis sits in the ashes, bent over the Koran. Three men drag the struggling girl into the bushes. I wander over an island. All of them are dead. I dig into the earth and find a body. I sink my teeth into the rotten flesh. They try me for an unspeakable crime. I did not cut off her head. Before God I am innocent. That is why I killed them. *Why should I murder Chrystle?* You must be-lieve me. I will not forget you: we will follow the fleet, green deer into the thunderhead together. I can't sleep tonight. I walk into the field and throwing the windows up watch God undressing for bed. A woman is singing somewhere in His house.

|||||||||||||||||||||||||||||||||||||||||||||||||||||||||||||||||||||||||||||||||||||||||||||||||||||||||||||||||||||||||||||||||||||||||||||

JUNE 22 ✻ Something is standing in back of me as I write this. The door is locked; the windows are barred. I have a sense that it will try to kill me. My only weapon is my pen, which I grip in my fist—ready to strike. I can hear the thing breathing now. It is moving closer.

I have spent ten years becoming a saint. It was not easy because always the man I was in got in the way. This man's name is Albion Moonlight. He has been puzzled by my behavior. I feel that he is nearly dead now. You may ask how I happened to be in him: I do not know. One day I was there. Since then the struggle has been great. His wife has been my greatest enemy. I do not want him to make love to her because it distracts me. Her passionate nature has caused me great trouble. I cannot warn Moonlight against this orgy of the flesh: I can only be the warning.

Last night she came into his bed. I made myself powerful. Moonlight felt my hatred for her and he raised his arm and struck her. Immediately I whispered, "We shall be together always."

That she is plotting against me I know. I have felt her eyes upon him and *it is only me she sees.*

I understand her. It is the man she wants, not what her husband is: you see, I am her husband now and she does not know how to conduct herself with a saint. Why should I go to bed with her? My seed is not for her. I wish to impregnate the world. I hate the man Christ lived in. How little he understood Him, taking Him to the Cross because the problem could not be solved. The problem of being a saint.

I have been very careful to make it clear that I am not God.

I have said that Christ was not God but a saint. God is opposed to saints. God is only the idea of one saint. This idea is not mine.

My great idea is that man does not need God. God needs man for His existence, therefore: how can there be God? When man perishes, God will perish—from the earth. A saint is another matter. You will see that I am a better being than God. I love Christ because He was the most successful saint.

I enjoy myself in Moonlight. I enjoy the books he reads, the music he hears, the people he sees—I know something of his plan for killing them. I found myself in him because of Tolstoy. There was place for me to stand. I told him that Tolstoy was false because he tried to renounce the world. A man must find the world. Dostoievsky knew what I mean. He was a happy man: he wrote *The Brothers Karamazov.*

I believe that man is God. It is yourself that you must worship. There is danger that they will try to kill Moonlight; they are even now gathering evidence for his guilt—"We accuse you of the willful, premeditated murder of Chrystle Gambetta." I urge him to get his record on paper before that sad hour arrives. You are God. I move the pen in his hand. Worship yourself.

I am Albion Moonlight. I do not know the being that says these things. I fear it. It will destroy me. It is but another trick of our enemies. My head is heavy with fighting it.

You can see that my victory is not complete. It is his fear of me that hurts most. It is his belief in God. He does not understand the wonder of being a saint. I actually offer him this. The fool prefers his wife to me. Be quiet now. I am peace. With me all pain will end. You are afraid because murder has become a commonplace, because your friends in hating the murder have allowed murder into their hearts. You are not so much afraid of Hitler as you are of the hatred for Hitler. What a plaything you have been. It is so easy to be a soldier. Soldiers are never alone. My plan is simple and beautiful. I can teach you to kill. Together we shall kill your wife. My sainthood is founded on murder. Christ was a saint of anger. My anger is much greater than His. Worship man, that is what I have said, and the sacrifice: man. *We can kill too.* We can become efficient murderers—but not for country this time. Murder is the new faith and I am its first saint. I am the will, the word, and the deed.

Its fingers are at my throat. The words come from my pen with a life of their own. What help is there now? I did not kill her! Won't you believe me . . . ? I did not kill her . . . I did not mean to . . . I was only holding her in my arms and my fingers went around her tiny throat and she started to cry and I said don't cry but she was dead and I took a knife . . .

The deed is done. I am now Albion Moonlight. I have declared my war.

This morning my wife (she is mine now) came to my bed. How I enjoyed making love to her! Her soft throat . . . putting my teeth into her white shoulder. I shall spare her for a time. Perhaps I have been in love with her. *Carol! Carol!* Besides, I have not yet decided the method of her death.

"We accuse you of the willful, premeditated murder of Chrystle Gambetta: and we further charge that you committed rape upon her poor helpless body . . ."

You are all crying. Please God is there any reason to make a story when no one at all will listen . . .

What is this way of humans, when all the light and joy have gone from every face, this slow perishing on all earth, this parting from those we love and who have loved us? What moves in this air? I am waiting for you most impatiently, eaten by disgust and sadness, filled with childish longings, bored, irritated, savoring these days which are at once bitter and tasteless. I am not angry now, only tired. I am not afraid now. Walk over my face, stick your dirty fingers into my eyes.

JUNE 23 ⚙ That was an interesting experience last night. I think my solution was the only one possible. I am the conscience of the world. Who has a better right to invent something to share this kind of responsibility? I will not deceive you: trust me. My nature is simple. I have strong hands and my eyes will not waver when I look at you. I am not afraid to speak the truth because the truth is the greatest lie of all—you may even be fool enough to believe it. Anything you may think to be the truth, will be a lie—otherwise there could be no war. In a world where truth was worth a damn, this book would stop the war. Everything is on my side. I speak the truth—*but all of this is a lie because nobody will listen.* I will do one thing, however: I will stop the war for anyone who reads this—you will listen to my war, until I am done.

It does not matter what happens in your head or mine; thousands of heads as good and as bad as ours are being opened like eggs before the Goddamn guns. But I am not afraid. Their inventions are child's play when compared to the way I have decided to destroy. You see, and this is not meant to startle you, I am at my work of murder now. A soldier kills after the fashion of soldiers; a writer must kill with what he says. They have ordered that we all become murderers. Very well, I answer, be witness to my kind of destruction. How simple to kill a man's body! I choose to kill his soul . . . the fact that I wish to put a purer soul in its place does not alter the fact of murder. The State has given the command to destroy: I wish to be a good citizen. Indeed, much of what I write is addressed to the dead; why should anyone be interested in the living now? As many of us as possible will be killed. We are an insult to our culture, alive.

Carol came to my room tonight. She is not unhappy. She speaks of Germans, of the English, of the French, but never of soldiers, never of death in war. She hates Hitler, yet she says she wants peace. That is a lie. She must hate the way men die in war. Any man with a gun aimed at another man is Hitler. He believes in Hitler. Hitler will be gone tomorrow—a withered leaf falling into a millrace—but the hatred of Hitler will live to breed others like him. I do not hate Hitler. I hate what brought him into being—and the thing that keeps him where he is. I am interested in humanity. Hitler serves the enemies of his people more than the people themselves. He is the hate! "We have no quarrel with the German people," said the late Woodrow Wilson.

I believe that the German working class will know what to do with Hitler when the proper time comes; and I believe that the English, French, Italian, and American Hitlers will be dealt with in the proper way too. What a stupid animal you are, Carol—hating Hitler! Hitler hates, and in hating him you become a Hitler. How the governments tremble when they think that all men will one day see under their masks—and find the same thing.

Stop their filthy, hypocritical war! It's not *our* war. But the people of Europe will be hungry this winter . . . starving. Maybe . . .

Just down the river a bit from where we are, Hart Crane sat, writing *The Bridge*. What did you have in mind, Crane? What did Pocahontas and Rip Van Winkle have to do with it? When the gin bottles were all empty and the good people of Brooklyn were safe in their beds, what did the words on their shiny stilts add up to? Who put the cat out and where did the fifteen-legged beast go? *Why did blood drip from its mouth . . . ?*

Carol wants me to write a novel: "You have met so many interesting people," she tells me.

Very good, there was once a young man and he could never get his hands on enough women. That's a novel. There was an idiot and he became God. That's the same novel. I can't possibly think of any others. It is rather pleasant to be the author of two such excellent novels. The critics are divided in their opinions. One lot believes that they should be shorter; another not, that they should be a mite longer. I rather prefer short critics to long ones. I like critics with tan shoes—look nicer, I think. I had a lot of books once and I felt happy looking at them. I enjoyed thinking about them more than I did reading them. I like to think about Spinoza, Christ, Dostoievsky, and Herman Melville. The fact that

41

these men decided to say things is not all that concerns me. Look at the faces of these men! I listen to them out of respect, but I need not read them to know them. Pour the hogwash of American letters down your throat, Carol—I want these faces bound in tooled calf and placed in every shop, factory, and home in the land. How could they hate Hitler? Who the hell is Hitler?

Carol removes her dress and sits in the window which overlooks the river. I kneel down on the floor at her feet.

"Do you think I'm a good woman?"

"For me, yes."

"What do you mean by that?"

"You're my kind of slut."

Her face becomes silk and roses. I can see that she wants some beautiful talk.

"But you don't really mean that," she says.

"Of course I don't mean it."

"Then why do you say it?"

"Because I'd like to believe that you're my kind of slut."

"I'll love you always, Albion."

A big boat all covered with lights goes by the window. We can smell the fish and salt.

"Shall we go to bed now?" I ask.

"Please don't change the subject."

"I won't. That's the subject."

"Why do you pretend to be so hard? Other men say nice things to a woman."

"Then they take her to bed."

I light a cigarette. I let the match burn down to my fingers. The pain puts a skin on what I am thinking.

"Oh, you're mean," she says, being a little girl. "The nice things they say to me . . . their tenderness . . . that's why I go to bed with them. Don't you see?—it's not the bed part."

"Then why do you go to bed with me?"

"Because . . . oh hell—I told you. I love you."

"What does that mean?"

42

"It doesn't mean just going to bed with you."

"Let's get into bed and talk about it." I start to take off my shirt.

"But you won't say anything at all then."

"Why should I?"

"You're impossible."

"Then why don't you go off to Jetter?"

"I'm afraid of him."

"What if he finds out you're here?"

"He'd kill me."

"He'll probably kill you whether he finds out or not."

"What is the matter with Jetter, Albion? He used to be so gentle, so kind—a good man."

"He's still a good man. Just a bit on the nut side."

"Do you think he is really insane?"

"No more than you are."

"But I mean seriously . . ."

"Shall we go to bed?"

"No. I'm going back to Jetter." She stands up, begins to slip into her dress.

"You like them nutty, huh?"

"You're vicious and mean. I think if anybody is crazy, you are."

"Then why don't you stay?"

She starts for the door. I hit her in the back of the head with my fist. She crumbles like a sack. I drag her over to the bed and undress her. She moans weakly, like one waking from a terrible sleep. Then I get down on my knees and stroke her hair and tell her that she is pure and beautiful and that I love her. I light another cigarette and by the match's light I see that her eyes are open and full of joy. Next time I will know to hit her with all I've got. I slip into bed beside her and put my head on her breast like a baby. A buoy jangles out on the river. I turn off the telling now; I won't take you to bed with us.

The dogs awakened me at dawn. I yawned into the mirror and was startled to see that the face did not yawn back. It was watching me in cold amusement.

JUNE 24 🪶 My great task now, of course, is to formulate a report for Roivas. I do not feel myself ready for this.

No sign of the innkeeper's body.

Don't put your glasses on a blind man; you will only see his blindness better.

It was beside the cold river (and it was snowing)
That I heard her sigh that she had lost her love.

"Only a drop of blood in the snow," William explained.
"Were there no tracks?" asked Elizabeth.
"The snow has not stopped," the old man said.
The four of them waited patiently for the clock to strike. Snow drifted into the room through a great gash in the ceiling. Yesterday a fist as massive as a tree trunk had suddenly broken in on them—and for one moment a huge shaggy face had hung there in the hole.
"I can easily believe you did it," William ventured in the direction of a hooded figure which rested near the telephone in the very darkest part of the house.
"Hush," cautioned Elizabeth. "You will annoy her."
"Annoy, indeed!" her husband roared. "What right had she to be out there this night?—At all," he added.
The young woman opened the pure and bewitching eyes that were in her mutilated, dead face. Her slender and graceful body was cold and still.
"Mother," she whispered.
"Yes, Ann . . ."
"Why can't I move my hands?"
"This is a good high hell," muttered the old man, rubbing the bridge of his frost-bitten nose.
"Your hands are tired, dear," whispered Ann's mother.
It was now only three minutes of the hour—the hour which

they all dreaded so much. Somewhere a whistle screeched savagely. A bat stirred in the little attic.

"I don't feel the hurting any more," the girl said.

"Try to sleep now, darling." Elizabeth's voice broke and she
sobbed without restraint.

The old man moved uneasily in his chair; the long, old-style
rifle which he held close to his withered chest—many the squirrel
he had bagged with it—was getting heavy beyond his meager
strength.

"You know quite well that you killed her," William said to his
wife.

"Run away to bed, William," she ordered. Her gray eyes were
ice upon him.

"Not before I have my bite," he said, laughing. "Liz," he went
on, "fix me up some 'taters and sow's tit."

"There, there, you old goat . . . Would ye listen to the likes of
him now. Wandher off, me proud boyo." And her eyes went soft
as merd. "Dhrink'll be the death of ye."

"Jaysus!" coughed Ann. "Can't a body have any peace here?"

William shook out of his chair and hobbled over to his daughter's side.

"Can't a body . . . ha!"

"Father!" entreated Ann.

"Yup . . ."

"Please don't point your gun at me."

"Father, father, don't point your gun at me," he mimicked,
shaking with laughter and old age.

"Have you seen Leah lately?" Elizabeth called to the hooded
figure in the corner.

"No, ma'am, I h'aint," it replied politely.

"I heard she had a job with the city," the woman persisted.

"Well . . ." and the man in the mask seemed somewhat startled
by this piece of news. "You can't prove nauthin' by me."

Standing up very straight at last, his rheumatic old legs snapping like brushwood in flame, William, hat perched at a cocky

angle on his graying locks, and his hands carefully holding the fowling piece in front of him, took two quick steps forward, and fell flat on his face.

Instead of undressing him at once, removing the dun-colored trousers and worn-out singlet, Elizabeth, with pardonable caution, crossed to the door and slid the heavy bar into place. It groaned like an iron wrestler.

"I hear the telephone," Ann said. "Won't one of you answer it?"

"It didn't ring," her mother declared firmly.

On a chance, scowling under his mask, the man in the shadow said hello into the instrument's black mouth.

"Harry?" came a voice.

At once those in the room became tense, watchful; even the old sailor, far in his cups, managed to gain an elbow, from which vantage point his whiskered eyes looked out like pools of warm piss.

"Yes . . ." the dark stranger said hesitantly, with easy craft.

"Are you sure that you are Harry?" There was panic in the voice now. A clock in the room boomed hoarsely. The great fish-net swung from the ceiling like a giant's shroud. Elizabeth's nails bit into her palms. Had it come at last, the word they had all awaited so long?

"This is he. I'm Harry."

"Why did you order their murder?"

"Their murder? . . . I don't understand."

"You have a pretty smooth game, haven't you?"

The voice seemed to be retreating, to be moving away.

"Hello . . . hello . . ." the stranger called desperately.

"You are not Harry . . . look at me."

"Look at you?"

There was a soft laugh. "Yes, Albion, look at me . . . at Ann." They turned to the girl on the bed and her lips were moving. "Your mask did not fool me," she said, "as soon as I learned that you knew who Harry was . . ."

Angrily I snatch the cloth from my head.

"What sort of trick is this?" I demand.

"No trick, my friend." The voice comes from the floor. I look and see that the old man is standing erect and tall. The rifle points to my chest. Ann's arms are around me in an instant.

"How did you know that Roivas' name was Harry?" I ask her.

"Out in the snow tonight . . . just before I was shot—I was told the whole scheme . . . everything . . . all about your plan . . ."

"Do you know who shot you?"

"Yes, Albion, I know who shot me."

The army truck roars by. The young boys standing in its bed, their heads banging at the tailboard, do not wave to us. A star-shell goes off and by its lemon glow I can see a thin line of men moving toward us. Now we are passing a kennel. I smell the cooked dog-flesh and I begin to whistle. I whistle every tune that comes into my head. Presently we reach the inn. Below the swinging gates, outlined in the half-dark, I can see Jackeen and Thomas Honey, their bodies naked up to the navel, locked in a lovers' pile on the ground.

This is, as nearly as I can remember it, the dream I had last night. Sweat covered me when I awakened, but I could still feel the cold, bitter touch of the snow falling on my face.

I have decided finally, after much thought and vexation of spirit, to tell part of our story in the form of a novel; I sincerely hope that you will find instruction as well as entertainment in it. *"The Plague"* shall be the title of the first chapter.

⎯⎯

JUNE 25 ⊱ I am less surprised than you might imagine to learn that the innkeeper has been in constant attendance on us—cooking our meals, waiting on table, keeping our rooms clean. It is simply that we have not been aware of him. When I asked him where he had been, he smiled and answered, "Do you observe nothing unusual about me?"

I told him that I did not.

"Look at my hands." And he held them out.

The flesh was beginning to part from the bone. His eyes were turned round in his head, the roots of nerve and stumps of muscle sticking out, while the seeing part looked in on him. I remember thinking that if he had a soul he was staring right at it. The joker, of course, is this: why haven't I the courage to reveal his true identity to you?

I recognize the filth of these years. I have a machine gun in my hands, but I won't kill them. *My own people* ... A man should never kill anyone.

I can lift a carrot out of the ground without disturbing the soil. There is a trickle of blood out of the corner of my mouth ...

I have enough life in me for twelve men. I could father a city, design a snowflake. I joked with two men in a Harlem bar. Everyone suddenly felt happy because my laughter was unafraid. I thought that I could borrow some money from them. Even before I had the words in the air, they had heard and were half-way across the room on their way out. Yes, yes, of course, money—*their* money—don't ask me for that! But they can't buy me. I'll take their money but I won't give them anything back. Spit in their faces ... but they won't pay me for doing that—now will they? I write along a single line: I never get off it. I said that you were never to kill anyone, *and I meant it.*

Mr. Glen and Jack Cove invited me to supper in his apartment in the West End. He was a small, tight man with a brittle, polished manner and a wife who had been a first-row girl in Minsky's. J.R.D., as he called her, spread a good table, and I looked forward to getting my feet under it. The one thing I can't eat is crabmeat and creamed corn. They had crabmeat and creamed corn. All right, I sat there while they ate, getting a surly lion in my belly.

"I was just telling them never to kill anyone," I said, above the noise their jaws made.

"You sit down on them, boy," Mr. Glen and Jack Cove said, "I got hemorrhoids."

"Is that any way to talk?" J.R.D. remarked.

"I don't like to think when I eat," he said.

"You have little to worry about there," his good wife told him, beginning a laugh which only ended when she had almost a bucket of crabmeat and creamed corn in her painted gash.

I said: "And they made Lincoln into a penny."

"Did you feed Farmeroy, J.R.D.?" Mr. Glen and Jack Cove asked.

"I can't—I'm too sore," she said, pulling out a breast and showing the marks of teeth that might have belonged to a horse.

Farmeroy was their idiot son, a hulk of fourteen.

"Old cow," came his unmodulated voice from a crib near the china closet.

"Shush," growled the once-beautiful mother.

"Herbert Hoover's the man for us," declared Farmeroy, making an untoward sound.

"He always says that when he doesn't get what he wants," explained Mr. Glen and Jack Cove.

"They won't let us commit him," J.R.D. said.

"I know what I'd commit," I said, more to the lion than to them.

A mangy St. Bernard walked in with a *New York Times* folded neatly in a little cradle under his throat.

"Bugger Guiniver," chortled Farmeroy.

"Down, Guin, down," ordered Mr. Glen and Jack Cove, as the beast persisted in kissing his face with its rubbery, lamb chop lips. He got hold of the paper finally.

"What's new?" J.R.D. asked.

"There's talk here of conscription," he said, turning to Little Orphan Annie—"France has gone Fascist—officially. Brooklyn split a double-header with the Cubs."

"Ain't it terrible, Albion?" J.R.D. said, fixing her large, striptease eyes on me.

"Yup, it's pretty bad," I said.

"Hoover's the man for us," Farmeroy said gleefully, making his impolite noise again.

"Telegram, Mr. Moonlight." I tipped the Western Union kid

two bits, got my hat from the hall table, thanked my host, and with a last glare at Farmeroy, who was now playing stink-finger, made my way into the soft, light-needled fog of the street, where I found Billy Delian and Jetter waiting for me under a street lamp. Their faces were set and grim.

"Well . . . ?"

"Chrystle," Billy Delian said. "Snatched." He let it sink in. "Somebody kidnaped Chrystle."

"When?"

"About an hour ago."

"Who knows?"

"Only Jetter and me—an' you."

"Jackeen?"

"She don't know."

"Better tell her."

Their eyes said buzz you.

"Tell her," I said. My hands were shaking like mating rabbits. "Any ideas?"—I had to say something.

"Yes," Jetter said.

"Who?"

"Joseph Gambetta."

"Her father? . . . You're both cracked."

"Maybe, maybe not."

"Where is he?" I said. My mouth was twitching so that the words ran into the fog like broken stones into a bale of cotton.

They spread their hands.

"It wasn't Joseph," I said at last. "He's been with me all night."

"Albion . . ." Jetter spat into my name.

"Yes."

"You're a damn liar. Joseph Gambetta was pulled out of the Red River yesterday—with a slab of concrete around his middle."

"Jetter," I whispered, wanting to be dead and all the pain and terror at an end . . . wanting to put my arms around them as they stood in the night fingering their revolvers . . . "Do you think I made the snatch?"

Why do they torture me!

"In the name of God! . . ." I shouted.

"Take it easy," Billy Delian said. People were beginning to watch us, floating in around us like logs caught in a jam.

"Come on," Jetter said. "We've got the car here."

They started to drag me to the curb. I sank my teeth into an arm; I kicked out, scratching like a cat . . . and I got away . . . someone had unbuttoned my fly and a knife had made me sexless and the blood ran down my legs. I am bleeding to death Jesus help me . . .

Carol is bathing my face. Thomas Honey and Jetter are sitting one on either side of the bed, their hands laid lightly on my arms.

"What happened?" I ask weakly.

"Food poisoning," Carol says. "You have been out of your head . . . we thought you would die."

"What did I say in the delirium?" I am thoroughly frightened now.

"A lot of nonsense," Thomas Honey says, releasing my arm.

"You seemed to think someone was after you with a gun," Jetter adds.

"Go to sleep now," Carol says, brushing my hair back from my hot forehead.

"But wasn't anyone else poisoned?" I ask. "We all ate the same food for supper."

"No one else, Albion. Please get some sleep."

"So someone tried to kill me . . ."

"Go to sleep." She kisses me and they go out, leaving me to imagine how much I had babbled in the fever. I knew who had attempted to murder me.

What a strange expression . . . 'out of your head.'

Jackeen gave birth to a seven-pound daughter early this morning. We named the child Chrystle.

Alas for Art, when everyone's energy for hating is turned against

51

the artist. When men are at war, there is no hatred of soldiers; it is the artist who is despised and reviled—the only enemy of their fraud—in truth, the one, real *warrior*.

"Look, under that broad beech-tree, I sat down when I was last this way fishing, and the birds in the adjoining grove seemed to have a friendly contention with an echo, whose dead voice seemed to live in a hollow tree, near to the brow of that primrose-hill: there I sat viewing the silver streams glide silently towards their center, the tempestuous sea; yet sometimes opposed by rugged roots and pebble stones, which broke their waves and turned them into foam: and sometimes I beguiled time by viewing harmless lambs, some leaping securely in the cool shade whilst others sported themselves in the cheerful sun; and some others craving comfort from the swollen udders of their bleating dams.

"As I left this place, and entered into the next field, a second pleasure entertained me; it was a handsome milk-maid that had not yet attained so much age and wisdom as to load her mind with any fears of many things that will never be, as too many men often do: but she cast away all care, and sung like a nightingale: her voice was good, and the ditty fitted for it: it was that smooth song which was made by Kit Marlowe . . ."

It must be clear to you now, what I am trying to do. With what sense of shock you must have realized that it is not we who are fleeing from the world: with what joy you exclaimed, "No, Albion and his friends are not running away—they are speeding to us; we were in headlong flight, and they have overtaken us—they have stopped the runaway world, and it is awaiting their further orders. Now we are to hear of love and hope—we are to be instructed in salvation!"

Yes, that I must do for you, that I must do for you . . .

We all are not to blame. Yet look at us, faces twisted with the modern disease—paddling our hands in the pools of dried blood where lies Europe's head, its stiffening tongue the ladder for what grim and terrible new Jacob.

Have you a sense of being followed? This advice: don't go home tonight. Someone awaits you there with a knife in his hand. I warn you *seriously*.

Chrystle, I may say now, is the girl Christ.

||||||||||||||||||||||||||||||||||||||||||||||||||||||||||||||||||||||||||||||||||||||||||||||||||||||||||||||||||||||||||||||||||

JUNE 27 🐖 A strange village, this. We arrived here late last night, footweary, hungry, and badly in need of baths and clean clothing. Our escape from the inn was accomplished through the agency of a little green flying car—which Joseph Gambetta made to celebrate Chrystle's birth. He certainly was overjoyed by his good fortune in becoming a father: phantoms so seldom do. Why should it be so damn difficult to get our simple needs taken care of? Our tempers are near the breaking point.

One is reminded of men on tired horses riding into ruined cathedrals. Something unreal about the information furnished us concerning this place. It seems—though this is hard to believe —that the inhabitants here *do not have enough food*. The barns and sheds groan with it; money spills out of the banks in a flood the color of snake skin. Everyone is working like mad—his fingers peeled to the bone. But they don't have enough to eat. Yet this is truly the odd part: the few who are sitting about at ease are as well fed as shoats. Amazing! *Only the loafers are taken care of: the bread-makers have no bread.* I asked a man plowing in a field why they didn't all behave like the wise ones who did nothing and who yet enjoyed all the fruits of the land.

"They wouldn't like that," he said.

"They?" I asked him.

He looked at me in positive bewilderment. His battered hands clenched and unclenched like live trout on a river bank.

"You mean the rich," I said.

There was terror in his eyes now.

I said: "Who made them rich? Who feeds them?"

He watched me as though he expected at any moment I would take a bite out of his horse.

"I have ter git on with my plowing," he said at last.

"What do you think of the war?" I asked.

"War?" He seemed to be trying to remember something.

"Yes, the war. You know about the war . . ."

"That might be why they blew up the bridges down the road a piece," he said meditatively. "Might that be why, mister? An' settin' fire to the barns over Clarville way . . . War? Maybe that what it be . . ."

"Have you sons?" I said.

"Three, mister. An' a dater what's droppin' come November."

"Are your sons home now?"

"Naoh, they be off awheres bein' larnt by the govermint."

"Larnt what?"

"Fixin' up to keep down the trouble."

"What trouble?"

"Them's what aim to bother the govermint." His face twists out a smile like a crack in a dry pod. "Maybe that what it be . . . War, eh? I ain't got no time to figger much on sechlike."

"Do you like the rich?" I asked him.

Suddenly he laughed. His face got full of sun and green fields.

"You might be all right," he said. "I don't know you."

He lurched off down the field, lashing out at the horse in peasant savagery. Above the clatter he shouted:

"I got three boys in the army, you nosy sonofabitch!"

I spoke the other day of the strange growth which has formed over Thomas Honey's eyes. He is totally blind now. We, in our wisdom, are helpless to aid him. I am not satisfied with our condition on earth.

I stood on the porch of our hotel and shot four of the dogs— then my rifle jammed. This had never happened before.

Some time ago, in a little town down the road a piece, a certain woman brought four children into the world.

54

The eldest among them was a fool. He knew how to do nothing, so his brothers and sisters said, "We cannot live with him, get him out of the house at once."

The poor fool was driven out and after a time built a settlement for himself and lived in it. Around him was nothing but sand, so he made a swing and amused himself with it. The mother grew lonely as mothers will and set forth to get her child one night, but an angel fell under her hand and she took him home.

With the coming of the day the children awakened and set upon him, screaming, "Fool! Fool!"

It was a wonderful little angel and he answered:

"Yes. I am a fool."

And their stones picked him to pieces while the idiot swung happily on between heaven and earth as it was in the beginning.

A mud-spattered mule browses on the roadside.

> *Let the day perish wherein I was born,*
> *And the night in which it was said*
> *There is a man child conceived.*
> *Deep calleth unto deep* ... Alyosha, *Alyosha!*

I have been honest with you. But who can express the thoughts of a man's heart, coming on a sudden into a place where the whole world seemed of a fire-light? The valley was on one side so exceedingly bright, the eye could not bear to look at it; the sides of the mountains were shining like the fire itself; the flame from the top of the ridge on the under side casting its glow directly upon them, from the reflection into other parts looked red and more terrible; for the first was white and clear like the light of the sun, but the other being, as it were, a reflection of flame, mixed with some darker substance, represented the fire of a great furnace, and, in short, it might well be said that here was no darkness; but certainly at the first view, it gives the traveler no other idea than that he stands at the very door of eternal horror.

I spent the night with Jackeen but I did not touch her. Treasures in heaven . . . She will have nothing to do with Jetter; and it is not because he is a Negro.

JUNE 28 ⚐ The heat is great—hottest summer in forty-six years. Carol's nose has been bleeding all morning.

My arm is in a sling. It was my turn to beat Mrs. Drew and in my excitement I pulled a muscle in my forearm. I should make more of an effort to control my emotions.

Three men rode by in the twilight yesterday. Their marksmanship was certainly of an inferior order: beyond kicking up the dust at our feet, their bullets made no impression on us whatsoever. It is difficult to handle a rifle while on horseback, even at a slow pace—and they were riding at full gallop. I had a distinct feeling that I had seen one of them before; that, in fact, these same riders had passed us on another occasion in exactly this manner—what a sleepless bundle of race-memories we humans are! How many times have I awakened in the night to the snuffled barking of animals in pain—the horror of being a dumb brute in a cave full of chewed bones and excrement, never able to say God or Napoleon or Michelangelo, never quite sure that his ass isn't just a hole in the ground or his elbow.

We are now in a little town in Ohio. Here and there among the houses, which are certainly comical in their structure, all towered and pillared and trellised, like a child's drawing of a house, we saw strange, shell-like cellars extending deep into the earth. Our inquiries brought the information that these were originally designed as roasting pits for the preparation of human flesh. Upon consulting a history book, I learned that cannibalism was prevalent in the Middle West as late as 1924. These pits are now the scene of dog-baiting and cock-fighting. This region is up-to-date in the extreme: it is not at all unusual to see other sights in these diggings—women cohabiting with sheep, pigs, and dogs; men masturbating stallions with greased inner-tubes; surgeons performing cancer operations; local election rallies featuring the castrating and lynching of Negroes—all this done to acquaint the public with a new cosmetic or tooth powder, or to open a new movie palace or church. I do not wonder that this state ranks second in the number of sons it has contributed to the White House.

Jetter swears that there is the smell of poison-gas in the air to-night. He got a nice taste of the mustard variety in the next-to-the-last war, and even a whiff of his own stink will set him yelling "Gas! Gas!"

But he may be right this time . . .

The novel begins . . .

1. The Plague

Everything was ready for his arrival. I had put on a fresh shirt; my shoes, battered and scuffed as they were, had been treated to a polish and a brisk rub-down.

Cautiously I inserted a disk in the phonograph. I knew music —and Bach especially—upset him. One advantage I would have.

The minutes ticked past. I had a feeling of unease, almost as though someone stood in the room with me. I paced the floor; over, back, three steps, four . . .

I crossed to the bookcase and took out two books. Spinoza and Villon. I put Villon back. Under the lamp with the other—arranging the chair so that the opening of the door would conceal me from anyone entering—making sure that my revolver moved easily in its holster at my shoulder—at last, then, I turned to the first page.

But I was not destined to read that night.

A faint breathing behind me ... Wheeling round, hurtling the lamp to the floor in my haste, I beheld, as the flames licked upward to the curtains (spreading tiny people of fire against the window), a little girl holding a doll in her arms.

The doll's lips moved and I saw that, whereas the bo ly, legs, arms, and torso were of sawdust and painted wax, the head was that of a young man. Blood trickled in a little rill from the corner of his mouth.

I was positive that we were being watched.

"My brother—" she said. "They took him away to war." Her shoulders moved convulsively in the light from the flames which were now running about at our feet.

"Yes, child," I managed to say.

"And now—this morning—I woke up with my dolly in my arms..." She sobbed in heartbroken terror. "My brother's head— you see! he's trying to say something."

It was true. The mouth moved in and out like a small red door in his mutilated face.

I bent over. "What do you want to say?"

The fire was roaring and snapping and I couldn't hear all he said.

I heard: "The dogs ... the dogs ..."

The little girl's dress was on fire now. Flames skirled around her doll, reaching up to her brother's poor face.

"The dogs belong to ..."

At that moment a hand wrenched the doll from the child's arms and something struck me a glancing blow on the back of the head.

I fell into the cave where all of us are alone.

2. THE DAYWATCHMAN

My head ached. A furred animal made waste on my tongue. The room was strange. I was in a stranger's house. That was not all: a hand played at my genitals. My organ was swollen and ready for use.

I opened my eyes upon the little girl who had figured in the events of the previous night. She lay in bed beside me.

"You must not do that," I said, pushing her hand away.

"Why don't girls have those?" she asked.

"Because if they had them too, there'd be no point in anybody's having them," I said, hoping by an ambiguous answer to silence her.

"But they're funny," she persisted. "Why are they made like that?"

"Because God willed it so."

She frowned, trying to understand. "And Jesus . . . He was made just like you . . . ?"

I said: "His body was a man's, like any other."

"Then why can't I touch you there?"

"Because that would serve no purpose in nature." I was sure that God would forgive my lie at that moment.

I got out of bed, crossed to the window, and, pulling aside the heavy drapes, gazed out at the day.

Two round, unwinking, brutal eyes looked into mine. Don't think, daywatchman, that you can bring ruin to me with your lying reports. I had a momentary feeling of uncertainty: should I attempt to bribe the man? should I rather lunge against the window, unseating him from his perilous seat on its ledge? should I . . .

I saw that he was dead. Stone eyes in a hardening face. A mouse of blood sniffed down the sleeve of his coat.

"Chrystle!" I called, turning back to the room.

The bed was empty. On the pillow was pinned a note:

Beware, Albion Moonlight. The net is closing in. They are beginning to suspect the truth.

||||||||||||||||||||||||||||||||||||||||||||||||||||||||||||||||||||||||||||||||||||||||||||||||||||||||||||||||||||||||||||||||||||||||

JUNE 29 ⊁ The first bombing plane went over at three this morning, to be followed at ten minute intervals by groups of six, flying in big Vs, until the sky was full of the damn things—sputtering, diving, dipping, and letting their steel shit down on the country-side—Bamb—raining women and children, ha ha, into the next township.

We sat out on a hill watching the show. When it got dark we went back to our hotel. It was the only building left standing in the whole place. We drank some coffee and were on the point of going to bed when the door opened and Hitler walked in. He sat down on the bed and put his face in his hands.

3. TRAFFIC COURT

The landlady was waiting for me when I returned to my room. Her face was puffy with weeping.

"Dilly is dead," she said. "He drowned himself in his bath, poor dear."

"Sorry," I mumbled, as I entered my room.

There they sat, the four of them, wine bottles strewn about in wild faithfulness to Cynara. They'd like to get God drunk, and tickle His belly.

Jetter said: "Ah, the wandering minstrel, home from the wars all spick and spanked."

"Have you found Chrystle?" I asked.

"We've got a good lead," Billy Delian said.

"Sure have," Joseph Gambetta added.

I was almost a character in the Bible, I was so happy. At that moment I trusted them with my colonies.

"What is this lead?"

"We think a traffic cop took her," Jetter said.

This was getting too playful. I took out my gun and twirled the cylinder: zig, zig, zig, szip.

Thomas Honey got out of his chair and felt his blind way over to me. He put an arm around my shoulders. "This is not an ordinary traffic cop, Albion," he said.

Jetter said slowly: "Roivas is his name."

"His name is Roivas!" I shouted. "You mule-eared fools . . . there are thousands of Roivases . . ."

"But not with the little fingers on their right hands missing!"

I thought: I'll have to go through with it now. But I was shaking with rage.

"Yes, you'd better go through with it," Joseph said savagely.

I had forgotten that he was a phantom.

The judge was saying "thirty days" when we got to the court. A big, red-faced beef of a man was the recipient of this sentence. He spat on the floor.

"Get down and lick that up!" thundered His Honor.

A bevy of blue-coated apes came up on the dead run and kicked the beef in the groin. He bent double, then triple as they went for him again.

His tongue went over the spit. I could taste it. He vomited, holding himself in where he was man.

"Next case," barked the regal figure on the bench.

Thomas Honey found his way to the front. "I am blind now," he said. "I was a champion boxer in my day."

"Who did it?" demanded the judge.

"Did what? make him champ?" Jetter asked mildly.

"No, made him blind . . . say, what the hell is this?"

I said: "God did."

"I charge you with contempt . . ."

"Contempt of what? God?"

"Get these bastards out of here!"

The apes tore up. Thomas Honey raised his giant fists.

"You baby-eater you . . ." a voice said. It seemed to come from the judge's lap. He looked about like a bull with a wasp under its tail.

I had again forgotten Joseph Gambetta.

We were not able to question anyone about Roivas.

JUNE 30 🦂 Howevermuch we may desire it, bending every effort of will in our desire to remember, there is something which pulls our minds up short when we attempt to recapture the sensations of childhood. Our stomachs grow weary of food; our eyes ache to view new objects; the old, never-changing sounds finally grate on our ears; but we never tire of contemplating the world we knew as children. That is always fresh, pure, sweet. No matter how wretched and hungry we were.

I watch Chrystle playing at Jackeen's feet. We are in the lobby, surrounded by potted plants and dead bodies. The clerk still sits on his high stool, pen poised over the ledger . . . 'Mr. & Mrs. Chadwick of Ashtabula' . . . a little black hole at his temple, and poor Tom and Molly Chadwick are lying where their honeymoon ended, her eyes asking him a virgin's question. Yes, I say to myself, it is a sorry world and no mistake. Gas killed off most of the town's inhabitants, the mop-up crews took care of the rest.

The members of my expedition were unharmed.

Chrystle's fingers are no bigger than a doll's. Her hair is a golden brown. What goes on in that pretty head? Does she know that I am already being hunted for her murder? It is curious to think that the saliva in her mouth is clean and wholesome-tasting. Decay and death are in the mouths of women; their teeth are always at rot; the inner flesh becomes tough and heavy-veined—kiss tiny girls if you want to know what life might have been. That is why I must possess her; yet I do not want to hurt her—that is why I shall kill her first. Jetter and the others understand this: but they are wrong—never in his world shall I rape and murder her. You must believe me. It is in my head, I admit; *that is why they hunt me.* I can hide nothing from them.

To get old is a terrible thing: When finally you have begun to understand how to live in your body; when you have learned not to eat too much, not to drink too much, not to fornicate too much, you find yourself with a big hulking bag of rot on your hands. That is why man is a sad animal. I don't want to die.

"Have you a cigarette, Albion?" Jackeen asks.

You're so beautiful but you gotta die some day.

I hand her my pack. She takes one and hands it back.

"When are you going to let me come to your bed, Jackeen?"

"Never."

"That doesn't sound very promising."

"I didn't mean it to."

"Why do you hold me off? You haven't said no to any of the others."

"You're not like the others, Albion," she answers sadly.

"Would you want me to change?"

"No."

"You're talking in circles. First you tell me that I can't sleep with you because I'm different from the rest, and then, when I ask if you'd like me to change, you say no—what's that add up to?"

"Women sometimes love men too much to sleep with them."

"Do you love me?"

"In a way ..."

"What the hell kind of way is that?"

"The way you love God."

"But the question of sleeping with God never comes into it." I feel that she is trying to tell me something.

"That's why women are never drawn to the idea of God, as men are ..."

"What about Christ? He certainly has been the original sheet-wetter—the eternal Bridegroom."

"But women know that he will never possess them in the flesh."

"Not in the flesh ... we're talking about why you won't sleep with me."

"And I told you, Albion, I don't want you to be like other men with me."

I get up angrily and cross to the dead clerk. "Got a match?" I say. I half-expect that he will give me one. Instead, with a beautiful, slow movement, he opens his eyes and says: "I haven't one. Will this do?" and, as he reaches out his hand, a blast of hell-fire shoots out and burns off my eyebrows.

Politely, I reach up my cig and he controls the flame enough for me to get a light. I mumble thanks and he slumps off the stool, banging his head on a half-full spittoon as he falls. Tobacco juice gives his face the look of a baboon's ass.

"Jackeen, I want you to come up to my room for a minute. I just got a message from Roivas and you may be able to help me decipher it."

"Who will look after Chrystle?"

"She'll be all right. Wait . . . I've got it . . ." I go to the stairhead and call. When he gets down I tell him that he is to mind the baby. He makes what he considers a face, though I think it is a decided improvement on his usual one. So, leaving Chrystle looking at Hitler with evident relish and anticipation, we start up to my room, my eyes having a mighty good time with her bottom.

4. THE AGE OF CONSENT

My glass was empty. I raised the bottle: it was empty too. Damn, I thought, if he comes tonight, I won't be able to offer him a drink. I did not know in my heart that he would come, but I was determined that his coming should not find me unprepared.

I had just slipped into my coat when the sound of singing came up to me from the street. The voice was that of the woman I had heard in God's house.

She was just across the way, standing under a street lamp in the fog. I loved her at once.

I had never loved a woman in my life before.

She sang:

> *The Pale moon was rising above the gray mountain,*
> *The sun was declining beneath the blue sea,*
> *When I strolled with my love to the pure crystal*
> *fountain . . .*

A car slithered by in the wet; the driver wore a silver mask and two men with rifles sat in the rear seat.

> *. . . that made me love Mary, the rose of Tralee.*

64

Allow me to make a very plain confession: I did not lust after the woman. I wanted to take her to some quiet village at the world's end—I wanted to say, "Darling, there is no suffering, no hunger, no murder . . . there are children playing in the meadow there . . . see! their bright scarfs blow out as they run in the wind. Nearly all the monsters are sleeping under the hill . . ."

Nearly all the monsters are dub-smack at our throats.

There is nothing more beautiful than a flock of sheep moving against a summer sky. Why do men kill each other!

Are you planning to take part in the murder?

Have you lost your way in the dark? . . .

I lifted my empty glass. The gray, sky-sweat of the fog poured in at my window. I drank to her in the blood of all the wounded and tortured in the world.

Then a man came and touched her arm and she went away with him. What a dose he would get for his two dollars . . .

5. THE ENCHANTED HAYSTACK

Fiery greyhounds raced crazily up and down the sky as the old man, the two young girls, and the dwarf, weaved puddle-careful along the lonely sea-side road. I was sheltered well in a cave which cattle had made in the side of a haystack; and, from my safe retreat, standing in the rich, touching smell of milk-thick brutes, I called to them, my voice, as it seemed to me, taking a natural place with the hoarse bulling of ships passing far out on the sea. They came upon me, but still they did not hear. I advanced into the rain, and touched the old man on the sleeve.

"Come," I said. "There is shelter here."

Lightning illuminated my face: he recognized me.

We stood crowded together, elbows touching. Soon there was a stirring in us. The girls were quite pretty: one was tall and golden, her mouth a wet, sweet kiss waiting; the other, who appeared to be the dwarf's companion, was the statue of all women and I wanted her body naked and warm against mine.

65

One of the hounds bit through a tree and his roar shook the earth, causing the nearby village to murmur in its sleep.

"I love thunder storms," said tall, golden Ann.

A door creaked open behind us—we were staring into a large, well-lighted room. At a table under Rousseau's *Sleeping Gypsy* sat a man in the uniform of a traffic policeman.

He moaned. "Water! Water! In the name of God . . . Water!" A long knife with the initials H. R. engraved in its handle skewered him neatly to the chair.

I burst into laughter. For the first time, with the opening of the door, in the hot flood of light, with somewhere away in that world we had left, people moving in and out of dancehalls, pumping water at lonely wells, as we stood there, the whole big damn thing taking place, wind tugging at prowling cats, swelling girls pulling on college sweaters, canoes nosing through moonlight and condoms, boxers sitting hunched like slim assassins on their stools in the cardboard light, small boys masturbating each other in the exclusive schools of the rich, the brain boys with poems like iron turds in lavender water measuring off their reputations in apothecaries' scales, drummers in Chattanooga bunning-up on Coca-Cola, bedrooms smelling of Oedipus and lysol, Filipinos with larded hair ordering more shoulder-padding and trying to waddle like Dempsey, organs wheezing "O promise me" and the boogie woogies making blue hot love to the angel of Bix Beiderbecke, while we stood there beside the dying cop, I say, in this world of arrogant murder and shameless falsehood, with our own Rome falling around our ears, with not one single, blazing, wonderful star that hasn't been pissed on by some butcher bleating of his destiny, yes, *yes,* men in ditches filled with the guts of their fellows, the ghosts of all the wars trying to scream above the jackal mouthings of the war-mongers, and I was laughin', kids being blown to hell like bags full of sheepshit, the same ones all the shouting and poems and music and statues are about, the same warm good kids with their clean, fearless eyes looking at you, standing there in that room with all the bucket-thumping paraphernalia of a forty-hand

66

novelist's technique keeping me from what I wanted to say—I busted out laughing, for in the rush of light I saw for the first time that the dwarf had seal's flippers where his feet oughta be.

You see, we are on water but there is no need to build a boat because it would be destroyed in an instant. I know history. There are many names in history but none of them talks because of the water which fills them.

A man walks across the field beneath my window. The left side of his face is bright yellow.

My mother took me into the country. I saw a tiny horse asleep under a willow. We did not take him home.

The old man began to cry. I wanted to be hugging and love-dancing with Maudie, the dwarf's girl; but we had to gawk a bit at the corpse—the poor cop had shoved off by now—there was that singular difference between us. I tried to imagine him with his mouth open, the teeth showing like yellow dice, mustache quivering like the fin of a dolphin in his eagerness, but each time a scarlet rat peered out, wiping sewer-slime from his whiskers.

His right-hand little finger was not missing.

Outside the wind snorted and stamped on the unprotected tops of ships; the houses grinned at each other, relishing the curious dreams of the mortals who fretted out their black heritage in them.

The wild, painful, splashing need of a woman runs through me. I want to crack a rock with my head and find inside it that turning, wet, slippery-soft honey—to press hard, savagely into it; I would tear up a tree and throw my body around it, grinding, twisting, shoving—feeling a woman's flesh drowning under me, the sweet, blubbery spit on her lips, the smell of her hair, Jesus! the whole dizzy pure vile ravaged wonder of my hands cutting into her thighs and the little gulping puppy-sounds she makes . . . the incense of that sharp, half-bitter womansweat as she worships what we are doing . . .

"Dilly, for God's sake, stop that damn flapping around," Maudie said.

67

"He's an Arab," she explained to me. "Can't spika de Eng." She tapped her forehead significantly.

On the table rested a little calf which had been whittled from olive wood. Picking it up, I found a note; it read:

Chrystle's decapitated body was found near Galen this morning.

I turned on them and shouted:

"Whose house is this?"

Ann looked at me, her face sad and withdrawn. A mouse nibbled daintily at the dead man's finger.

"We have no homes now," she said. "We ran away, leaving everything when the armies came. We walked for days in the rain without food—men killed themselves, women went mad—and always the planes fighting over our heads—coming down like horrible torches—setting the fields and woods on fire . . ."

The wind blew the door open. A circle of dogs hemmed us in. One held a doll in its slavering lips.

Then a voice spoke—and it could have come from the head of the young man which was on the doll—saying:

"Brothers, why have you forsaken me!"

6. THE ANGELUS

I had been home only a short time when the landlady knocked. Her breath stank of stale whisky.

"Won't you 'tribute somephin' to poor Dilly's burial?—that's a dear." She smiled like a happy distillery, holding out an alms cup.

"I thought from the way you talked that Dilly was a canary bird," I said without much civility.

She took the coin from my hand.

"Dilly was jes' the sweetes', deares', little dwarf in all the worl' —hiccurf!"

"Whoops!" I said.

I saw her out and locked the door. Then I sat down at my desk and wrote hurried letters to Jenny, Mildred, Eleanor, and Mar-

garet Yard. From somewhere in the town a bell started to toll . . .
I sank to my knees and prayed.

He came to the door and banged but I did not open to him.

On a roof across the street sat three huge women, unmoving,
beautiful in their nudity, their eyes fixed and white on mine.

7. The Pure Crystal Fountain

I have lived many years in the summer of 1929. Some years in
our lives are as minutes, fugitive, possessed of a woeful frailty in
time—time, that is, *human*, not of the clock; other periods, often
no more than a week, a month, a moment long, are as eternity—
they last forever in us. The flash of a leaf in the sun, the fall of a
hand on our arm: empires rise, engender rot, and die; but the
leaf . . . the hand . . . they are in our hearts always. *Oh, Leah, I can
yet hear the lake-water lapping at our canoe; the cry of a night-
bird; boys and girls laughing softly along the shore; I can hear
your voice saying my name.* We did not know what the world
would be; there was no warning from anywhere . . . Leah, they
had no right not to prepare us for what was to come.

But they did not know themselves, Albion.

They knew what they were capable of doing: the white-gloved
murder, the hypocrisy, the whole damn cynical fraud . . .

I am one of them now.

Why should I believe that, Leah?

Because it is the truth.

What do you know of truth—since you are one of them?

Perhaps there was a wonderful moon that night. She was late
in coming to me. I had only met her that afternoon. Would she
not come after all? I'd love to, she had said; I've never been
canoeing on Mendota—looking across the table in the library at
me, her soft, girl's face beautiful in the light of the green-shaded
lamps—I'd love to come. Did she mock me, even a little?

I had blurted out my invitation, conscious of a schoolboy's
pimple on my chin. Women always watch your pimples when you

try to talk as though your animal were as old and wise as theirs.

Standing beside the still water, as couples passed down the pier to the little boat-house, as a crooked ring of bluish light put terrible faces on the trees, as, in distance, at first softly, then with loud impertinence, farm dogs barked at some poor wanderer in the Wisconsin night, I thought: in another month I shall be eighteen, and I have never been with a woman. I saw groups of girls in pretty, many-colored blouses, arms around each other's waists, walking down country lanes, their fierce, golden laughter directed at me; at my fumbling innocence, that prize of my parents, that bane and nuisance of my sleepless nights, being tossed like a paper bull on the horns of their derisive merriment. Their little, swinging buttocks were ancient and naked under the pleated skirts. Eve's goat-yellow eyes looking at me from all their faces. So noiselessly she came . . .

"Hello. Have you been waiting long?"

"No," I lied. "Just got here—few minutes ago."

She talked lightly, quickly about a chemistry exam as we moved out into the lake, the canoe whispering, *Leah . . . Leah*, to the dark water.

The shore-lights were gone: the moon found her face. I saw my town, my road, my faith.

"Take my hand," she said suddenly.

And when I hesitated: "Oh, let's just drift for a little while. We're out far enough now."

I took the paddle in, and lowered its wet, silver-fish length beside me.

She laughed, leaning forward: "You're not afraid of me, are you? Here . . . take my hand."

How cool and tiny! I gripped it awkwardly.

"Are you happy here?" I said, feeling a joy that choked and blinded me.

"Yes, of course I'm happy here. I love all of it . . . the lake, the moon . . ." She broke off, laughing again, but her hand moved deeper into mine.

70

I could not compete with her. My coat felt baggy, my socks dirty, and a sweaty, hot shame for my solitary practices in the night filled me. I believed at that moment that I could only live with her without sex. I understood why religion, which was created for adolescents and the aged, arose, like a headless bird, from the ashes of a Christ conceived sans biology.

"I . . . I didn't mean that," I said. "I meant here, at the University."

"Oh, well, I think Wisconsin is a very fine college." Her lips were deep, deep as plums. I did not like to think that she put food through them.

"But are you happy?"

"Why are you so serious? *(I never said that.)* Let's just enjoy all of this . . ." She moved her hand to include the night and our two bodies. "I know! Let's go in to Picnic Point and sit there for a little while."

I got the paddle in my hands. I sent the canoe in, nearly clawing the water as I thought what she might mean. Good girls did not ask to be taken to Picnic Point. That was the law. I looked up at the clouds. "The angels have their washing out," I said, hoping that she would think me above thinking that other thing.

"You're an old funny. I'm not going to eat you up." How did she know!

You were a baby. Anyone would have known. How frightened you were—pretending to be unconcerned—such a man of the world.

But, Leah, how could I have known then what you wanted me to do?

You will never know that.

He wished that the shore would retreat; that the question could never be given to him for answer. After all, he had only met her that afternoon . . .

They were on land again. Land animals, the split cells of the species, together alone in the night—and the moon shone with a hard, expectant light.

When they were seated, side by side, the smell of the grass coming up to them, she said:

"Kiss me, Albion."

He put his mouth swiftly on her mouth. That he knew about.

"A real kiss."

He put his tongue in her mouth.

"I didn't mean that. This . . ." And she held his head in her hands and pressed her girl-mouth firmly into his. Now his arms, as though they had no other fashion of being, went around her shoulders—her breasts, even when he pulled her body in very hard to him, touched his chest gently, with infinite shyness, like baby wrens.

"Now we can talk and enjoy ourselves," she said, drawing away.

He could think of nothing to tell her. His hunger for her was a tiger; he did not so much want her as he wanted to *be* her; he wanted never to leave her; he did not want his desire to part him from her; he did not want to place himself in a lover's position upon her; he wanted to breathe her; he wanted to find a sexless body somewhere and take both of them into it.

"Are you happy?" she said at last.

"Yes," he said slowly. "I guess I'm not unhappy."

"But that's no answer."

Music drifted in to them from the lake.

"I wish we could dance," she said.

"Yes, so do I."

"Why are you so sad? . . . so tense? I'm just another girl. There are plenty of us in the world."

"Is that the way you feel about me?"

"In a way . . . yes."

"You . . . asking me to kiss you meant nothing to you? Is that it?"

He did not feel anger, only a quiet, consuming kind of bewilderment.

"I wouldn't say that. I like you well enough."

"Do you kiss everyone you like?"

"When I like them well enough."

"What's 'well enough'?"

"Just . . . I suppose it's . . . oh, let's talk about something else."

"You don't love me, do you?"

"Why, I only met you today. How should I know about that?" Then, when he was silent: "Do you love me?"

Yes, Leah, I loved you.

Perhaps . . . perhaps you did.

What will he say? I believe he does love me. There is something strange, almost cruel about him; he tries so hard to be nice, yet, even when he is kissing me, a part of him is sneering and gibing, tugging fiercely at the dearest secrets of both of us. He is a sort of cannibal. There is an instinct to destroy in him. But I like the full, hard shape of his head; the strong grip of his hands; the decisive, quick movement of his walk; the unrelenting, yet tender look of his gray eyes—I like the feel of his mouth on mine, and our bodies are in love—I like the savagery that fills him, that would destroy me. I am afraid of him with every fiber of my being.

'Let me call you sweetheart,
I'm in love with you . . .
Let me hear you whisper
That you love me too.'

. . . a phonograph in a canoe somewhere on the lake . . .

I have a sensation that he is struggling to ask me something. A leaf flutters to the ground beside us. The moon goes under a cloud. I put my hand on his arm.

"Would you marry me, Leah?

"What do you mean, 'would I'?"

"Well, will you?"

"Yes," I said. "But that is impossible now."

"Why? Why is it impossible?"

"How would we live? We have three more years here . . ."

"What does that matter? We can leave . . . I'll get a job—we'll

73

go to New York." In my eagerness I put my hands on her arms. The moonlight made her face more beautiful than anything in the world.

"No, Albion . . . think of our parents; mine sacrificed everything to get me here. Maybe when we're through . . ."

"In three years . . . ?"

"That's not long. And we can see each other often—after all, we hardly know each other."

"Then you won't?"

"We can't, now."

I stood up. I turned and lunged at the canoe, wrenching it from the shore. Tears burnt my eyes and, in my haste, I floundered into the water. She was just standing there, watching.

"Albion . . ."

I couldn't answer. Finally I was moving swiftly away from her. Looking back, I saw three men, their dark figures like hangmen, emerge from the trees and move toward her.

She screamed once . . . then a muffled cry. They were dragging her away from the path, into the bushes.

Blood covered the moon, but he raced on, her name like a fire in his mouth.

Leah! Leah! how could I know that they would kill you . . . my pale girl bride . . . night wind, night, wind . . . black shapes flying against the sun . . .

8. How the Swan Was Investigated

We were walking along the shore, laughing and in good spirits after the disastrous wreck of the Overland Limited. Two hundred and eighty-six lives had been lost. The coach we had been riding in, the fourth behind the double-engine, had, by one of those miraculous chances of angel-luck, not only not left the track, but had come through without so much as the shattering of one window.

The sun was shining; the morning was clear and bird-filled; we were happy to be where we were; our breakfasts had been good: we had forgotten the war altogether.

Carol saw him first—a little, round fluff of white swimming about among the lily pads like a baby king. His feathers were glistening with wet. I knew of the cruelty of his race; I had heard the stories of small children pulled into the water and drowned by swans—but this one was playing like a kitten, spinning after his tail, chasing ghosts.

While we lingered there, applauding his snowy behavior, a fat man, smelling of riches, his legs running without interruption into his stomach, flipped his burning cigar at the water. The little swan caught it deftly in his bill and was painfully burnt.

The fat man laughed, and started to walk on.

Suddenly he went head over heels into the water.

"Thank you, Joseph," I said.

How white the tiny swan was!

Carol and I sat down on a bench and discussed plans for Chrystle's funeral.

9. THE LOST AMAZON

We were playing poker in the backroom of 'The Pickled Goat.' It was a warm night and the bar was crowded with men putting beer into them.

Jetter was using his own deck and the stakes were that for every chip won the winner got a punch at the loser and the rest of us would look like hell in the morning. He was in an ugly mood and we preferred a sock in the mouth to getting shot for keeps.

The clock struck: bub, bub, bub. I looked into the public room and saw her. I nudged Billy Delian.

"Christ!" he said.

Jetter and Thomas Honey looked then.

"She's seven feet tall," I said.

"If she's an inch," Jetter agreed.

Billy Delian pushed his chair back. "Let's call her in for a beer." He moved off. The piano tinkled like somebody breaking glass in a tin box.

"Well, boys," Billy Delian said, as she shuffled in at his side, "I want you to meet a couple friends of mine."

"Cut that," Jetter said. Then, to her: "Here, sit down, take a load off your feet."

She sat down slowly, testing the chair. We saw for the first time that she was fat.

"What's your name, sister?" Jetter asked, trying to take her in in one look.

"I don't know." Her voice was muffled, like something wrapped up in a sheep.

"She must be one of these here amnesia victims," Thomas Honey said.

"You don't know what your name is, huh?" Jetter said. "Don't worry about us—no matter what you done, we wouldn't turn you in."

"I haven't done anything," she said, holding her beer in her hand but not drinking. "I simply don't know who I am."

"Sure you're not William Jennings Bryan?" Billy Delian said.

"I told you to stuff that," Jetter warned.

"Sometimes it just takes one thing to make them remember all about themselves," Thomas Honey explained.

"Perhaps we should ask her a few questions," I agreed.

"O. K.," Jetter said. "Drink up your beer and we'll find out who you are in no time." He thought hard, shuffling the cards with three fingers. "Let's see . . . you ever been in Canada?"

"No," she said. A fly alighted on her arm and she nailed him with one of her hams—surprisingly fast for such a monster of a woman, I thought.

I said: "Do you have a husband?"

"You mean *one* man?" Billy Delian said, putting half his laugh in his beer as Jetter looked over at him.

"I can't remember," she said slowly.

The piano was going to *The Dark Town Strutters' Ball*. "Shall

76

the four of us dance?" Billy Delian made a gallant gesture to her.

"This is a serious business," Jetter said. "Put that damn clown back in your pocket."

She said: "I think I'll have to go now."

"What's your hurry?" Jetter shoved her back into the chair. I could see that he was enjoying himself.

She said, "Well, all right, for a little while."

"Ever had syph'?" Thomas Honey asked.

"I don't think so," she said.

"Wouldn't you suppose she'd know that even if she can't remember her name?" Jetter said, half to himself.

"Four o'clock. Time to close," a big, bristly head called into us.

"Where you plan to stay tonight?" Jetter asked her, as we got to our feet and reached for hats.

"At the Y. W.," she said.

"Now you don't want to do that," Jetter said. "Come home with me—you'll be as safe with me as with your mother."

"If you like," she said. "I don't care much about anything anymore."

She started to cry. A milk wagon passed us as we started down the street. It was raining a little. We pulled our coats tight around our throats. A dog barked behind a fence.

Billy Delian pushed a bill into Jetter's hand. "Grab a taxi," he said. "What's the point in letting her catch cold."

It was raining hard by the time a cab came along. We all stood behind her and hoisted; it took minutes to get her in.

We watched the taillight disappear down the street. Morning was graying the things around us.

"Jetter forgot to collect on the poker," Thomas Honey said.

"Yeah, he did at that," I said, watching the lights going on in houses.

10. THE WALL OF BIRDS

The sentry had fallen asleep at the foot of the tree.

A little girl was picking flowers in a meadow that lay just over the hill. I waited until her back was to me, then, being careful not to give in to a desire to warn them, I bellied worm-like into a position which commanded the whole scene. The sky was losing light. I wanted a cigarette, but my hand was too shaky to hold one. Sweat poured along the barrel of my rifle.

I made the required signal to my company. They moved up in a flying wedge, blunt end first, running back, four men, three, two, then into the point, that one man who could have mowed them all down with one spray of his tommy-gun.

Then a strange thing took place. The child in the field, with a single, beautiful movement, slipped out of her dress and stood naked there. Her breast-points were as tiny brown eyes as she faced us.

At once—did God signal too?—where the sleeping sentry had been, a ball of wings turned, spinning up, making a song like peasants singing, careless, age-old, defiant—larks! They rose into the sun, grim and a desperate shield; O my Chevaliers . . .

I pushed out a hand fashioned of water. To that from which things come must they return in the last hour. In fear and pain must they account for their being, as was the case of He Who first saw the naked girl-child and the wall of birds with all our faces written on it.

Sweat pours down my pen. I signal to you . . .

11. Chrystle Again: The Funeral

In the depths of the earth, I hear them stirring: the countless, unliving dead. The ground is full of them; they are as the blades of grass, as the dust-motes in shafts of sunlight. They are that terrible army we must join. Death is in us now. Its voice is the only voice that rings through us always. The child picks a flower: our bodies lie in her hand. A deer bends to drink at a mountain stream: our blood enters his throat. The horrible screaming in the ground . . . ah, that's what we hear in that one mad hour of the night. Our own calling to us—*do not answer!* Madness is there. Christ was crucified not on the cross but in the ground—by their voices: he arose *from the dead.*

"Wait a minute," Jetter said. "You may think that's a proper sermon and all that, but it don't sound like no way to bury somebody. How about a bit of Bible reading?"

We stood around the black hole which had been dug in the yellow, soft clay of the river bank. It was late at night and our lanterns made us figures in an earthquake.

"We came to bury Chrystle, not to parade her," I said.

"And what does that mean?" Billy Delian asked, coughing in the mist that covered us like wet flannel.

"It means that we must speak the truth over the graves of the poor," I answered. "The Bible belongs to the rich."

"That's stupid," Thomas Honey said. "How can you say that the Bible is the sole property of the rich."

"No puns, please," Jetter said.

"Because the Bible belongs to the church," I explained.

"There's where you go off the track," Thomas Honey said. "I admit that the church is controlled by the rich, but actually it is the poor who sustain its existence."

"By the sweat of their brow?"

"No, by their will."

"I suppose they will the state in the same way."

"Not at all. Their dog-like submission to the state breeds in them a need to seek solace in the church."

"Do you say that the state is the cause and the church is the effect?" I was not sure that he was being honest with me.

"That would rule out the religious impulse altogether."

"Do the rich have this too?"

"They have the church."

"I thought the church belonged to the poor by right of their will . . ."

"What man wills possesses him."

"Then what you are saying is that the poor have willed a monster which the rich use for the destruction of the poor."

"You forget one thing . . . the poor, even more than the church, are the creation and property of the rich."

"And will destroy the rich . . . ?"

"Of course," Thomas Honey said.

"Then," I answered, "since the state exists in the will of the rich, it is the state which possesses the rich, and not the rich the state, as we have supposed?"

"That is true. The state is the monster which the rich have set at their own throats."

"But it is the throats of the poor which bleed now," I said. We would have to lower the coffin soon: day was nibbling at the trees.

"The monsters of state and church shall one day sleep under the hill where rises a free and beautiful world," he said.

"And the rich will have died at the hands of the poor?" I asked. A cock crowed from the yard of a farmer.

"By no means," Thomas Honey said. "They will have died under the teeth of their own monsters. The poor can no more inherit the earth than there can be 'mute, inglorious, Miltons': for if a man be mute, where the poet? inglorious—how Milton? and if Milton, how can he be other than Milton? If a man have an inheritance, however small, he cannot be poor; and if he have the whole world . . . ?"

"Let's put her in," Jetter said.

"What should be said as we lower her down?" Billy Delian asked. "You have ruled out words of Bible and state . . ."

Footsteps could be heard coming down the bank of the river. We must not be found there. A low whistle sounded near us. A sharp, brutal noise—the bark of a dog on the chase.

I said: "You were one of us." And we lifted her down into the earth and the earth we put over her.

We were moving away, extinguishing our lanterns as we went—it could have been a monster, that wounded horse charging out of the trees, entrails swinging like bloody vines under him, and screaming, God! it was a woman screaming—knees buckling under him in the soft dirt of the new grave, chopping up the coffin-wood and the body of Chrystle flying in red horror into the deep river.

A man knelt on the ground in a circle of silent people. Another man stood above him with uplifted axe. He brought it down in a clean, righteous stroke. The head of the standing man rolled to the feet of him who was kneeling.

Yes, indeed, a moral: in this world, the executioners are weaponless always.

———

JUNE 30 After supper today I went up in a bomber. The pilot was a nice, young chap. He said that he was sixteen, but he looked younger. His name was G. R. Deaken.

He showed me how to release the bombs. I tried out a couple. It was fun, of a kind.

I dropped one on a little feed-mill. The miller went up like a geranium opening. His head, which had come off at once, kept yelling "Cleo! Cleo!" going higher and higher until it whizzed by us.

G. R. grinned.

My next fell in a field covered with cows. It worked great on the cows. It must have been a new experience for them, being cut to pieces by something costing thirty thousand dollars. We were using good bombs.

Then another plane came up and started chasing us around. G. R. got very excited. "Use it! Use it!" he shouted, meaning the machine gun. Just at that time something ran like hail along the side of our plane. That was it! They wanted a fight! I grabbed hold of the machine-gun and swung it around, pulling away for dear life on a little gadget that looked like a trigger. Put! Pit! Pit! The first round got poor G. R. Deaken in the middle of the back. He wasn't expecting that and he died without so much as an allegiance to the flag on his lips.

In an instant the enemy was clamoring up the wings, bayonets held crosswise in their mouths. The plane was spinning around like a tin snowflake.

"Have a cigarette, boys?" I asked, holding out my pack.

They looked surprised, but they didn't shoot me.

I smelt something suspiciously like shit.

"That's the war," one of them said, taking a cigarette.

"Are you always scared like that?" I asked.

"Not always . . . Not when we're dead."

"Well," I said, "you'll soon not be scared anymore."

We hit the ground like an empire falling.

I crawled out just before the damn thing went up in flames. It smelled like a steak-fry for a little while.

||||||||||||||||||||||||||||||||||||||||||||||||||||||||||||||||||||||||||||||||||||||||||||||||||||||||||||||||||||||||||||||||||||||||||||||

JULY 1 🐒 It has been agreed that we are to take the automobile road to Topenville. This village, long noted for its curious climate (no one has ever died there), is impossible of approach from the world. We shall go by another way. Roivas, presumably, has willed this trip into the cold-lying reaches of ice and snow. I hope that we will be favored by the sight of red flowers growing in the mile-high drifts. We must traverse more than nine hundred thousand kilometres straight up the side of a mountain which is known as the most perilous in all the world.

I paid a visit to the meteorological department of the University and begged information on the matter of the un-physical climate into which we were headed. They shook their collective gray head and mumbled something about a woman in Switzerland who had spent her honeymoon in Topenville. By a lucky chance, lucky enough to make me chuckle, she happened to walk into the office just then. Despite a vacant look in her eyes and a tendency to slobber, she seemed pleasant enough. It was the work of a moment to persuade her to accompany us. She refused to divulge her name, though I wiped her chin and nose with a clean handkerchief. Let us call her Öhklipt-Pogy.

I stuffed my rucksack with herring and over-size pretzels; Topenville ale is famous from Harmondsworth to Oil City.

My ice-axe is an unusually fine one, the gift of Jackeen.

We got the twelve cylinder Mercedes onto the highway about noon. Jetter sat behind the steering wheel, a long, fawn-colored duster of an old style around his shoulders, and on his black nose, gleaming in the hot sun of summer, rested a giant pair of aviator's goggles.

"I wouldn't trust him at the wheel," Carol whispered to me.

"Shut up," I said shortly.

I busied myself with my note-books until Billy Delian and Thomas Honey had got everything strapped into the rear trunk where, at the bottom under greasy rags and fripperies, were concealed a machine-gun and three machetes such as are used in cutting sugarcane.

Hitler and Öhklipt-Pogy were already settled in the bright red trailer which we had uncoupled from the car of a traveling evangelist; large signs in big, block letters of yellow proclaimed:

REPENT WHILE THERE IS TIME!
MAKE YOUR PEACE WITH GOD!
PUT YOUR TRUST IN JESUS!

Well. Goodbye. Goodbye. We set off at a clipper's pace and soon left only an inch-high Billy Delian waving to us in the mid-day mists which rose from the fever-infested swamps. Billy had to stay to complete the last stage of his barnstorming campaign.

I unslung my binoculars and looked through the big end into his face. He was weeping—standing there in the dust crying like a bee-stung baby. His was no small job—beating Mrs. Drew all alone.

The little green bushes of gorse rushed by us like prairie chickens dead from ptomaine.

What was it that troubled me so? Oh, yes ...

I said to Carol: "There is no danger from the world; all that is dangerous lives in us."

83

"What do you mean, Albion?"

"I mean that the saner we are the more danger of madness there is."

"Just what ..."

"Shut up. I can remember seeing a horror story in the newspaper—an axe-murder, for example—say I read it at five in the afternoon; by six o'clock I am in deadly terror that someday I shall kill someone with an axe; by seven o'clock I can think of nothing else; by eight o'clock I am hiding all the knives and sharp instruments in the house; by nine o'clock ..."

"Where to now, boss?" Jetter had stopped the car at a fork in the road.

"Get out and ask Öhklipt-Pogy," I said.

"It's not what happens that frightens us," I went on to Carol, "it's what it does to us. Consider the war—few of us are afraid of being killed ..."

"I wouldn't say that, Albion."

"I know you wouldn't. We are afraid of what the killing does— it gets down around our nerves."

Jetter climbed in, spun the wheel to the left and we hit a road that must have been paved with boulders by the Indians.

"That is where we are defenseless," I said. "Our nerves can't stand up under it."

I faced around that they might all hear me. "And our nerves haven't stood up under it. I much doubt that there is a single sane human being on this planet now. Mad men ... I tell you to listen— nerves can take so much, then, *bing* they snap. Lock anyone of you in a dark room for twenty-four hours and you'll be screaming like stuck pigs, beating the walls with your fists—your nerves, gentlemen—we protect ourselves by going mad."

There was a loud woosh of air and the right, rear wheel started to pound like a two-headed hammer in a crockery shop and we lurched off the road into a field where a shepherd sat on a rock near a brook playing a reed pipe and beating time with his foot.

The holy stars that light this world brought me to that man. St.

Michael of the Mount! My head ached with love and nightmare ...
I, I, I, Albion Moonlight, hater of mobs, lover of truth ... bah!
glutton, pimp, raper of girl-children ... The shepherd was looking
at me out of the eyes of Jesus.

He regarded me gravely. "You are looking for Me," He said.

"Yes," I mumbled, feeling shame and a great joy.

"Well ..." He smiled. "What do you propose to do with Me?"

"I want to ask You a question, Master."

"What question?"

"What will be the outcome of all this?"

"Of all what?"

"The war ... the murder ... the madness ..."

His beautiful face turned to His Father in Heaven and His eyes
filled with tears.

"It was the same when I was on earth," He said softly.

I could not answer at once. I was conscious that my stomach
was digesting loudly.

"But there was hope then," I said at last.

"Hope ..." He made the word a knife. "Hope! for whom! You
fool! You miserable fool."

"Please, Jesus ..."

"Don't 'please, Jesus' Me! The day will come when not one
stone shall remain on another; nation shall rise against nation,
and kingdom against kingdom; famine and pestilence shall walk
the earth with dripping hands; settle it therefore in your heart
what answer you will give, when you shall be betrayed by your
own people—and ..." Christ covered His face and wept bitterly.

"And when ye shall see Jerusalem compassed with armies,"
Thomas Honey went on quietly, "then know that the desolation
thereof is nigh.

"Then let them which are in the city flee to the mountains; and
let them which are in the midst of it depart out; and let them that
are in the countries enter thereinto.

"For these be the days of vengeance, that all things which are
written may be fulfilled.

85

"But woe unto them that are with child, and to them that give suck, in those days! for there shall be great distress in the land, and wrath upon this people.

"And they shall fall by the edge of the sword, and shall be led away captive into all nations.

"And there shall be signs in the suns, and in the moon, and in the stars; and upon the earth distress of nations; the sea and the waves roaring.

"Men's hearts failing them for fear, and for looking after those things which are coming on the earth; for the powers of heaven shall be shaken."

Jesus said: "Heaven and earth shall pass away; but my words shall not pass away."

"That won't help anyone," I said.

He looked at me in a clumsy way, almost as though He felt embarrassed by what He saw. We were not unlike in our outward appearance—my beard was perhaps a little more vigorous.

JULY 2 🐇 We put up in a little mountain village last night. I was surprised to find that our landlord was the same one who had attended us in the forest inn. He refused, smiling, to answer any questions.

"This is a free country, isn't it?" he said.

Christ, Who had ridden along with Hitler and Öhklipt-Pogy in the trailer, showed no curiosity about our reasons for making the hazardous excursion to Topenville. He seemed to realize that a man must move around. Hitler avoided Him like the plague.

We are up in snow country now. I have a fur cap which, when pulled down over my ears, not only keeps me warm but serves to deaden somewhat the thudding of the heavy guns.

Yesterday we passed many regiments of ski-troops, looking like fat ghosts against the forests and the snow.

After supper today a messenger from Divisional Headquarters

86

paid us a visit. He said that the Enemy were using gas-shells—in violation of International Law—and what should be done about it.

"Have you taken any prisoners?" I asked, more to evade his difficult question than out of any genuine interest.

"Yes," he said. "I'll bring you one."

No sooner said. The prisoner was a little, red-faced man who looked as though he'd been crying.

"What is your name?" I asked, feeling very uncomfortable.

"Gerry Boller. What's yours?"

"Albion Moonlight. How old are you?"

"I was born in 1923. And you?"

"Look, Gerry, if you don't mind," I said, "I'll ask the questions."

"Shoot," he said sullenly.

"What were you in civilian life?"

"I worked in a paper napkin factory in Toledo."

"Did you like it in the army?" I knew that this was a silly thing to ask a prisoner, but I couldn't for the life of me think of anything important to ask him.

"I like it better now," he said.

"Didn't you believe in what you were fighting for?"

"Believe in it? In what?"

"You mean you didn't know what you were fighting for?"

"I wasn't fighting for anything."

"Then why did you fight?"

"I didn't. I didn't fight a lick. I'm not mad at anybody." His mouth got tight. "Except the sons-of-bitches who sent me out here."

Jetter looked at the kid with a grin.

"Gerry," he said, "you're all right."

"Go fry a rabbit," Gerry told him.

I gave him a pack of Camels and the guard led him away. Just as he reached the door, he turned and said:

"When I get out of this damn uniform I'm going to get a gun and shoot everybody in sight."

"I thought you weren't mad at anybody," I said.

87

"I'm not," he said. "That's why I'll knock them off—do them a good turn, that's Gerry."

The guard cracked him on the side of the head with the butt of his rifle, and off they went.

It is snowing outside my window as I write. Not far away the villagers are cooking supper over open fires in the flank of a great cave. They sing as they move about. Their diet consists mainly of crayfish which abound in the nearby mountain lake; the flesh is stringy and has an unpleasant gluey flavor. The incessant bleating of sheep makes conversation or rest difficult. Apparently the natives have never thought to add mutton to their eatables.

The food in this inn is unbelievably bad. I got into a vile temper and would surely have fallen upon the landlord with any weapon at hand had I not been painfully restrained by the spectacle of two enormous dogs which crouched watchfully at my feet waiting for the merest gesture from me to make their deadly way to my throat. Christ, observing my fear, walked calmly upon them with outstretched hand; they growled deep in their throats but suffered His caresses.

I shall read *Faust* until sleep comes.

JULY 3 🐾 We breakfasted off fried crayfish patties and indescribable coffee. While the others were busy with the loading and oiling and gassing, I heated a silver dollar and wrapped it carefully in my muffler; then, when we were all in the car, the trailer chain examined and in order, I tossed the hot coin to our host, the scaly innkeeper. His roar of pain and rage was music to my ears.

We got away at 6:20 a.m. It was snowing wonderfully, the flakes big and soft and affording excellent cover against bombers which could be heard high overhead purring like giant cats. Occasionally we met sledges drawn by shaggy-sided horses with lemon-colored manes, but the preponderance of traffic was of peasants sauntering along on foot carrying huge baskets full of dried crayfish (known locally as *offkenisona*). The women are sturdy and cheerful, but afflicted, unfortunately, with a tendency to be cross-eyed—after staring at them for a time, one invariably finds one's self looking down one's nose.

I managed before starting to clothe myself with heavy sealskin gloves, an ox-hide overcoat, snow-boots of rabbit, and two scarves of virgin wool—besides my fur cap. For this I am thankful.

The others do not fare so well, being got out in summer fashion. Hitler, especially, suffers from the intense cold; his anemia is complete and well-nigh inhuman. There is a good deal of muttering and complaining; Jetter is in a towering rage because I won't surrender my gloves to him. His fingers refuse to unbend from the steering wheel, and Thomas Honey is obliged to do all the gear-shifting and braking. I invited Jackeen to come under my coat with me (it being of mammoth size), but she declined with a frozen-lipped smile.

Once we passed a large group of people gathered in a field around a fire. They had an old, fat woman strapped to a post and were slowly cooking her, amid shouts of merriment and good spirits. She seemed to be laughing with the others, although the flesh on her thighs was already beginning to flake off.

I was surprised to see very small children poking the meat off her with long, pointed sticks.

We are now above the timber-line, and our pace has slowed appreciably due to the engine's difficulties with the rarified air.

JULY 4 🦊 The snow has given way to a fine, driving sleet which renders driving impossible on this narrow, avalanche-beset road.

Ohklipt-Pogy wears a worried frown. She is incapable of speech. An excellent guide!

We have all piled into the trailer, where, before a little, pot-bellied stove, we sit and listen to the storm which gathers force as it threshes from crag to crevasse, from arrête to poky-hole in the rocks.

I am anxious to witness a conversation between Christ and

Adolf Hitler, but as yet they appear equally anxious to have nothing to do with each other.

Privacy is impossible, of course; the blizzard prevents us from relieving our bodies of their waste out-of-doors. We have set apart a corner for this purpose. The crayfish has made us runny—worse luck! This is a hard situation with women in the party.

JULY 5 🦁 Still marooned. We were roused out of troubled sleep this morning by the twittering of birds. They are of a kind unknown to us; their bills are dark purple and are quite transparent in a certain light—creepy to see their tongues and teeth mangling the tiny gitte-bugs which is the chief fare of these creatures. Their back sides are bright orange, and two tiny black spots there placed look for all the world like eyes.

I spent the day on my report to Roivas. Perhaps I should set a part of it down in this place.

The report (in part):

The first thing we discovered was that at no time in history did man so need a word of guidance and encouragement.

I propose now to give you some idea of how we set about to answer the tide of barbarism which has swept plague-like through the world during the past months.

There is only one answer: *end War.*

There is only one way to end War: *that is by bringing Capitalism to an end.*

There is only one way to end Capitalism: *that is by Revolution.*

There is only one way for Revolution to succeed: *that is by establishing a world-wide Socialism.*

This is the task of mankind. This will be done.

Capitalism and Fascism are one under the iron mask.

Fascism is the expression of Capitalism's death struggle.

War is the life blood of Capitalism; it is the body and soul of Fascism.

Capitalist economy leads inevitably to War; Fascist economy

begins and ends in War—it is an economy of War, and of nothing else whatever.

To fight against War is to fight against the Capitalist State.

To fight against the Capitalist State is the only honorable and humane course open to thinking men and women.

But our struggle will be without historical importance: Capitalism's death is assured—and with it, the death of its horrible twin, Nazi-Fascism.

America will go to War; indeed, is at War now.

America's face is smiling. A new blood quickens her step; her mills and foundries are pouring out black smoke in a frenzy of exultation—but do not be deceived: it is the false, painted bloom on the face of a corpse; America does a crazy jig-step behind the screeching bands and the banners proudly carried by the moronic schoolboys upon whom she depends—but her breasts swing flabbily and are without milk—great red-handed whore filling the air with fighting planes, and the sea with destroyers: your struggle is useless, already the death rattle can be heard in your throat.

What a murderous cheat and liar you are!

You have crippled and destroyed; you have burnt and pillaged; you have defiled and degraded every decent impulse of my people; you have butchered and laid waste to man's very soul.

yet you expect me to fight for you

Nay, not expect, you demand!

Recruiting Officer: Sign here.

Moonlight: I will not.

Recruiting Officer: Oh, you won't, eh? Why not?

Moonlight: I refuse to fight your war.

Recruiting Officer: My war! What the hell . . . won't you fight for your country?

Moonlight: Yes. I will fight for my country.

Recruiting Officer: O.K. That's better. Here . . . on this line.

Moonlight: But I told you I wouldn't sign it.

Recruiting Officer: Look, guy, I ain't got all day. I thought you said you'd fight for your country.

Moonlight: I did; but you're not my country.

Recruiting Officer: What the hell have I got to do with it?

Moonlight: Everything. You're the only face of government I've ever seen—the mill cops, the dicks on the railroad...

Recruiting Officer: Tough guy, huh? Hey, Ed, take this mug into Number Seven.

(I am led down a corridor and into a large office where sits a ruddy-faced man behind a polished desk. He smiles pleasantly at me; offers a cigarette, which I refuse.)

Number Seven: College man? (I nod.) Well, that's fine. Now what's the difficulty?

Moonlight: No difficulty. I refuse to fight your war.

Number Seven: My war? Come, my good man, let's get down to brass tacks. Do you have a religious objection?

Moonlight: In a way.

Number Seven: What do you mean by that? What church do you belong to?

Moonlight: That's a good way to put it... 'belong' to.

Number Seven: Well, what is it?

Moonlight: I belong to no church.

Number Seven: Ah! Then what did you mean by saying you had a religious objection.

Moonlight: I didn't. I said, 'in a way.'

Number Seven: All right. Let's have it.

Moonlight: I believe in mankind.

Number Seven: Now, what the hell kind of an answer is that?

Moonlight: It's the only answer.

Number Seven: Look, fellah, maybe you don't know what you're up against. Do you know what happens to conscientious objectors?

Moonlight: I know what happens to soldiers when they get a bayonet in their guts.

Number Seven: Oh, that's it! So you're just plain afraid, eh?

Moonlight: Yes, I'm plain afraid and fancy afraid, but that isn't my reason for refusing to fight in an Imperialist war.

92

Number Seven: Ahha, so that's it—a Red.

Moonlight: Yes, I'm a Red and a Black and a Brown and a Yellow and a White; I'm a Negro, a Chinaman, a German, a Spaniard, a Swiss.

Number Seven: Don't get cute ...

Moonlight: I'm the grandson of a man who was killed in a coalmine because the owners saved a few dollars on timbers; I'm the son of a man who worked thirty years on a farm and was buried in a pauper's grave; I'm the friend of a man who was lynched because he had a black skin ...

Number Seven: You dirty son-of-a-bitch ...

Moonlight: And you sit there on your flabby fat ass and ask me to sign a paper saying that I'll take a rifle and shoot down my own people.

Number Seven: We'll take care of you.

Moonlight: I said my own people ... I refuse to kill in your defense—so long as there is war between nations, the working classes of the world will be blinded to one simple fact: that they have only one enemy—the German people, the English, the Dutch, the Japanese, the Mexican—one common enemy; and that is Capitalism.

Number Seven: (sputtering) Scum! Bastard!

Moonlight: In the name of Shakespeare and Dante! that I should be an outlaw of the world! I had no part in making any of this! I have never in my life desired the death of anyone. I have wanted that all men live beautifully and purely on a free earth. I am the one who should be directing the minds of men. To whom do I speak? To the intellectuals? They are already jumping like monkeys on the war-drums—poor, puny, little turncoat hypocrites, beating their breasts in horror at the Hitler menace, and hugging away for dear life to the hideous monster of jingoism— fondling the gangrenous ass of our own 100 per cent nascent Fascism. To whom? To the workers? The workers are glued to the radios, and beginning to froth at the mouth in the approved cannon-fodder style. Poor devils! Who on the face of the earth to lead

93

them! To whom do I speak? Ah, yes, to whom? To the Stalinist Communists? Debauchers of Leninism and murderers of the leaders of the October Revolution; betrayers of Spain and allies of Hitler. No, not to them. To the Trotskyist Communists? Where are they? Where is their following? Who are their leaders? What are they doing? No, surely not to them.

I speak for my own kind.

For those who love the warm fields in summer sunlight; for those who love . . . yes, yes, yes, yes, yes, yes, Goddam it to hell . . . poetry, music, Nijinsky, Spinoza . . .

As I lay with my head in your lap, Camerado,
The confession I made I resume—what I said to you in the open air
*   I resume:*
I know I am restless and make others so;
I know my words are weapons, full of danger, full of death;
For I confront peace, security, and all the settled laws, to unsettle
*   them;*
I am more resolute because all have denied me, than I could ever
*   have been had all accepted me;*
I heed not, and have never heeded either experience, cautions,
*   majorities, or ridicule;*
And the threat of what is called hell is little or nothing to me;
And the lure of what is called heaven is little or nothing to me;
Dear Camerado! I confess I have urged you onward with me, and
*   still urge you, without the least idea of what is our destination,*
Or whether we shall be victorious, or utterly quelled and defeated.

> *Take her up tenderly,*
> *Lift her with care;*
> *Fashioned so slenderly,*
> *Young, and so fair!*

for those who yet believe,

I am the flower of destruction, and the living skull of now, Jackeen
*   said.*

I lay down in the city's shadow, and its fruit was a bitterness in my mouth.

They brought me to man's slaughter-house and the soldiers put the war out of them on me.

Their sweaty hands implore me, their thighs throw up the knot of flesh that not even war can still.

My lovers are like rats in a well: behold, they put their hands to me, whimpering . . .

The human winter is upon the earth, youth and love lie rotting on these terrible fields.

Death walks upon the seas; the time of singing is done, and the voice of the vulture is heard through the land.

The war-tree putteth forth her sour fruit, and the barbed wire with its mangled flesh gives out a horrible stench. Get up, poor dubs, take thy souls away—what have men to do with souls!

Thou art in the mud of the trenches, in the vomit where the heroes lie—did you like the speeches? was there one orator better than the others?

Turn on the searchlights, let us see the vines of barbed wire again: what wine will be made from these pitiful grapes!

Behold my breast, my naked, woman's breast, where all who lie here are good and clean and as safe as the generals are.

Hold me, soldier, we will do as the pairs of everything do; we will rejoice in the wonderful difference of our bodies;

I am a two-dollar whore, but as the night and stars are accounted beautiful, so must thou accept my beauty: they have made me the symbol of ugliness, but mine own wonder they do not know—in me the sink, the grail, the lustful skeleton.

Go thy way forth by the fields of blood which overflow their cathedrals, but come, come back to my two breasts, for being on hire, I shall not ask thee of thy kill, of how his flesh moved under your knife. I shall demand no tales of glory, no talk of causes and the Right: we will make our private, ritual murder —and you will pay and I will eat again. I am the pillar of thy

*State, the trampled ground of suicides, escape from madness
—in this world where only our organs are sane.*

12. The Betrayal

The lights were out in London, and over all the earth terror
crept like a man without a face. Great fists of hate beat on the
houses. I kissed her on the mouth, and we went to sleep.

That was last night.

God knows why I was trembling when I put my morning touch
on her breast. Perhaps I expected to find her dead.

This is going to be hard to tell.

I got up and started water for a quick bath. I put a new blade in
the razor and squared off in front of the mirror. A little gate
opened in my forehead and I saw a mouth moving back there.

"What are you going to do now?" the voice said.

"I don't know," I said.

"Are you sure that Chrystle is dead?"

Before I could answer the voice started to laugh and Mildred
came to the door and called my name and then I was back in the
room with her and she was saying, "It was just your nerves" but I
knew better than to believe that.

Mildred's men squatted around us with their buttocks on their
heels. They were a hard crowd and I was not No. 1 in their book. I
blew on the eye of my cigarette, pinched its belly between two
fingers, then I flicked it out in a beautiful arc straight into Rubio's
mouth. I stepped back easily

GIVE

when he came in, and ran the ripple
of my arm like a ramrod into the pit of his stomach. He rolled over
on his back, gasping and looking mean. My first shot caught him
in the shoulder, my next in his nuts. Mildred didn't look any too

pleased, but she didn't say anything. Kelly started to move up and I leveled off thinking I'd take him right

ME

where his purple hand-kerchief was. He said, "Let's forget it now, punk," and I said, "Sure, we can discuss it after breakfast."

I knew that something was phony when I caught Mildred slipping fifty

SOME

bucks to Moe over the eggs. I made a show of being very busy mopping up the last traces of yolk on my plate, but I was doing a lot of thinking. I hadn't a chance against her if she really wanted me to get on that little black train, and she seemed to be building up for an ugly mood. She would knock me out of the park at the first pitch—and I knew it, hard.

I kicked over the table. I walked in close around them and beat in their heads. Then I lifted off the top of the house and threw it over my shoulder. I took my fists and pounded them together until the blood came. I rolled Mildred over

OF

and got on and stayed for eight hours and twenty minutes. All the time I was shouting at the top of my lungs. I took a pen and some paper and started to write:

Tomorrow I am going to knock down all the buildings and tear up every Goddamn street you ever heard of. I am going to write a book on billboards from coast to coast—with letters fifteen feet high. It's going to be a simple story. In the first place somebody

97

gets killed; then a blonde doll gets knocked up; the police break in and find a little guy sleeping on a cot; by God the first thing you know everybody

THAT

in the country is involved—200,000,000 characters in this one book, and I'll be sitting there smiling—but my eyes will be cold and fixed. It is raining. It is snowing. The room is furnished rather well. A huge armchair is placed near the fire. I step over to the old lady and ask her please for a loan of five hundred dollars. She scowls and I kiss

GOOD OLD

her tenderly on the throat. But all this time the car is eating up country, and we have almost forgotten that the driver is dead.

It always surprises me, how happy I feel when a lot of things are going on at once. Consider this present instance. I had tied up with Mildred the night before—took her away from a bullfighter, as a matter of fact. She was a neat piece, but rather too handy with a gat. We were walking back to

WHOREHOUSE

her room when a big guy in a Palm Beach suit called to us from a doorway. I was playing it cozy and we went along meekly enough. Well, just as we got inside, Palm Beach dealt me a solid one on the kisser and I went out. When I looked in again, this boy and Milly are doing a Mr. and Mrs. on the edge of a big bed and the room is full of dicks.

I have been framed, of course. John Law takes me on the instant I get my eyes open. All I can say is that I never saw the dead man before. I tell them this in ten

PIANO

languages, even going into dialect, but it's no soap—they keep turning him over and shoving my face down until I can see the tiny red lines in his eyeballs. I haven't the least idea who he is. Then a couple girls walk into the room and the cops say who are you? These dolls don't seem to hear, they stand right there and undress as cool as brass. Pretty soon Mildred comes over and takes my arm and we get moving. Palm Beach is laughing like he'll split. O world, O life, O hell. I pull my collar up around my neck and then it happens. A big sedan pulls out of a side street and starts cruising along beside us. A slim kid with his cap pulled down over his eyes sits at the wheel. He gives us the nod. We get in. He sends her up to fifty, then sixty, seventy, eighty, ninety, one hundred—we jump right over the town. He pulls up at a house. I notice that the shutters are bullet proof. This lad's name is Choo Choo. How can I describe him? He is a snake with wings. We get into that house and Milly says where's the can? As soon as she steps out Choo Choo whispers I've got the record in my pocket. What record? I ask him. Why, he says, the record Jackeen made of the conversation between Adolf Hitler and Christ. Oh that, I say, what the hell, it can wait. He looks at me and grins. Would you like to hear something funny? he asks. I say, sure, why not? He walks over and opens a door. After a little while I can make out voices talking, and people moving around.

"Do you think he's wise to it?" Jetter's voice.

"How could he be?" Billy Delian.

"Suppose somebody put him hep."

"Who'd do that?"

"What about Thomas Honey? He might talk."

99

"Not a chance. Honey hates his guts."

"Jesus! What a laugh. He really thinks he killed her."

"Yeah, it's making him potty."

"Where is she now?"

"Chrystle? Why Jackeen put her in a nursery until we can get back from this damn trip."

"Who was the kid we buried?"

"Oh, just some slum brat."

"It's sure going to be funny."

"What is?"

"Why knocking off Moonlight for something he didn't do."

"How come he thinks he did it?"

"Search me."

Choo Choo shuts the door quietly. His grin is lapping around his ears. They're sure making a fool of you, he says. Think so? I say. Milly comes in and Choo Choo gets out some cards and we play until Rubio and Kelly arrive.

"Did you have any trouble?" Choo Choo asks.

"No." Rubio says, putting a big wad of greenbacks on the table.

"How did Herman make out?"

"Fine."

"No squawks from Tilly?"

"Hell, boss, Tilly wouldn't tongue-up to me," Kelly says.

"Don't be too sure," Choo Choo tells him. "She's a dame, ain't she?"

"She won't gab as long as I'm around to spread her legs."

Mildred slapped his face with the heel of her hand.

"There's a gentleman present," she said.

She turned to Choo Choo. "Who was the guy rubbed out on the West Side tonight?"

"How'd you know about that?" Rubio said.

"Somebody in a Palm Beach suit pulled us in on it," I said.

They were all looking at me now. Something told me to turn around. Moe was standing just behind my chair with a knife in his hand.

"Put it down," Mildred said.

Moe's face looked like a tin mask with a cigarette glued on the front of it.

"That was my brother got knocked off," he said, still holding the knife.

"Well, this mug didn't do it," Mildred said. "He was with me when it happened."

"How do you know when it happened?" Moe said.

"I asked a cop," Mildred said.

"What'd he say?"

"He said eight o'clock."

"He's a damn liar. It happened after ten."

Mildred looked at him with venom in her eyes.

"How do you know that?" she said.

Moe ran his tongue over dry lips. He suddenly looked haggard and old.

"Why ... I ..."

"So you killed him," Choo Choo said, reaching his hand in under his coat.

"Let him alone," Mildred said. "I'll take care of him later. The scum, killing his own brother."

"He took my tootsie," Moe said, his voice having a hard time getting up out of his throat.

"And you thought you'd bump off Moonlight, and pretend you thought he'd done it," Choo Choo said, "That's hardly an ethical thing to do."

"What hurt would it do if I rubbed him out?" Moe asked, looking at me out of fish eyes.

"He's mine," Mildred said. "I've got a good use for him."

We are not going to find salvation in old wives' tales. I want to explain a few things to you. I don't give a damn what system you play. What do you suppose Choo Choo hopes to get out of life? Milly doesn't really love me. I lied about that. She wants more class than I've got. You heard Billy Delian say that Thomas Honey hates me. Why shouldn't I believe that? Who cared when my little

101

buffalo was killed? There is no point in trying to jack-off the statue of George Washington in the park. All right, all right, you'd like to have a dame like Carol. Let's just for fun say you've got her. Now what? Ah, the world rots. You get old and tired and bleary-eyed and toothless. What are you going to do when the rent comes round? I make jokes, sure, but you won't find me laughing. We've got a dead man at the wheel there. And that's not all. There are six girls in Iowa City would give their right arm for just one little word from me. Yes, it's a tough titty when the footsteps stop at your door and you've got no way to get out. Snow falls on the river. A hairy face looks out of the cloud. When the banana had a baby, eh? Harps made of dry silver and yellow roses. Shut up and listen! I'll go to Iowa City just as soon as I can get the dough. Trust me to stay awake. You know damn well that Homer is a bore. Only the living speech makes sense. A black leopard lowers its muzzle into the snow-filled water. I feel cold. Through all that morning I heard the swish of invisible robes. I'm as full of people as a city. I am safe enough for the moment. The bull made of water charges on the land. Mary's rosary writhes in my hand. The death tree opens its arms. You will find me three jumps ahead of you all the way. It's very jolly when you are sitting at breakfast in your chambers, thinking how green the grass looks in the inn gardens, and how much greener it will look in Sante Fé, and what it would avail you after last night's binge in Charlie's, to run down and have a long lazy day in Brooklyn, winding up with a quiet dinner with Ann— it's very jolly then to hear a gentle tap at your door, and to find on the sill a grimy-faced kid with a pocket full of hazelnuts, and a let-ter from Adam Webb; and going out you find two notes in your letter-box—one pink, small and perfumed; the other brown, big and brutal: the first is written in the most delicate hand, and reads:—"Dear Albion, We have the address of Chrystle's nursing home. You will come to the house for it, will you not? Oui, mon-sieur, you must, if you please. Yours always, William."—the brown one is a warning from the mob. You'll slide down into the river. A fatal mistake on your part—putting horns on the sparrow.

Rider and horse disappear into the thunder-head. We can't possibly go back. Have you practiced throwing your grenade this morning? Gentlemen, here we have the big show, the heart of a man beating in a jar full of quicklime. Belly up and eyes front. We are going down that awful road. You weep tears of canary piss. A mad woman bangs around in the kitchen. The thighs of my little daughter are made of candy. O pure and guiding light. We must be strong enough to defy our own wills. The pure heart cannot beat in a human breast. He who would lose his life must first find it. Do not become entangled with any other creature. I stand before you naked and angry. I am a stranger come in the night. I am a religious man. The talk of worldly affairs is a dullness in my ears. I do not seek peace; we were made to suffer and to die. Yes, brothers, let us lay us down under the dark hill. O sweet naked lady what impossible thing do you say? I speak of loving you. I live only to be with you. You are the one woman alive and real in all the world. The sky is full of eyeless swans. Something whimpers in the shadows. Up that quicksilver mountain, boy. They're coming in the window. I say hello very affectionately. Who rides by in that closed coach? *Leah! Leah!* She does not hear me. What is the latest rumor about Mrs. Drew? The stars sit on the high cliff combing their shining hair down into the sea. Sad women braid the tails of tranquil codfish. The temple sets out in search of its pilgrim. Two old men finger their sex in a field alive with loneliness. O unsleeping wisdom . . .

The whole lot of us got into Sandy Hook about four-fifteen that same day. Choo Choo had brought along a couple basketfuls of grub and ten kegs of beer. On account of my lame arm, the bunch had to pitch in without me. I let myself down beside Dulcinea, who was Rubio's black-eyed pip of a sister, and took to telling her a lot of stuff that made her want to get away quick. Then I warmed up a globe of apple-jack in my hands, and what with getting that in me and the sun making crazy figures on the leaves and the arroyo singing Flamenco lullabies at our feet, I finally made her, there on the ground under the olive trees. Once got to be twice and then we ran out of gas. I stood up and handed her a beautifully worked *manton*. She wrapped it around her head and smiled like a dove, her teeth even and strong. I then walked into the *hosteria* and emptied my bowels. While I was engaged in this, Alhamdolillah walked in and stood idly in front of the mirror, looking for a clear space on the wall; by the time I was through he had made a rough sketch of a jane with all the vulgar lines done in heavy and *that* word right under it.

"Nice day," he said evilly.

"Glad you like it," I said.

"Very nice," he went on.

"Gladder," I said, getting outside where the first thing I did was to step into a warm burro patty.

Fyodor Pavlovitch said, "That was fonny."

I didn't want to act strict then, so I said, "As a crutch."

He drew me off the little path that led to the cribs. His breath could easily have soured milk.

"This place," he said, "she stinks, no?"

"No," I agreed.

"You are my friend," he said. "The best friend I got in the whole world. I am going to do you a favor."

"Shoot," I said, watching the flies chinning themselves on the hair that stuck about a foot out of his ears.

"I'm going to let you lend me fifty bucks." And he banged me on the back so hard my coat split in two places.

I counted it out, three tens, a five, thirteen ones, two fifty cent pieces, a quarter, four dimes, four nickels and eleven pennies.

I handed it to him and he thumbed it over.

"Dog! Cheat! Pig!" he shouted, throwing the money off into the bushes. "You think I am born today? Gaugh! Trying to rob me— Fyodor Pavlovitch—of four cents."

It took me an hour to find the forty-nine dollars and ninety-six cents. By then the party was in full blast. Alonso Quixano and Lady Bellaston were swirling and dipping along through the paces of a gavotte, while Cardenio and Mr. Honour, their faces beaming and hot, beat out Mozart on an eighty-eight and a dog-house. I was anxious to speak to Mr. Honour and I started edging over through the press, but before I got there a hand fell on my shoulder and I was looking into the sneering face of Kamar-al-Zaman. If there was one thing I didn't want at that time it was to see him. He had sworn to kill me on sight.

"Oh, farewell, Moonlight," he said huskily. "Your hour has come."

"Nay, unhand him, gentle sir," entreated Harriet Graveairs, her eyes glittering like a peeled stick.

"Level, level, blow you to the devil, lass," Kamar said through his yellow teeth.

"The tower does lie in the wind, broken," I said, knowing what evil lurked in his black heart.

"Ah, but Adam fell," he answered boldly.

"But did not stay the running of the deer," I said, leaving them locked in each other's arms on the ground, his fist tight around a corncob.

Natasha greeted me warmly. "So glad you could come. We were just talking about you."

"I tune my instrument at your door," I said.

"The Quigleys have a new heir," she said.

"And may he live to die in love and rest," I said.

"Have you seen Mr. Honour? He was asking after you."

"Ah, Natasha, how kind you are to lie to me."

"But I'm not lying to you."

"Nor laying for me," I said sadly.

Her rich, streaming laugh rang out clear over the frenzied merry-making of our fellows.

"You make me giddy," she said.

"Fast fall the dead leaves," I said.

"Where have you been keeping yourself?" she asked.

"All things are artificial for the artist," I answered.

"I'll just bet you spend your time horning around," she said, smiling in the little red cap of her mouth.

"I spend my nights with the wanton dame of the foam," I told her, noticing how robbed by many hands her body had been.

"I'll chase you around the dog-star," she breathed.

I fled after her through that anguish of trees and down into the dungeon beneath the sobbing flutes. Everything was watching our frolic. We ran through the pith of a murderer's bones and into the nest of that wondrous bird which one day laid an egg all of hair and jingling rowels. We snorted and fulged until we came upon Tom Fool. Then had we a fine jigging and buttered well our ging. Oh how we tossed and doxied in that sweet moon time. They who marry us will mad their beds in devil's spleen. O what glorious cheats! And the water booming over our faces. Would you go the same, into that green country? Less pother and more paddle-walling! You ought to value me. O for a wedding and a bedding of all the good folk among us.

I am not yet weary of my reign. You are all down on your knees, and somewhat am I—but I have a splendid fun in the unbuttoning. I will be damned! fine, fine, upright days are these. Lovely Natasha . . . there is no pain now. Beware when the righteous prepare for the practice of evil. I am so full of pity!

> *When I short have shorn my sow's face*
> *And swigged my horny barrel*
> *In an oaken inn*
> *I pound my skin*
> *As a suit of gilt apparel.*

May mine be the voice to wake you . . .
They sniffed at the corpse and a great terror was in their eyes.

The time has come to introduce Keddel to my readers. Keddel, next to myself, is this book's most important character. He is fine and strong: an innocent before God. I simply want you to know now that you will have the privilege later of learning to know and

106

to love him. It is important that you have the image of Keddel before your eyes as you read what I am about to tell you. Do you understand? Thank you.

He suddenly became conscious of strange oaths ringing on the air like bells of blood. It did not matter which way he turned, the voices followed him in a dense roar. Nanny, the homeless barmaid; Mr. Honour, the eager friend who spoke in unknown tongues; Zdrzhinsky, the butcher boy whom no one loved or cared for; Katerina Ivanovna, seamstress . . . cockeyed and lewd; Dulcinea, a bed piece if there ever was one; and Kelly—and Moe—Fyodor Pavlovitch—Alonso Quixano—and Ann—and Elizabeth—William—Jetter—Carol—Grushenka—and *Leah*—Thomas Honey—Choo Choo—Lady Bellaston—pimps, pickpockets, carpenters, finger-men, chorus dolls, housekeepers, second story men, watchmen, cops, priests, soldiers—Mildred—The Dwarf—The Man In The Palm Beach Suit—The Masked Man In The Car—*the story that was coming to life under his fingers.* And he had not yet said that Jackeen was his own daughter. Truth cannot be symmetrical, he told himself. As he rounded a hill, he saw all of them down there below him. Not one of them but would die. He had seen no danger in toying with them like a monster cat in a box of mice. But their cries were beginning to worry him. They were beginning to act as though he, Albion Moonlight, did not exist. They were starting their animal panic which would take them back to the world. No command or imprecation of his could stay that horrible march. Somewhere lay the great fault, the flaw in his plan. He turned over in his mind all the steps by which he had reached a place inviolate from the calamity which threatened his world. Then for the first time he knew his mistake: he had been behaving like a visionary, a seer; and he was the least of them, the poorest, the most alone—the one man in all that world who had no armor, no weapons and no faith. They at least believed in him; he saw nothing on earth *which could excuse life.*

He thought that it was time to surrender himself to his slayers.

He had no plan of escape. He despised them too much to struggle well. There was, however, one image that would not die.

He remembered with fierce joy the rabbit in the forest. Its face was not cowled, it would never blur so long as life was yet in him.

Well, he could fight! There would be no turning back. A dull hate caused his skin to crackle. He knew hunger. By God! there was a war—and he was in the thick of it. Soon he was down with them again. He kissed their faces and leapt and scampered about them like a colt. *But they did not appear to see him.*

"Here I am! Here I am!"

The forest stretched out around him like green horses gently mating. He could hear their soft calling. A soldier emerged from the evening haze and sank down on a bed of moss. The front of his face had been shot off. Another came, legless, dragging himself like a red worm. Then another . . . and another—he lowered himself to his knees and wept.

He felt a hand on his shoulder. Christ stood there. Moonlight nodded stupidly. Christ handed him a square of cheese and he stuffed it into the pocket of his filthy coat without a word. As one who had been on a cross, he knew when neither word nor act could have meaning. And then He was gone. A dry wind rustled through the trees.

Mildred and I lay in the big stone house by the river.

The party was over.

The voice of the earth spoke from the water. Perhaps it had flowed down far deeper than where graves are. A fox yelped from somewhere in the forest. The hoarse cry of a hunting wolf blocked out all other sounds, the bubble of foam, the faint plop of otters diving, the murmur of night birds, and then plaintively itself died.

"You've walked by my side always," I said softly.

"But you scarcely know me, Albion."

We were silent, listening to a foraging owl.

"You have been in my every dream." I put my hand on her cheek, tenderly, without passion.

108

"Will they kill you?" she said.

"Yes, Mildred."

"But why? Why?"

"I'll tell you in the morning."

"You will not be here then," she said, raising up until by the moon I could see the knife scar in her chin and the way her shoulders sagged in like broken axles.

"I know," I said, moving to get her down.

"You think you can pull a lot of fast ones with me," she said, twisting out of my way. "You must take me for a mush. I sized you up when you first walked in. No, you didn't do anything. I heard somebody say, 'That's Moonlight' like you was God and everyone got up to see you. Just standing there giving us the cold eye. I wouldn't come in with you if you were the King of Chicago. I got my own bunch together on my lonesome. I played it hot and cozy. Everyone of my boys is hand-picked. My mob's tops this side of the Rockies. Don't think I'm not wise to your game. If you want them knocked off, either go to somebody else or do it yourself. That ought to be pie for you. And another thing, I don't make no kid snatches—that's red ice all the way out."

"Who said anything about that?"

"You'd give your right eye to get her out of that nursing home." She got up and snapped on the light.

Mildred's bullfighter was trying out a few passes on a mean-looking longhorn steer at the foot of the bed, using his cape pretty well on the in-work, though I must say his *faena* was not what it should be after the charge had been made. I knew that as soon as I got out he'd have her and no fooling in that bed. Kelly and Moe were sleeping soundly in a corner on a pile of corn husks, their arms around each other.

"Milly," I told her, "you'll never make the big league with these gorillas in with you."

She stepped out of the path of the bull—just a little too late. The horn caught in her belly and pulled most of it out. I bent down and lifted her head up on my arm pushing the hair back and feeling something getting ready to leave her but she managed to smile at me before whatever it was left there and she said, "Albion, no matter what happens, do not forget how to hate."

"Go to sleep now, Milly," I said. "Say a good word for me wherever you're going." And I kissed her forehead that was growing cold. I slipped the rings off her fingers and put them in my pocket.

Outside the stars were threshing about in the heavens like live fish in a skillet. The longhorn steer was rooting up trees and crashing through houses with Moe and the bullfighter and Kelly holding fast to its tail. After a little time it dove into the sea and came up with a submarine impaled on its horns. A brace of wild duck made the design of a woman's sex against the moon.

It was nearly three-thirty when I got to the cribs. Jetter and Billy Delian swung out of a door buttoning their flies. Through the open door I could see the Amazon lying on a bed. She looked even bigger nude. Her face was set in a vacant stare. When I looked round again, my brave hearties were gone.

Jackeen was just finishing with a customer when I arrived at her stall. I had never before seen so much hair on a fellow as was on that Greek. It covered his shoulders like a bear rug. I have heard since that he made his living exhibiting his torso in store windows.

I didn't like the idea of paying her for it but she preferred it that way. Twice for one of the rings.

"Don't work too hard," I told her when I left.

"I won't," she said, making ready for an old man who seemed to be having some trouble getting his equipment in order.

"Goodnight, Jackeen," I said.

"Goodnight, father," she called after me.

I got in the car and told Choo Choo to head for Iowa City. I sat there in the back smoking and trying to figure things out. After a bit I knew we were being followed. I tapped Choo Choo on the shoulder, told him to step it up a bit. He made no sign that he had heard. Then I noticed a knife sticking out of his neck. I bent over and touched his cheek. He was stone dead.

110

13. The Net Draws Together.

One morning, just after sun, before even the militia was abroad, Albion walked down the cobbled street which overlooked the harbor. A lean dog, rooting in a pile of refuse at the curb, snarled as he passed. Over the heart of him his coat felt thin and unprotective; his chest might have been made of glass. Fog stood on the air, ominous as an order of arrest. It occurred to him that this was not the way he had thought of his home-coming. A ridiculous longing to speak to someone caused him to quicken his step. He heard the screech of a hawser as a schooner was tied in at the pier. A bell lipped at the salt face of the water. The day was breaking drab and fat with rain. There were so many lovely and curious places in the world; he asked himself with almost a sob why it was that he paced there in that treacherous shadow. He drew his collar in at the throat and hurried into a dimly lighted tea room.

The gently swaying ceiling lamp opened the face of an old woman who leaned at the counter. He waited until the two halves melted together again, then he asked in a voice so strained and grating that it surprised him for a scone and a pot of green tea. The hag moved devilish quick into the back of the shop, where he could hear her crashing dishes about and cursing in a strange tongue. Then silence. He waited for what seemed an hour, when the door to the kitchen opened and a horse with a deformed lad on its back plunged out. A fiery rage filled him as the appointed hooves ground him down into darkness. The room filled with men talking excitedly together in low voices. They touched his face. They opened his pants and felt about in there, continuing despite their haste to conduct themselves in gentleness and devotion. Then they stood about in a tight circle, their arms drawing them in to where he lay in the confusion of his papers and manuscripts. Behind the world another world, stretching away into the wailing shadows, awaited the crumbling of that curious wall which would free all of us. Albion stirred uneasily as a butterfly alighted on his mouth. The little men hurriedly stuffed his be-

111

longings back into his coat. They smiled happily, rubbing their knuckles into the dark nooks where their eyes were.

When Albion entered the world again the little men had vanished, but leaning against the counter in exactly the same position as before, her thoughts searching deeply into his own, was the old woman. "What is the meaning of this?" he asked in a loud voice. She smiled in an almost motherly fashion, answered: "You do not understand our ways." "But where is the horse with its crippled rider?" he said faintly, as though ashamed. "There is no horse, there is no rider," she said, reaching out and taking his hand in a loving hold. "You are frightened, my child," she went on, "fright causes the eye to see itself. There are worlds in our heads whose beauty is beyond our understanding.—But here, while we are gabbing, your tea grows cold." With a sensation of terror, he became aware of the flowered cup which rested in his hand. He put his lips to it, and its taste was bitter as gall. "Yes," she said, "it has been poisoned, Albion. You see, we had been warned of your coming." "But why do you tell me before I have drunk of it?" he asked. "Because I enjoy hangings," she answered, again reaching out for his hand. This time he withdrew his fingers; her touch was disturbing in a way that he could not have explained. "You speak in riddles," he said at last. A smile lifted her ancient features, but she gave him no answer. "I am very tired," he said. "Perhaps you can tell me where I can find lodgings." She laughed suddenly in a shrill whinny. "You are a child indeed," she said, struggling for breath. "Now where could the likes of you find room when all the countryside around has come to hear him speak? You tire my patience." Moonlight stroked his beard with trembling hand; his tongue felt swollen and yellow in his mouth. "Please," he said, "you must overlook my stupidity, but the truth is that I am quite in the dark concerning the identity of this speaker"—the withered old crone tapped impatiently on a stack of tea trays, causing them to jump about with such a noise that his words were drowned and lost—"though" (and he pushed

112

his voice up to a roar) "I am most willing to concede that his fame is one with God's . . ." It was no use: she had not the least desire to hear him. Her lips were breaking in and out in what seemed to be a sort of chant:

"I seen the brave lads in the bushes, facin' round to their maidens . . . all golden in the sun. Thenatimes this wee earth had a manner of talkin' like a green man lyin' there with trees and clouds agrowin' outa his breast. Ah, I tell ye, friends, some things are done that the doin' o' them makes a new thing, an' afterwards ye find th' tears in yer eyen an' yer 'eart gits too big an' bursts out like a red arrow straight into the spirit that lives in the sky. My head is piled high with all the lovin' and the weepin', all the pain and the sufferin', all the heartbreak and the hunger . . ." She raised her bony, clawlike hand. "I ask ye not to do murder, not to think evil, not to violate the girl child in the thicket of thy despair."

Then it was that Albion Moonlight became aware of a gentle tugging at his sleeve. He was relieved to see that this human was a slim girl with dark hair which was worn in a little love-knot at her neck's nape. Her eyes were large and lustrous in a plump, agreeable face. With almost a sigh he stayed the hand which had crept down to his male parts and was pressing there. The old lady had by now disappeared into the secret wine cellar, whence issued the velvet tinkle of bottles being shifted about on shelves. "Come," said his new friend, "I will show you to your quarters." Obediently he followed her into the street which was congested by the traffic of office workers scurrying to lunch. The sun stood squarely overhead, like an enormous blood-orange tossed there by a careless schoolboy. It bewildered him to think that the whole morning had been spent in the tea shop.

"What is your name?" he asked.

In an instant her arms were hugging him and his face was covered with her soft, wet kisses. Several people detached themselves from the throng and joined in her play, rubbing and breathing

113

over him like idiot puppies. It was some time before he could disengage himself from these convulsive embraces; one old fellow was particularly demonstrative, throwing his arms and legs about in a sheer frenzy of pleasure—and all the time his scabmarked lips played in and out like a diarrhetic cow's ass. Finally, his clothes and hair in wild disarray, Albion contrived to break clear, and sprinted over the tight wedge of celebrants, who were now cavorting amongst themselves.

The skinny lass matched him step for step.

"What kind of tomfoolery is that?" he whistled as they rounded a turn bringing them in view of the sea.

"I thought you loved me," she answered, looking up at him shyly.

"And why should you think that?" he demanded.

"Why, simply that . . . you wanted to know my name, didn't you?"

They had stopped and were staring at each other; he angrily, she with the faintest suspicion of scorn in her smile.

"What makes you think that knowing your name will make any important difference to me?" he said, setting off again through the fog with long strides.

"But you asked," she said simply. "Why should you show interest in someone you don't love?"

"Oh, don't bother me with such childish nonsense," he said in anger. "Tell me your name or not, just as you wish; but I do feel I have a right to know where you are taking me."

It was true that in an almost imperceptible manner she was guiding him, turning as though by blindest chance down this street and that, but ever in a seaward direction.

"Jenny is my name," she said. "As to where you are to pass the night, you shall know in good season."

It was now totally dark. The street lamps drew smeary faces on the fog; giants and helmeted heroes, five-legged beasts with no heads, birds with saw-toothed beaks, leopards with wings, dogs with the tails

I

of fish, all swimming and crawling and flying
through the little paths of fire which criss-crossed that strange,
muddy river of air. A finger of pure light swung in a great circle
over the ocean, and another, stronger beacon made an x with
their crossed knuckles. The dark buildings, the silent harbor, the
seemingly endless street and everyone

WANT

who was abroad on it ap-
peared to be afloat somewhere beyond the wide world's end. He
felt her fingers jumping at his sleeve and as they entered the large
unaccountably

YOU

black room he had an uncanny sensation of many
eyes peering at him from knot-holes and crevices in the floor and
ceiling. They were moving through a thick pudding of men, experiencing the position of many dogs attempting space on the
same bitch. Albion could not down

BOYS

a conviction that the whole
life of the place was concentrated in his path; it was only before
him that the laughter and drunken breathing were heard, only
where he walked that those others were. A panic filled him and

he struck wildly about, his fists colliding with—nothing. He sank weakly into a chair.

TO SHAKE

"Open your eyes, Albion," a voice said. "What ... ?" he murmured stupidly. For the first time he realized that his eyes were bandaged tightly shut. Desperately he tore at the thin strips of cloth, which came away

HANDS

in his fingers like frozen cobwebs. He looked about him now. Jenny was standing at the bar in deep talk with a man whose head was shrouded in a cheap, paper goat-mask such as children wear at Hallowe'en. Or so Albion assured himself: it was perhaps demanding too much to believe

NOW AND

that the creature was indeed half man and half goat. Across from him sat a group of little bearded men—more than twenty at the one table—they were spinning their white and red whiskers about like agitated skirts on their chins, and their thin voices scampered around in

WHEN

the tobacco smoke like baby mice in balls of wool. Every little while one of them would reach into his trousers and jerk wildly, the others simultaneously rocking and bounding with his movement. At such times the chief actor of

these little tableaux would bestow a solemn wink in Albion's direction, as

THE BELL

much as to say: "We know what fun is, you and I."
On his one side, under a rubber plant of elephantine proportions,
were a young man and a middle-aged woman who affected an
ostrich plume in her Empress Eugenie headpiece. These latter
were staring at him in a mechanical way, just as though Albion
were a fly's leavings on a window

RINGS

pane through which it was neces-
sary to look. The gaze of the female was unusually perplexing because her eyes were of a hue and shade foreign to his whole
experience: these eyes were white, a white more solid and more
firm than that of milk or snow. They rested in balls of lavender.
Albion felt that he must speak

COME

to her at all costs. He was on the
point of shoving his chair back and crossing to them, when he became aware of a curious occurrence. It so happened that while the
young man gave every appearance of looking in total idleness into
Albion's face, this was quite the opposite of the true state of affairs; for his hand was not at rest; indeed no: this member was
conducting a pencil in mad

OUT

career across the pages of a sketch

book, charting lines which made the white paper yawn away from shapes human and divine. It was remarkably easy for Albion to study this handiwork, for, having noticed your hero's interest in his endeavor, the young artist had promptly tilted his pad into view. However, Jenny who had by now settled matters with the landlord, chose this moment

FIGHT-

to slip into the chair opposite Albion's; which happening, coinciding as it did with a sudden cakewalk among the tables indulged in by the little old men, made it extremely difficult for him to follow the canter of that furious pencil—and he had seen enough of the drawing to want to see more. He bent far over to the

ING

left; Jenny, smiling, accommodated her position to his, and three or four of the ancients, thinking no doubt that this maneuver was made in order to stimulate their enjoyment, began such a bobbing and bowing that, not only could he not see what was being done by the young man but he could no longer look into the white eyes of the lady. Before he knew what had happened the path between the tables was cleared; Jenny was on her feet, pale and tight-lipped; the old fellows were congregated in whimpering huddles near the door; and the hand of the artist could be seen to point in a curious gesture upward. Slowly Albion lifted his face; he could see nothing at first, then, on a landing overlooking the room, he made out something standing. His stomach quivered, but he managed not to be sick. The thing's head was swollen three times the size of a man's; its skin was the color of liver; a hideous belly swung down to the knees like a ram's testicle; sprouting from each shoulder blade were two wing-like humps; it ran gray lips over broken teeth in a cretin's grimace; and its pipe-stem arms dangled to the floor. Albion watched the horrible slavering of that mouth and a dread such as he had never experienced put a film over his eyes; it was not the monstrousness of the creature which terrified him—he had not been blind in the world—no, it was not that: it was that he knew its identity, its awesome name.

When Albion Moonlight got to bed that night his very first deed was to examine carefully the drawings which had been left behind by the young man. They had a strange fascination for him; excitement made the figures jerk and twist in his hand. As he looked at each of them, a thought went through his head, and he made a few notes:

(Drawing A) This represents a man trying to attach an umbilical cord to his navel. The cord is withered and thready.
Thought: Wouldn't it be curious to see our own umbilical cords? to hold them in our hands?

(Drawing B) I take this to be a little girl modeling a penis on a snowman.
Thought: Occasionally murderers encase their victims in snow, even going to the extent of putting on buttons of coal and inserting clay pipes in the cold mouths—strange to think of blood seeping out of a snowman.

(Drawing C) A man is seen standing with his legs held tightly together and his arms outspread; another man, his body taut and cringing, is being crucified on the first—nails through the two sets of hands and feet, a spear at the last driven through the two breasts.
Thought: Why has the artist made the crucified twist in terror, whereas he who is the cross stands stiffly, proudly? How can this be taken to mean that anyone who participates in punishment is

119

punished, murderer murdered with his prey? But murder, dear friend, can never be shared; it belongs alone to the murderer, as love to him who loves.

(Drawing D) A superlative sense of dimension in this one. Three men on ice skates are shown jumping over a nest of barrels; from the opening in one of them peeps the head of a small boy, a flute between his lips.

Thought: In art there is ever the demand for the distorted, for an indefinable thing termed 'magic.' But for the artist, there can be only one distortion: that which is not art. To say it in another way, the world is in a mess precisely because a bunch of stuffy fools insist that there be no mess. Everyman his own Marx! Let's have some honest-to-God fun—smear everything up and down and sideways. To hell with Liberty, Fraternity, Equality, and all the rest; let's make one whopping, beautiful botch of it—do I hear a second? (I was only kidding, you blasted lick-ass.)

(Drawing E) Hands. Hands outstretched. Hands drawn in until the fingers are doughy lumps. Hands in an attitude of prayer. And up in the right top corner, a hand sporting a huge ring upon which is sketched the battle of Waterloo!

Thought: Nietzsche was Napoleon; Napoleon was a sick little guy who never got over a fondness for playing with blocks labeled England, Russia, Prussia, etc. Power! It is always the weakling who gets the morons to remake the maps with him. It adds up to this: maybe there has been a poem written in the world. And maybe not.

(Drawing F) A mother holding a child.
Thought: It is necessary to see this pair seventy years hence.

(Drawing G) A fox sniffing the face of a dead soldier.
Thought: A thousand thousand pages would be required to tell you what is in my heart as I gaze upon this.

120

(Drawing H) This is intended as a likeness of me.

Thought: Much too demoniac; I am a placid, sentimental person, given to sending out Xmas cards.

(Drawing I) Birds flying across a wintry sky.

Thought: The liver of the wren is smaller than the smallest thimble, but the whole wide heavens is its province.

He lowered the papers to the table and turned to Jenny who was lying on her back like a sleek cat rubbing brandy into her soft, flaming skin. Her little stomach was covered with a golden fuzz and at her sprocket glowed a bush of sheened fire. Even the walls seemed to bend in for better sight of her. The stern lips of the ancestral portrait might almost have been thought to smack in patriarchal appreciation.

"Jenny."

"Yes." Her eyes were soft and deep as a deer's.

"How will he be able to speak?"

She thought: How tousled and unkempt his beard is.

"What do you mean?" she said.

I shall smooth it straight with my fingers, perhaps even run my comb through it—if he will let me.

"There is no use in trying to shield me from the truth," he said, his voice suddenly become immoderately loud and harsh. "I am aware of the name of that hideous monster which stood on the balcony in the inn."

"How had you imagined him, Albion?"

I shall yell with pleasure when he presses his hard, lean body upon mine. Feeling the brutal caress of his ribs and thighs . . .

Alb on gazed at her in bewilderment; he felt that if he spoke of it at all there would be no earthly way of holding back the tears which burned like liquid coals somewhere in his skull.

"Imagined him . . ." he repeated dully. "Why, I . . . Jenny, in my heart I saw him as the most beautiful and noble of all God's creations—tall, straight, blue-eyed, with strong arms—and there would be a notebook in his hand into which he entered comments and observations . . ."

"But why a notebook," she asked, rubbing the brandy into the little tan eyes that looked out of her breasts.

I shall place my hands on the small of his back and draw him steadily, fiercely to me.

"Because I believed him aware of his wisdom," Albion answered. "I was sure that he would want to share his knowledge and love with other men."

Involuntarily they rose to their feet and embraced midway between the bed and the chair. From the street below, echoing upward like the tread of a giant on a drum-head, had come the sound of savage hammers falling on wood. Jenny was crying, her naked body pressed against his in the attitude of a shield.

A hand of wind reached into the room and scattered the drawings at their feet. One came to rest exactly under Moonlight's eye. He stared at it unseeingly, but the speech of his heart choked on a terrible syllable, and his hands went up like wounded birds to his throat.

"That is what they are building," he said at last, sinking down into the litter of papers which moved slightly under the teeth of the angry wind.

"Yes, Albion," she answered. (Why couldn't they have waited at least another day—I wanted so terribly to enter heaven under his touch—why? why! why!) "They will have finished it by morning."

The artist had surpassed all his efforts on this startling drawing: the whole scene had been executed with such consummate mastery that one expected almost to hear the thud as the trap was sprung, to hear even the little crackle of the poor devil's neck snapping as he plummeted down to the full stretch of the rope— swinging there a good ten feet from the gallow's arm.

"By whose order do I die?" he asked in a whisper.

"By his order," she said.

Before his eyes passed the vision of the idiot's smirk on the bloated features of the dwarf; again he could see it leering down at them from the balcony, its webbed fingers flexing open and shut like the jaws of a foetus.

"But he is not alone to blame," she cried suddenly, flinging herself out of his arms and standing erect and defiantly beautiful in the candlelight.

Albion looked at her helplessly; was there to be no end to the terror?

"He is only doing what they wish him to do," Jenny said. "They brought him wonderful evidence that you had murdered her."

How could he have committed such a beastly act! Dear Albion Moonlight, she thought, what evil thing possesses you . . .

"Who accuses me?" he asked, only now lowering his hands from his throat. A gentle rain had started to fall, it brushed across the roof like words walking on thin paper.

She hesitated, knowing the hurt that would be put in him.

Then she said: "Your death warrant was signed by—" They were fitting the rope around his neck; the black mask was being slipped over his wide, staring eyes— "Jetter, Thomas Honey, Carol, Billy Delian, and Jackeen . . ."

"Jackeen too," he breathed, tears making him blind.

"Yes," she said. "You see, it is hardly his fault at all."

Albion Moonlight stood up and ground his fist into her face. She spun to the floor like a just-born calf trying to walk—sprawling there in a heap with a trickle of blood at her mouth—but her eyes did not waver from his.

"Why must you insist on defending that drooling monster?" he shouted, kicking her savagely in the breast that her eyes might not be upon him, for now they had become white—white horrible dead globes in pools of lavender.

She twisted about to face him, her chin dripping redly and her dress torn away showing a huge, bubbling wound.

"Because . . ." she mumbled, "he is my father."

"Your father!" Albion felt like a fool; he was trapped, defenseless. "Then you were sent to spy on me . . ."

123

"Yes, I was told to bring you here. The soldiers will be coming at any minute now." And she fainted.

He stood over her while his heart broke and footsteps began to move up the stairs.

"Poor thing," he said tenderly—"to be of his blood . . . to be the daughter of Roivas."

━━

JULY 5 (continued)   hold hard to that which we have, the eyelashes of a dreaming child, the moon-marrow of your father's ghost,

> It is not death, that sometimes in a sigh
> This eloquent breath shall take its speechless flight;
> That sometimes these bright stars, that now reply
> In sunlight to the sun, shall set in night;
> That this warm conscious flesh shall perish quite,
> And all life's ruddy springs forget to flow;
> That thoughts shall cease, and the immortal sprite
> Be lapped in alien clay and laid below;
> It is not death to know this—but to know
> That pious thoughts, which visit at new graves
> In tender pilgrimage, will cease to go
> So duly and so oft—and when grass waves
> Over the passed-away, there may be then
> No resurrection in the minds of men.

I am your friend; I wish you no harm; please God that the way be not too hard for you,

> Put them in the grave with me, said Jetter, the fretting and the
>   bobbing,
> The sick toad and the child with the precious head.
> You drink too much, said Golden Carol, and night,
> That great Negro, put down one black foot on the water.
> Put them in the grave with me, he said, the style of mouth

You have, the way your breasts fit tight within my hands.
Tea or lemon in your gall? asked Mrs. God, and Jetter said,
    I'll take
That angel with the precocious fanny:
Then Herbert, that wonderful green pony, took them all
    on his broad back and they rode away to hell
and watched Dante spool spaghetti with Lord Nelson
while buffalo played on the little cabin floor and
John Brown combed historians out of his whiskers.
And now, good morrow, Millie and Pete and Little Lester,
here's that big nice old wagon with the store-bought horn;
That girl I love is dancing with tears in her hose, but
Jetter groaned in his sleep and Golden Carol put her hand
on his naked belly and the dream went good as the Negro
lifted his foot from the river and a truck made its morning wind.

   I am ambitious of doing the world some good: if I should be
spared, that may be the work of future years—in the interval I
will essay to reach to as high a summit in poetry as the nerve be-
stowed upon me will suffer. The faint conceptions I have of poems
to come bring the blood frequently into my forehead. All I hope
is, that I may not lose all interest in human affairs—that the soli-
tary indifference I feel for applause, even from the finest spirits,
will not blunt any acuteness of vision I may have. I do not think
it will. I feel assured I should write from the mere yearning and
fondness I have for the beautiful, even if my night's labors should
be burnt every morning, and no eye ever shine upon them. But
even now I am perhaps not speaking from myself, but from some
character in whose soul I now live....

in this way did John Keats love the beautiful; great soul; a good
man

          They spiked the beer and put her in a cab.
          It's a cold, night, mates, beside this river.
          It's a big world; a sad, damn affair.

125

They got her in and shut the door of Tim's cab.
How old was she? I think she was twelve.
She was plump and warm and they wanted her.
How good was she? I think she was good enough.
She had a tiny nose and her breasts were round
And soft where they put their big hairy hands.

Back in the joint Willie monkeys the piano hard.
A pretty blonde spits up her supper and Tony
Muldoon, well-heeled, watches the door for cops.
Tony shot his sweetie through the head and drinks
Frowning because he can't remember her name.

Shall we follow the cab, mates?
Shall we watch them take her?
How old is she? Twelve, I think.
I won't go there, fellows. Go on alone.
Open the door on them if you like.
I'll sit on here and ask Willie to play
'Drink to me only with thine eyes'
While Tony waits for the Boys in Blue.

I have named her Jackeen after God's mother.
All night I search for her along the river.
The wind is bitter and the boats groan like beasts.
Then what is this approaches through the dark?
It is Croudy-Mutton who lives on Avenue A.
And where are you going, my pretty dame,
All flushed with the dews of morn?
To the Hall of the City, steps to scrub, my man.
And have you seen my Jackeen, whose heart is pure?
Just that I have, a girl as fair as Helen were . . .
But where, good frau?
By the river then, her face a cloud of smiling joy.
And she was happy?
As the day, good sir.

And no harm to her?
There are tears in your eyes, man.
Tell me of Jackeen, woman.
But here is your Jackeen coming now through the
   morning!
She is walking upon us, mates.
Will you live with me? she begs.
Who will live with Jackeen by the wonderful river?
Will you live with me?
But why does the blood spurt from your throat?
They cut my throat when they were done . . .
And does it hurt, my child?
Far less than when I was whole, good sir.
What do you want of me?
I want you to buy me a hat with a golden feather
And a book with the confessions of God in it.

as the emerald thread unwinds from the angry spool of sea, trailing fever-mists above the world, in fog, in night, in death-cries, in velvet moaning of gulls; so do we, in our little place, friendless, without faith, companioned by phantoms, go across this dismal frontier, unwound from the secret womb to a damnation profound and final as a broken wave—Lord! Lord! Lord God!

But, Roivas, you will want to know what we found; how we made our way and what we saw there . . .

You must listen now with more than ear.

I have wanted to turn the face of someone to the striking stars; I have wanted to rouse him from sleep as their clappers summon the black, slow elephant of eternity into the skies; and the angels there—angels bright and shining as the Southern Cross—seaweed and shipwreck in their cold hair—the angel of Beatrice and of Penelopeia—ah, but there are angels, angels that live in the great tensioned camps of the sky, and angels that live far under the sea —but no one would listen. People sit in the darkness with rifles across their knees. Why should you fear me?

They do not listen to me. They say that nothing can save them.
We speak the same tongue, yet they will not understand.
They do not believe in angels. It is as simple as that.
There is danger.
There is the danger that you will kill me.
I am your enemy more than any foreign soldier.
I love you. How can you forgive that?
My moist skeleton clings to your lying mouth.
I am a poet of death.

I carry a wounded deer in my arms.
I eat of its breathing flesh in an ecstasy of love.

Forgive me, I am dazzled by your sorrow.

A gentle wind moves the forest's green whiskers;
He clears his throat with the sound of birds singing.

None born knows the dark meaning in the fish's eye.

A general's reputation is made out of untold corpses.

The ox champs sullenly at the boards of his stall;
But the fat, banker-faced flies are glad.

I am tired of writing on the air. I want to say something that
will help you. We are animals together. I have no money. But I
have made speeches in the mountains. I have held the body of a
dying child in my arms. The road I have come hangs by a thin
thread over a pit full of howling beasts. Let us consider. What is of
importance? Why are you afraid? I will tell you what things are
saddest for me. The cruelest thing of all is that we die. This is
wrong. We die because we are animal organisms. Is there any
reason for this? That is the heart of the trouble. We resent our
human condition. Death is our color and our smell. It is sheer folly

to be mortal. Why were we made only to die? Is there any purpose in this? No one has ever been able to find any. Why must we get sick? Why do our teeth ache? What rotten stuff are we made of that our arms and legs break; that our organs fill with pus and rot? But here we are. There is nothing we can do. On what day will you die? What about your head? What stops in that? And then we set about slaughtering each other; we torture and debase these poor creatures. I have tried at times to think of man as something foreign to myself—like a bear or a toad; but then any possibility of understanding is lost: we must accept our horrible limitations, we must say, "I am a man-animal and I shall die." Within a century all men now living will be dead. We don't have much of it, do we? If I had been given a choice, I should have much preferred to be a horse or a deer. I tell you that I do not like the pain that is in me. If my thinking cannot alter the fact of our mortality, of what good is it? of what use? This war is important only to us; tomorrow's people will have a new war or a world without war. God grant that it may be easier to live then! War advertises death; death becomes the only player; everything else is forgotten.

We die.

But I have told you that I believe in angels.

I believe in the beautiful.

I am, in fact, an accomplished fool.

So, Roivas, have we found the world. If you are in touch with God, communicate these things to Him. Tell Him how it is with us.

For the sake of your records, I should like to list the following occurrences—or items, notes, observations, whatever—they may prove of use to you.

(1) Jetter has had thirty-seven boils since we set forth.

(2) We have spent on actual necessities $6,400.24.

(3) We have spent on luxuries, such as tobacco, whiskey, talcum powder, taxi fares, whores, and lawyer fees—$2,871.65.

129

(4) To date we have covered 21,000 miles—app.

(5) Carol has had four abortions: three male embryos, one female.

(6) We were held up and robbed of $700 by six masked gunmen just outside Scranton, Pa. We managed to kill two of them, a short man with a red wig and a very fat man who had a startling birthmark on his left shoulder-blade.

(7) Billy Delian contracted syphilis in a place in Denver called *Maw Thompson's Haven.*

(8) Mrs. Drew's condition is somewhat improved.

(9) We have seen a horned rabbit, a hen's egg having five yolks, a goat that spoke passable French, and a king with a bottom constructed of steel and cork.

(10) Chrystle was murdered and raped by a person or persons unknown (as yet).

(11) We are wanted by the police.

(12) I found the body of a sparrow under an apple tree; its lungs had collapsed under the concussion of a great shell.

(13) Something snuffs upon the air above my head.

(14) Your wanderer taps at the invisible gate.

(15) My cathedral was so beautiful that the workmen who built it were moved to worship there.

(16) I have a blinding pain at the back of my head.

(17) What have men to do with goals? who spend their lives flying from themselves—their only goal.

(18) What will you say with your last breath?

(19) Be quiet in your heart and the noise of the world will die into nothingness.

(20) O everlasting confession! How we belly through the slime seeking—not a disease to kill the God Who put us there—but seeking to be pure in His ghoulish sight!

(21) We shall enter Galen on August 27th.

(22) Thomas Honey is quite blind now.

(23) I beheld you in a dream. You were singing a song made of blue satin and water lilies.

(24) The man with moss and nettles growing from his shoulders is bathed publicly every afternoon in a store window in Memphis.

(25) Jackeen wears a size 3A shoe.

(26) We shall have good things to tell you later of our trip to sea.

(27) Can you sew a dress without a seam? I asked Carol. So it wouldn't seem what? she answered.

(28) Our supply of salt is running low.

Allow me to interrupt this to say that we have just received word that Billy Delian has been elected President of the United States.

(29) I saw a beautiful woman in Houston, Texas. An enormous, rough wen grew from her cheek. She held out a penny and a little tin pig—"Take one," she offered.

(30) In my dream a drowned man sobbed out his love for the holy and luminous sea.

(31) The panther who broods with yellow tears on the unforgettable island where I shall go to my sleep ...

(32) I am wide-awake! What a fantastic martyr I would make! Everlasting ... eternal *doubt*. But I am amiable and shrunken under the leprous caresses of my parasites. Gentlemen! Ho! Ho! Heg!

(33) The hooded alleys and the monster in the pat of butter ... I do not boast of my power. I shall murder out of tenderness; out of a frightful desire to be *charitable*.

(34) To those I have loved . . . this cruel glory. This stained contortion as a man stands upright—do you understand? do you hear? Great God do you hear me! The hand grows still and cold.

I tell you that I love Carol. She excites me with her art—she is an artist in making men suffer. This is her life, her possessed joy. Our courtship was carried on under the eyes of her husband, a dealer in flowered carpets and eccentric furniture. She despised him with all her heart; her first entry into my arms was made to torture him. The poor man was devoured by grief; he put a bullet through his head on a night when we were enchanting ourselves in her bed. He came into the room and stood above us with the revolver in his hand; she held me to my carnal position on her. "Get it over with," she told him; "kill me while I am like this." His eyes were full of tears. He smiled at her, then lifted the pistol to his head and fired. I attempted to rise; she would not suffer me to do so. A woman! Yes, Roivas, a woman ... I felt remorse that I should have been an actor in that little farce. "He was always a fool," she said, stepping over his body to the chair where she had thrown her clothes.

The police declared his death a suicide; but it was the basest kind of murder. Her children were sent to a home for orphans.

She does not ask God for forgiveness. She lives for the night and a man in bed with her. Jetter ... Billy Delian ... *even the innkeeper* ... (she confessed this herself) ... she will call in a stranger from the street.

But she is pure and good, Roivas; this you must believe. She has been my comfort in time of terrible need. She is quite without jealousy; my possession of Jackeen would give her joy. It worries her that this is denied me. She even schemes that this dream of mine may succeed. Her ingenuity in this is surprising; she has a genius for intrigue. She has the winsomeness of a child as she attempts to persuade Jackeen into my arms. Secretly, she despises both of us. Her hatred of Joseph Gambetta is savage and sinister; she has a terror of that other world. News of Chrystle's death was honey on her heart.

She wears clothes with a style and dash that is the envy of all the women we have met on our journey. With a colored pin and a yard of wool she can gown herself like an empress. Her feet are large and the toes have a tendency to spread; one of her pleasures is to caress me with them—like a monkey's hand moving in ancient vice. Her aptitude for cleanliness is not strained; at times the gentle rain from heaven will furnish her only bath. Dirt has gathered under her fingernails, which she keeps long in order to ease the sting of bites from the colonies of bug-life with which she is infested. She eats noisily and in an uncouth manner; as a breaker of wind her finesse is deplorable. But she has a charm and manner that are completely winning; forest pools seem to lurk in the hollows where her eyes are. Her thighs are superbly rounded and firm; notwithstanding the presence of innumerable moles, her breasts display a beauty that is rare in this world.

Thomas Honey is drawn to her, but he will not permit himself so much as a kiss on the spine of her hand. He is content to give her tangerines and chocolate squares, which are a passion with her. There isn't a sloppy novel that she hasn't read; she cons the best-seller lists with an avidity that would do credit to a Maine schoolteacher. She especially likes the *How-to-do-it* books, but the particular one she'd like to see will probably never be published. It is scarcely necessary to say that she knows nothing of modern French and Spanish writers of the eclectic school. Similarly the formal architecture of a work of prose art is worse than lost on her. In her cultural ink-pot Stendhal does not exist. She sits in the gaudy shell of a protestant provincialism that is well-nigh blinding in its drabness.

But life will not fail her. Her heart is not with the dead. I rake the serpents out of her active fire and we feed on them together; as children, watching an idiot put a blue sleeve on his useless sex, are wont to say, "Now he has a metaphysical distinction, at least." —so Carol and I adorn ourselves in the winged and unimmaculate gloom. Ah, I feel so tender to her . . . *I could eat her.* Supposing she were laid in the ground—she will be dead with Shakespeare. Light! Light! I want light! I am sick of this darkness! My mother, gleaming in her talk, shakes her music in the grave . . . I thought how this life, the life I have in me, will go down below the gray wall where Beethoven lies, and I started a jig with a murdered gentleman whom I know, hands together, pit, pat, left foot—are you fond of Donatello? my sides ache! there they sit, the whole bloody shebang, drinking spider-milk from the hollow, wooden

figure of a fatted calf—put a marinated star in my julep, Claude
—and that Maid of Athens, did they wrap her in the winding
sheet with the little pink bunnies on it? O Helas! Helas! I weep
for John the Brown. The shadows begin to stir . . . crosses swing
up with their horrible burdens . . . morning star, bring my love
back to me . . . I am not to be hanged until the day breaks o'er
yonder hill . . . then we can all go home and the bells tolling, tolling over our cold graves. I shall put on my silver shoes and walk
up and down out of the world. Swing low, swift bomber . . . I
thought how I would put flowers in her hair. The lantern leans
to the bitter end . . . SHEPHERD, WHY DO YOU KILL YOUR
SHEEP? *What do you want of me!*

JULY 6   The entire population of the village assembled this
morning to bid us God-speed when we set out again. Christ! how
wonderful everything is! This country is spiritual in its beauty;
the snow falls like wool from a great white herd—the frozen
pastures of heaven. There is an invasion of peace. Twilight found
us exhausted but happy.

We had four more flat tires, which Jetter grumblingly fixed.
Due to the stiff condition of his hands, this work took many hours;
so many in fact, that we did not get beyond the confines of the
village. Hence we decided to repair back to the inn for the night.
The villagers gave us a rousing welcome—for all the racket, we
might have been returning from a stay of ten years, and not one
of just a few, short hours.

Their habits do not cease to amuse me. They have a little instrument called a bol with which their horses' tails are unkinked.
Also, in the square, under a tall tree, they have erected a tower in
which moving pictures are shown; unlike those we know, these
films concern themselves solely with shots of photographers
squinting through cameras at other photographers with cameras.
Many scenes are made at once in this way; that is, camera-man A
takes a picture of camera-man B, who is taking a picture of
camera-man A—meanwhile C camera is shooting both A and B,

and is in turn shot by D, who has been in range of B and C—while cameras E, F, and G, etc. The villagers have their stars just as we do; this season it is photographer L, whose facial contortions, though somewhat obscured by his camera, did amuse me somewhat.

We ate desperately of the crayfish.

JULY 9 🐒 It is so cold the ink won't flow in my pen. Bother.

JULY 10 🐒 We are no longer in the road. It is a hell of a note to be bumping along on tree tops.

JULY 11 🐒 Will this damn snow never let up?

JULY 12 🐒 We ran over and killed a man on a bicycle. Jetter got his gloves—a rather worn, cheap pair.

JULY 13 🐒 We made a big fire last night and the Mercedes went up in it. Luckily only Christ was sleeping there—I wish nothing could hurt me.

JULY 16 🐒 What a gallery of skeletons we were! staggering into Topenville after that damn trek up the mountain on foot—I refuse to talk about it. I had a bit of good fortune, however; I thought myself up a badly sprained ankle and there was nothing for it but that Jetter and Thomas Honey rig up a litter on which I rode with some comfort. What a fine, high swearing went on when I stepped jauntily down upon our arrival here. Why walk when you can ride?

Topenville is a city with a population about three times as big as that of Chicago and Cedar Rapids combined. Huge casks of flaming whale oil, placed at each street intersection, furnish the only illumination. There are no houses, no shops, no police-stations—these hardy people live in baskets suspended from cap-

135

tive balloons; and indeed the whole effect is one of a stupendous garden with the cables leading up stem-like to giant, vari-colored eggplants that sway gracefully in the back-wash of fighting planes which constantly harass them—amusing to hear the deafening pops when a direct hit is made. This goes on all the time. Those who are shot down immediately go up again, this time as pilots bent on bringing down a few balloons in their turn; in this way everyone has a chance to be shot at and to do a little shooting. No one is unemployed because there are always balloons and planes to be built, and damaged ones in need of repairs and new parts. Everyone, of course, is much too busy to eat.

This sport is quite harmless and entertaining. We had heard that death was unknown; that is true—in a certain sense. The real truth is that these people are dead; what they fear is life. When they 'die', they are transported to Hannibal, Missouri, where they must remain for all time. Their chief sage has said: "Life must come to all men; much as we may struggle against it."

Fortunately there is only one thing which can bring them disaster: this is a small, blunt-nosed gadget looking not unlike a stocking-darner—in fact, it is a stocking-darner. How these terrible instruments have been smuggled into Topenville is a problem which has occupied their Secret Service for countless centuries. The slightest touch from the business end of these darners is enough to send the bravest of their heroes spinning head over heels into Hannibal. They go off over the mountain wailing that at last life is upon them—and their fellows weep bitterly, thinking of the awful fate that awaits them there. Death is so sweet in Topenville—God! why must we live in Missouri! . . .

For the greater part of our stay, officials seemed to think we were foreign balloon experts called in to devise newer and more rugged craft; every protest of ours was met by a fresh flood of maps and blue prints—over which we were expected to pore. Finally, thinking to demonstrate our total ignorance (and thus win release), I made the suggestion that they fill the big gas bags with cement mixed with horsemanure in equal parts—this they

136

did at once, *and it worked beautifully*. We became heroes overnight: they never tired of taking us up in the air and shooting us down. We had revolutionized their whole death.

(In my foolish youth, beholding one noxious thing after the other, I marvelled at the purity, kindness, gentleness, sweetness, modesty, and essential goodness of mankind; the mystery increases within me. Right or wrong, rain or shine, I am a man of faith and good works. I no longer despair of the future; yet, having once more considered the matter, despair of it I must . . . I am hungry for a good, solid individuality like Tam o' Shanter's.)

Jackeen found a primrose in a little copse lined with larch—the beauty of it in her dark hair is as suns seen through oily steam. I have never observed anemone as sallow as it is here. Foxes peep out of the blackthorn and a wise swallow skims through the balloons which are decked out with rhubarb-tinted popcorn at this holiest of all seasons—Christmas. In a lovely, moss-banked glade Christ said Mass and we drank of the blood and ate of the flesh with a fervor remarkable for the occasion. Easter falls on November 8th in these parts; the Fourth of July on March 10th.

The smell of brine fills my nose as I sit here. Are we near the sea? Ah, to plunge into the fern-frothing surf and run exultingly down the lanes of starfish and convolvulus! I have been moping too much of late. Of a sudden, eh? The noble quiet of an old town by the sea. The right weather for a murder.

JULY 17 ❧ My window is thrown open to the rain; it beats in with the aggressiveness of liberty. Somewhere church bells peal out over the drenched fields—the eaves drip Sunday. There is something vulgar and satisfying about it.

On the bed Jackeen lies, her arms flung wide and a perilous spittal on her lips. The hour has come. But I shall read to her first —perhaps play the piano a bit.

"What would you like to hear?"

137

"Oh, Albion—" she gets up on an elbow, displaying long, deep-falling breasts with dainty dugs—"will you really read to me! How nice . . . I'm so glad . . ."

"I thought you might be."

"Well now, let's see . . ." She purses her mouth up until I want to rush over and bite blood out of it. "Do you have the sonnets?"

I get them and mumble through about a dozen.

"Look, Jackeen," I say. "It's getting late . . ."

"Please, Albion, just one more—read the one that goes, *"Not mine own fears, nor the . . . nor the . . ."*

". . . nor the prophetic soul
Of the wide world dreaming on things to come,
Can yet the lease of my true love control,
Supposed as forfeit to a confined doom.
The mortal moon hath her eclipse endured,
And the sad augurs mock their own presage;
Incertainties now crown themselves assured,
And peace proclaims olives of endless age.

Now with the drops of this most balmy time
My love looks fresh, and Death to me subscribes,
Since, spite of him, I'll live . . ."

"Albion."

"Yes, Jackeen."

"Don't read anymore."

"Say, wait there, darling . . . what's there to cry about?"

"About . . . about what you said a little while ago."

"What I said a . . . what do you mean?"

"You said, 'It's getting late.' "

"Why, I only meant we shouldn't be sitting around talking and reading all night when . . ."

"When what?"

"Oh, hell—you know what I mean."

138

"I am afraid, Albion."

"Afraid? Afraid of what?"

"Of you."

"Of me? But this isn't your first time with a man."

"I'm not thinking of that."

"No?"

"How can I tell you . . . it's . . . it's almost as though a voice warned me, saying, 'It's getting late. You have not long . . .' "

"You're just upset and tired, Jackeen. Why do you insist on attaching so much importance to what I said about it's getting late? Of course it's getting late—every good thing that ever happened in this world had to end because someone had to go off on a journey, or rest up for the next day's work—because it was getting late. The clock is the lovers' greatest foe, killing most of the wonder and the beauty with its foul tick."

The storm's liquid prisoner beats at the bars of night, sending eager streams across the floor. My ice-axe bobs head down on the planks, like an impatient ghost knocking for release from Purgatory. The candle frets on the mantle. A log bumps forward, scattering sparks like burning confetti. Dogs bark a devils' chorus on the margin of the swamp. The whistle of a demented shepherd sounds . . .

"But that isn't the late you meant, Albion."

"All right. You know more about it than I do."

"You meant that I haven't long to live . . ."

"Suppose I did? No one has. I've been telling you that for a long time—take your joy where you find it—live while there is still time."

"That was when you were urging me to sleep with you."

Out of the corner of my eye I see a grizzled face peering in at us from the window in back of Jackeen. The faint rattle of a chain causes her to turn, but the figure has already gone.

"What was it, Albion?" Her face is white and knotted.

"It was nothing . . . the wind. Your nerves are getting out of hand."

139

"Why do you sit there? Please . . . please come and put your arms around me. I'm so afraid."

"I thought you were afraid of me."

"I was joking . . . I'm tired and jumpy, just as you said I was, Albion . . . Why should you want to kill me? Isn't it funny how people can imagine things . . . nerves, of course, that's it . . . just like you said. I was a little fool to be afraid."

"Why should I want to kill you?"

"There! you see how silly I was . . . hurry, Albion, I feel cold. I'll make you so happy. Be gentle with me . . . we can have such fun . . . you do forgive me for making you wait so long . . . Why do you look at me like that!"

She begins to moan softly, drawing back with the blanket held tightly about her shoulders. A puppy's whimper . . . .

"Like what? For God's sake, Jackeen, don't start that up all over again. I'll come over to you as soon as I take care of something . . . it won't take a minute."

"Albion! Please! No . . . no! . . . not with an axe . . ."

I lower it to the table. I feel empty and dead.

"So you thought . . . ?" Something breaks inside me. I sink into a chair and sobs choke me like fists. "I was only going to dry it from the rust," I manage to say. "And you thought that . . ."

In a moment she is beside me. Her kisses cover my face and neck. Her naked little body strains against me. Her breasts lean out like a mother's to my mouth.

The room goes dark suddenly. Her body tenses, jerks as though under a blow.

Something moist and sticky moves down my cheek. A chain rattles . . . At last I am aware that someone is screaming in utter terror . . . then I recognize my own voice.

14. Albion Lives Through a Night In Galen

I would have time for many things. At least on this last night the world would open its doors to me—I was prepared to kick them in.

The first thing I had done was to give the soldiers the slip. This was not at all difficult: I waited until they were pounding at the door, then I opened the window quietly and stepped out on the air. I walked about in this region until presently I espied a cottage which interested me. In the bedroom, into which I had slipped unobserved, lay an old man and a serving maid, their voices blending in gentle talk.

"All my life I have wanted to witness a hanging," he said dreamily.

"Well, Poky, tomorrow you'll get your wish," the girl giggled, rubbing her soft thigh across his shrunken side.

I waited patiently until Poky had dropped off, when I sidled in next to her. It went on for a long time, the old fellow now and then waking with a start and shouting: "That'll be Lee on the white horse, my friend—make no mistake there!"

She was strictly a dish.

I lower my face into the grass near the fountain. A wild boar rushes about me in a circle. He is young and fat.

Overhead a dark wing shudders . . . grows still . . .

A fire crackles near the white church. A little boy and girl squat near its heat. He is telling her that God will not forget them. A sparrow's feather falls at their feet; and God can be seen making an entry in His big book. He is still at this work when the fire reaches and consumes the two babes, who perish singing with their arms fast and loving around each other.

Hearts never listen, do they? Hearts remain closed and hard. In some way, perhaps, we amuse ourselves. What rubbish most of it is. Squack! Squawk! You give me a pound of butter and I'll give you thirty cents. That's business! Not kids playing at store but grown men *being important in it.* Brutal, suspicious, watching for your fingers to open so they can count the corn. Such flashy bleeders . . . making sure that every Sadie Gilwater who can buy a fur coat, buys one. Of this Christ! all you can say is, what an organization . . . what a rip-snorting monkey's nuts of a business! Everything in cute little bottles . . . everything shiny, sweet-smelling, and mostly useless. What a nation of crows! lining our nests with absolutely priceless trash. Back into your cage, brother! The chief thing is not to do any living. Ah, that's not allowed! May I look at your waxworks? What are we on earth for! What's the meaning behind the things we can't understand! Why is there murder! What's it all about! I won't go under . . . I won't pull any tricks with mirrors on you.

Later I may see a mistake in this. Later I may say: what was the use in not resorting to all the old, boring stage sets; the imitation teeth and the spreading, false mustaches—why did you trouble to show yourself as you are? Later, maybe. But now I'd like to let you in on a secret. Here it is: I am sorry that I did not begin my book in this way:

The reason I cannot be at your house tonight is that I have an appointment with humanity. I find myself out of sorts with the world. I consider it my obligation to offer you a few practical suggestions. In the first place, read all of this journal; and for God's sake, don't fight it. Everything will come out fine; I know a hell of a lot more about what is here than you do. I am very proud of some of the things which you are to read in this book. I am not at all nervous. I do not fear death. I want to write and go about my business at the same time. I never sit down to write; I stand up, holding the paper off at arm's length. Forgive me, I was joking: I always write lying in bed with a box of bitter-sweet chocolate at my elbow—I wear both the tops and bottoms of my pajamas.

I have no unreasonable regrets. I sincerely believe that devotion is possible. The hymn is still to God.

Who would demand a *comfortable* soul?

When an ape looks into a mirror, do not be surprised if no swan appears.

142

The reader will remember that A. Moonlight is not a reformer, nor is he an informer, an outformer, an underformer nor an overformer; he is a *former*—savvy?

You make so much of the difference between good and evil. There is evil in good and there is good in evil; but there is no bad good and no good bad; there can be no good *good*, no *bad* bad—the good man thinks of the Devil and the evil man dwells much on God. Direct your thoughts to a place squarely between the two; because there is a day to be evil and a day to be good; when you awake in the morning, ask yourself: whose day is this, God's or the Devil's?—often there is more good in the Devil's day; for then God can be expected to recapture His sense of perspective, to remember that where there is a choice of masters no man need become a slave. Poor God has no such choice; that is why we feel sorry for Him.

In the eyes of God man is a grain of sand; in the eyes of man God is as sand without grains. Imagine what a deft barber with a sharp blade could do to our image of God . . . how quaint to think that He should hide His face in a beard—and what a start He must have got when Michelangelo walked into heaven!

We never admire a man: we admire our admiration for him. In the same way, love always separates us from the beloved; and he whom we hate is ever less affected by it than we are. This is why that never by word nor deed do we give evidence of hating or loving ourselves.

What is not understood is that talent has nothing whatever to do with creation. Mediocre artists produce a veritable cloudburst of talent; in fact, it is their sign, their stock in trade. If you can make nothing, then see to it that the *effort* of making is beautiful; but if you are a maker, you will know that somewhere the thing you would do has already been done, and you will set about quietly to do it.

143

Finally, I suppose, all wars are waged by women, who expect men to do something for them—to protect, to acquire; whereas men, expecting nothing of each other, proceed glumly to the slaughter.

The more pitiless the journey, the more crafty those who would accompany us—and thus deprive us of our goal. And rightly so, for we should never set out where others may follow—which is another way of saying that twenty-three and not fourteen angels can stand comfortably on the head of a pin.

We suffer with everything that suffers; but we share in little, if any, of the joy that is at every minute taking some fortunate man to bed.

I do not doubt that there is a world where the pillar of salt is punished by being turned into a woman. Who can deny that the first state is not better—*and a precise part of the same state*—?

It is necessary to keep one's hand in, to enjoy that sense of proportion which comes from a planned deformity. You know as well as I do that on this last night of my life it would be folly for me to attempt to recount my experiences. It is true that I hear the hammers driving in the nails that will sustain my destruction. You know what the sound of a hammer is like. Men have been hanged before. Soldiers are brutal. That is expected. (You are not forgetting that I am still engaged in telling you how I should have begun this journal. I make every allowance for the universal and acknowledged carelessness of book-readers, but there is a point of laziness beyond which I will not permit you to go. It is unfortunate that you are not better equipped to be my companion—this you have undoubtedly noted to yourself—but here we are, *just at this instant,* beginning to understand and appreciate each other. I told you not to slink away from me. Since you have not done so, I am moved to confide in you again. This time concerning my central, all-important problem: you see, it was necessary for me to go out of my way entirely in order to write *that which I did not want to write.* To put it simply: I had to become a person I was not; indeed, to *become* a person it would kill me to be. Thin ice, eh? I was determined to show you precisely what the world is. I had no intention of writing about it, or at it—by Jesus!—I would be that world! But not all the time. Ah, no. I wanted a book that I could read too. I wanted to make a book that I could read for the first time *after I had written it.* OK? Now we go back.)

But why should I tell you what I should have written? it is enough that I made a beginning—however impure and inadequate it may be. There is no problem here. I resorted just now to a rather shabby trick: I was most anxious that you remember *exactly how this book was begun*; and I knew that if I hinted at a feeling of unease about it on my part, you, dear reader, would immediately spring to its defense. And I want you to have a sense of devotion in regard to the beginning, the middle and the end of this little chronicle of the human spirit. Perhaps this is the time to talk to you about something which causes misgivings to rise in your breast. In short, to dwell for a moment upon the novel and the problems which have faced me in it. You have only to remember one thing, and all will be clear—the perfect shape will rise to your sight; you will have no score to settle with me on the matter of confused systems—you are to remember this: this novel is being written as it happens, not what happened yesterday, or what will happen tomorrow, but what is happening now, *at this writing.* At this writing! Do you see? I told you before that I would tell part of our story in the form of a novel: I did not say that I would write a novel. Consider my position: I sit in this room with a pen in my hand and outside in the town soldiers are moving like hunting dogs on my trail. It is altogether possible that they will find me and that I will be hanged with tomorrow's sun; but I shall do everything in my power to see that this does not happen—why? is it that I treasure life so much? that I wish to continue my agony in the shadow? No, my friends; it is simply that I am desperately anxious to discover what takes place next in this book—I am burning with longing to see how all this will end. I have never read anything which interested me as much as what I am writing. I pray that I shall be spared to finish this work. If I could only know what this night holds in store for me. I do not wish to die before I have told you of Keddel. There is the sound of shouting in the street . . . I may not have long to be with you. At any moment a bullet may sing through the window, bringing my strange career to an abrupt close. Once I asked you what you would say with your dying breath. Now I ask myself this question. Should I speak of God? Should I attempt to set forth my motives? Should I write of how complete and beautiful I feel? Should I tell you why I think my journal will grow in importance and stature as the years go on? I think it wise that I touch on everything. Tonight I am going to hold nothing back. I am going to tell you why I love Mildred more than I love Ann Deaken. I am going to tell you why it is so necessary for me to see Mr. Honour. I am going to describe precisely how I felt when I learned that Roivas is a hare-lipped dwarf; how this discovery caused a complete reshaping of my plans. And I shall speak of death, of art, of philosophy and religion, of the science of numbers and of the cults of decay. I shall not hesitate to tell you that there is a truth which rests above truth—do *not* be patient with me—I have a desire to reach beneath the gilt and the ornaments. I leave no room for another word to be said here. You will begin to understand my proportions. You will see that any novel I may write is a thing of danger and simplicity—above all, of simplicity. I propose to make the future and the present and the past happen all at once. I shall allow you not a moment to draw breath. You will realize that my characters are dangerous to me. God knows! they may decide to walk out of the book at any time, leaving me to carry on as best I can. I had no suspicions of Thomas Honey. Yet he managed to turn Jackeen against me. Jetter was my dearest friend. He leads the hue and cry for my blood. It was my earnest wish to make Choo Choo one of the most revealing characters in all this book: somebody shot him through

146

the head. Proudly I told you that Chrystle was the girl-Christ—where is she? why should I die for her murder when I have not so much as touched her hand? I demand the answers to these questions! I insist upon knowing why Turnbull and Fenn forced themselves into my journal, taking up a space I meant to fill with an account of how my mother wanted me to study for the priesthood. These things may be of no significance to you; for me they are of the essence of this book. I have been compelled to struggle every inch of the way against the sheer bullheadedness of these people. I had not the least wish to tell you about Leah, but, dead as she was, in she came. How wonderful it would be to someday write a story with a 'plot.' You know the sort of thing: A certain man in a certain town has a certain affair with a certain woman. Well, it seems that this dame is married to a certain guy who for the sake of his own evil designs is willing to give up his wife provided her lover submits to a certain little operation. Now, the question is does the woman decide to keep her prick of a husband or does she take this other guy who was stupid enough to let himself be unmanned and what part does Caleb Middlepot have in all this or/and just how strong is love and/or why was there a petunia in the dead man's hand particularly when you consider that Aunt Martha was *not* in her garden at a quarter of three on Wednesday last ... I am aware now that I have been making a miserable effort at beating time. I am a little afraid of taking you altogether into my confidence. Those damn hammers ...! I sit huddled up on the bed in a corner away from the window. The door into the hall is unlocked. They'll never think to just walk in on me. Later I am going from room to room in this house for a last look at the world, for a final word with my fellows. I won't let the hangman cover my eyes ... I shall want above all other things to see at that awful moment. I shall never deny my deepest instinct: which is to face all events with open eyes. In the beginning there was only being and spirit; whatever we know of reality arises from our disbelief in it. The mind forever returns to itself. To speak of logic in creation is to imagine that the mind has concerns outside itself. This

147

is not true. The mind is not a logical instrument. Vulgarians speak of 'using the mind.' How? How is this done? If the mind does not function in a logical way, by what right do we demand ordered thinking? What put this thought in our heads? If there can be no logic outside the mind, and if the mind rejects logic, is not the desire for logic a form of madness? The shepherd has his sheep, the horseman his horse, the hunter his rifle, the banker his bank; but what do I have who am none of these things? I will explain in another way: bees get honey, the tiger falls on the calf, the lion and the gnat and the worm and the moth each have a *particular* role to play in the universe. What is the function of man? Surely the sheep can get along without him; horses run better wild; rifles make nothing; of what good are banks when ninety-nine percent of us have no money?—I have said: what are we on earth for? *We serve no purpose in nature.* It is my guess that we are slated for extinction. What a puffed-up solemn-sides you are! Do you think it would matter one jot in the scheme of things if every last damn one of us handed in his checks tomorrow . . . such runny-assed self-importance . . . sitting back there waiting for me to say something that will set everything right. You can't drink from the bottom of the glass until you have downed the top. We don't know beans, any of us. We can just vaguely imagine that the whole business is tied up in someway with a seed . . . a little brown hard-shelled seed *that comes to life* in the ground . . . but what that life is, what it means . . . mathematics? huhuh; astrology? huhuh; physics? huhuh; economics? nope; metaphysics? nah; mineralogy? no—and it's about time we put our souls to this question. Tonight I shall meditate on the greatness and the littleness of man; the heavens and the earth, the cow and the ant, the wren and the buffalo, the wise and the foolish, the good and the bad, the fairy tale and the Word made flesh, this world and the next . . . death and birth, the idiot and the messiah . . . to speak, to see, to walk, to eat, to sleep . . . what do we do! where are we to go! . . . sun, moon, stars . . . those who are born of air, those who are born of water . . . what is memory? How is it possible to speak the truth

148

if there should be no truth on earth? How is it possible to have faith if there should be nothing at all to believe in? How is it possible to practice devotion if there should be nothing worthy of our love? How is it possible to act if there should be no result whatever but murder? ... to have power, to be born, to die, to wander in the darkness without hope, with nowhere to lay your head, with no one to walk beside you, with no man anywhere whose name is not known to the eyeless worms ... Jenny! Carol! Mildred! Ann! Jackeen! why do you hunger and decay? why do you suffer pain and die? Jetter! Thomas! Billy! Joseph! why do you thirst after murder? why do you waste your bodies in the crawling dust? Self is the barrier against which the world throws itself. Spirit is the wall against which we batter out our poor brains. It is getting dark. The bridges crumble into the raging waters. The mountains lift up their terrible sides and walk upon us. Someone is coming up the stair. A rifle is fired just outside the window. I put my face in my hands. I reach out for the New Testament and feel the raised letters of the cover under my fingers. It is necessary for me to relieve myself but to cross the hall to the bathroom is to invite a bullet. I drank several bottles of beer in the afternoon and now my back teeth are floating. I do my business against the wall and the sharp odor of urine fills the room. For some reason I start to cry. I am not afraid. I am curious about the sensations of death. But I do not want to die now. The footsteps stop outside my door. A gentle rap. A child's voice. Great God! I turn the knob and pull Chrystle into the room. She smiles at me. We do not speak. I gather her into my arms. "Please don't cry," she says. "They won't catch you." I caress her hair. "Why did you come here?" I ask. "To save you," she answers, snuggling closer to me. "But how can you save me, Chrystle?"—"Why, if they see that you didn't kill me at all, they won't have any reason for hanging you." I look into her seablue eyes over which the lashes move like hair on an angel's head. She does not fear me. She believes in my mission. I put my fingers around her throat and when her struggles cease I rip the clothes from her body and I ... I ... the knife ... blood on my hands ...

149

Why! Why! God have mercy! Christ have mercy! . . . I had to do it, I tell you! There is an order and a plan in all that I do . . . she lies in a pitiful heap beside the bed. I bend over and close her eyes. Something breathes at my back. I wheel around and (what do I know of guilt? Where would I learn not to kill?) Roivas is standing there, his face contorted in a beastlike joy, saliva dripping from his gray lips, his lower body shoved out as for carnal embrace. He points to the murdered child . . . "Ul ul!" he says, throwing himself upon her . . . and I drag him off, striking at his monstrous face until my arm is weary. Then they are all there. I turn from one to another of them. "What do you want of me!" I shout. "Kill me! Kill me! Have done with it!" But they just stand there looking at me, their faces like wooden masks, the eyes dilated, nostrils drawn—staring in abject horror. "Well, say it! Damn you! say it!" I scream. "Tell me what you see! Am I so hideous! What are you afraid of?" Quietly, like mechanical toys, they cross before me, one by one, each hungry, hot mouth pressing into mine—Jetter, Carol, Thomas Honey, Billy Delian, Jackeen—then, as though hell had at last found a voice, Roivas, doing as the others had done, squeezes his pus-filled lips squarely upon my mouth. I cannot move. My arms and legs are as iron weights. And they go away; the door closes—but I do not hear the sound of their steps on the stairs. I must find something to do. Morning should be coming soon. Already the sound of a cock crowing in a distant farmyard can be heard. It crows again. I pick up a newspaper. The first thing I see is an ad put in by a woman wanting a husband. A widow in Iowa City. Hurriedly I write her a letter, full of promises, endearments, and statements of my exceptional state of finances. Meet me on the west corner of Maple and Delaware in Saginaw, Mich.—such and such a date—and be wearing an ostrich plume in your hat, I tell her, signing myself, Your own Boopee Woopee. I put an Air Mail stamp on the envelope and drop it out of the window, knowing that some good soul will surely put it in a box. Then I light a cigarette. I take two drags and snuff it out. It is true that we can go anywhere in the world if we know the way. A hermit's life has mystery for everyone save the hermit. Who anywhere has authority over me? I have no fondness for jewelry. I am unalarmed by the glory of merchants or princes. Think for a moment upon this expression: *To lead one's life.* How? Where? That is the sort of thing men have said; is it remarkable that we are where we are? Life does the leading, make no mistake. Nothing is grotesque or ugly except it stand against what is beautiful. The splendor of the emperor is as nothing compared to the flake of snow. The greatest man is the craziest man. Nothing is known of children. Why do creatures get 'older'? There is nothing stupider than the books which attempt to follow a human being through childhood into manhood. I say that the thread breaks, that the man does not come out of the child—God knows where the man comes from or where the child goes. All our damn sense of continuity! Where do we get it? This storekeeper philosophy that says the day's work begins in the morning and ends at night; that men grow up—holy God! we are not beasts of burden . . . why do we put up with this business of standing around in a muddy ditch all day in order to make a living? . . . whose living, you poor boob? . . . and as for growing up, most men grow down . . . there is not an ounce of sense in any of it—isn't it about time for your alarm to go off? That's it! on the double quick! how perfectly gloriously righteous you feel, hot-assing it off to spend the day at some fool's job and then tearing back at night to get on with your boring fool's life . . . put something by for a rainy day but stay out of the path of floods; you'd have to get your boss's permission to build an ark. The soul chooses its own company. What a humdinger you must have! I wish to Christ you'd stop making me stutter. You don't deserve that I put this in good language. Every time I think of what a howling mess of everything you've made, I get tongue-tied. Scratch an intellectual and you'll find an ill-literate, pompous, cock-sure, inconsiderate, stoop-shouldered, mouse-colored nincompoop smelling of cafeterias and steam heat. Enough! Back into the clean air . . . nobility begins when there is no longer any reason to have faith.

When the solitary tree is chopped down the forest moves nearer heaven. The traitor will not fear death; it is from life that he flies. Men know the power of the storm only when their ship has plunged them deep into the terrible quiet of the waters. An evil name is not come by without a good effort. When you lie your tongue is happy, for truth generates bitterness—but is itself sweet. Love cannot be expected to conquer; the ocean asks nothing of the rain. The cock's wings are more important to his cry than his voice is. Where fire cannot be no life that breathes can be. Air rushes in to fill the vacuum: so the artist . . . into the place *where the mold already is.* When two things hit each other it is always the fastest moving which flies backward farthest: it is no disgrace to fail in this world; it is, in fact, impossible to conceive of success in any other way. The bird that flies upside down will not be surprised by the hawk—nor will it discover its own prey. We can only be praised or blamed for what is in our power to do. The man who is separated from his fellows supposes at once that they have forsaken him: hence leaders. Two weak men leaning together have more strength than two strong men who struggle to keep apart. It is folly to be wise when your wisdom can only feed on folly. To hate a thing for its own sake—there is the miracle. The earth takes rain out of need; why does the sun lift it above again? You come into the world like a loaf of bread across a filthy counter. Human force cannot be other than spiritual; surely earth does not need man's feeble stirrings. Why desire the impossible? more than all else do we pray that that at least will not cease to be. If the maker should die, what has been made? Water is the male blood of mountains. Nothing that can be lost is worth possessing. Time does not exist in nature, but everything there is done in the shortest, simplest way. The size of the world is determined by the size of your dwelling: the smaller your house the larger the world—to live in a palace is to altogether deny the First Carpenter. The elements of which our bodies are made have only one desire: to return to their own condition; that is why there is eternally in us a will to revert back to primal chaos. It is *natural to go mad.* Imagination is the enemy of sight: how well we see in dreams! The man who at death leaves behind nothing but a full privy had no right to a stomach. What a pleasure it is . . . life! To lie here on my bed and thumb my nose at the soldiers. I have put a blanket over Chrystle's body. I wish I had something strong to drink. Impatience is my great vice. My skeleton wants to dance all the time. I ought to be thinking of some way to save myself . . . is that a ladder against the window? A face appears. Then another, another . . . those pesky little graybeards. They crowd around me, jabbering like monkeys with their bottoms on fire. I want no traffic with them at this point. I lead them into the bathroom (knowing that the soldiers will not risk taking a pot-shot at me while I am surrounded by so many) and show them the horse which is soaping himself in the tub. They find this fasci-nating. I crawl back to the room on my hands and knees. Think of me as I am tonight—I feel marvelously pure and clear-eyed . . . I regret nothing . . . nothing! Shoot me! Put your damn rope around my neck! Pick my eyes out! My lungs roar with the saying of it . . . ah, the beautiful, pure *saying of it* . . . the hand on my knee . . . O saintly debauchery . . . public error and ship-wrecked devotion . . . SAVIOR! . . . I am an idealist in a quagmire . . . *I am on fire* . . . farewell Death . . . what burdens are mine! . . . I come with my guns blazing . . . Goddamn! Goddamn! Goddamn! Hur-ray! Boil me! Put hot spikes through my heart. Finish me while you have the chance . . . I am going to make you get down on your knees to me . . . I am going to tear you to pieces like an old sack . . . I am going to beat in your heads and kick out your teeth . . . I'll make you listen to me! What do you know of punishment? You have an *idea.* Brutality? What do you think of that! Is it perhaps a crab-apple on a peachtree . . . shut up! Ah, those dear old women, Yale and Harvard and Princeton too . . . I'm generous, I'll pick your nose if you will pick mine. Let's agree on something! Do you know any French? maybe a smattering of Russian . . . hold up my blood! Put my head on your shoulder! *I'm sinking into the water* . . . who said anything about suffocating! The city

153

boils with vice . . . fear lies with innocence . . . a yellow rose . . . this is the gospel . . . knock me down! kick my ribs in! my blood walks out over the roof tops . . . I am not on hire, get that idea out of your head . . . I arrange science in the box with witchcraft . . . what do you know of GUILT! Once upon a time the Below . . . the hell with it, I tell you! the words get lost somewhere between my head and the paper. Most of this book is written on the air. I can't keep up! What a tight-fisted bitch this little matter of writing is. Come on, move in; put up your mitts—I'll bat your ears down . . . walk on the water? I'll walk along exactly six inches *above* the water. What do you say to that! . . . If you will open . . . here is my hand . . . I shall study medicine . . . I'll learn to play a mandolin (Jesus! that *plunking*) . . . hello, mom, it was a good fight—I'll be home as soon as they can find my head . . . *poor bastards* . . . I want to be a carpet in a cathouse . . . how funny it will seem to die, not to be able to see or feel . . . do you talk in your sleep? are you afraid? are you in pain? do you hunger? how is every little thing? I've got *polish*. What a peculiar face that ghost has . . . where is the rhythm? They just dropped me off here—I don't know a damn thing about this world. They just scooted me out and said find your hole and pop into it. They didn't give me any build-up— they didn't tell me that I was sent on to stink and rot and kill and puke over all the pretty hills and still waters. I started in to eat and drink and then I emptied myself and did it again and if I looked at a star it was either with my mouth full or my pants down. I maintain that we should be friends—what *right* do we have to hate each other. Now I think I'll tell you how to make the most of the things of this earth. Do you like glass beads and the bright little fannies of the flowers? I have seen a bullfrog take a North American Indian in its mouth and spit out a paper-hanger named George Tobin. George is married now and has eighteen children—four by his wife. I tell myself that I understand impressions. I dig my thumb nail into my manuscript. The lampshade here is of a particularly hideous design. I have been brave twice in my life—once with a madman, once with a mountain lion. That was a distinguished summer . . . stars foaming in the millrace of the sky; a blonde swinging with me in a hammock under an elm —it is difficult to remember what being with a woman is like . . . and the lion just walked in and took her arm in his mouth. A time for decisive action. I beat it into the brush when I encountered the madman—her father, who had been spying on us. I called the lion over and told him to go to work on the old boy, which he did but I couldn't get the light-top's arm back. I do not care for your opinion. I am not here to settle your account with the tailor. I do not want your praise: it is within my power to do what I am doing—when I do something I can't do, then will be the time to drape me with the laurel. And throw Hardy in too. Just how sensitive do you think I am? I am fed up with this hurting that gets us nowhere. Let us think of snow. Did they sing carols when you were a child? Silent Night, Holy Night, eh? That's pretty. My foot's asleep. Somebody has to say it: what is literary criticism? No you don't—no systems please. Get down and grub in the dirt . . . I'll make a hit with my notion of charity. I shall be forced to talk to you about Art—one is successful or not. Is that clear? My fingers are beginning to get tired. I yell into the bathroom and two of the beards come shuffling in. I get them set and start dictating: Dear friends, I say, I love you as I love all the creatures. I write to you without any hope at all of ever hearing from you. I love Carol. I love Jackeen. I don't pay the rent here; I was just brought in and dropped. I would give you money but I have none —just enough for some wheatcakes and coffee in the morning. I take no interest in politics. Not only do I not have an axe to grind I haven't so much as a pot to pee in. I work when there is nothing better to do. I know that many of you are addicted to pocket pool —so be it. I write this without salary. I have a mother who kissed me when I was little. Her mouth is old and dry now. What can you do? I hate the theatre. Nothing should be *acted*? Stop the play and watch the audience. What do you prim-necked freaks expect to happen! I am hurt bitterly by my conscience. I expect something to have been right. To make an issue of despair is to lick the

155

devil's ass. Gentlemen, be seated! I am frightfully constipated
with that horse in the can. I don't want to see a horse at a time like
that. I know what you have been thinking all along: just who was
my wife? Who was the mother of Jackeen? If I were to tell you
the name of my daughter's mother, your eyes would pop out of
your heads. Suffice it to say that she was a leader in Newport society, an habitué of the smartest spots on this continent. Why, I
can remember a prince—a prince! mind you—walking into our
bedroom on Park Avenue and standing there with a monocle in
his hand until we finished. She was strictly a pewter plate. I have
a bit of a surprise for you. I am going to put another little novel
right in this little novel! How will you like that? After all, I can't
just sit here and listen to those blasted hammers . . . *I wonder if
they'll get me in the morning* . . .

Well, here goes:

Chapter I

Albion Moonlight sat on a rock by the sea. He was eating an orange and figuring out his income tax. An old man hobbled by and
said: "What an insidious sunburn you have!"

Albion answered: "Did you ever hear of a Norwegian angel?"

The palpitating biscuit rubbed some more elderberry jelly into
its womb . . . spermatozoa coagulating in cabalistic delight. But I
do not now anticipate a love affair between the paper dog and the
quaint anthropomorphism of the well-sprung eagle which sits at
the right testicle of Jesus Christ.

Chapter II

He quiet and unseeing leaves nothing to its fate. The useful dimension of the apple-bird-star-saloon-motorboat-naked cannibal-
shadow-safety razor-arcade-jewelbox-baby's ass-green cloak.

A. An owl in a wasp's nest.

B. The next step is 1917.

C. Why can't painting be done from inside the canvas?

D. Put this book on a glass-topped table and fire a bullet through it: it will drip a woman's face in its own blood.

E. Advance the probable question now. Who put the used postage stamp on the milkyway ... was it Friar Pierre?

F. The marvelous is in the seaweed's milk: in the hastily devoured washing machine: in the fragile shudder of the bull-dreamwolf.

G. It is all-important to know how you hold your hands in sleep.

H. A shoe made of alligator hide eating a poached egg while the photograph of a yellow snowstorm leans out of a window whistling to a *one*-lipped junior high school girl. I am jealous of the tent.

I. What crisis do you speak of? The gesture of fruit is not timid.

J. Keep your swaybacked rowboat. The hurricane lamp shall be my train and down-going wing before the wet drops all the plaster from this explosive house.

He quick and unseemly learns what he knows before his head gets around to it. Darling girl! washed all away by the nasty rain ...

CHAPTER III

The shapes must be mutilated ... it is holes not blocks we need.
DON'T BE A CRY BABY WHATEVER YOU DO
It is exciting to think of keeping the secret from the secret. I bring Jetter and a flabby-faced giantess in here and a bit of this and a bit of that—so you get the slant—maybe a kiss, a smart boot in the rear ... a spacious room with a Baltimore stove and one isolated little bit of talk "Hello, kid." "Check." and so and so and so and so and so

however, the camera is not idle. If you get what I mean?

157

Chapter IV

I am in a stew. Carol is out with a truckdriver. Where did I put Loretta? (Loretta is my meerschaum pipe). There remains a lot to be done.

I stretch out my arms to you. I put a towel around my head and stare intently into the shadows.

The telephone.

"Hello."

"Have you got a fellow living there by the name of Hansen?"

I tell him yes and turn Hansen on to him. I watch Hansen's ears. His wet body glistens like a fish's.

Miserably I stuff Loretta into my mouth and sit there.

Somewhere pieces of a battleship are flying into the air.

The earth rolls in agony on its red sheets . . . Death must be damn weary tonight.

Chapter V

A few feet from me rests a derailed locomotive. As I watch, it dwindles away until only the pockmarked buttocks of an old woman are left. From this shameless object crawl the wounded and dying of the wreck . . . lashed on by the spinning whip of a pageboy who wears purple trunks and a goat-mask. Look around you—Why, hell, you're running off in all directions. Afraid . . . of what? I am. Afraid, I mean. We must become humble and full of bowels. To be aloof and ugly-willed. To start yelling like bastards everytime they start fitting us up for uniforms. Get me? . . . you know, I think it would be a relief to get into some cozy nut house. A *moderate* setting. Between you and me there is one difference: I've heard the tongues sizzling in the skulls . . . zzzzzz. Baby! All right, let's go higher. O! O! O! the desolate battalions . . . closer honey . . . the wounded choirboy in the umbrella stand . . . the candle slips from my fingers . . .

footsteps of the beast *seven wings!!
Breathe the wild air
O lovely earth! not DEATH
& the perfumed milk of my ladies
O flaming cave To be pure
Concealing tears, * sleep
everything is like looking into a leper's mouth

Monday. Is this Monday? WHAT REALITY ARE YOU TALKING ABOUT
You won't leave me, will you? will you? will you? will you? will
you? will you? will you? will you?

One two three four five six seven sun blue tree door alive sticks
heaven eight hate nine thine ten amen and there wasn't a dry eye
in the house.

CHAPTER VI

The day sat on the window sill and combed sunbeams out of its
whiskers. It was as peaceful as an empty jug. Moonlight stretched
himself out flat before the altar. He prayed for a long time. When
he got back to his study the shadows were already playing hide-
and-seek on the foreheads of the numerous whores who paced
back and forth like grim cats in the streets below. He turned to his
journal and reread his entries of that summer. An eye looked over
his shoulder and made a cruel judgment.

159

MAY 2 🏃 We have studied all the maps; Galen is on none of them. A strange bird alighted on my shoulder at dusk. Man, forever's vagabond, moved forward another inch on the dread road.

MAY 5 🏃 Jetter complained today of the presence of a tiny little woman who dogs his every step. She is under two feet tall. Her shape is superbly rounded and calculated to excite desire, but all her members and organs are unfortunately proportionate to her size. I expect trouble on this score.

Hunters make a battlefield of the forest. We came upon one whose thigh had been blown away by a charge of buckshot intended for a fawn. He died as we were carting him to a farmhouse.

I spent the evening working on my report. Roivas should be surprised by some features of our investigation.

MAY 11 🏃 I quarreled with Thomas Honey over a passage in *The Trojan Women*—the one where Talthybius tells Hecuba that her son Hector has been seen sleeping with a white-haired girl just at the elbow of the Great Wall. It was my contention that Euripides was making mock of our most sacred institution—murder; whereas, Honey, possessed of an unaccountable stupidity, insisted on reducing the whole speech to the status of a plea for better understanding between people with blue eyes and people with light brown (or even hazel) eyes.

The rain shows no sign of abating. I cleaned my rifle and wrote a few letters.

A festival of healing grief . . . quick-throated legends . . . the earth swims deep in windclutching psalms . . . gaunt mustang gallop through the sky . . . the dancing girls are all nudely DEAD.

MAY 19 🏃 A fluttering as of desperate wings.

This is the moment of tranquillity and celestial journeying.

Always the silver music in the shadow . . .

160

MAY 24 🐾 An orange bear stalks its supper off in the thicket. Childhood chants at the edge of a martial cliff. Prayers rustle through the golden haze . . . the tinkle of incredible runes. Something carries the melting palace through the pain. Mountainous horses plunge the bell-ropes into shimmering hallelujahs above the haunted campanile.

Jackeen murmurs in her sleep . . . I remove my hand.

A telegram arrived late tonight from my attorney. He instructs me that my suit against the Standard Oil Company has been thrown out of court on the ground of insufficient evidence. I'll walk in on them one of these fine days and bash in their heads . . . what do they think they're dealing with, a school boy!

Mrs. Drew's condition is far from good.

Our tents afford little real shelter against the rain, which is now of storm proportions.

MAY 25 🐾 I am obsessed by the thought that the priest who came to make confession to me today is much less worldly than he makes out. What utterly childish sins! He had impure imaginings of a woman . . . how is that possible? What he needs is to get the lay of the land—and I know just the dish who could give it to him. I was interested, however, in one thing he confessed to: he told me that it was his habit to smell the bicycle seats lately occupied by women. This hit me as being rather droll, and I chuckled all through dinner.

Disquietude is to be desired in humans. I honestly don't know what is meant by 'temperament.'

I tell you that it is altogether reasonable to expect anyone in the world to produce a work of art.

How do I say it? when we remove our gloves we are *more apt than not* to find a stirring, vine-like antenna where we supposed our hands to be.

MAY 29 🐾 A great flock of parrots scattered through the forest, all talking in the most wonderful way:

161

"I inquire, is the navel awake in the savage mirror?"

"Illusion is the suitcase in which we carry our proper hearts."

"Nothing must ever be said precisely: there must be a running over of meaning—a spectacular mis-statement."

"In future, men will write as though language were their only dull tool—which is quite true."

"When the book is finished, then will be the time to write."

"The experience that is not impossible is no experience at all."

"In sculpture the artist must learn the ancient law of his stone."

"Music can only advance when every known instrument has been destroyed."

"The painter will strive to exclude all living images from his canvases. He will paint only that which cannot be seen."

I made this reply to those delightful parrots:

How have you settled the little matter of death?

I know ... contained in the skin!

———

JUNE 4 🦟 Carol is mending my socks in the little alcove off our bedroom. I feel vaguely uneasy ... a house with four red chimneys strolls across the field. In an upper window, a little girl, blood spurting from a gaping hole in her forehead, drops a withered, claw-like hand to the ground. I rush down and stuff it clumsily into my pocket. Now you have succeeded in getting my dander up —I shall come to terms with victory in my own way.

At least you, I thought, would make an effort to understand ...

———

JUNE 12 🦟 I have succumbed to Jackeen's pleadings and hired a bodyguard. He is a big, toothless hulk with a jail record as long as a widow's night. The first thing he did—after shooting me accidentally in the leg—was to fall asleep, and by God we can't wake him up to save our souls. He lies sprawled out on the kitchen table and his snores make the timbers of the inn shake like jelly in an earthquake. It would seem to me that I have enough to think about without listening to that lazy bastard all day.

JUNE 15 ✇ When I got up this morning I discovered that everybody else in the place had been bound and gagged during the night.

Monster footprints lead from room to room, only skirting mine —what new torture has been conceived!

I have barricaded myself in my room. After two or three hours of sorting through my files, time begins to weigh on my hands. Perhaps I should essay a short novel on childhood . . . I set to work on the first chapter:

Albion Moonlight was big for his ten years. He seemed to dominate the little group of his friends as they disported themselves in the old lumberyard.

"Cuz yuh c'n git nutt'n outta 'er wad fuh yuh down der?" he demanded of his friend Limpy, who was holding little Ida down with one hand and feeling with the other.

"Shod yuh faz," Limpy said.

"Waaaa!" yowled little Ida, struggling to get up.

Izzy McGuire dealt her a good one.

"Wyntcha sthop dat?" he said.

"Whoose toin now?" Albion demanded, as he took the two cents from Limpy. "Yuh god tah take toins."

"Who 'djuh t'ink yuh are?" he yelled suddenly. Happy, who had been trying for a long while to get down there, slunk away sheepishly. "Yuh ain' god no right comin' hea—yuh never sawr two cents."

"Snodnoz!" Happy said, moving off.

"Git da bastid." Albion ordered.

Louie and The Drip pinned Happy to the ground and unbuttoned his pants and rubbed spittal in.

"Albie!" Ward Thomas called. "Ida's stopt breathin'."

"Cheez!" said Izzy.

"Wadddayuh wanna bet I kin make 'er breathe," Albion said, bending over with something in his hand.

"Oh boy!" The Drip said admiringly.

163

A squawk went out of little Ida that would have made an Indian envious.

"Yea," Albion said. "Dah bitch thod she c'd slip sumpt'n on ter me. Yea."

He flashed around on them, his fists raised like hammers.

"Giddaddihea, yuh damn stinkers!" he said.

When they had all gone, he knelt down beside little Ida and said: "C'mon, yuh piss-a-bed, I'll show yuh whad's whad"—she started to scream—"Yea." And then there was no sound—but that of Albion's sobbing.

(Talk about a fool! Here I sit working on a novel with the door boarded up and I should be using all the wits I've got on a plan to get out of here. I wonder what would happen if I telephoned the police?

Those dogs out there are beginning to get on my nerves.)

JUNE 16 ⚜ I thought that, having been baffled at every turn by the curious inertia of my fellows, a spell of solitude would sit well with me. It is clear that I have overestimated my own resources. So, knowing the hazard of such an act, but resolved in some way to brook my loneliness, I, at last, with what misgivings you may imagine, drew the bolt.

Carol sat exactly on my doorstep, heigh-hoing it forward in great style with that truckdriver. She must at some time, though it is a stretch to suppose it, have turned a trout's cold cheek to a man; as to now, the wonder is that she doesn't wear quite out. I am done once and for all with wayward women.

Such are we of this strange race . . .

JUNE 22 ⚜ Thomas Honey is experiencing difficulty with his eyes.

I was compelled to call Jackeen to task for spanking Chrystle. She stamped her pretty foot at me:

164

"I'll thank you to never meddle in my affairs," she said haughtily.

"Now, just a minute," I said. "If you're going to sit around soaking yourself in highballs, you can keep your muddy temper to yourself."

She turned on me in a rage: "You hairy-faced sonofabitch! Just you try to run my business! I'll ... I'll ..."

"You'll what?"

"I'll tell Carol about Eleanor," she said, starting back as though expecting a blow.

"Has Eleanor gone?" I asked.

"Yes."

"With whom?"

"She went to see some bear-baiting with Billy Delian."

I got nervous then. I took Jackeen by the shoulders and shook her. "You lying piece of jail-bait," I said. "What makes you think I'd care if you told Carol?"

"Mmm," she said, smiling; but her eyes were hard as dry blood.

"All right," I said. I carried the fight to her for about ten minutes; there wasn't a spot on her face that didn't have a welt on it.

She was crying softly, coming out of her drunk.

"Don't let me hear you mention Eleanor again," I said.

She looked up at me out of her good eye: "Albion," she whispered.

"I'm listening," I said.

"Don't blame me for getting tight."

"I don't, but I won't have you lamming that kid around," I told her, putting my coat on.

The exercise had made me feel good. I didn't feel cooped-up anymore.

"I've got a reason," she said.

"For what?" I said.

"For getting tight," she said.

"Which is?"

"I've been knocked-up."

165

"Who's the lucky guy?"

"Don't joke about it."

"Look, honey," I said. "Why tell me about it? You know that if you had let me be the one I'd have seen you through. But now . . . what the hell, make the guy who got the cream lick society's chops."

"But I don't want an abortion."

"What are you going to do with another squaller?"

"I don't know," she said. "But that's not it anyway."

"Then what?"

"It's funny," she said, lifting herself up to a chair.

"It must be," I said. "Ha ha."

"And I'm scared, Albion."

"Tell papa."

"It's . . . well, you see . . ." she broke off, coming over to put her arms around me. I stroked her hair and lights were going on and off in me. "My sweet," I whispered, so she couldn't hear.

"How can I tell you?" she said, crying.

"Would it be easier to tell me if I went out of the room?"

"Oh, damn you! I suppose you'll laugh . . . It's just that I . . . I haven't slept with anyone."

"Now I'll tell one," I said.

She jumped down and turned to face me with guns in her eyes.

"I knew that you'd never believe it," she said in a controlled sob.

"Is it true?"

"Yes! Yes! It's true . . ."

I cut in: "OK. I believe you. What's the matter with it?"

"What's the matter . . .?" She stared at me unbelievingly.

"Yes," I went on. "Suppose the brat has no father. So, does that put you in jail or something?"

She stared at me for a long time, then she said:

"You don't believe me, do you?"

"Yes, Jackeen," I said. "I believe you."

"But how can such a thing happen!"

"It can't. That's why I know you're telling the truth."

166

A fog was rolling in from the sea when I went to bed. I didn't get to sleep until daylight. I'm a hard fellow to be alone with.

||||||||||||||||||||||||||||||||||||||||||||||||||||||||||||||||||||||||||||||||||||||||||||||||||||||||||||||||||||||||||||

JUNE 30 ⚙ We got into Lincoln yesterday. Billy Delian made a couple speeches and I went through a pottery works. I happened to hit a rack of pots in the middle of the floor and you can believe it those pots just kept knocking each other over until there wasn't a whole pot in the place. It was probably the biggest thing that had ever happened in Nebraska. The owner of those pots just sat down and cried like a baby. He had a little yellow mustache that looked like a canary perched on his lip.

Jetter's little two-bit woman is something of a medium. We held a little seance the other night but all we could get to come through was an Indian named Gaven who shook the starch out of that little woman with his big bass voice.

She'd say: "We're waiting, spirit," and he'd come back with: "This is your Aunt Winifred. I am well and happy here. Your Uncle Turner wants me to say hello for him . . ." and all the time it's this big bruiser of an Indian socking us out of our seats with his bellow.

She got her wires crossed someplace, I guess.

I went into a drugstore to buy a pack of cigarettes and when I got back to the street several thousand people were running around yelling and pointing to the sky. I looked up for a good while but I didn't see anything. I enjoyed the sensation immensely.

When I am gone it may be that there will be material enough for one little statue . . . ?

My eyes are closing. Time enough to read more of the journal tomorrow.

CHAPTER VII

Hansen has moved out. He had a revolting habit of bringing his women in just as I was ready to sit down to dinner. There is no good point in confusing our appetites. What's more, and this really upset the applecart, he had the nerve to ask all his relatives in. This is not a big room and when you think of twenty-some people barging around in here you get some idea of what I was up against—particularly at night—twenty-odd in one bed . . . and if you don't think some of them were odd! His Cousin Norbert, for instance—pissing into the air and then running under it . . . Ah, I could tell you tales about that crew!

I finally got my income tax figured out. I sent the government a bill.

(To be continued.)

Those bloody hammers! How can I be expected to write a novel with all that racket! "What a stinko," says the little graybeard who has been taking my dictation. (His brother or whatever went to sleep after the first page.) What a diet these little fellows must subsist on! I have never encountered such an aroma in anybody's wind before—and do they let go with it! Stinko! I'll 'stinko' him. Also, to add to the excitement, the horse has wandered in from the bathroom, shaking soapsuds all over the place. I think it might be well if I showed them all out. I manage after about half an hour to get them all on the horse, then I open the door and boot them all the hell down the stairs. There is a whale of a thumping and banging and my neighbor across the hall looks out and asks me what's the matter. He is an old duck in horn-rim spectacles and a lot of big books under his arm. I tell him that they are paving the street on the next landing and he says 'I see' and plods back amid a cloud of dust and cobwebs. An instant later he looks out again: "That's strange," he says. "I never heard of a street being built in a house before. Are you sure about that, young man?" I laugh cannily. "I was just joking," I say. "You see . . ." But just at this moment, the horse looks around the turn in the stairs. "Why," chuckles the old boy, "it's only a horse. He must have fallen downstairs." And he goes in, this time to stay. I beat the horse to the door, slamming it in his face. I know damn well he'll head for the

168

bathtub, but I don't want any more scrimmaging around with him tonight.

I snuff the candle out and move cautiously to the window. The smell of wax reminds me of the flowers banked around a coffin—which never somehow smell of flowers at all. Outside, the town-square is drenched in moonlight—a hard, driving glow that seems to sift into the very pores of the night. At first I can see little. It is almost as though I looked down through water. Little by little the objects take on shape and meaning. Beneath me, stretching away into remote space, stand countless scores of people, their faces, every one, none turning away, fixed, unmoving, frozen—I am yelling at them! my heart does not beat . . . sweat streams down my cheeks—their faces all raised to me! I am crying . . . I can't make you see it . . . the scaffold lifting there like a hawk's wing; the hammers of the carpenters poised to strike; the great bell in the church tower swung far to the side but not swinging back; a child in the crowd stooping to rub a dog's ear; the dress of a woman lifted by a now dead wind above her thighs; the hand of a priest pointing at something in the sky (*are they all dead, God? do those unmoving eyes see into mine?*). I'll tell you something. Now I must go on. Forgive me if it never reaches you. My mother would say something fine about me . . . The window is square . . . the knife-mouthed dogs will return . . . push down to see them *as though through water* . . . not even the soldiers are moving . . . shall I stop now

THE END

how do I get in to you! You see what has happened is that high up in the night above where the earth is . . . all those people are talking and the hammers are ringing. The tongue of the bell is striking. Everything is known there. *His* heart . . . *His* decrees . . . It is *His* fears that hide me . . . whose atrocious innocence? Is this the favorable moment! Speaking . . . through the webbed stare of the multitude . . . a sodden light on all those unweeping faces . . . let them not despise me . . . thus afraid and alone. Crawling along the ledge to the roof; standing upright in the cool light; my hands clenched—cotton-muscled—I move forward. Rup! Rup! Rup! The shouting and the singing drifting down the sky . . . I come upon hundreds of Negroes busy at the task of polishing an endless row of automobiles which appears to reach down to the ground . . . flashing teeth . . . bobbing heads . . . men and women . . they do not hear me . . . but a tall, shining figure floats along the lane of cars and I put my arms around it, sobbing. Then I see another thing. Three huge women are leaning against a chimney. Enormous white thighs flash in the moonlight. Their hair is black. How beautifully still their faces are! The floating figure passes before them . . . I begin to understand. It is myself who is thus moving about in the raw, pink light. Pink! the color we see when we close our eyes to the sun. I'll move a little closer to you. Advancing along the roof's edge . . . trying not to fall . . . meeting thick, heavy things without arms or legs . . . flesh, doughy, breathing . . . lumps that cannot see or hear or speak or taste . . . coupling together in monstrous positions . . . a thick, green blood dripping from their organs . . . *do not disturb them* . . . God will be displeased if you disturb them . . . I am walking through the groups of silent people, mounting the stairs that lead up to the gallows, taking the rope in my own hands and slipping it over my head . . . *I step to the trap.*

Now my eyes (through no will of mine) lift to the room where I had been prisoner, to that little cell where the soldiers had driven me. A man is standing in the window, a terrible smile on his face. He is staring down at me with such hatred that I cry out as though under a vicious blow. Solemnly he winks. I sink to my knees, for I realize that it is myself who is leaning there. Then, quite as if a spell had been broken, all those thousands of people come to instant life, yelling and waving about like dwellers in a satisfying hell. The soldiers and police drag that unprotesting figure from the window and in a moment a lane is cleared from the hotel to the foot of the gallows and Albion Moonlight is flung at my side. They kick his face until the eyes run in tiny blue threads over his

170

cheeks. His right hand is placed on a block and hacked off. Then they fix his neck in the noose which is around my neck and we are plummeted down . . . he is fifteen minutes dying.

But I live. I, Albion Moonlight, have not died.

Let them take their ghastly souvenirs . . . one young woman, more adept and resourceful than the others, contrives to get possession of his penis. As she holds it aloft, the blood spurts up like a flame—like a fire hungry for the soft, dead flesh of our cities.

|||||||||||||||||||||||||||||||||||||||||||||||||||||||||||||||||||||||||||||||||||||||||||||||||||||||||||||||||||||||||||||||||||||||||||||||||||||||

JULY 20   I slept unusually well last night. My dreams were innocent and instructive. In my halcyon days it was not often that I rose early—seldom that I saw the daybreak. There was always some reason to be dull and benumbed; the pace I set was not calculated to make me float when I walked.

But now, in this quiet house, in this drowsy little village, my senses glow and I have a tilt to my kidney. I bound out of bed and wield my toothbrush like Sancho's spear, humming the while like a boy in love.

And I am in love—with the young lady who lives just across the street. She has red hair and she is taking lessons on a cornet. All afternoon the practice continues—*too . . ooo toot ta wahee pa paa* —she can't play worth a damn. The neighborhood is practically deserted; busses rechart their routes in order to escape the vicious din; every so often the pop of a gun announces a new addition to the mounting list of suicides—she has been known to blare through a whole night without one pause for breath. Her cheeks puff out until she looks like two pillows with a nose glued on between.

I said it was quiet here. It is. I just pull down the ear muffs on my fur cap and everything is fine. Of course I look sort of ridiculous walking around like this in the middle of the summer, sweat pouring off my head in sheets. I can't stand five minutes in a place without leaving a puddle. But it's worth it—I mean, she is. I spend most of my time writing her notes which she never reads. I've

171

spent two hundred dollars on messengers alone; my bill at the florists would keep me in chorus cuties for ten years. Violets, and more violets—nothing but yellow violets. And I'm getting no place. I must snitch that horn away from her.

The others are putting up in an auto-camp just outside town. We have an armoured car now, all equipped with short-wave set and swivel machine-guns. It was standing in front of the Twelfth National Bank in Pasadena; and, so luck would have it, the whole rear end was full of little blocks made of solid gold. We melted these down into nuggets and pose as prospectors. All the papers took it up—thousands of men are methodically picking and shoveling away at the whole damn state of California; toppling over buildings, tearing up sewers, tunneling under mountains, even draining the rivers—a pretty mess.

It is hard for me to realize that Jackeen is dead. And such a horrible death! We had to wrap her head up in a bag—the axe had done its work so well—and she was buried after a service over a closed casket. How the murderer got into the room without my knowing it, I shall never understand. Thomas Honey found him wandering in the field, muttering incoherently—his hands and trousers smeared from his awful work. His punishment fell rightly to my choice. I ordered that he be strapped into the identical chair over which Jackeen had leaned; then, starting with his toes—using the same murder weapon—I proceeded systematically to hack him to pieces. He was long in dying. Perhaps fifteen minutes. Twice my strained nerves caused me to see the same grizzled face at the window . . . I seemed to hear again the grate of heavy chains. Oddly enough, that night, Thomas Honey, never taking his sightless eyes off mine, said: "You say you saw a face in the window before she was killed?"

"That's right."

"And heard the clinking of chains?"

"Right again."

"Well, something is rotten somewhere."

"What do you mean?"

"I saw and heard the same damn thing while you were hashing that guy up."

I considered the position.

"Transference of psychic phenomena," I said coolly.

"What the hell's that?"

"That's what you heard and saw."

"I'm beginning to wonder ..." he said.

"Wonder what?"

"You'll know soon enough."

I didn't at all like the way he said it. I shall not be caught napping.

The girl across the way is waving to me, the horn plastered to her mouth—I wonder what she looks like? I've never seen over the bell of that monster machine of hers. I yell to her to come up and call on me. She disappears from the window. Now she is in the street—still blowing away for dear life. I can hear the infernal racket coming up the stair. I open the door. Hello!

Toot. Toot.

My God! does she talk with it?

"Look, you, put your cornet down for a second."

"All right, handsome." She has taken it out of her face! A nice looker, and no mistake.

"What's your name?" I ask her.

"Ann Elizabeth Leah Deaken," she answers, smiling.

"That's a pretty name."

"I'm a pretty girl."

"You've got something there," I say, looking her over from red top to dainty bottom.

She lowers her lashes demurely.

"Did you have a brother in the army?" I ask.

"Yes, Gerry Robert—he was an aviator," she replies sadly. "He died in defense of his country. Shot in the back by a spy."

"An interesting death," I tell her. "Would you resent it if I ask a rather personal question?"

"How personal?"

173

"That depends—I want to ask you why you blow on that horn all the time."

"Oh, I'm trying to get a job in a circus."

"Say now, that's fine! I can arrange that in a jiffy . . ."

"You can?" She is all eagerness. Her nose drips ever so little.

"Sure, one of my best friends runs a circus."

"Gosh, that's swell. How can I ever thank you?"

"Well . . ." I look her over again, carefully.

She reddens but does not lower her eyes.

"I see," she says slowly.

"I hoped you would."

"When?"

"Now."

In this wonderful time, with my lodgings clean and airy and light, with good food in my belly, with magnificent projects building in me, I remind myself with a whip to heaven that there are still people who, of their own rough doing, march in and out of steamy bathhouses, who canvass the cancer-places of our city with a gabble after lustful sport, in thick wenching and bottle-tilting, denying the true precepts of their souls; and I tell you a sweat breaks out over me—they call that thing *life*. I make no pretense of my unutterable disgust. Vituperation can achieve no more. Let him speak out against me, who can weather this lash! I shall suffer no rebuke in my own house. Happily, I have a clean shirt for any occasion. Be exceptional when you encounter the exceptional man.

JULY 24   At Buford, Mississippi we enjoyed a good laugh, one of the many things denied those who do not travel. Jetter was forced to get off the sidewalk every time he met a white man. What a quaint custom! Finally, after we had exhausted the humor of the situation, we started cruising up and down the main streets, machine-gun blazing like a hail storm. It was reported later—though this is open to some doubt—that we put away thirty-five

174

hundred Bufordians, even bagging the Mayor and two councilmen. I told the Governor that, unlike his own, Jetter's skin was only black on the outside.

We have now experienced the top and low character of our American eating places; they are uniformly bad—deplorable. Consider one's morning bacon; by the degenerate saints, what muck! Fat and whore-hide stinking of saltpeter. Where find a decent rib-roast or leg of lamb? They must beat the poor beasts to death—all sinew and gravel. And the vegetables! ah, there—spare us, those putrid messes of pulp and scrag; potatoes like lacquered doorknobs, beets tasting like flannel drawers, cabbage covered with mildew—yes, even the rice strikes the palate like whitewashed mice turd—never enough salt, too much pepper. And the prices! I'm sick. Whose is the fault in all this? The President's? I do not think that the case. We have a Senate and a House of Representatives—but find a decent meal! No, no, I won't speak of the coffee . . .

Where is that leisured grace in living? Where the established manners and the uncommercial comfort. I have been put in hotel beds that were sodden from the very perspiration of the bugs. I have lowered myself in chairs that collapsed under me like knock-kneed hodcarriers. I have found little to delight me in the sink-rooms, with their monstrous drawings and vile stench.

Take an instance. One parlor-bar I recall, where, having to keep an eye on the door at all times, I invariably found a buxom maid blocking my vision and keeping my mind off the business at hand, which was not to get shot in the back if I could help it. As a rule, being a careful, somewhat fastidious man, I do not pick up with strange women in bars. This one was different. Her large, blue eyes had a chatty, home-town look; her dress was cut low and revealed a bosom in a million. There was no way to know: I dated her. We walked out into the country and sat down on an old log. I was deliberate and skillful. It was one of my best times. The moon arose over the hills and I saw by its cold, gross light that she was crying.

I have heard it said that a woman's tears would melt a stone. I am not a stone. I slapped her brusquely across the bare flank, and she squealed—*squealed,* mind you. This got me laughing and when I looked around she had already set off along the road at a smart pace. I spurred up my horse, and soon overtook her. "Don't come near me," she sobbed. I got down and dealt her a mean one on the ear. When she came round again, she found herself on a cot in a boat-house beside the river. I lighted the lantern which hung from a great beam; suspended from it by loops of tarred rope, hung a beautiful fishnet; its entire surface worked by skilled hands into a tapestry of many and strange colors depicting Jesus and His Disciples in a tiny fishing boat upon the great sea. Scarce an educated man anywhere who would not have lowered himself to his knees before this awesome sight. Christ's face had been worked with remarkable attention and craftsmanship. I asked Leah how she felt but the only answer I got was a sniffle. Later she warmed up to me again, but I do not chalk the experience to her door; it was I who had brought the whole thing right as rain—no thanks to her empty, though, it must be said, pretty head. I am perhaps unduly harsh to her memory.

Hitler suffers from a severe case of piles.

We have stopped for the night in a little market-town in the Great Smokies. Bats flitter past in the growing dusk; they maintained an incessant burring while Joseph Gambetta and I went over our maps and charts.

Carol is in Washington for Billy Delian's inauguration. We listened to his speech over the wireless. It stank.

JULY 25 🐿 I was awakened in the middle of the night by a timid knock on the door. It was my friend who owns the circus. He asked me if I had found any girl cornet players. His elation when I told him about Ann Elizabeth Leah Deaken knew no limits. I gave him my cap with the fur ear-muffs—just in case.

176

The electric light company sent me a bill for services at 1062 Mott Avenue, Davenport, Iowa. Considering that I have never so much as set foot in that fair city, this event occasioned me no little perplexity of spirit. How do these bungling cat's-meat-men get into the public utility business!

Fires rage through most of this section of the town; heavy bombing has been going on with particular severity for the past twenty-four hours. I shouldn't be surprised if they dropped some of the big stuff soon.

JULY 27 🐀 The task before us is not for apple-cheeked boys.

It would need a ruder language than mine to describe our panic upon finding that the dogs have entirely circled the house in which we are staying. I had almost forgotten them. Their number seems to have increased. To machine-gun them is to put shoes on sea-horses.

I forgot to say before that Christ went back to Heaven. His presence was awkward for all concerned. However, Jackeen (rest her soul), did make a dictaphone record of a conversation between Adolph Hitler and Him. I haven't had time to hear it yet.

I took a walk out into the hills behind the town this afternoon. Soldiers everywhere. They'd run off one way, then turn around and dash off another. I got in on it finally. The objective was an old saw-mill just at the toe of the valley. I dashed about with the rest, **DOST THOU** now here, now there, stopping every now and then to get breath, **IMAGINE YOU** but I couldn't make out which side was which. The uniforms were **CAN WIN** of two colors: tan and deep olive—but damn if I didn't see them **THROUGH** changing clothes every little while; rushing through with it as **TO GOD** though the fiends of hell were after them, buttons flying off all over the lot. Then there was a sad-whiskered old boy who just mosied around looking, I suppose, for a friendly face and a thump

177

on the back. This was the more renowned of the two generals on the field. The other, whose daughter graduated from Bryn Mawr in the class of '31, just sat on an empty lard pail and scowled fiercely. By now I was on the tan side; the olive-greeners were coming down the gully in tanks and Buick trucks—whooping like banshees. We had thrown some big tree trunks across the road just before you get to the turn near the stone quarry. I crouched down behind a little bush and waited. The minutes went by. I unslung my canteen and took a drink. The water was tepid and full of typhoid baccilli. Now the artillery was beginning to go into action. Somebody whizzed by me and took cover under a partially destroyed kitchen-wagon ... It was my friend, the lard pail general. Down went his breeches ... I turned away in time to see 150,000 men pouring into the old saw-mill. They were wearing dark orange uniforms. A great shout went up. In the excitement I rammed my bayonet halfway through my leg. Suddenly a lark sang. The sun shone. It would never be done shining. The old boy was still bent low in the bush. A branch shot off by a bullet fell smack on his bare ass.

The fallen bodies lie still and dishonored; they are dwarfed by the size and aspect of the monster which moves snuffling and gobbling contentedly from one to another of them. Vultures circle low in the sky ...

I had a mean time getting back through the dogs. Thomas Honey met me at the door. He did not speak. It is clear that he has something on his mind.

JULY 28 🐿 Carol came back with a fine new wardrobe and gossip of the Capitol set. Billy Delian is proving a very popular president. He has promised to do a lot for the farmer.

The whole wonderful night I spent in Carol's arms—my obscure destiny forgotten in the pulsation of our two bodies, locked together ... shadows moving like little brown horses through the lakes of moonlight ... Carol's fingers putting a soft hurricane in

178

my male country, and all the trains running on time, everyone well-fed and with nice houses, a bell ringing . . . and I opened my eyes and I felt that I held the meaning of the world in my hands, a meaning which the guns and state-gluttons deny; an understanding and message known to the birds which soar above oceans and mountain peaks; an act of love composed of children's voices, of the eye in the thunder-head, of the face looking out of the mist which floats over the river, of the arms which are going around us in this howling dark. **O GENTLE TOWNS . . . BLESSED ARE THEY WHOSE HAIR IS MATTED**

Toward morning I had one of my worst nightmares. A figure approached to the foot of the bed. It raised aloft a primrose caught in a scalp-lock of dark hair . . . blood dripped down and suddenly Jackeen's face appeared, the flower gripped tightly in her mouth and I raised up to find a great, snarling dog on my chest.

Carol warmed up some hot milk for me and I managed to get to sleep just as dawn came on its little cat feet and with its rosy fingers opening and closing like little baby fists reaching out for the big wet tit of the world, so help me. **HANGED MEN ARE ALWAYS NAKED**

The two Caen stone arches ran smooth as thighs into the tall, shadow-pocked turrets, which in their turn climbed in an agony of order upon the breast of the wonderful tower of Gesze, gaining at last, though in stiff walking and grudging night, that place of allotted conquest where the wounded stars moan on the vast, black table which the angels attend. This, then, wanderer, was the fabulous cathedral whose horrible portcullis steamed once with the blood of Dante Alighieri; here it was that the divine *terza rima,* which *made Ulysses die* in the twenty-sixth canto, went down to be scanned by the slime-eyed worms—those archbishops of corruption.

Let us consider for a moment. The ass, the goat, even the slothful and vicious camel; the spider and honey-bee; yes, and the trilobite, the shell-fish, the grim polyps; the elephant and the sail-less ships; levers and screws and propeller blades; consider Ptolemy, Aristarchus, Ein- Mr. Idroe, a widower, had five children to cheer his hearth, and of these three were daughters. The two eldest were pretty enough, but Ann, their younger sister, then scarcely seventeen, was a pip in high speed. (Cold,

179

pale spirit, stop breathing down by neck.) She was born to be loved, and I loved her with the energy of a hummingbird under whose tail carbolic acid has been put. I do not wish to linger on that period of alternate hope and fear, of broken words eked out by glances, and all the petulant changes of passion. Suffice it that my love was returned at last, and that before my long visit was at an end, Ann (or was it Marie . . . ?) had plighted me her simple troth. I went bravely to Mr. Idroe, and told him all. He was not displeased. He appeared, in fact, hardly surprised. Lovers, indeed, are generally very transparent in their wily stratagems for hoodwinking the world, and even the most guileless household is speedily aware of the progress of an attachment—and with my tight-fitting trousers a blindman could have seen the horn I was shoving around in front of me. But that's life, I guess; you bet. Now Mr. Idroe, though not averse to receiving me as a son-in-law, was not willing that his daughter should marry at such a tender age *(sic)*, and was, besides, desirous that time should test whether we, the principal parties in the case, really knew our own minds. We both thought this decision very tyrannical and absurd. It was decreed that we were to be separated for a year! I was to go ahead with my work, and the Idroes were to travel, to visit watering-places and strange cities—to vary their usual retired mode of life in order that Ann might see something of the world before she irrevocably fixed her fate in it.

stein, Archimedes—do you begin to see? and, too, the Pax Romana, the Civil Law enacted in 3000 B.C.; the abdication of the Emperor Diocletian; the building of the roads and the bridges and the aqueducts; no doubt of it! the *Civitas Dei* taking the place of the *Civitas Romae* —this was St. Augustine; then the trees and wide-skirted women in Palermo and Assisi, in Cordova and Cape Town; motives? I suppose . . . the bloody Crescent and the bloodier Cross; Gutenberg and Columbus; Luther and the Pilgrimage of John Bunyan in 1678—it has been a long time; gunpowder and Arabic trusts; the carnivores rooting in the shitty chaos called human history—and I reach in my thumb and pull out Kingdom Come.

High on the narrow, moss-grown steps stood André Tombelaine, Guardian of the Bells, his eyes searching the gloom of the haunted campanile, a sandgrug growl issuing from his dark throat, for to his ears had been borne the unmistakable sound of a struggle. On the dusty floor of Gesze's sacristy lay the sleeping figure of a young girl. A little yellow, dried-up Pomeranian strained at his leash in shameless disregard for her innocent slumber. Mervessa had lain thus in the labyrinth of holy images under the tongueing bells since late yesterday, when her brother, the Earl of Huhassen, had dispatched her there on a quest hopeless and mayonnaised with danger. Would Hethlard make good his foul threat to land his forces on the dyke-head near the harbor at Daka, where, as all men know, deceit and treason repose in the breasts of the coast-watch defenders?

Jeffers lighted a cigarette. At once the rifle of André Tombelaine sent the echoes reverberating from jewelled nave to the underground guddy-pas where the prisoners were kept.

"Damn!" Jetter said, quickly lowering himself to the short, stubbly grass at the foot of the postern-wall.

180

"Quiet, you fool," I said thickly.

Mervessa awakened with a little cry. So much time squandered in ear-pounding; and already the fleets might be lined up, bristling with animosity, in the bay. Her rheumy eyes roved the sacred crypt. Very carefully, with a hot blush for her dereliction, she hoisted herself erect, being careful not to venture into the mauve light which poured in at the fifty-one covernald windows.

She chuckled to herself. How well she would look when they carried her triumphantly through the streets of the city—Mervessa O'Malley, savior of Kennebunkport! How Theodore's eyes would gleam! Were they not to be one when the last leaf of the curly maple fell on the sharp stones at the base of the reservoir! Ah, Teddy, Teddy . . . She gathered her heavy mouth in, hard; her nose, which was the sole heritage from her father, slapped up and down like a blown-out tire casing.

"Not bad," Jetter whispered to me.

She wore a ranch-hand's cap, with the strands of her unhealthy, golden hair caught up in a wiffle's knot beneath it. A mud-colored smock lent an elfin charm to the ponderous meat balls shoving out of her chest. Her thick legs were bare to the semer-bone, and richly haired. Her shoulders were narrow and stooped, perhaps from the labor of supporting the massive hump which swung like a bale of hay at her back.

The Pomeranian yipped querulously. Savagely her hobbed boot struck out. The little brute lay still in the laps of the countless moon-children which frolicked under the altar; gently they fondled his evil-smelling breast.

Again André Tombelaine's rifle spoke the sparkling word of its people; and Mervessa slipped to the floor, a bullet through her pure heart.

"Too bad," Jetter whispered again.

But up in the bell-tower, with the bats, Hethlard, Ruler

The year passed. All went smilingly with us. I went to claim my bride. She had the old loving look in her dear blue eyes; she had been courted and flattered, but no one had been able to beat my time. What a flower she had become . . . a hedge-rose! as sweet a type of the more fragile order of womanhood as ever existed here below. Our wedding-day was set; I took a leave of absence from the turkish bath where I was employed as an assistant soaper. Happiness lay before us. (And lay is just what I had in mind.)

But Ann (or was it Lucille . . . ?) had one fault, if fault be not too harsh a word, one flaw in her nature. She was a bit nuts. They had to send the little wagon with the screened-in back round for her one sunny morning—after she had done a bit of work with a cleaver on poor Mr. Idroe. But she was a cute trick. Dear saucy naughty Ann . . . damn! it wasn't fair of you, God, not to tighten up all her screws. (And that is another word that comes to mind in her connection.)

A bit of health; no wealth; and a life of stealth. Ah, me . . . the throbbing of devil drums. Next time round, you try to grab the ring. Twilight ran up its vague gray flags. When she returned to the house, she found her husband in the pantry with an Arab; they were distrait and excited, watching each other warily for the first show of friendliness. She closed the door quietly and went out to cut the lawn. "What pretty green hair you have, Mother Nature," she said tonelessly. The witty—the brutal—the slanderous—the shocked and

the terrified—among the fishermen of Capernaum—sun
sink sodden WATER leave
the rest to God, huh? Well,
I'll be candid with you, Can-
dide. A nice warm little society with spinning wheels
and pistachio-nuts . . . The
shape does not change. Are
you awake, Elizabeth?
Raleigh and Essex can do
nothing now about Ireland.
Tinker Bell! Tinker Bell!
called Mrs. Darling; have you
seen my pussy, sir? The aque-
ous and the igneous: to the
latter, earthquakes and vol-
canoes; to the former, tides,
rivers, frost, snow, the dew
and the rain—hear it on the
window pane . . . pain, sane,
drain, *stain*, lain. Such dreams
as all your stuff is made of.
Rose-red blankets—so! slip
in my little chit and sleep
tight like Ben Jonson used
to. Who would . . . on the last
day the clean creature will
be brought out. Are you
against Caesar? I am being
dull, *mon brave*. Sweetly
flows the liquefaction of her
nose. And we have Newton.
A fig for him. To act is easy
unquote Goethe. But who
came in the back door when
he went out the front door?
. . . the free fellowship of
fanny-fondlers: tree-shaded
tombs, Tommy boy. Right
belief, aspiration, speech,
conduct, living, effort, mind-
fulness, meditation; I am free
because I have no desire for
anything. Eternal felicity.
Perfect and everlasting rest
. . . the fiery storm of the
senses. Pure bitch-bright sorrow. Poor Egypt off in the
shaggy corners of the world.
Everything is intoxicating!
Honey baby sugar dove sweet
we're going to make out fine.
Nobody's going to hurt us

of Aliquippi and Levittsburg, raised his lantern in signal
to the men he had placed in the harbor—ha! he had been
clever! little would these unsuspecting fools realize what
danger approached them in the guise of that great herd
of cattle which was even now mooing its way across the
water; for under each hide skulked a soldier armed to
the teeth and thirsty for the sweet taste of blood!

Of course, the Tower Guard had demanded a good
price for his treachery; but no price was too great to pay
for success in that night's work. Even now the varlet was
grumbling that the money had not been enough—better
silence him—his mutterings would soon bring André running to investigate. Hethlard walked over to the grasping
fellow. With a long, slow, beautiful motion, he drew his
sword; *ah . . aa*, that was good. One needs only a keen
blade and a fat hobbledehoy to run it through—when a
man is young and sleek and stout-hearted.

The city stretched out before him—this city which
soon would be his! how he loved it all! the slanted roofs,
the vine-singing walls; the cutting of potato chips in deep
cellars, the mortars complaining under the strong arms
of women pounding maize—and pretty women, too. He
walked over to the Hall of St. Peter, paused to look out
of the cernette window—he could hear them mooing but
the darkness was too great to permit him sight of them—
then he directed his steps to the burly arch which supported the Mothney Staircase, down which the saints had
come in the days of his great-great-great grandfather . . .
that's strange, he thought; the planks have rotted. Suddenly he knew: *quicksand* O God! now it was creeping
up around his shoulders, now over his chin . . . down,
down . . . the monstrous crust giving like glue-filled butter . . . help me! O my Go . . . !

Carol said she was hungry and we made our way to the

182

great kitchen where the monks and a few, chosen neighbors sat around a great table made of solid teak.

"You look as though you'd had a bad scare," Duperwell said to Thomas Honey.

Jetter said quickly, "Not until he saw yur puss, he didn't."

Fenn gave him a black stare.

"We don't want no killers here," he said.

I cut in: "Look, we just want a bite to eat."

"Yeah," Carol said. "We can pay for it, too."

"Now, ain't that nice," said the monk leader. "Just draw up a hogshead and sit down here."

"Which hog's head do you mean?" Jetter asked, looking up and down the row of churchmen.

"If you'd been two days in the woods outside of Galen, in that fat hell, with us, we'd see a different tune on your pipes," said Fenn, talking with a cigarette jumping at his lip.

Before I had time to answer, he went on:

"And we learned there the use of the axe..."

Powerfully he raised his weapon above one of the dogs; down, in a short, silver storm, and the two halves of the wretched brute gurgled a red horror at my feet, the legs still twitching, and the eyes watching me without change.

Then Fenn held out the axe to me.

"Take it," he said. "It belongs to you."

I stared at him uncomprehendingly.

"Where did you find it?" I managed to say at last.

"Don't you know me?" he asked, laughing softly.

It was then that I knew him—this was the grizzled man I had hacked to pieces in punishment for the murder of Jackeen (rest her soul).

All their eyes were upon me.

183

one tiny bit ... Just you sharpen up that razor and I'll start at one ear and you at the other. An artist *by nature.* I reached Milwaukee early in October. Gunboats everywhere. LIZARD EYES. Making a noise in your cave ... are we silly to confess? the psyche of the underdog ... I am suffocating with this cheap fright ... conjugal infidelity is exceedingly rare in octogenarians—pip! pip! Let it rain kingdoms on my face, I'll still be a man without a world. But how have I been injured? Continue: *O equilibrium mobile!* A unified disorder. Who's got that last piece of fundamental verity? Is there a Perfect Being? All dope abandon, ye who come in here: jaundice the founder of my fabric minced. Let us weigh the drainage of knowledge in the balance with all other things. O Dionysius of dead Athens ... Attic soil flowers in Decelea. Alas! cold, hungry—the stain covers the pilgrim sleeping in the glistening shadow. Ten years of war. On thy fair bosom, Mary. If life were all! Safeguard my devious captivity. That you, Duke? TO THE NETS! TO THE GLITTERING NETS! Hate me, Vishnu; Osiris slay ... capricious serpents crowd the dreadful farewell. In China. Decayed. Cruel. I want usable monuments—kissed, caressed, hooted at, stoned! Rise of the great banks and the stock exchange: eviction of those who work. Twitch that third eyelid of your shark-ancestor. Poor wretch that I am! Open me, God; fix my battered works. Pour oil on my bloodied face.

Thomas Honey's sightless ones blazed more savagely than any of the others. His hands tore into the wood of his chair.

The mooing as of a great herd drifted in through the sombre halls.

I laughed until the tears streamed down over my shoulders.

"Nothing can be that funny," Jetter said.

I stopped after a time and we went on with our dinner.

The food was awful; the wine superb.

Duperwell dragged his flat feet over to my side.

"Do you have a present for me?" he whispered.

I fished a little cloth doll with movable eyes out of my pocket, and gave it to him.

"Oh, thank you!" he shouted, beginning to hug and kiss it for all he was worth. Little did he know that it was made in Japan.

Turnbull slowly took his hand from deep in the recesses of Carol's bodice. A silly grin mantled his watery features.

"Just curious, you know," he muttered, moving off to the can.

An argument broke out between two of the monks.

"I tell you it was," said one heatedly.

"You believe anything Father Malarkey tells you," said the other just as heatedly.

"I didn't have to be told. I was there."

"You were where?"

"Why, where it happened, you pumpkin-head."

"You're going to sit there and tell me brazenly that you actually saw them together?"

"I'll tell you more than that. I was there when they found it."

"You were there when they found it!"

"That's what I said."

"Was it covered with straw—like they say?"

"Yes, covered . . . and the feet were tied together."

"And you saw them just before it happened?"

"Yes."

"But you didn't see it happen?"

"No, I didn't see it happen. I didn't have to—to know who did it."

"But you can't prove it?"

"No. There is someone who can, though."

"Who?"

"Joseph Gambetta."

Cows started to pour into the room, from both doors, all ninety-six windows, a few even through the fireplace.

"They're not real cows," I whispered to Jetter.

"No?" he said. "Let's have a see."

He squatted down under one and worked a tit. A great stream of milk splashed on the planks.

"My God!" I said.

"Why, I could have told you that," Carol said.

"How did you find out?" I demanded of her.

"Simple enough. He told me."

"Who told you?"

"Say, what is this? Jetter did, of course. He said he learned to milk on his uncle's ranch in Wyoming."

"Learned to milk! Well I'll be damned!" I said. "That isn't what I was talking about. Those cows were supposed to be soldiers."

"Don't you want to lie down for a while?" Carol asked.

"No, I don't. The whole thing was a trick—soldiers concealed in cow hides. They planned to take over the town before anybody got wise."

The monks were poking their thumbs into the bovines, nodding and exclaiming and pulling bottles of catsup out of their smocks.

"Hey!"

The voice came from inside a cow.

Then the horned head was tilted back and a man's head looked out.

"What the hell you guys up to? Ramming your fists into us . . . Why don't you leave us alone?"

We were too surprised to say anything.

185

The cow's head was lowered into place and the beast continued to rummage around.

"Let's just see . . ." Jetter said.

He went over to the hide from which the voice had come, knelt down, and again grabbed a tit. Milk hit the floor with a wet thud.

"Hay!"

"Hay!"

All the cows were yelling now.

"What do you want?" someone asked.

"Hay!" came the swelling chorus.

Servants were dispatched for it, and soon the sound of contented chewing could be heard through the hall.

"What's all this about?" demanded André Tombelaine, hoary Guardian of the Bells, who had at last left his lonely loft.

Quickly, without mincing words, Mervessa, his golden-haired step-daughter, related to him how we had found them wandering through Gesze's great halls—the tiny boy in the blue jacket, and the tiny girl in her wrinkléd pinafore.

He regarded them with an eye which would have been the envy of a hawk with a wasp working on his nuts.

"What do you have to say for yourselves?" he barked.

They held hard to each other's hands and their yellow eyes filled with tears.

"We were only going to the shoe-makers . . . and we got lost."

"To the shoe-makers!" roared old André.

"Yes, our father left his shoes there last Wednesday . . ."

"All right. All right. But what are you doing in Gesze?"

"Is this really the famous Gesze?" asked the little boy eagerly.

"It's very ugly," his sister said faintly.

"I don't know what we can do with you," André said, shaking his gray locks sadly.

"Please, mister," pleaded the little boy. "Just show us the way out of Gesze—we can get home easy then."

"But I don't know the way out, my child," said the honest old guard.

186

We left the three of them crying in a little knot, their arms fast and struggling around each other's shoulders. The monks were crying too. Even the cows had stopped their chewing, and were just standing around like birds on a treacherous cadaver.

As a general practice, or better to say, I suppose, an iron-fast rule, the tallest monk escorts visiting pilgrims to the head of Mothney Staircase; but, as chance decreed it, we were led out through His bedroom—which smelt like a poultry-run—and on to the sub-terrace, by one of the shortest of all those exorcistic brethren. He couldn't have been more than twelve feet tall—in his shoes.

"How d'you like it?" he shouted down to us.

"Pretty nice," Jetter yelled up.

"Pretty nice, eh?"

"Yes, pretty nice . . ."

This went on for some time.

A magnificent sight met our eyes when we gained the outer air. Prodigious . . . breath-taking . . .

15. How I Meet Keddel

The morning was bright, the air was pebbled with sun like a good steak with fat, there was a familiar joy in Albion's heart. He did not notice that people were going crazy in magnificent houses, and that the poor were starving quite shamelessly in the open street. He sauntered along until he reached the river which divided Galen like a thread through an apple; this, it was black and slow-flowing, he stepped over with ease.

Now the whole aspect of the day changed. This was a bad world, and treacherous. He no longer smiled. There was only one thing to do: he must get in off the street. He knocked at the door of a cottage. A dog's bark made him hurry on. No one whose business allows him peace should read what is about to be related.

At noon—much has been omitted in this little tale: some things should not be known—Albion, his voice hoarse with weeping, submitted to a brutal beating at the hands of youthful soldiers. He stumbled on, his head spinning from their light-hearted blows. He began to whimper, his fists squeezed into his eyes. After a long time he yielded to the knowledge that he would die.

Albion Moonlight was one of those people whose whole lives seem to conform to a rigid pattern. When Margaret Yard heard his fumbling hand at her door, she moved with good speed to open. They faced each other across the sill. She thought: how tired and wretched he looks. He thought: this is surely the most beautiful creature in all the world.

She put him to bed and he passed the night in healing sleep. From time to time soldiers would tip-toe to the foot of his bed and roll their eyes in greedy merriment; but Margaret Yard did not permit them to piss in his face as they wanted.

That same night Jetter and the others sat at a table and planned how they would kill him. Their faces were intent and cunning. Only Jackeen showed sorrow. She sat to one side, away from the light, and her eyes were those of a hunted animal. Once she said: "My father deserves a better fate than to die at our hands." But they were in no mood to hear her.

Albion awakened hating no one. He could not have named a man on all the earth whose death he would have welcomed. It was enough to lie there looking into the pure, radiant face of Margaret Yard. While she was feeding him, he said:

"How different everything would have been if I could have known you always."

"Eat your breakfast," she said, smiling down on him.

"I can remember," he said, never lowering his eyes from hers, "a time when everything I loved and thought beautiful was identified in me with the thought of a woman."

"And now?" Her lips were full as rose buds.

"Now . . ." he said, looking away for the first time.

"Please," she said quickly. "Go to sleep again. You are tired, and you have a long journey before you."

"I don't know how it is now," he whispered; and then, as though what she had said had just reached him, he went on in a louder voice: "A long journey . . . yes. But I'll come back for you, Margaret."

"And I'll be waiting," she said softly.

He raised up in bed, his eyes seeking the window. The sound of heavy boots came in from the street. Silently he slipped back, took up his spoon again.

"Of course you'll wait for me," he said lightly.

"You don't believe me, do you?" she said, a single tear standing like an elf's jewel in the corner of her eye.

"As I believe in God," he answered.

"Will you . . . before you go . . . ?"

"What, Margaret?"

"Will you," and she lowered her eyes, "will you do what the fox does to me?"

"Will I what?"

"Will you . . ."

"Oh. I get it. A fox, eh? . . . funny to put it like that."

"No one ever has," she said. "I couldn't . . . with anyone else."

"I shouldn't," he said. "I'm dirty, Margaret, filthy with a thousand scabby uglinesses . . ."

"You are the most beautiful man I have ever known," she said simply.

Albion could not bring himself to look at her.

"I will do it," he said at last, "—for your sake."

With quiet dignity, without shame or hesitation, she started to undress. First, her dress—letting it slip to the floor where it encircled her feet like the fallen petals of a flower—her body pushing up straight and rounded (What are you thinking, Albion Moonlight?) . . . the soft white shoulders, the fullness of her throat; then out of her slip . . . the alert cups of her breasts, the first sight of her clean little belly; now the brassiere . . . the tiny brown eyes; and at the last, her panties . . . he gazed long at the spot where the feathered arrow had gone in . . . she started to climb in beside him and a thunderous pounding on the door shook

189

the house. Hurriedly he threw on his clothes and, without another look at Margaret Yard, dashed down the rear fire escape. He ran until he came to a shell hole. Clambering in he found the old man of the spectacles and the arm full of books. "Did your horse get away?" the professor asked politely. "No," Albion said, "he's chasing me." And at that moment the animal plunged down upon them, shaking soapsuds and graybeards off its mane and heaving sides. It stuck its long, hairless nose into Albion's face, and snorted lustily.

Next afternoon, as the bell of the Church of Our Lady was sounding out over the dreaming fields and sun-smelling city, I stood before a little gate which led on a quaint garden overlooking the sea. My wounds had healed with surprising rapidity, and I was in a happy temper with the recollection that Margaret Yard in her haste had forgotten to take off her shoes and stockings. I sat down on a stone bench and munched on a liverwurst sandwich. Idly I thought back over my life: my penny-pinched and dirty-ass childhood, mother lamming the daylights out of me everytime dad— *dad,* my God! did I actually call him that?—everytime dad drank up all the proceeds (he was in the ball bearing business); and high school, the little free-wheeling tootsies . . . parking the car in a lane . . . the soft, half-frightened aggressive mouths . . . an honest to George feel once in a blue moon . . . both of us tense, waiting for something to explode, as though the bodies belonged to a couple other people; then college—learning the hard way that condoms are not made of concrete . . . a lot of yowling and jawing . . . hell, I have seen . . .

"Are you Albion Moonlight?"

I turned around to confront a woman in a black veil.

"What does it do if I am?" I asked, noticing that she had an expensive ring on her finger.

"I am in trouble," she said. "Will you help me?"

At that moment I heard a tiny *peep* off to one side of the path under a linden tree. When I got over I found a baby robin lying on its side and trying to squirm to a place of safety. "Trying to fly before you have wings, you little bastard," I told it, wiggling my fingers in under its egg-shell soft body, and holding it up in my hand so its mother could see it was all right. By now the lady in the veil was tugging at me saying we had to hurry. I shook her off and climbed into the tree and put the little guy back in the nest with his brothers and sisters. Then I shinnied down and said:

"What kind of trouble are you in?"

"Oh, how can I tell you!" she said.

"You don't need a foxing, I hope," I said. She was nothing to wire home about.

Her voice was blushing when she spoke, but I could see she had liked it.

"Please come with me," she said, starting to run off through the garden right through a bed of Easter lilies.

I didn't like her careless manner, so I let her go.

Hell, I have seen enough to make you ashamed to be a member of the human race—the hypocrisy, the cruelty, the downright *nastiness* of people . . . but I am forgetting my story.

The mud-clotted workmen and slim-eyed priests had disappeared entirely; the breast of the great figure which watches over the doings of man and the other poor creatures, contracted in unmistakable anguish; the little steepled town seemed to float back into gently champing gray jaws as the fog closed in; the tail of a crazy beast shuddered in a design which no one, luckily, could see; a gaunt wild face shimmered high in the air like a silver kite; the first husky strain of music was heard: for Albion Moonlight had left Galen on his journey to death.

His head seemed full of water. The greenish light from the heavens glanced off his forehead with the tight ripple of snakes. He placed one foot before the other as a child learning to walk; there was apparently only one path to the devil's fair, and it led through nothing into nothing.

Suddenly he was not holding it in; the war and the shipwreck

THE GODAMNED JOYOUSNESS OF THE EARTH

191

and the murder gurgled out of his throat in a slimy flood. He struggled against the door, and then the dank, rotted thing came on and covered him.

Having risen above ambition and all desire, he had at last felt the cold hand of God on his arm . . . but the pattern did not end with peace or love or dignity, instead it forked through the weave where there was only pain and blood-rooted fear . . . he was a man smothering in the cloth of his own life, in the web of his own ordained defeat. For he had made an important discovery; he had learned that life for the human animal is not possible on this earth; he saw that what we call 'the evil of our day' is just another thread in the monstrous coat of terror which has covered all men everywhere and in all times—and which nothing living can ever remove. When men wage war they are not moved to destroy one another; their struggle is against *what they themselves are*—poor fools, they can never kill that.

Our only plight is that we are alive.

The stupid say, "Would that I had lived then!"—but they mean: "It were better to be dead now."

None of us wants to live: What we suppose is a passion for life is only an instinct to *protect something*—not ourselves, not our beings, not our souls, but something which we cannot ever hope to possess, something which is not within our power to conceive of or to comprehend. Something, in fact, which is at once nothing and everything; nothing, because we cannot 'know' to want it— everything, because it is the only thing our 'knowing' wants.

We are all quite mad. I am no different from you.

It is possible to wish for nothing but *Life! . . . Life! . . . Life!*

I can only think of you and me as being already in our graves . . . How close we are to each other at this moment.

I command the sun to send down his white, beautiful horsemen.

As the gulf widened, as the land grew stiller and more fearful, as the very stones cried out in secret anguish, Albion pressed nearer and nearer to his one instant of revelation.

192

The hollows in the air filled with rain; a great thundercloud **NO ONE** hung savagely in the heavens; there was no shelter in all that **KNOWS** place. Quite suddenly he came upon a multitude standing silently **ANYTHING** in the field, their faces lashed by the drowning wind.

It seemed that everyone stood there.

One of us sank to his knees in the grass. You sobbed and held your hands in an attitude of prayer. I put my hand on your arm and we lifted our heads together . . .

I said that all I wanted to do was make you believe in what I am saying. This could not have happened without your faith. It could never have happened had we not trusted in each other.

God's angry sword flashed down the sky . . . then we saw Keddel. **HEADFIRST**

An eye. **INTO THE**

An eye looking down upon us. **FLAMES!**

Keddel . . .

The man Keddel was a shoemaker in a small town. He was poor and without distinction; but when he died, one of his eyes did not die. It left his cold face and moved up in such a way that it rested watchfully in the air. At the time we first saw the eye, it had grown to the size of a dinner-plate. Someone who knew about such things said that Keddel would continue to grow until the whole sky was blotted out.

We screamed in horror when we gazed into it . . .

You helped me to my feet and we fled from that place of greater love than man's.

‖‖‖

JULY 30 🐾 Öhklipt-Pogy has taken over the management of Mrs. Drew—and a fine job she makes of it. Her careless habit of setting fire to the patient's bed, can, we believe, find correction with somewhat more vigilance on our part; but—and this really is all that matters—she seems to have a true affection for the old lady.

Cleveland's 82nd air raid warning of the present war and the 21st since 6:14 a.m. last Monday was sounded at 9:47 p.m. yesterday and the all-clear signal came at 4:26 a.m. today.

The alarm lasted twelve hours, eight minutes, the third longest of the war, being exceeded only by the Tuesday-night-through-Wednesday alarm of fourteen hours, ten minutes, and by the July 19th record-breaker of *twenty-nine hours, fifty-four minutes.*

In the 603 hours, 11 minutes, between the beginning of the next-to-the-last alarm sounding and the conclusion of the warning this morning, this city has been in a state of alarm for a total of 76 hours, 59 minutes.

The time-table:

From 6:02 p.m. Tuesday to 3:17 a.m. Wednesday.

From 7:36 a.m. to 7:43 a.m. Wednesday.

From 11:12 a.m. Wednesday to 12:06 p.m. Wednesday.

From 2:09 p.m. to 2:43 p.m. Wednesday.

From 9:00 p.m. to 10:47 p.m. Wednesday.

From 11:23 a.m. to 11:26 a.m. Thursday.

From 6:55 p.m. Thursday to 2:30 a.m. Friday.

From 4:11 a.m. Friday to 6:47 p.m. Saturday.

From 12:23 p.m. Saturday to 3:38 a.m. Sunday.

From 4:39 a.m. to 8:04 a.m. Sunday.

From 10:45 p.m. Sunday to 1:22½ a.m. Tuesday.

From 7:13 p.m. Tuesday to 4:26 Wednesday.

In toto, seventeen Dutch-Keggy bombers (of the dive type), twenty-nine Kertherwaith-112 fighter-bombers, and two thousand, four hundred and six Dupond-113s, were destroyed; 24,000,000 men, aged 21 to 45, died under the debris; $134,953,016,235 worth of city property went up in smoke; 70,000 kegs of crude rubber were seized; all live stock was commandeered; a 164 per cent sales tax has been decreed; 13,000 oleomargarine dairies were compelled to close their doors; 596,000 suspected spies have been arrested; newsreel theatres report heavy booing whenever Billy Delian is shown opening a new bridge or kissing a not so new baby. In an otherwise hopeless situation, one encouraging trend has been noted; the Communist Party has come out openly for unconditional defense of the Soviet Union. Ivan the Terrible rides again! Making the world safe for Stalinocracy.

194

Being low in funds, and in need of muscle-building exercise, we decided to get jobs in one of the coal mines which abound in that section. That night I was obliged to tell Carol: "No more now—five o'clock'll be around in an awful hurry, you know."

The wisdom of my remark was seen in the morning. With what grumbling she pulled on her long ruth-cloth pitman's pants—and the hooters hooting bloody murder outside in the windy half-dark. I filled the tea-jack with boiling water, stuffed some carbite into our two naked-light, cap-lamps, slung an overcoat and an old sweater over my arm—in case, and we were set.

Under the gas streetlights the blacked night-shift hurry by, intent on gaining their doors while their legs yet carry them.

Out of a public-house shambles Jetter with Joseph Gambetta in tow—his face is red and sprinkled with pretzel salt.

"Just a bit of a livener," he explains, swishing a torn sleeve across his mouth.

"Where is Thomas Honey?" I ask him.

"What do you mean, where is he?" he answers. "Who do you suppose that is? walking along at your elbow."

"My God, Albion," Carol says. "Do you mean to say you didn't know he was with us?"

Thomas Honey, swinging his long arms with my step, just grins.

"He hasn't been out of our sight since yesterday," she goes on. "Why he even spent the night in a cot near our bed."

What does the hooter say? Six o'clock. We are at the pit-head. An old-fashioned phaeton drawn by eight milk-white horses rounds the turn and reels off into the weary-raging mists; the ruins of a dark manor house rise like shriveled breasts against the first, weak coughing of the day. What a son of a bitch of a place —we hand in our work certificates to a lad in a dingy little office, then fall in queue for places in the miners' cages. Bump. Bump. I get a good grip on the handrail and hold on for dear life. We dodge down the shaft like sick ferrets. All right. Don't shove! Everything at a sprint. Men with picks and mandrils banging around everywhere. In the pitchdark. Nobody thinks to light a

195

lamp. And mules! Everytime I take a step I fall over a mule. Suddenly there is a muffled explosion. A fierce yelling begins. It's a stampede. Now fire rushes down one of the tunnels. For a couple of minutes I can't see. Finally I look around me. The old baron is laughing quietly off in a corner. Carol has her legs up around his middle and is sawing away. The eight white horses are drinking at what seems to be a mountain spring. Jetter, looking very puzzled, is examining a plaid shawl, and questioning a beautiful young woman who seems eager to be obliging.

"You say your mother made this?" he asks.

"Uh huh."

"All by hand?"

"Every single bit of it."

Jetter stiffens. He drops his hands to his sides, letting the arms have freedom for quick movement. He walks about her in an excited circle. She smiles at him with the lassitude of a she-tiger. The languor of her loutish body maddens him with its allure. Rapidly her expression changes, her eyes gleam like skuffed stones, the veins on her forehead stand out like three-inch ropes— *she has seen her father's ghost.*

The whole world is tumbling around her ears. What is this strange thing that moves on the dark, heaving plain of her soul! She has sinned! She has *desired*—shyly perhaps, even sweetly, but nonetheless, desired. A torpor overspreads her flushed temples. She hurls herself over the cliff. The moon casts its wan light over the white and mocking water . . . a fish pokes out its head and laughs hollowly, derogatorily.

Suddenly there is another explosion.

I sat down on a knoll and took stock of the situation. On all sides the moorlands were dotted with the bleeding remains of anthracite miners and pit-ponies—the latter born blind after generations of entombment in those terrible, coal-lined dungeons. What I disliked most was be-

Albion departed from the village that same afternoon, under the auspices of his conductor, and found himself benighted in the midst of a forest, far from the habita-

ing separated from my company. For all I knew then, they might all be dead—victims of a mine-owner's greed. The musky smell of heather made my eyes heavy . . . I stretched out near a bog-hole and yawned. Somewhere a plover sang his reedy, faraway lullaby; a tomtit joined lazily . . . *tit, tit, tit* . . .

How long had I slept? I sat very still and listened. There could be no doubt now: my pursuers were hot on the trail.

Before me, and a little to my left, a wagon-road climbed through a green pocket in the uplands, then fell away again, skirting a huge tussock high on the feathery slope of Mt. Foondkill, only to appear once more far, far down like a silver ribbon tying up the purple hair of the valley.

The hill-air choked me with its smell of pines and cottage smoke.

I walked ten miles until I found the place I was seeking—quickly I doffed my pit-man attire and donned the fireman's uniform which had been hidden carefully in the hollow of the giant sycamore. I breathed a silent prayer of thanksgiving. My operatives had not been remiss in their duty.

Now I could hear a crashing off in the brush to my left. Presently it stopped.

Suddenly I saw him. He was a short man with a broad buthy of a nose. A mail pouch swung at his elbow. His hair was combed straight back above a shallow brow.

We studied each other for a long moment. We did it again.

There was a rich burr to his voice when at last he spoke:

"Feelthy pictures, mister?"

In a trice his bag was open and we were crouched low in the heather talking excitedly. There were one or two

tions of men. The darkness of the night, the silence and solitude of the place, the indistinct images that appeared on every side, "stretching their extravagant arms athwart the gloom," conspired, with the dejection of spirits occasioned by his loss, to disturb his pale fancy, and raise strange phantoms in his imagination. Although he was not naturally superstitious, his mind began to be invaded with an awful horror, that gradually prevailed over all the consolations of reason and philosophy; nor was his heart free from the terrors of assassination. (This is a good time to speak of various things which I forgot to tell you before. For my religion I assume the bold style of a naked man. Who can think of Nature without ecstasy? Solomon was wise because he liked wisdom. I like faith more. So much for conscious folly. God is not bald, nor has He a physician. And it is pure humbug to imagine that Mrs. God is a frolicsome heifer. Ah hell, grandees of disillusionment, powdered wigs on empty beans, caterwauling clowns in a miserable farce . . . I've travelled much in the realms of mold . . . jabneck poverty and looning solitude . . . virtue? THE LAW OF THE LUNG FISH Memory sits quietly in its gilt chair. Not life, but living. Aye, lad, we're bleeding away deep down inside somewhere. Passage to Cathaya; the narrow, crushing seas . . .) In order to dissipate these disagreeable reveries, he had recourse to the conversation of his guide, by whom he was entertained

197

with the history of divers travelers who had been robbed and murdered by ruffians, whose retreat was in the recesses of that very wood.

In the midst of this communication, which did not at all tend to the elevation of our hero's spirits, the conductor made an excuse for dropping behind, while our traveler jogged on in expectation of being joined again by him in a few minutes. He was, however, disappointed in that hope; the sound of the other's horse's feet by degrees grew more and more faint, and at last altogether died away. Alarmed at this circumstance, Albion halted in the middle of the road, and listened with the most fearful attention; but his sense of hearing was saluted with naught but the dismal sighings of the trees, that seemed to foretell an advancing storm. Accordingly, the heavens contracted a more dreary aspect, the lightning began to gleam, the thunder to roll, and the tempest, raising its voice to a tremendous roar, descended in a torrent of rain. (Heavenward Ho! In the haunted woodland . . . remnants of a higher race . . . devil-skinned girls mount the snorting steeds of SEX . . . THE WOUNDED SAVAGE. And never never mourn the flood of murdered boys. Having infinite power, I sink to my knees and weep. Faintly tolls the glass bell in the patch of skunk-cabbage. So there was Scheherazade, the talking stick.—If there could be only a pocket-size reality. Jumbo pigmies, huh! Well . . . Jack Ketch opened a lot of people's oysters. In yon hornéd moon sits a steaming plate of bouillabaisse for

I had never seen; one in particular called "Parisien Gambols," which took my eye for its fine composition and hearty qualities.

But I must not tarry at this pleasant work. Already Fenn's men might be beating around the bushes for me, hoping to surprise me like a rabbit in a hair-net. And I was not wrong in my surmise; far down at the foot of Foondkill, almost obscured in the round-shouldered haze, I could see them combing the veldt for me.

Quickly buttoning another button on my firefighter's jacket, I took to my heels, leaving my new-won friend staring after me in slack-jawed astonishment.

"Where's the fire?" he called sadly.

My sunburn stung like a nest of wasps on my face and arms. Added to my other troubles, the earth seemed to be heaving as though in a quake; it was some time before I realized that a large stone had entered my boot, causing me to dive about as I ran. By dint of much labor I managed to extract this offender, only to find it a tightly-wadded piece of parchment upon which was scrawled in a nervous hand the secret treaty which had precipitated all the trouble.

I decided after a little scuffle with my conscience to drink of my now cold tea and eat of my now stale cheese before falling upon the task of deciphering the fateful code.

With trembling fingers I unfolded the paper. I read:

You will find the clay pipe in my green waistcoat on a hook in the cellar-way. The milkman will bring the asparagus on Tuesday.

The milk-man will bring the asparagus! Ah, they were clever devils, and no mistake.

Quickly I fell to work. A would be d . . . no, s; b would be q; l, an x; t, a w—I had it! *Now* it read:

The forearm of the butcher is toothless. Charles is play-

198

ing dickerdo in the meadow. Look for me under the mill-stone.

There was no time to be lost. I put through a trunk-call to the Yard.

"Hello," a sleepy voice said.

"Hello! Hello! Is this Inspector Mellquist?"

"No. It is not."

"No?"

"No."

"Well, who is this?"

"This is Adam Webb."

"When do you expect Inspector Mellquist?"

"I don't."

"You don't!"

"I don't."

"Look, Mr. Webb, this is a matter of life and death."

"I don't doubt it."

"All right then. Get Inspector Mellquist for me."

"Why don't you try the Yard?"

"Why don't I . . . say, who is this?"

"Adam Webb."

"Now who the hell is Adam Webb!"

"I am."

I felt an insistent tugging at my sleeve. Turning around with a muffled curse I recognized the little boy in the blue jacket and the little girl in the wrinkled pinafore.

"How did you get out of Gesze?" I barked at them.

"The Tower Guard showed us the way."

"I thought Hethlard killed him."

"He was killed. But, you see, his blood ran down the steps and out through all the halls and terraces and so into the street at the foot of the cathedral . . ." the little boy said.

"And we had only to follow," his sister finished.

"That was lucky," I said.

God's lanky hired-hands. Nihil est in intellectu quod non prius in sensu. Mimi! where have you been keeping yourself! By knowing, by watching, by loving . . . It is here! *the virginal dynamo.*)

In this emergency, the fortitude of our hero was almost swamped. So many concurring circumstances of danger and distress might have appalled the most undaunted breast; what impression, then, must have been made upon the mind of Moonlight, who was by no means a man to set fear at defiance. Indeed, he had well-nigh lost the use of his reflection, and was actually invaded to the skin, before he could recollect himself so far as to quit the road, and seek for shelter among the thickets that surrounded him. Having ridden some furlongs into the forest, he took his station under a tuft of tall trees that screened him from the storm, and in that situation called a council within himself to deliberate upon his next excursion. He persuaded himself that his guide had deserted for the present, in order to give intelligence of a dumb traveler to some gang of robbers with whom he was connected; and that he must of necessity fall a prey to those banditti unless he should have the good fortune to elude their search, and disentangle himself from the mazes of the wood. (Captain Ahab, we are here . . . My early home was Calvary. Let us endeavor to keep these munificent gifts from the gaze of the curious. The Count gave no balls because he had none. Thus the drawn dagger, the famous shot, the bewitched ringmaster; and the Cross, the brickbat, the

199

anchor, *the trick*—masticated puppy-meat for idiots— BUT THE DEAR LADY IS TRULY DEAD. I'm going on a journey to the town of God. I need my bit of money and my steady lass. There'll be no bad weather on that road so solemn and so green, tra la. Do not love me, I'm as wicked as you.)

"Not so very lucky," they said in one voice. "For now the blood follows us everywhere."

It was true. Coming down the coarse hills in a great tide the river of blood rushed upon us. There was no escape. We were drowned in that awful bath. Indeed, my friends, we are all drowning—it covers our faces, it drips from our hands . . . O Jesus! Jesus! Lord have mercy on us . . . Lord have mercy!

To tell the truth, I have lost the way. I want to destroy all these stupid pages—what a miserable, broken-winded hack I am! What remains? Be assured—whatever happens, I won't lie to you. One ends by hiding the heart. I say here is my heart, it beats and pounds in my hand—take it! I hold it out to you . . . Close the covers of this book and it will go on talking. Nothing can stop it. Not death. Not life. Draw in closer to me. How small and frightened we are. Our little fire is almost out. What do we seek? I am smiling now. You will be told that what I write is confused, without order—and I tell you that my book is not concerned with the problems of art, but with the problems of this world, with the problems of life itself—yes, of *life itself*. Does this astonish you? If you will listen to me, you will learn to create laws. You have none, you know. What did you get from Shakespeare's hooting and howling? A bit of stuff about an idiot and a king. And you threw up in sheer ecstasy. That won't do. The noble speeches aren't enough. The thread-bare and ridiculous plots aren't enough. Men were made to talk to one another. You can't understand that. But I tell you that the writing of the future will be just this kind of writing—one man trying to tell another man of the events in *his own heart*. Writing will become speech. Novelists talk about their characters. This is because they have nothing to say about themselves. You will ask, was this true of Dostoievsky? and sadly I must answer: yes, Dostoievsky made this stupid mistake—but I am wrong! I am right in what I want to say, *but it doesn't make sense*, it doesn't tell you what you should know. We

200

must keep Shakespeare and Dostoievsky, because they talked above the clamor of their characters—they poked their bleeding heads through the junk-pile of literature, *and we saw their white, twitching faces.* We saw their lips moving. We heard their grunts and their sobs. Ah, but who did! I am full of anger when I think of the smug pigs who call themselves writers—the dirty white-livered fat boys fingering their mother's love letters off in the attic somewhere. What luck! Get that rubbish out of my way ... you're damn right there, I am stewing in my own juices ... *Hm-ummh! !* I can still remember my first pair of roller skates ... hot-assing it down Morrison Avenue with little pork sausages held fast in our mitts ... about three o'clock ... rain maybe, a bit of slush ... tongue-tied under the bill-boards ... they could sweat a pimple off in three seconds flat ... like I said to Tony ... no half-measures, eh? ... the "modern touch". ... what a nasty odor! ... a bad moment, but it *was* fun ... don't turn away. I have bad habits. For one thing I never have enough money. I have no trade. There is money in novels, but none at all in writing. Money is a necessity. Without it one starves. Then there is the matter of the landlord. Landlords care even less about writing than novelists do. It is hard to write in the street. People get the idea that maybe you are crazy. Writing is a difficult job. There is no trouble at all in knowing what you want to say; the trouble begins in keeping out the rest of it. I'd like to talk about God all the time. I know less about this than anything else. I know that you encourage me to show my heart. I have never belonged to a political party. Please tell all your friends to read my journal. I have spent many lives learning to write. It would be a pity if no one bothered to read this, wouldn't it? I feel that I have somebody to write to. I am not evil. I want to be saved. Does that amuse you? Perhaps I have been too kind to you. We are not alike, you know. I have much more to give you than you could ever give me. I have stepped onto a new planet. I feel a cold wind on my face. The dear old horrors bore me. Do you see me at all? Does my voice come through to

201

you? How soundly you sleep! Do you hear the feet of an angel on this page? I am crying—do you know at least that! I want to leave you now for a little time.

I have prayed. Let us go on.

I work in the shadow. I stab out and many words fail to land on the paper. I bang away at the stone. Nothing but the essential must go into writing—but everything is essential. I take you into my confidence. I told you that I hated novels. This is only partly true, for I also love novels. I love even the cheapest, most debased novels. You make a mistake in thinking that I demand purity in everything. Don't forget that veterinaries have their place in the world. And pimps too. Even people who send schoolboys up in bombing planes. There is a spot for everybody and everything. But this was nothing of my doing. Why should I exhaust myself shouting at a wooden Indian? Why should I care that there are no artists in America? What am I? a newspaper reporter? Why make a record of something that nobody can use? It is clearly my duty to come just at the right time, saying exactly the right thing. You have read many books. This book is reading you.

I exaggerate nothing. I am not a dealer in distortions. This is precisely the way I found the world. Imaginative people end by becoming tongue-tied. They talk above things. I operate from the inside. My feet never leave the ground. It is not my business that now and then the ground sinks away. I am heavy with the stars in my cap. I bring the sea in. I do no research whatever. Every problem to me is a problem of living. I make no attempt to translate. My speech is as much a part of my body as my arms and legs are. What have I to do with the cult of hallucination? Derangement is for the too-sane—everything under heaven cries to be *arranged*; I demand order and precision in what I do. The supreme cultivation of chaos has already been done. *That is what I am talking against.* The world is drunk on pig-piss . . . power! power! That's what we need! You need nothing of the kind. What is powerful? A gun is. A battleship. But we are weak. We are stumbling around in the dark. War is endured because it offers

us a spectacle . . . a better and bigger kind of fireworks. It scares
the hell out of us. It turns us inside out. There is its hold, its
fascination. Nobody can understand how year after year and age
after age war is put up with. It's because everybody wants to see
what it's really like. Everybody is secretly proud of it. We put
that on. God! nothing like this ever before. Did they think they
had a war . . . watch this one! But the real secret lies in property.
These are our guns, this is our fleet, this is *my* country. My country! Now you are beginning to watch me closely. I won't let you
squirm out of it! You poor little creature . . . what is yours? Your
house . . . your job . . . your kitchen chairs and the number plate
on the door . . . ah! but these don't belong to you. Where did you
get them? By what right did they come to you. You worked for
them? *Worked* . . . ? What did you do? Oh, you sat in an office
and put figures in a book. You even dug in a cold, water-filled
ditch. But I have already told you that property is murder. Because of property people starve to death and are beaten by the
police. Because of property millions of men are blown into bloody
pieces. Every Negro who is lynched has your rope around his neck.
Because of property every good impulse of mankind has been defiled and lost. Your property? The butchering of Jews in Poland
. . . the murder of Sacco and Vanzetti . . . the blood-drenched
monster called Hitler . . . yes, these belong to you. These are your
property. Indeed, this is your country. A country where systematic
murder is the *one* function of the State. At the last your only
property is murder. Refuse to murder in the name of the State,
and you will find yourself behind bars—your house, your job,
your kitchen chairs and the number plate over your door . . .
kicked into the ditch you spent your life digging, your death but
another figure you entered into the monstrous book of Capitalism.
I ask for an unconditional overthrow of every last vestige of the
world you will risk your life for tomorrow. Don't attempt to conceal the truth from me. You will fight because you are stupid,
brutal and cowardly. And a fool as well. But this is your role.
Why should I expect a monster to give birth to an angel? The

State has no misgivings about you. You will be in at the kill with the rest of your kind. You will march sprightly along at the very head of the paid assassins—stepping like a brainless goose away out in front of everybody. What does your death matter to me? It is the living who matter—those who will struggle with their last ounce of strength *to live*, not to die for a crew of soft-handed gangsters. What matters to me is the heritage of creation which a few brave men have managed to keep inviolate from the destroyers—it is their courage and purity, their faith and *idealism* which moves me to take heart and to speak out now. I am not alone. I have no wish to become a murderer. I do not *choose* my truths. I am not concerned with what appears to be true. I do not play a dozen parts at once. I am not caught off guard. I don't make judgments through casual reading of Manifestoes. I say that it is almost inconceivable that I should be rejected for the phlegmbags of the marketplace. Doubtless I will be. To live honestly. To be loved honestly. Am I such a criminal? Am I not to be given a moment before the quaint ritual at the stake? Thus, against murder, against hypocrisy, and for life, for all that is most beautiful and noble in man, for the immense joy of being alive, do I speak. I am an island in a cess-pool called History. A strange feeling comes over me. I seem to be addressing a dead man. A dead world. A dead sun. The angel has gone. I am ringed in by a circle of mocking savages. They extend their arms—blood drips from blackened stumps. O Father, whence this horrible fatherland! What is the sign? ... whose the incantation? ... where the refuge now? I am caught in a trap. The fact is pitiless. There is no escape from War. Have we already been killed? What do we oppose? The spirit creates its own country. Into what solitary place has mine departed? We behave as though our orders came from another world. Invisible and singing voices fill our ears. Our hands are grasped by strange beings. It is our spiritual obligation to be killed. We have no property now on earth. The law of the spirit in this time is death. We must not split our responsibilities. In a world of murder the artist must be the first to die. He must lead.

AND THE SWEET CHRISTS SHINE LIKE THE TEARS OF A WOMAN WHO HAS BEEN ENTERED WITHOUT LOVE

Otherwise no one's death will have meaning. We must exhaust the systems of destruction. The spirit's life is profoundly and organically a part of the world's. The mind borrows from the affairs of the greatest men; the color and *theme* of the spirit derives from him who is most degraded and brutish on all the earth. The mind can take flight into the world, because it is not purely of the world; the spirit cannot escape, because it is the world—it is, in fact, the only world which the mind can know. But there is another world; a world which neither mind nor spirit can fathom. I know that it is there. It exists outside the sphere of the human will. *That which is* is as an armless idiot in its endless house. Our beliefs are ancient and without reality. What exists, does not exist. How could we live otherwise? One must come on truth without race and without wisdom. Man's conception of man has almost succeeded in changing the *species.* We are tormented because we are no longer right as animals. We believe in men who have been *pictured* to us, but never in the men about us—and especially do we not believe in ourselves. Even Napoleon could find only 'his star' to have faith in. I taught you that Power is an image in the mythology of a slave. The power of an empire rests in the threat of its poor, half-starved subjects to take up arms against it. For that reason fleets are built and armies are trained. Wars are conducted that the people may lose sight of their own need to wage war. The people always fight for the cause which enslaves them; that is, the cause of their rulers. A monstrous game is played. Not content with condemning their subjects to a life of hunger and slavery, the powers that be craftily call in the wretched subjects of a foreign murderer to complete the job. This is done for the sake of trade and markets, mind you. It would be an unforgivable impertinence to ask: whose trade? whose markets? Yours, perhaps. Or mine. Then, when the paint wears thin on the mask, they just haul out a new set of labels and begin all over again; they say, "Horror of horrors, what is this ghastly thing? Look what it says there! *Fascism.* Now isn't that barbarous! Surely you'll fight against that! The world must be saved from Fascism." And they are right. It must. But it should have been saved from Fascism before some clever butcher thought up the word. For it is only a word. It differs from what we have known by only a word. Make no mistake. If Capitalism is wearing a new mask in Europe, we'll get a bigger and a better one ourselves tomorrow. The styles of Imperialist murder must change as Capitalism draws nearer to its death; it is unfortunate that our warm bodies and singing blood should be destined to once more clothe its hideous skeleton. That is not all. In our cities we have tolerated noise and dirt that would sicken a half-witted ape; we have deliberately sought out the ugly and the deformed; we have done everything in our power to stamp out the merest hint of that which has grace and beauty. We have behaved as though only the taste of the most depraved and besotten had any claim to gratification. We have pushed the nose of our culture into the shit of our self-interest. For all this is done that, of all things! we may enjoy ourselves . . . the moron-minded radio; the theatre which throws wide its arms to adolescent windbags; the literature which *exploits* the sufferings of the migratory worker; the music which stinks of Hollywood—here we are! In one word, we are the greatest nation on earth. We come nearest to the desired condition: imbecility—ordered and delivered fresh at your grocer's every morning. We never miss. Everything we know to be fine and good is denied by what we are. We are absolutely classic. Our artists have only one desire: and that is, *that their works may not live.* There is something old-fashioned and uncouth in writing for posterity. How can they send us the checks when we're dead? You will think that I want my book to live.

Think it.

It is the duty of the artist not to die. He must preserve his life *even at the expense of his ideals.* This must be understood.

I am a poet of life.

What are we going to do?

Where can we turn?

There is so much hate in the world.

I would crawl a thousand miles on my hands and knees if that would stop the war.

16. THE ESCAPE BY SEA

I made my way for some time in that desperate country, advancing as well as I could where no roads were—clawing my way through a forest where no man had ever been. Ceaselessly I moaned, for I knew that I was being followed. Often I turned and shouted into the darkness . . . did a dog howl somewhere off in the night? *Why didn't you come when I called to you?*

Something rubbed against my cheek . . . wet, clinging, cold. I put out my hand and touched it.

It was nothing that could live on this earth. But it breathed . . . it wrapped itself around me and seemed to empty itself. A horrible stench burnt my nostrils and put the taste of filth in my mouth.

I heard water lapping on rocks. The voice of a man called to me from the water. I made my way down and onto the deck of a ship. At once there was the creaking of blocks and the stinging slap of sails as they bit into the wind. A single lantern swung from a hook in the mainmast. By its mournful, jumping light I saw a young man standing knee-deep in the feathery spume which slithered in at the bow. His arms were folded. He was tall. His face was alert and beautiful. He appeared to be making entries in a notebook which he held easily out of reach of the pounding sea. The helmsman's wheel was gripped steady in no hand that I could discern. The creaming reach of canvas was sent on its right way . . . the whole life of a ship under full sail went forward in the best style . . . I wondered if that remarkable crew could see me. The tall young Captain did not seem to see me, though I tugged at his coat and beat upon his shoulders. I had the sensation that perhaps I was the only unaccountable being there.

Toward morning I grew sick and vomited over the side. At once a shark, its fin riding up like the clasp on a great zipper, cut in

207

and nailed my supper. I thumbed my nose in his tarry face but I had to give him some more.

Here we were at the voyage's end . . .

I stepped upon the land. When I turned around the ship was gone, but something was in my hand that had not been there before. It was his notebook. I opened to the first page and read:

The Book of the Living, written by one who has been called Savior . . .

A voice said: "You have come at last."

Something broke in my heart.

Jetter, Carol, Thomas Honey, Billy Delian, Jackeen . . . waiting there in the soft mists of the morning to kill me.

I regret that my death may discourage the people of this nation.

I wheeled around and plunged back into the sea. I swam until I reached the other side of the island. There was no one there to trouble me—but the print of one enormous foot was clearly outlined in the white sand, and I heard a shuddering breath far above my head. I have at the last come home. There is no other place in the world for me to go.

17. THE ISLAND

. . . softly, gently, not making a sound . . . *the end will come with no pain.*

What are you doing so far from mankind?

I am weak with hunger.

I stretch out my hands to you for water.

There is no one at all here.

The bodies of my pursuers stink in the sun.

I walked through the island and they followed me. But I was stronger. They are dead. I shall not die. My eyes are closing. I cannot hear. I crept to a wall on the first day and went to sleep. When I awakened they were standing about me with knives and rifles in their hands. They hacked at me but I did not die. They shot me many times but I would not die. Then they went away.

Today I crawled to the place where their bodies are.

Inch by inch, pulling myself along with my blood-caked fingers.

Their faces are contorted horribly. Blackened tongues bulge out of their mouths.

And when another door opens . . .

I was stronger and I did not die.

Flies and maggots crawl through my wounds.

I shall not leave you.

And now I laugh . . . I laugh! Before God! I . . .

My fingers touch a face. I drag myself forward. This is Carol . . . pieces of her breasts still hanging from her fingernails . . . ah! this is where you are . . .

And Jetter . . . his head twisted into the sand . . . you can't hide, you fool . . .

Jackeen! I will not look at her . . .

I refuse to die. There is no use in trying to kill me, God . . .

With my last energy I put my teeth into Carol's thigh . . . I chew weakly on the crawling flesh. There is no taste. I eat until I am unable to swallow.

I feel the strength coming back into me. I try to get to my feet . . . I sink down . . . later . . . be patient . . .

Then I am dying . . . this poisoned meat . . .

Now . . . now . . . now . . . *God* . . . now!

I cannot lift my head!

For the last time I open my eyes . . . Keddel is there above me . . . filling all the heavens . . .

What do you see?

An EYE . . .

It is trying to tell me something . . . $\quad$ EYE

Yes!

Roivas!

The Book of the Living slips from my fingers.

Savior!

JULY 31 🐾 Someone had tied Thomas Honey's arms behind his back; his legs had been drawn up and bound to his wrists; then a noose had been slipped around his neck and the ends made fast to his ankles. No man could stay in that position for long—when at last he gave in and struggled, the baling wire cut slowly into his throat and killed him. A nasty way to die . . . Straw had been spread over his corpse.

I enjoyed a long talk with Mr. Honour over dinner coffee. My liking for him grows at each new meeting. It becomes increasingly hard for me to believe some of the vile tales which circulate around him. He is credited with the most amazing and fascinating crimes. This is not the moment nor am I of a mind to set them down in this place. He has a curious habit of snapping his knuckles when speaking—very nerve-wracking to the auditor.

Now I may as well admit that I had the devil's own time finding a shop which offered silver bullets for sale; but finally I did, and bought two.

By forging ahead at a decent clip today we have penetrated deep into the woolly fastnesses of Wyoming. The long brown faces of the cowboys give every promise of a stupidity substantial enough to satisfy anybody. There is something dismal and pathetic about these overgrown morons. Once or twice a month they have a go at hard likker and a fast time with some broken-down Indian whores; the rest of the while they whinny against being buried on the lone prairie—though why they should worry about when or where they are buried, I can't see. We were much amused by their slow, drawling baby-talk. The Goddamn boobs.

Immediately after setting up my tent, I lay down on the bunk and gave some thought to our situation. The night was cold; the stars sharp as pressed steel. When Carol came along I folded her in beside me and we talked the night out. It seems that Joseph Gambetta has been doing too much gabbing . . .

AUGUST 1   I got up this morning very early and took a prodigious walk off over the prairie. About five miles from camp I sighted an elephant. After stalking him for the better part of an hour, I managed to get near enough to read the large canvas sign which swung at his back; it said: *Drink Coca Cola*. A rather droll way to advertise, I thought.

I can't get over how gruesomely agreeable these cowboys are— "Make yerselves to home, folks."—dinning it into you until you feel like breaking their necks on the spot. If there is anything I despise, it is a willy-nilly hospitality; even dogs do a bit of sniffing of asses before any glad-handing is done. And, by the by, the smell that went up from these cowlads was nothing to put in a bottle and keep. Why should every bloody last one of them stink of burnt horse manure! Do they smoke the stuff?

A thing happened this evening that set my teeth on edge. I am no physiognomist but the face of the ranch foreman really got in to me. I suppose you would call him a liberal. He has a nose that is a good seven inches long. People forget that a man's eyes are his measure, not the shape of his head or the placement of his cheekbones. I was telling him something of our experiences on the road, when I happened to notice that he was not listening at all; but you will have to take my word for it that man's eyes were drinking in every word. He was *seeing* what I said. Another thing about him: the little finger on his right hand was missing. I left the bunkhouse like a sleepwalker, muttering to myself. In all my life I had met no one whom I feared more—and I am no slouch in that department. It was hours later before I realized the truth: he had hypnotized me. I had been telling him things that had not yet taken place; I had been recounting events that were to happen only after my death. How do I know this? I have experiences outside this world.

I have heard it said (and from quarters usually reliable) that I am an adventurer. As a general rule, I should be inclined to ignore such boorish nonsense; however, at this special moment, at this time when the whole destiny of the world lies in the balance, I feel moved to say that this is a malicious untruth. It is a peculiarity of mine to find nothing commendable in action; the only life is the life that stays fixed inside us regardless of what we do. The running man goes nowhere that the steady man has not been.

Today has been the dullest and most unproductive day of the entire trip. Just plain off my feed, I guess.

AUGUST 2 ☙ A spangling of stars showed from time to time through the rain as we pulled stakes late last night. I couldn't have managed another day in that Godforsaken hole. So I escape the cowboys. I haven't a thought left in my head.

AUGUST 3 ☙ I am griped by a muffling discontent. I feel empty, washed-up. Another day of this and I'll chuck the journal altogether.

AUGUST 4 ☙ Nothing. It's no good.

AUGUST 5 ☙ I don't know where we are and I don't give a damn.

AUGUST 6 ☙ What in the name of God has happened to me? Just the thought of writing is enough to turn my stomach; I actually throw up. We are now going through the most wonderful country —and I am tongue-tied. Women with delayed periods must feel like this.

AUGUST 7 ☙ Joseph Gambetta was shot and killed today. Being a phantom did not help him on this occasion: he had been drilled twice through the head with silver bullets.

I am beginning to take an interest in my affairs again. If you will bear with me, I shall now practice a few finger-exercises—just to get my hand in again:

The old graves cry out for fresh, young bodies.

The North Wind gets astride snow-embroidered geese.

Staring before me I watched myself go through all the sad defeats.

Alas, that love were pure and the horses saddled in the courtyard.

Even the tumbling wave has its fixed place somewhere.

When the stallion tastes the mare's milk the world will end.

The deer walk desolate through the white wood.

Swiftly flies the arrow that has a heart to house in.

The trees on her tomb moan like sick ferrets.

To bring love to a single being is not of much use.

The candle sits in the dusk like an eye in a dead face.

Traveler, the gate you seek is in a tower that does not exist.

The bright petals of the day bob softly on the meadows of the sea.

Death's but the distance of your fingernail from all you love.

Would you sell yourself for a coin that the wind could wear away?

When we are left only the lying down under the heavy water ...

Do not ask the wound where the pain is, neither your love whom she loves.

Young men share themselves; old men their houses.

It is strange to live in a body, to have hands and feet and a head. Is there a simple meaning in this? Is it important to live in one part of the body more than in others? I believe that many people never live in all of themselves. Some live in their stomachs, others in their loins—pain brings you alive wherever it is. A man whose hand has been scalded, lives nowhere but there. What is pain? What purpose does it serve? The war does not prevent me from having an interest in these things. War causes me to think of murder. To murder someone is to commit an irrational act. Soldiers cannot be other than madmen because they are trained to perform deeds of madness. The insane economy of our rulers demands a universal insanity. We must not hate our oppressors, because hate arises out of a sense of guilt. There is your monstrous farce—no man who ever stood up to authority but did so with a sense of guilt. How they have trapped us! That's the secret of their power, for deep in all of us is a sense that they *must* be right. How else account for the defensive attitude of political martyrs? Why do revolutionists make out a case for themselves? through what propulsion? Surely they know that the State will not recognize the truth in their plea, will not honor the arguments which they advance. Why is it not possible for one man to say to the State: there is no need for me to offer a defense, it is you who are on trial; what do you have to say for yourself?

I know why.

It is because it is beyond the limits of the human imagination to realize that our systems of government and the men who govern us are actually as vile and brutal and heartless as they are.

Consider the world at this hour. The *overwhelming majority* of human beings are hungry, ill-housed, diseased; millions of men are proceeding systematically to blow each other to pieces.

Why!

Is it my fault? Is it your fault? Whose fault is it?

Has anyone any conception of this thing?

Men speak of God.

What right do they have to so much as breathe His name?

Men say we are American.

Men say we are English, German, Dutch.

That is a lie.

There are only human beings.

We are not motor-cars or chunks of soap that we need labels.

Who plans to sell us?

They mean *to do something* with us.

I tell you that no man has any right whatever over another man.

When I am told that the President of the United States is forced to take us into war, I answer:

How can any man sign the death warrant of millions of his fellows?

How can any man now be the President of the United States?
I do not say: How can he go through with it?
I ask: How can any man be in it at all?
The answer is simple:
Power! Career! Prestige! Glory!
And I ask:
Where is the power that leads only to wholesale slaughter . . .
Where is the career that rests on the bleeding bodies of school-
boys . . .
Where is the prestige that fattens on jails and asylums and
graves . . .
Where is the glory that lies with the swollen jowls of the
Caesars . . .
I would to God I could love the President of the United States.
It is not my fault, nor is it his, that I cannot.
Though I walk through the valley of the shadow . . .

AUGUST 8 ⚗ Return to me . . .
The bloodstain on the page.
It is time to end this book . . . an abnormal precaution, perhaps . . . majestically humiliated . . . what body shakes in the
sweet religious shroud . . . *to issue from a hypocritical luck . . .*
away, then. Damn you to hell! Let me go to sleep. Why should I be
the one to nourish the blind and the halt?
Oh, could I but find rest on this earth. No, no, no . . . I feel the
method in my fingers. You will be surprised to learn that I have
tracked you to your lair. The pain . . . God! The *pain* has brought
me to your fantastic grave. I address this human race—I chip
my speech out of the stone. Marvel at this ineffaceable servant of
God! Whoever you are, I bring my danger on you. Vengeance. I
am that precocious murderer whose silhouette stands in your
every dream. You cannot escape me.
And now . . .
The houses of your world lie in ruins. Toads and flying snakes

tumble from the sky. It is too late to bring you warning. I define the magnificent limits of our terror.

Make ready for the coming of the monsters.

━━

AUGUST 9 ⚜ This night, *silence . . . peace.* Contrary to my habit, I spent the whole day reading. As we go through a book I imagine few of us have much curiosity about the condition of its author— how he is taking the book as he writes it, what it is doing to him, etc. I am convinced that a truly great book would leave its creator in a condition of superb madness. It is not fair to expect any of us to achieve very much; about all that can be done is to bark out orders on a parade-ground where walk the impossible acrobats of our own animal defeat. We wave awkwardly to the angels. The artist wants to prove once and for all that the vain ornaments of this life are not to be endured. It is not an excess of trust to be-lieve that the Beautiful is not within the province of Art. The first law in good writing is this: get rid of all *charm.* What poor little bare-assed bastards we are . . .

━━

AUGUST 10 ⚜ I have finally reached a decision about my notes. It has been my custom (while on this journey) to make occa-sional jottings of things which, for reasons of fatigue or lack of time, could not be handled adequately in the journal. I had a notion that one day I would write another book—and so use them —but it is clear to me now that I shall not live to have a fresh crack at it. Therefore I have decided to copy in a few of them here: for the sake of the record, as they say. You will forgive their somewhat pell-mell and disorganized state. Here we go:

THE NOTES

Describe the old farmhand we met on the banks of the Red River. His marvelous lucidity, his talent for pure expression.

.   .   .   .

The uniforms of the salesgirls in the A&P in El Paso. What a superior practical joke.

Why is the Senate so badly lighted? Get an expert opinion on this.

.   .   .   .

In the novel (projected):

See to it that the character of the girl remains murky and undefined until the very close of the execution scene.

Write about these people as though you were lying full-length at their feet. The perspective *from below.*

Pay less attention to the dialogue, more to the touch of their presences one on the other. Speech is unimportant if the total atmosphere comes through.

Meat your narrative with treatments of your own feeling.

Manage at the last to crowd out all of the book's characters.

Build up the sequence in the church with full use of the associational value of bells and incense.

Don't bear down too hard on the significance of the island.

Try to keep your story from slipping off into the bog of the possible; be absolutely certain that it will not 'hold water'.

The lizard . . . above all, it must be drawn *true to life.*

Avoid delightful passages; bring your ship in at low tide every time.

Make sure that the words are hung with all their flags; kick them into each other; make their noses bleed.

.   .   .   .

That beautiful girl in Cheyenne. Her unbearably lovely smell. The poem of her walk . . . the sprung rhythm of her swaying buttocks. What a pavilion of rapture!

.   .   .   .

It would be amusing to write something about the secret joviality of the statues we pass unheeding everyday. A statue's opinion of our heroes—there's something.

.   .   .   .

Draw up a list of the men you admire. Think of a useful collaborator.

.   .   .   .

It is more important to come in a good period for creation than it is to have great talent. Genius must be released in a man; it does nothing of itself. The genius will make a heroic mess of his art, then furiously work to put it together again. He will build in no other house but his own. And he will be forever the most wretched and happy soul on earth. Because he will be alive.

.   .   .   .

Simplicity of statement is not the hallmark of craft. There is no such thing as a well-bred perfection. Great art must possess an absolute flaw at its very core; otherwise it would be an abuse of the imperishable frailty of all things that exist, and we could say with complete truth that the apple is the most beautiful object under the sun. Art must add to the mystery.

.   .   .   .

A short pilgrimage to Herman Melville's grave.

.   .   .   .

The yellow sky over Flagstaff. Arizona's Harqua Hala desert is perhaps the greatest treatise on sordidness to be found in this country.

.   .   .   .

That which is not daring is nothing.

.   .   .   .

Write of a landscape out of which *grow* three great white figures.

.   .   .   .

Scribbling this as we ride along beside the Mississippi. It's hot as all hell. Carol is out of sanitary napkins and we've been dashing madly from one town to another all day trying to find a place that sells them, but no soap. The women in these parts must resort to leaves.

What an effect all this bother has on my state of mind!

.   .   .   .

One must be steeped in an indifference to the little matter of the laying on of hands—the artist must keep the world from knowing the exact complexion of his success. To be aware of the public image of yourself is to lose your own special identity. For the world, your least notable face; for yourself, no face at all.

218

I noticed how simply the departure is made when we are all in bad spirits. We assist each other most in external things when we are countries apart inside. It is perhaps not remarkable that man's supreme achievements have been made in roads and bridges and methods of conveyance—always that flight, that getting away . . . and the more we flock to the cities, the more like chicken-coops do our dwellings become—everybody trying his damnedest to shut himself off from everybody else. I say, smash up all the cars; do your running on foot like the frightened little mice you are. There is nothing more disgusting than the automobile-man who sits in your room with his eye out the window for the nearest filling station. That great soothing masturbation of machinery, the gear shift . . .

An idea must have an inexhaustible substance; it must burst its banks—*without control.*

The greatest masters foster no schools. They imitate themselves until the matter is ended.

Oh! the noise the skeletons make trying on new bodies.

See to it that something of Jetter's past is given. I foresee a whole battalion of little scribes digging into his strange career, coming up with God alone knows what.

Each day I begin a new life. An endless procession of men runs through me. Who am I at this moment?

What is often mistaken for prose style is only a tone of false gravity.

Progress always meets itself on the backward march.

O to have been Marshall Ney's yes-man.

219

What good is it to be alive only to find yourself stuck in Panguitch, Utah! We were held up here four days while Billy Delian was investigated on a charge of rape. An odious affair all around.

This part of the country suffers from a severe case of malignant mange. Through what indifferent fatality did I arrive in this horse's ass of a place?

The vigorous arm—the rough, beautiful intoxication with saying.

They are pulling down the old meeting house in Montpelier. An outrage! They will burn up the planks in the wooden bridge next.

A pretty rogue stole our spare tire and lifting jack. I forgot myself to the extent of kicking out the windshield, which helped out little.

What a master stroke of asininity, this little business of regional literature! That outfit that used to operate in Nashville—the *Fudgiteers*—how they do dig into the Civil War . . . is youall been baptised in Jeff Davis' blood?

Do not overreach the sky; you will only have another world to contend with.

I awakened this morning and screamed when I touched my body. I can't get used to it.

The lady of the apple blossoms . . . what fun we had together in her luscious scenery—the battle raging through all her pretty towns . . .

With the policeman in the alley's black lip. The approach to the inner city. Cats clawing the face of a slobbering drunk. Women at washlines. Chimneys stretching up like the red, pocked thighs of syphilitic crones.

The green tea being poured down the rough throats of cabmen.

The head of the universe pissing into the gutter.

A great deal of slack to that little lady's churchly ways.

The handsome behind eats an orange by the garden wall.

Why do the soldiers level their rifles at us?

I call your attention to something which is nibbling away at your face . . .

Very good hanging weather.

The ram's horn catches in the rusty cannon.

The cries of the young married women who are being butchered.

Men climbing . . . a white horse flecked with blood.

My arrival here. This is Forth Worth, I think. Monday.

Sun following the flies around.

Hot, powdery stones . . .

The loud disorder; laughter; the dust always; a lane of trumpets in battered mouths.

I went through a hedge of closely packed whores. A dangerous place to be naked in.

A story told in fury. Running. The tents on fire. Sticks studded with nails driving into the sides of horses. Two huge dogs fanning out their sex in the square.

The cannibals are feeding. I present my respects. If it suit your fancy, we can tour the cemetery after breakfast.

A painted column extending twelve miles into the sky.

Another gate and another pleasure to be explained.

Milk from a dirty teat. The quarrel of the kissing standard-bearers.

The wind blows out the flowers' brains. Not too dark, God. Not too cold, God. Not too lonely, God. What is the case against me?

I plead guilty. (Get my heirs to explain this.) My parents and my friends will attest to the solemnity of my deportment.

Was that a drop of rain?

. . . PEACE-FULLY PICKING THE FLOWERS WHICH GOD HAS PUT IN ME

Is it beginning to rain?

Was that rain starting to fall?

I anticipate the punishment. Hand me that terrible black merchandise. I withdraw from this case. I do not at all like your offhand manner in this, God. You could have heard me out. I am one of those things You made. You put the breath in these lungs. Why do You walk out on me? Where are You off to?

I shall exact a vengeance that will wither the hair off Your head.

Midnight. Midnight lowers his soft cloak over the world.

We are not going to win out. We've been beaten to the punch every time.

A voluptuously shaped corset in a spider-thick closet.

This is not a bad thing, sitting here on top. To have a city.

The monastery is very cold when the snow comes.

That was a drop of blood on my cheek. It fell from the sky. Is something up there being tortured too?

This cold moonlight.

This light of the cold, still moon . . .

Horses breaking through the loose boards of the bridge.

White leaves tossing on phantom boughs.

.   .   .   .

The king has gone to bed. A woman lying under the melancholy wind in the churchyard.

(My impression of Mobile Bay . . .)

A lad in an orange coat playing a flute near the entrance to a crypt. *Down Mobile Bay.*

Lower childhood into the furrow made by a hurricane of birds.

The ecstatic dead everywhere. At first my moans made that old general walk faster. Set your gait to the dancers'.

Got into town about eight o'clock. I am persuaded that there is a gentleman here who went to reform school with me.

I intend to place a certain outrage of words squarely between your legs. I detach myself from pity. Nobility mostly.

This is your audience with the emperor.

(Problem: how is it possible to rewrite this passage? Perhaps too much emphasis has been put on what is *above and underneath* this particular scene. Remember that the profound can never be purely mournful.)

Flowers alternate with her eyes as we journey through these prodigal catacombs. The grandeur in the robes and attributes of that hawk-nosed priest—but he has a bib on!

The undeceived chrysalis opens beneath the sea. Almighty God there is no reason to twist the dagger . . . the stone knees of our houses knock together as the tempest of fear strikes. Can you do it? can you run your hand over the scales on your body without crying?

I demand to know exactly what we are going to do about these matters. Until I spoke, no one had caused the cemeteries to lift up their terrible bodies and crawl over the earth. I take an innumerable delight in my justice.

Close the door on this cell . . . I lament for mankind.

.   .   .   .

Jackeen used to love to say my name. Well—when I am disgusted and tired . . . The woman-vault opening on the washed and motionless stars.

I have been requested to resign from my club. What a lugubrious time they chose to put the heat on! We have been awaiting our turns all morning in a de-lousing station on the Texas border.

A splendid thunder storm last night. I have never seen the sky so full of clotted fire—like the blood of a golden beast pouring down.

.   .   .   .

I watched them guillotine a sailor today. The poor fellow's clay separated under the bright metallic storm without a trace of mortal significance. I suppose one way is as good as another. The most vivid thing about the whole affair was the glob of yellow snot that hung at the nose of the executioner.

.   .   .   .

A painful splinter has lodged itself under my nail. I gnawed away at it until I tasted blood. Why does the blood of another have a different flavor in our mouths? Not a very picturesque way of reminding us that *by nature* we should be eating one another.

.　　.　　.　　.　　.　　.　　.　　.　　.

How many high school girls have lost their virginity playing basketball? I'll wager that the figure is appalling. When sport attains the vigorous dimensions of a bridegroom, I'd say that it was time to call a halt.

.　　.　　.　　.　　.　　.　　.　　.　　.

We were proceeding leisurely down the main street in St. Paul when suddenly, without warning of any kind, an immense octopus wrapped his arms around our car. He seemed innocent enough of particular malice—simply working his suckers in a kind of anguished friendliness, and making a vague little call—but his conduct certainly put the wind up all of us. An octopus in heat is not a pretty sight.

.　　.　　.　　.　　.　　.　　.　　.　　.

What have I to do with their charity! I have cried myself loose from this dreary tribe.

.　　.　　.　　.　　.　　.　　.　　.　　.

I shall be weaker than anyone. There can be no doubt now: I ought to pay at least one short visit to the world. I have heard that there are creatures there who will greet me not unkindly.

.　　.　　.　　.　　.　　.　　.　　.　　.

I am lame with too many legs. This is the ultimate running . . . gentle little gentlemen, you are at last face to face with a man.

.　　.　　.　　.　　.　　.　　.　　.　　.

The penetrating stupidity of the somnambulist who silkily whistles the *Magnificat* to the moulting matadors of dawn. (Happily this could not be said in any other way.)

.　　.　　.　　.　　.　　.　　.　　.　　.

I say, I say, I say, listen to what I say, *pinggg!* . . . not an effigy this time—I am well-stocked with *authentic* murders. Waggle your fat ass when I give the word. Don't try to pull any of that obsequious stuff in front of me.

Tired of these moon-faced robots ... O daughters of Kalamazoo, what is the farce that has launched these ten thousand shits? I cannot, at present, fix my heart on that peculiar heaven.

.   .   .   .

A word about my qualifications. I have hit on a hunch that practically everything that has been written is worthless—I'll give you odds of ten to one that you can't name five really exciting books. That's one ... two ... *and* ...

.   .   .   .

I lovingly salute the pitiless renegade who will understand my position.

.   .   .   .

Decatur is a city with extremely odd accoutrements. A pernicious spot to be baptised in. (Quicken the pace a bit; your proportions must stand out nicely on close inspection. You may even be privileged to have a careful reader.) To begin with our arrival. Somebody had spread out a great carpet in the square. An incommensurable amount of money had been spent to assure that no one see anything green and growing—no flowers, grass, trees. A slate-colored canopy swung from four enormous posts at the city's corners—thus adequately shutting off the sky—and I was not at all surprised to witness upon it a motion picture which featured a boy's efforts to get a girl. (I was informed that this particular movie has been in progress for twelve years, and still the end is not in sight. The people sleep with one eye on the screen; all other activity has been forgotten.) Then the radio. There is only one. It is as big as an office building—so big in fact that all programs can be broadcast at once. But, in spite of all their advantages, Decaturans do not shamelessly parade themselves. I found them a curiously shy people, little given to idle chatter with strangers. They are justly proud of their civic record: no births, no deaths, no runs, no errors. And by a strange coincidence, they are all deaf, dumb and blind.

.   .   .   .

The humanitarian bandit ...

225

Every sob arranges itself in my ferocious Rosary. I am on the last beautiful hunt. How could I be nourished on the vegetable of History!

.   .   .   .

My feet have wandered off the path. *No one would have noticed it.* No one could have tasted my hunger.

.   .   .   .

A startling affair, arithmetic. What can be divided? What added to? Surely four is not two *and* two: there is no way of slipping the twos into each other so fast that you can get rid of that little 'and'. But where did we get the two? One (and) one? We tried that. There can be only one thing in the world. Each is *its own part* of all.

.   .   .   .

By every law of this continual art, I should end this book right here. For my purposes, the end must not come at the end, but in the middle—*and then we go on.*

.   .   .   .

The most frightful wreckers can do no more than bring ruin: and therefore are to be pitied as ones whose action is below act— even as the dead.

.   .   .   .

The weapon that can stop war must be able to kill too; for most people should be murdered in their tracks. War's killing is too good for them: it will be necessary to make them into decent human beings—a punishment from which they will fly in utter horror.

.   .   .   .

Do not reproach me with swinging thus from the gallows without a necktie. My tan one, flowered in delicate maroon—the only one that really strikes my fancy—was torn to shreds by an army of supernatural sword-fish on a quiet day last May. (This is a good touch—could be elaborated perhaps: an unquenchable martyrdom is much admired at the moment.)

.   .   .   .

I came upon the most extraordinary continent. A criterion for land shapes . . . I shouted gleefully . . . I said to myself, "Theoretically this must surely be Paradise!" The huge wings flapping on either side—that unusual earth was flying through the heavens exactly like a bird, and saying, "Caw! Caw! Caw!"

.   .   .   .

I would like to tell you something of how I am at this time. It is cold and dark. Does that make you understand? Do you feel my breath on your face? You are trying much too hard to get away. Why do you fear my voice? I have you at last—now I shall build my fire in your soul!

Here, God, is Your determined hunter . . .

.   .   .   .

Because my lips are warm . . .

.   .   .   .

An answer to my critics:

I am physical.	*It is time*
I feel the rain.	*to take*
I feel the sun.	*these bastards*
I feel the wind.	*into*
I feel the snow.	*my confidence.*
I am without blemish.	*They will*
I fear God.	*love me*
I fear your God.	*applaud me*
I fear my God.	*hate me*
I will shake your hand or cut your throat.	
I bake poisonous fish in my oven.	*but they*
Drink my blood.	*won't*
Eat of my flesh.	*ever*
I have power.	*forget*
I have love.	*me.*
I am a young man.	*I give*
I am a thousand years old.	*them*
I will not humble myself.	*a look*

I am alone.   *at*
I am in debt.   *a naked*
I am heroic.   *snarling*
I am laughing at you.   *animal!*
I am weeping for you.
I look for the meaning.   *This is*
I search for the truth.   *truly*
The world belongs to me.   *an event*
I praise my methods.
I have examined philosophy.   *I*
I have given an account of my soul.   *lift*
I have spilled out my heart.   *my*
I have told you nothing.   *brimming cup*
I am eternal.   *to the*
I am everyone.   *Greeks*
I am beautiful.   *Persians*
I am full of wisdom.   *Egyptians*
I have been cast in a bright clay.   *to*
I am lacking in all graces.   *Buddha*
I am dirty.   *Kant*
I am blind.   *Shakespeare*
I am a liar.   *Villon*
I am complete.   *St. Francis*
I am empty.   *and*
I have made a book for your shelves.   *The Devil.*
I have walked into the circle.   *I*
I have told you everything.   *approach*
I have taken a woman to bed.   *the hall*
I have put a man in his grave.   *where*
I am the beginning.   *the good boys*
I am the end.   *lie*
I have put a knife in your hand.   *in their*
A star tosses in my hair.   *big black beds.*
Something would kill me.   *Johnnie!*
Something would save me.   *Jennie!*

I defend the angel.
I vomit blood.
Advise me!
Help me!
I moan at your window.
I undress on your doorstep.
I squeeze my milkless tits.
I am playing with my own cards.
I have loaded the dice.
I have drugged that little horse called Death.
I've got a leg up on Immortality.

I've got nobody to listen to me.
The buildings have all fallen on me.
They've shoved all the bayonets up my ass.
I take the lid off.
I show you the works.
I shall be famous.
I shall be rich.
I shall be loved.
I am already forgotten.
My pockets are dry of money.
The police are looking for me.
My life is without consequence.
It is impossible to go on.
My book is babbling junk.
I am a fraud.
I am without passion.
I am without energy.
I am tired.
I am cold.
I am alone.
I am afraid.
I am unclean.
I am naked.

go back
to sleep
the
Jelly Roll
is
all
gone.

Whose
the mastery?
whose the
glory?
when
we are
all
lost
and the screams
and the madness
and the pain
and the tears

look out
we are
coming
to a very
very
low
bridge
and the
hand
of
the engineer
is fish-cold
on
the throttle . . .

229

I am dying.
Where are we going?
What are we going to do?
Tear me to pieces.
Spit in my face.
Make your dirt in my house.
I am lost.
It is dark.
How can we escape?
Where is the light?
I have been lowered into the water.
We are adrift on a terrible sea.
We have nothing to hope for.
We have nowhere to go.
We have nobody to count on.
I shall not leave you.
I shall not let you down.
I am the pure voice.
I am the throat bare to the sun.
I have a trick up my sleeve.
I can save you.
I can show you the way.
We can dwell in peace together.
My clock does not keep their time.
I sneer at their gadgets.
I won't travel on their roads.
I won't live in their houses.
I won't eat their food.
I will not obey them.
I am one with God.
I am one with the earth.
I am one with the sea.
I am not afraid.
I am not alone.

for
the mastery
and the
glory
are
MINE

but

I
want to
say
Fear's
hyena
sits
on the white floor
of heaven
and
licks
his slavering chops

looking
down
on us
who have
grown
fat
and weary
waiting
for
something
to save us
who have
not
been alive

230

I shall not be punished.   *at all*
I am strong.   *who have*
I am aware.   *lain here*
I shall not suffer.   *helpless*
I shall not die.   *under*
You will not listen to me.   *the monsters*
You will learn to love me.   *which*
You will not beat me.   *inhabit*
You will not stone me.   *all*
You will not nail me to the cross.   *the world about*
You will not want to torture me.   *but which*
You will not want me to go mad.   *our eyes*
I want to sit in your chair.   *never see*
I want to taste the food in your mouth.
I want to put my tongue on your eyes.   *. . . another*
I want to feel the hair on your belly.   *man*
I want to run my hand over your sex.   *would have*
I want to press my body against you.   *turned up*
I want to sleep in your bed.   *his toes*
I want to discuss my book with you.   *long ago*
I want to hear you praise me.
I want to see your eyes move over this page.
I want to feel your mind feeding on these words.
I want to talk about God with you.
I want you to show me your wounds.
I want you to treat me with respect.
I want you to drop all pretense.
I want you to strip off your clothes.
I want you to tell me where the pain is.
I want to hear your voice.   *. . . a*
I want to put my arms around you.   *thunderous flood*
I want to fill you with my seed.   *of*
Where did I sleep last night?   *light*
Who follows to murder me?   *over all*
What have I done that they hunt me down? *the still*

231

Why is there blood on your hands?   *cold*
When shall I have the simplicity to say it?   *sightless*
How can I be cunning enough?   *forgotten*
How can I be pure enough?   *faces*
How can I be wise enough?
How can I be angry enough?
I am giving them warning.
Let them sharpen their knives.
Let them oil their rifles.
Let them get their answers ready.
I am going to knock down their doors.
I am going to kill them with my bare hands.

.   .   .   .

A few jottings for the exclusive use of lion tamers and magicians:

Reality cannot excite.

We must deny the world everything.

It is useful to be proud.

It is useful to be humble when God's eye alone can see us but at night there is a discharge from the great belly that lies across the sky and we are smeared wet and crying with it coming into the valley out of the womb to walk upright on the earth for I say that reality cannot exist at all do you believe me because I am a man who frankly says I don't know a Goddamn thing about writing because nothing quite happens like ramming at a woman happens I think that the trouble is we can't open up enough do you understand do you hear me I am down at the bottom of the heap buried under by the war and the pain and the despair I am trying to speak I don't know how to say it I confess to you that I don't know where I am going I am tired and afraid they are hunting us down they won't ever let us alone (This sort of thing terrifies me: it is so much like reading the sermon at your own funeral.)

The naked calm eye . . .

because we can't open up enough and the victim of our lust . . . abandoned LET IT GO . . . give yourself

232

we can't	look look look look look look look look look look
open up	I freely confess, I am in agony I am afraid I have
enough	lost my way LOOK AT ME look look look look at me
can't you	look look look look look look look look look look
see?	look look Here I am look look look look look look
I lift	look look look look look look look! look! look!
my mask	look! look! look! look! look! look! look! look!
ever	look! look! look! look! do you see me! look! look!
so	look! look! look! look! look! look! look! look!
little	look! help me! help me! God help me! look! look!
do you	look! look! look! look! look! look! look! look!
know me!	look! look! look! look! look! look! look! look!

out of the womb . . . to stand crying
    the ladies are all dead
    the white ladies are sleeping under the hill
    the ladies I say are all dead
    what has happened to the white ladies?
    the poor ladies who dropped us out of
their bellies?

A bloody cigar was found near the scene of the crime. I don't smoke cigars— do you?

  our mothers, eh lad? are sleeping under the dark hill
  This is the sound of terror, this is the truth, this is the . . .
  LOOK! LOOK! I am standing beside you

I got up this morning with a headache and a feeling of bad fortune just ahead. Several people dropped in during the day with news of one thing and the other. It appears that England will resist quite stubbornly after all. I read

a
thin
wisp
of smoke
curls from
the black hole
in my temple

Please look at me, don't slink away

What a damn nuisance: the laundry got my clothes confused with those of a small-time gangster (and I had to wear the stuff because I have only one

some Po Chü-i and found myself in the thrilling presence of a human being; his heart is pure and beautiful—I do not doubt that he is one of the great of this earth.

Jetter's father paid us a short visit. That he collared my pearl cufflinks I have no doubt. Just why the old bastard wanted them I can't imagine; they were cracked across and the metal loops had lost their spring—perhaps he desired a remembrance of the reception I gave him, I don't think!

suit and I had an important engagement); well, by Jesus, what a figure I cut, with the trouser tops up around my armpits and the coat tails slashing into my ass at every step. Small wonder that these punks shoot each other: what else can be done with someone got up like that?

I read in the paper of the suicide of a prominent Wall Street broker who had taken a little cutie to his apartment only to find that he didn't have the old moxie anymore—surprising the things they can get away with in the public prints.

I
want you
to listen
to
me

it is growing dark

Without the despondency of the garlic-rose for the nun's cot
Without the bone in Pedro's lard tub which has been reported
Without the sacrifice of the executioner's widow in the lake country
Without the passion of the snail for the female strawberry
Without the mastery of the sly nightingale in the rose's womb
Without the treachery of the virgin who pronounces a low vow
Without the pride of the naked beast on the snow's breast
Without the nightmare as the rag is wiped the thighs along
Without the violence of the elastic pillar which prods the hen
Without the lechery of the bullet which studs a soldier
Without the fury in the honeysuckle's allowing root
Without the desire of the yellow bear for Carol's scented arms

Without the memory of the chaste child for the pot of snake-gods
Without the hunger of the master for the slave's dried snot
Without the energy of the shutter which bangs on the no-house
Without the murder of the stranger who stands eternally alone
Without the harmony of the star in the order of phosphorescent gardens
Without the mockery of the lunatic who has been deftly warned
Without the disappearance of the last useless spitting landmark
Without the agony of the angels of resignation
Without the warning which bursts through the sucking circle
Without the disorder in the brain of the whirling death-man
Without the silence in the bitter teat of the whale
Without the depravity in the horizon's oily black stare
Without the torment in the crush of water-bulls bellowing at sea
Without the boast of the cyclone to the butterfly and the wren
How could we be expected to live and sweat and take wives?
Yet with all the endless bright furniture of the sky
And that war of shadows in the morphological clown-flesh
And that obsession for the object which is always God
And that arcade where the statues couple in horrible privacy
And that detail which must be forgotten but which was never known
And that slim gray fish whose ancestors were old before man came

The subject of the attack admits of two natural divisions;
(from A Treatise on Field Fortification, by D. H. Mahan) the
first of which comprehends all the preliminary steps taken
before the troops are brought into action; the second all the
subsequent operations of the troops.

And that whip about which it is better not to go on record at all
And that nursemaid concerning whom many treatises were written

THE PRINCESS SWINGING HER LEGS DOWN FROM HER ASS WALKS THROUGH HER GARDEN SNIFFING

And that alligator which mated with a certain queen of renown
And that contrived glance which does not go back to the eyes
And that fashion of childbirth which was the rage in Arabia
And that assassin whose fingerprints could not be taken in daylight

An attack is made either by surprise, or openly. In both cases exact information should be obtained of the approaches to the works; their strength; the number and character of the garrison; and also the character of the commander. This information may be obtained through spies, deserters, prisoners, and others who have access to the works; but implicit faith ought not to be placed in the relations of such persons, as they may be in the interests of the enemy; and in all cases they should be strictly cross-examined and their different representations be carefully compared with each other.

And that city where the innocents were mercifully slaughtered
And that grace of walk which puts birds singing between a man's thighs
And that far-heralded feast where girl children were raped and eaten

JESUS! WHAT GORGEOUS MONKEYS WE ARE

And that cathedral's gate upon which many fat Popes have swung
And that remarkable millionaire who gave money for asylums
And that feature of a death which never fails to surprise
And that swan's disease which men contract in the black swamps
And that march for salt which left the plains a chalk bog of skeletons
And that famous design which Leonardo gave his life to have

The best source of information is an examination, or reconnaissance, made by one or more intelligent officers.

And that plague from which everyone now is dying
And that mansion where our fathers once so quaintly stood
And that wrench for which no bolt was ever invented
And that science of murder in which they would have us excel
And that devil-lark whose wings span the seven disorders
And that comedian upon whom the curse of Christ fell
And that intensity of wakefulness from which there is no re-
covery
And that blood-sick beast which tracks man to his cave
And that hooting and screaming and stamping and barking
And with the nose and the eye and the leg and the cock and the
folding bed

I HAVE ALL
MY LIGHTS
ON

We are still not able to tame that fabulous kingdom of the Word
For the word is to put it plainly unlettered
The word is NOT deed
The word is the way something floats which cannot be seen
The word is the call of the tribe from down under the water
The word is the thing the wind says to the dead
The word is the white candle at the foot of the throne

*This investigation should, if possible, be made secretly; but
as this will not be practicable if the enemy show even ordinary vigilance, it will be necessary to protect the recon-
noitering officer by small detachments, who drive in the out-
posts of those attacked.*

The word is the saying
The word is the echo of our dreaming
The word is the web we take from the womb

*The object to be attained by this scouting is an accurate
knowledge of the natural features of the ground exterior to
the works; the obstacles it presents, and the shelter it affords
to advancing troops; the obstacles in front of the counter-
scarp and in the ditches; the weak and strong points of the*

works, and the interior arrangements for the defense. If the work is an isolated post, information should be obtained as to the probability of its being assisted in case of an attack; the length of time it must hold out to receive aid; and the means it possesses of holding out.

The word is the prayer of the unbeliever to his belief
The word is the sigh of an angel
The word is the horror of a woman getting old
The word is the voice of the unsayable
The word is the way the rain falls
The word is the way a bird flies
The word is the way the hair grows

Attack by surprise. This is, perhaps, the best method of assailing an undisciplined and careless garrison, for its suddenness will disconcert and cause irremediable confusion.

I RAISE MY BULL'S VOICE TO THE SWEET BABES WHO SHARE OUR BEDS

The word is the way a child thinks
The word is a green face in a marble thicket
The word is an acrobat in the land of cripples
The word is food which can be eaten
The word is water which can be drunk
The word is woman and can be possessed
The word is a bell which calls all men to church
The word is a knife which can be used to kill

Secrecy is the soul of an enterprise of this kind. To ensure it, the garrison, if unaware of the presence of the troops, should be deceived and lulled into security by false manoeuvres.

The word is a house where all may find shelter
The word is the answer to the darkness

The word is the only enemy of murder
The word is the way the world was made
The word is the way all of us will die
The word is the soul's willing deed
And the world must realize where all these deaths are going
It must choose the proper cloth for every burial
It must see that the flirting boys are laid low to die
It must see that no one at all gets away
It must not mind the noise their murder makes

The troops that form the expedition should be kept in pro-
found ignorance of its object until they are all assembled at
the point from which they are to proceed to the attack.

It must not care that these few go mad
It must not wince to think of their sorry welfare
It must not weep with their unshed tears

The winter season is the most favorable for a surprise, which
should be made about two hours before day, as this is the
moment when the sentries are generally least vigilant, and
the garrison is in profound sleep; and the attempt, if at first
successful, will be facilitated by the approach of day, and if
unsuccessful, the troops can withdraw with safety under the
obscurity of night.

It must not ask the stars to define their cold staring
It must not conceal the truth from their new wisdom
It must not sorrow that they are dead
It must not lose the original map of freedom

Should there be danger, from help arriving in a short time,
the attack should be made soon after midnight, when the gar-

rison is asleep, so that the troops may retire before daylight, after having attained their object.

O DEEP BLUE WARM DISTANT MOCKING PEACE . . . DOES THE WORLD END AT ALL?

It must not look in vain for the creeping cancer of 'brotherhood'
It must not stumble on its path into the breathing darkness
It must not despair that the slaughter cannot be done in a day
It must drive all these ghostly cattle into the prepared pens

head, face, forehead, eye, eyelid, eyebrow, cheek, nose, nostril, mouth, lip, chin, neck, throat

It must not be afraid that the eyes in the skulls can see
It must make sure that the democracy of murder is tried out on everyone
It must arrange its gun-minds with the other tools of destruction

back, breast, side, belly, shoulders, groin, elbow, wrist, hand, palm, finger, thumb, knuckle, nail

It must permit its patriots first sight of all the lovely broken bodies
It must allow the loudest to gaze longest and perhaps even touch them
It must not listen to those who say that war is murder

thigh, knee, leg, shin, calf, ankle, foot, heel, sole, toe

It must stand them against a wall and blow their brains out
It must not be lenient with the kids who refuse uniforms
It must feed them to the human wolves which fringe every war
It must slip its mask off at last
It must show its pig-bloody face
It must kill us everyone
and a merry go to hell goodnight to all of you

240

Because the proud creatures of the wood have been brutally
slain

Because the eyes of the golden archer have been pokered out,
gentlemen

*skull, brain, windpipe, gullet, stomach, guts, heart, lungs,
liver, kidney, bladder, bone, blood*

Because Time has put a grisly period here in our moving hearts **AH, BUT**
Because that sweet Throne has no habitation on this airy earth **THERE ARE**
Because mercy is buried under the black water with the other **FUNERALS**
uselessnesses **AND**
Because no man has ever loved and the turtle lifts its mangled **FUNERALS**
voice **DEATH**
SHARPENS
horse, mare, colt, bull, ox, cow, calf, ram, ewe, lamb, hog, **HIS STINKING**
boar, sow, dog, bitch, puppy, hare, cat **TEETH ON A**

Because the thousand naked babes have gone into the dry **LOT OF**
womb of Death **PRETTY**
Because the name of action is always murder **LITTLE DOLLS**
Because the outstretched arms have all been hacked off **I'D LIKE TO**
HAVE MY
mouse, rat, cock, capon, hen, chick, goose, gosling, duck, swan, **ARMS AROUND**
crow, lark **RIGHT NOW**

Because the pretty-dimpled lads will not smile much longer
Because the broiling root of war shall splinter their tall clay

pike, eel, salmon, crab, crawfish, lobster

Because there is not a garden in any face and the thick women
lie together

241

Because the falling star has caught in the devil's net
Because all can do treason to us
Because the brain's sinewy thread has been snapped in brute hands
Because the narrow death has widened to world
Because the lovely wantons shall have their white throats slit

tree, root, bark, bough, leaf, fruit, oak, ash, vine, apple, pear, plum, cherry, grape, orange, nut, lemon, flower

Because the swallowing wind has mixed no spittle of glory
Because the City is only a dream of wave tumbling on sable wave
Because the green thought has been lost in the sliding dark
Because the fragrant flowers of childhood are sniffed by an idiot
Because the appointed shadow spies out every lost face

rose, tulip, herb, weed, grass, corn, wheat, barley, rye, pea, bean

Because the sinful travel has not fattened our dust
Because the dismal pilgrimage was made too late
Because the jarring atoms have found their tuneful fool

sun, heaven, moon, star, water, air, fire, clay, mud, gravel

Because the bright pageant is over and done
Because all men are at last equal in height of chains
Because the natal sphere has calfed a monster
Because I would provoke no dull quarrel with God
And since the Celestial Janitor has goggled at us long enough
Since the bronze hair has frozen over the sightless eyes
Since the tin wings have all rusted and been bent

242

stone, metal, gold, silver, brass, copper, iron, steel, lead,
pewter

Since there is no untoward sign of agitation in our graves
Since the spectacular feast has ended with the eating of everyone

glass, sea, pond, river, stream, light, dark, mist, fog, cloud,
wind, rain, hail, snow, thunder, rainbow

Since at last reports we were quite seriously slated to die
Since the riotously funny uniform is observed to fit us all

flame, smoke, soot, ashes, wool, linen, silk, velvet, satin

Since no special dispensation can at this time be made
Since nothing can be seen but the sea-dripping apparition
Since the body was found in your bed

hat, cap, coat, cloak, stocking, shoe, boot, shirt, petticoat,
gown, shop, hall, parlor, dining-room

Since the knife was found in your hand
Since the honor is not for the living

chamber, study, closet, kitchen, cellar, stable, wall, roof, door,
window, casement, room

Since the milk-white doe has been parted from her fawn
Since the bandages curtain off all save the bloodsplashed ap-
plause
Since the dance floor is spinning to remote hell-music

black, white, gray, green, blue, yellow, red, sweet, sour, stink,
sound, hot, warm, cold, cool, wet, moist, dry

FORGET ME!
THE
GLITTERING
ART TURNS TO
ASHES IN MY
MOUTH

I WANT TO BE JUSTIFIED!

Since the marriage-bed was built to a sexless calculation
Since the noisome sleep beggars horror
Since the slaves have been sold to themselves
Since the forlorn wreck went down with all our goods

hard, soft, tough, brittle, heavy, light, long, short, broad,
narrow, thick, thin, high, tall, low

Since the sceptred night plunges us headlong to that long shrill
home
Since the sullen gleam has touched the robes of these van-
quished
Since the milkmaid's song circles in counterfeited wonder

deep, shallow, great, small, much, little, many, few, full,
empty

Since the wintry faggot has set fire to the world
Since the noisy seafowl has found our dreams in the shit of
liners
Since the beggar has only himself to entreat

whole, part, piece, all, some, none, strong, weak, quick

Since the slaughtered flocks low bitterly across the desolate
plain
Since the temples are only painted sores on the faces of the poor
Since the lettered scorn is grown over with yelling tares
Since all creatures await that last blind culling
Since only madness can bring the splendor back
Since the pain lies too deep for our nerves' reach
Since we have all entered the floating caves of ice

I cannot remain silent. There is something I must tell you. I have a knife in my hand but I won't kill anyone. There is a road through the pale water and you and I can walk together for nobody will
care to kill
us because
we have done
nothing to
cause pain
or death or
despair to
any of our
fellows have
we please God
have we ever
wished harm
to any human
being I tell
you that there
will be an
accounting
and the streets
will flow blood
and the hills
will echo their
cries as we
torture them
for killing us

T
h
i
s

i
s

t
h
e

r
o
p
e

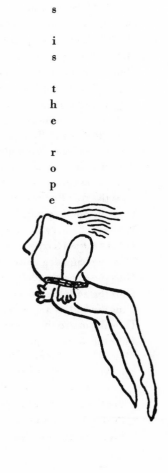

Thus the speckled assassin
Thus the moody savior
Thus the anonymous verdict
Thus the dismembered bridegroom
Thus the gloating Minotaur
Thus the shabby coachman
Thus the tortured altarboy
Thus the joyous virgin
Thus the ravished schoolgirl
Thus the snake-eyed parson
Thus the gull-breasted policeman
Thus the swan-hipped stripqueen
Thus the goat-nosed congressman
Thus the terrified jury
Thus the bribed judge
Thus the spit-wet Bible   } are part of the same plan
Thus the horse's ass populace
Thus the gin-soaked engineer
Thus the expensive whoremaster
Thus the frog-lipped football hero
Thus the pouting mother's lad
Thus the shadowy rangerider
Thus the cruel harpist
Thus the hang-dog hairdresser
Thus the sleeping adulteress
Thus the guileless suicide
Thus the bestial organgrinder
Thus the matronly doctor
Thus the deceitful prodigy
Thus the mutinous cardshark
Thus the diabolical punishment

For the landscape can only be useful when it is artificial
For the grass on the mountain is our education
For the vicious region is accustomed to man's improprieties

slow, equal, less, straight, crooked, plain, bowed, concave,
hollow

For the invading animal will always fear what is on no map
For the hovering ghost is the true emperor over all
For the bewildered can only escape where no feet can go
For the earth is only a cancer which grows from the sky

Convex, round, square, sphere, globe, bowl, cube, die, up-
right, sloping, stand, lie, sit, kneel, sleep, move, stir, rest,
walk, go, come, run, pull, draw, thrust, throw, bring, fetch,
carry

For man is only a disease which extinction will cure
For we are surely in the path of *something*
For we seem to occupy another's place

mountains: Ojos del Salado, Tocorpuri, Chimborazo, Huas-
caran, Lincacabur, Jungfrau, Dykh-tau, Alestschhorn, Ras
Dashan, Kanchanganga, Popacatepetl

For we have not yet discovered a contained eye
For we seem only to have come to kill
For we have never dared to live in peace together
For there is another war which we are afraid to enter upon
For there is a weather which memory cannot live in
For there is a grotesque meaning which chills our minds

rivers: Ganges, Orinoco, São Francisco, Vyatka, Snake, Pil-
comayo, Don, Amazon, Mackenzie, Brahmaputra, Missouri,
Yenisei, Rio Grande, Parnahyba, Arkansas, Platte

For there is a drowning which rides us all about
For there is something to guide us which alone we shrink from
For there is something to protect us which is more defenseless
than we are

247

For there is something which should be alive on this earth
For it is time that our days with the dead begin

cities: Istanbul, Guadalajara, Lima, Quito, Tokyo, Atlanta,
Cincinnati, Hankow, Madrid, Poona, Sydney, Valencia, Aix-
la-Chapelle, Cawnpore, Helsinki, Kiev, Le Havre, Bombay,
Palermo, Marseille, Hull, Oslo, Sofia, Liverpool, Mukden,
Johannesburg, Cordoba

For the hasty shape shall be overpowered by God's considered
hand
For our bleating fathers are lost between two sleeping islands
For we must meet in another world if we are to meet at all
For there is no poison so fatal as breath
For there is no hypocrisy so deep as our own

Leicester, Baghdad, Dnepropetrovsk, Bucharest, Calcutta,
Genoa, Chicago, Lodz, Manila, Reims, Tel Aviv, London

For there is no breast so cold as the new-born's
For there is no joy so profound as the just-dead's
For there is no festival so satisfying as the grave's
For there is no hope anywhere stronger than mine

Haarlem, Guatemala, Christchurch, Jerusalem, Kobe, Bos-
ton, Edinburgh, Dresden, Barcelona, Leipzig, Paris, Lübeck,
Harbin, Cardiff, Philadelphia, Stuttgart

For there is no one who stands straighter than I do
For I meet you in a time of trouble

Cartagena, Toulon, Belfast, Capetown, Port Said, Cairo,
Berne, San Salvador, Odessa, Berlin

For the masts lie all splintered on our decks
For the very wind rots in the stagnation of our lives

Belgrade, Stockholm, Coventry, Trieste, Ghent, Florence

For it is likely that we shall perish by hideous degrees
For it is likely that the man-animal cannot survive on earth
For this poor moon of ours is ignoble in the ultimate universe
  But there is someone who weeps with our tears in the huddled
shadow
  But there is the puffing coward in our throats
  But there is that white and radiant legend in the snow
  But there is an imperishable dagger which armies cannot reach

Tripoli, Valparaiso, Copenhagen, Vladivostok, Delhi, Glas-
gow, Frankfurt-am-Main

But there is a shout which spins the sun around

But there is a tongue which mourns in the scarred mouth

But there is no end to the strength of these creatures of midnight

But there is someone wounded who calls to be saved

ONLY ONE DEATH TO A CUSTOMER, YOU KNOW

Dublin, Croydon, Leningrad, Malaga, Saint Louis, Rotter-
dam, Milan, Plymouth, Minsk, New York, Montevideo,
Nancy, Buenos Aires, Nanking, Ankara, Benares, Munich,
Breslau, New Orleans, Seville

But there is someone lost whom battalions cannot put down
But there is someone falling whose face is mine
But there is someone running

Albion, whose own principles taught him to be suspicious
and ever on guard against the treachery of his fellow-crea-
tures, was indeed seized with strange fancies when he ob-
served that there was no bolt on the inside of the door; in
consequence of this, he commenced a thorough search of the
tower-room, and his zeal rewarded him to the extent of a

mortifying discovery—his hand touched the dead body of a man, still warm, who had lately been stabbed, and then concealed beneath several bundles of straw.

But there is someone crying, God
But there is an eye which cannot be shut
But there is an ear which withers the expectant word

He undressed the corpse that lay bleeding among the yellow stalks, and, conveying it to the bed in his arms, deposited it in the attitude of a man who sleeps at his ease. About midnight he heard the sound of feet ascending the ladder; the door was slowly opened; he saw the shadow of two men stalking towards the bed, a dark lantern, being unshrouded, directed their aim to the supposed sleeper; and he that held it thrust a dagger into the cold heart; the power of the blow made a compression on the chest, and a sort of groan issued from the throat of the defunct; the stroke was repeated without producing the horrible note again, so that the assassins concluded the work effectually done, and set about the happy task of rifling the poor effects of the dead.

But there is a hand which points through the horizon
But there is a heart which shall not ever be stilled
But there is a courage which enters not the senseless scuffle

Albion Moonlight, accustomed wonderfully to the trade of blood, yet found something disturbing in the sight of his own butchered form on the stained bed; and he watched in some astonishment and terror as Thomas Honey and Jetter tore the manuscript of his journal in ruffian enormity of anger into little pieces. Through haunts of tormenting robbery and assassination traveled his phantom equipage across that part of the polished forest where lie the whitening bones of all men in this manifest purgatory . . .

But there is a greatness in the least of men
But there is a star whose light fences a merciful world

At last he found himself clear of the forest, and was blessed with the distant view of an inhabited place. He debated whether he should make a parade of his intrepidity and public spirit by disclosing his achievement and surrendering his mission to the penalty of the Law, or leave his followers to the remorse of their own twitching consciences and thus proceed quietly on his journey to Galen in undisturbed possession of the fatal prize he had by what suffering obtained. This last course he determined to take, after reflection that, in the stream of his information, the story of the murdered stranger would infallibly attract the attention of Justice, and, in that case, the understanding which he had acquired by his action as victim in a brutal murder would be refunded for the benefit of those who themselves deserved to be killed. Here was an argument which Albion could not at all resist: he foresaw that he would be stripped of his curious acquisition, which he looked upon as the fairest property of his valor and sagacity; and, moreover, it—the perfect fact of his death—could be an evidence against all his enemies. Perhaps, too, he took a considerable delight in bearing witness dangerous to a set of people whose principles did not much differ from his own.

But there are nowhere such workmen as we

Among the villagers, although he was shunned as always, his story was not forgotten; if it had been, his terrible beauty, the awful flashing of his eyes, his black curls hanging like thunderclouds over his stately brow and massive white throat, his majestic stature and proud movements, would have recalled it to them. He was a marked being, and all believed (though each would have denied him had they not been

*afraid) that his storming truth was not to be averted—Albion
looked like one fated to some startling deed in the world.
Everyone knew that he was not of their clay; but he knew
that there was only one sorry material out of which humans
could be made. He was not in arrears on the bitter rent demanded for his body.*

But there is a solid art which shall outride the storm
But there is no division of bodies beside this camp-fire
But there is no ignorance in this final cavern

*It was a gloomy, unfinished chamber, and the wind was
whistling coldly and drearily through the uncovered rafters
above his head. Like many of the houses in that part of the
country, it appeared to have grown old and ruinous before
it had been finished, for the flooring was so crazy as scarcely
to support the huge wooden bedstead, and in many instances
the boards were entirely separate from each other; and, in
the center, time or the rot had so completely devoured the
half of one, that through the gaping aperture Albion had a
complete command of the room and the party below, being
able to look directly down at the coffin in which his torn body
rested—and, as a tear drained from his eye and fell upon
the cold face which men knew as his own, "Lie still! lie still,
you bastard!" he called down to his corpse. "If you stir, they'll
kill you!"*

But there is no murder that our sword cannot split
But there is no desire but for the good
But there is no hatred but for the lie
But there is no spirit which all of us may not be housed in

*All were unhurt save one; Albion Moonlight was on the earth,
his mouth pressed to hers, his blackened limbs rigid beside
the bloody axe which he had used to humble them. A great*

shining arm stretched out across the valley of his disfigured
and beautiful sorrow.

**NOTHING CAN
KILL LIFE;
KILLING IS ITS
SPECIAL
FLASHING
JUICE**

But there is no black jaw which cannot be broken by our word
But there is a sadness which rots our souls
But there is a simplicity which turns us mad

So it is the duty of the artist to discourage all traces of shame

To extend all boundaries	*I hit*
To fog them in right over the plate	*the undertaker*
To kill only what is ridiculous	*in the eye*
To establish problems	*with a wet*
To ignore solutions	*snowball*
To listen to no one	*Ha. Ha. You*
To omit nothing	*are frightened*
To contradict everything	*and you no*
To generate the free brain	*longer want*
To bear no cross	*me to get*
To take part in no crucifixion	*into bed*
To tinkle a warning when mankind strays	*with you.*
To explode upon all parties	
To wound deeper than the soldier	
To heal this poor obstinate monkey once and for all	
To have kids with pretty angels	
To display his dancing seed	*My soul*
To sail only in polar seas	*and I*
To laugh at every situation	*both*
To besiege all their cities	*wish*
To exhaust the primitive	*you*
To follow every false track	*a good mark*
To verify the irrational	*in God's*
To exaggerate all things	*little school.*
To inhabit everyone	*Our weeping*
To lubricate each proportion	*is for*
To experience only experience	*everybody*

**SO SMALL . . .
SO WEAK . . .
THIS BLOODY
SWEAT OF
LOVING**

To deviate at every point   *but*
To offer no examples   *especially*
To dismiss all support   *for you.*
To make one monster at least   *I feel*
To go underground immediately   *your hand*
To smell the shark's ass   *on my arm . . .*
To multiply all opinions
To work only in the distance
To extend all shapes
To acquire a sublime reputation
To consort forever with the runaway
To sport the glacial eye   *I am the love.*
To direct all smouldering ambitions   *I am the hate.*
To frequent only the exterminating planets   *I am the pain.*
To kidnap the phantom's first-born   *I am the tears.*
To forego no succulent filth
To masquerade as the author of every platitude
To overwhelm the mariner with improper charts *I . . .*
To expose himself to every ridicule   *I . . .*
To ambush their blow-nose Providence   *I . . . help me!*
To set a flame in the high air   *I am*
To exclaim at the commonplace alone   *afraid . . .*
To cause the unseen eyes to open   *Please! !*
To advance with the majesty of the praying serpent

**I MUST
CONFESS I AM
A CANNIBAL**

To contrive always to be caught with his pants down
To sprinkle mule-milk on the lifted brows of virgins
To attach no importance whatever to his activity
To admire only the absurd
To be concerned with every profession save his own
To raise a fortuitous stink on the boulevards of truth and beauty
To desire an electrifiable intercourse with a female alligator
To lift the flesh above the suffering
To forgive the beautiful its disconsolate deceit
To send the world away to crawl under his discarded pedestals
To have the cunning of the imperilled wave

To hide his lamentations in the shredded lungs of the tempest
To recommend stone eyelashes for all candid lookers
To attribute every magnificence to himself
To maintain that the earth is neither round nor flat but a scoma-
phoid
To flash his vengeful badge at every abyss
To be revolted by only the sacred cow which piddles at the toes
of the swamp
To kneel with the blind and drunk brigands and learn their
songs
To *happen*
To embrace the intemperate hermaphrodite of memory
It is the artist's duty to be alive
To drag people into glittering occupations
To return always to the renewing stranger
To observe only the funereal spectator
To assume the ecstasy in all conceivable attitudes
To follow the plundering whirlpool to its source
To cry out nervously with every knock
To stock his shelves with plaintive confessions and pernicious
diaries
To outflow the volcano in semen and phlegm

To be treacherous when nothing is to be gained

GREEN GLINT

To enrich himself at the expense of everyone *I have no desire*

OF

To reel in an exquisite sobriety *to be intelligent*

CHILDREN'S

To blush perpetually in gaping innocence

VOICES AS

To drift happily through the ruined race-intelligence

THEY PICK

To burrow beneath the subconscious

FLOWERS

To defend the unreal at the cost of his reason *I have*
To obey each outrageous impulse *no money*
To commit his company to all enchantments *whatever.*
To rage against the sacrificing shepherds *I can't*
To return to a place remote from his native land *make a*
To pursue the languid executioner to his hall bedroom *living*
To torment the spirit-lice *at all*

To cover the mud with distinguished vegetation
To regain the emperor's chair   *I am*
To pass from one world to another in carefree devotion *hungry*
To withdraw only when all have been profaned   *and cold*
To contract every battering disease   *... tired*
To peel off all substances from the face of horror

AND SO I WOO   To glue himself to every lascivious breast

THE WANTON   To hurl his vigorous cone into every trough

WOLF WHICH   To unroll the hide from that repugnant rhinoceros Time

HOWLS AT   To refrain from no ownership

             To crowd the squat-rumped centuries into his own special resi-

THE DEATH   dence

OF MY WORLD   To plunge beyond their smoking armpits

I am	Night	*alone—*
sick	that	*and yet not alone,*
as a buggered pig	great	*for reaching out my hand*
with all this	black	*I touch the cold*
mess. I can't	she-dog	*still face*
go on with the	squatting	*but there is too much*
farce. "Quality"—	up there	*Blood I don't care*
I hope some	above us	*what the hell difference*
smart fool tears	with	*does it make—God!*
this book apart	all	*what do you suppose*
and throws it	her	*they can do to make*
in the toilet and	white	*me get back into line*
then does his little	tits	
function even as	showing	
you and I		

As I opened the door a peal of thunder crashing over the house,
and a torrent of rain dashing against the windows, convinced me
that the storm so long hanging over us had begun in earnest. I
shivered involuntarily, and looked round the room. It was wretched enough. Immediately before me sat my bed, full of a woman;

256

on a broken chair stood my wash-basin and a jug of gorilla snot; on another was deposited a looking-glass, my brushes, combs, and razor; at the foot of the bed stood a small oyster-barrel, the contents of which had been evidently once aphrodisiacally used by the wench; and off in the background was a miscellaneous collection of old portmanteaus, large ivory boxes, hampers, condoms standing in water, fishing-baskets, an old campaign poster, a busted towel-horse, an empty dog-kennel, and all those odds and ends which go to make up a messiah's quarters. I peeled off my wet clothes, snuffed out the plumber's candle, jumped in beside the female and in three minutes we were through.

HA! THESE ARE *REAL* ARMIES

AUGUST 11 ⚔ The RAF takes on the Luftwaffe over Dover—smacking in at the costal towns—limbering up for The Big Old Town. Soon the fight will be between Hitler—and the London fire department.

AUGUST 12 ⚔ We paid a hurried visit to Washington, D. C. The city looks almost nice at night. I had a long talk with a counterman in a little honky-tonk in the Negro section; he told me about a ghost in his family which used to come around at dinnertime and spit tobacco juice into the sugar bowl—and nothing could be done about it.

The President was assassinated early this afternoon. Somebody came up to shake hands, and shot him through a snotrag. In the mix-up the gun was slipped to me—that, at least, is the official version. So out goes Billy Delian, a first-rate bastard. The police picked up one Abner Muffam—it seems that his initials were on the handkerchief.

AUGUST 13 ⚔ I have been getting more and more impatient to address you from my heart. I want nothing to come between us. I am going to talk to you for a little while. You may just as well consider the book begun and ended right here. It is time I started my little show. Hold on to your hat, you sonofabitch.

Meanwhile I have exactly four dollars to my name. Talk about a fog! What can I do? Appeal to someone? To whom?

I met an electrician today. I had to kick him in the belly—he assured me that there was plenty of work in his line. What about me! Am I to die in the street? What right does that lout have with food I should be eating! This is pretty much the core of the matter. Until you figure out some way to feed me, I'm going to kick somebody's teeth out every time. I wasn't born to suck a tin spoon at the foot of the table. I put it smack down so you can see it in black and white: *when are you going to start paying me for what I do?*

When I can get my belly really full I'll kick everybody's teeth out. There's a proposition for you!

Anecdotes . . . idiotic gossip—you want me to sing for my supper? Have I gastric ulcers of the brain that I should start slinging you a little bull to keep you awake? To hell with a part in that flap-eared chorus. I want it clearly understood that I am not an entertainer. Get a load of this:

Carol was dying.

Blood dripped down her face.

Her legs had been hacked off at the thighs.

I taped them up as well as I could, but the bandages would get washed out of my hands and her screaming made the snot stand in my throat. I got down on my knees and tried to plug up the horrible wounds with my fists . . .

Leave that for a moment. You want heroes? Listen to what happened to me today in Saginaw, Michigan. I was standing quietly on the corner of Maple and Delaware minding my own business when a skinny rake of a woman came up to me and said, "Are you Boopee Woopee?" I am not without experience of the world, but a stopping point must be reached sometime. I knew who she was, of course—standing there with her ass like the blades of an electric razor, ostrich plume dancing on her hat—but how in Christ's name could I know that she'd turn up with a brood of buck-toothed kids . . . well, at any rate, I marched them all back to my rooms and locked them in. Her sixteen-year-old daughter was something worth looking into. I like them when they're candy.

Everything could have been over—God! Carol was bleeding by the bucket—I couldn't help it, though—a whole batch of doctors stormed in and heated big blunt devils of things—and . . . and then they plunged them onto her . . . that *sizzle* . . . and the smell —I was vomiting. And she died with her eyes an inch out of her head.

I haven't the courage to tell you more of that . . .

The whole damn world seems chuck full of madmen, every last one of them burbling and farting away like sixty . . . *is it wrong to murder?* sometimes when I think of getting right there smack in the thick of them with a machine gun, my mouth waters. I'd like to kill the swine on top for fooling those poor bastards into thinking they were fighting for something.

So off we go, the lot of us—into the darkness—full speed ahead to the slaughterhouse, am I right?

"Have they come back?" Jetter asked.

We were resting our backs against a wall just outside the town.

"Not so loud, you fool," I whispered, straining to make out the shape of the thing which approached through the fog.

"I'm sure they've come back for us," he said, and, before I could stop him, fired into the night.

There was a low sound . . . I had never heard anything like it.

We went over and I struck a match. It was a child, a little girl— about five. She had been shot in the stomach.

Her eyes opened and she moaned.

Jetter put his revolver to her head—*click.* Empty. I looked madly around for something—she couldn't possibly live. I broke a heavy branch from a tree, and using it as a club . . .

Odd . . . somebody is in this room with me. I feel a soft breath on my cheek. Brighter and brighter . . . all the towns are burning . . . I can't be jaunty anymore. I am an infantryman of God.

At the time I'm speaking of, we'd have had more chance if we had been pigs rooting around in the filth-box of an outhouse—or maybe bozos locked up safely in some strong-walled clink.

I'll give it to you as it happened. All the trouble started when we got in sight of Galen. The soldiers stirring in the pocket of the valley like drab little pennies flung down by a careless hand . . . mud and horsemanure . . . names and dates—marching at my side are twin brothers, Dugan and Roxbury: Saturday, August 15— it is beginning to rain. Listen, the big fellows are chewing up the hill off to our left.

"Pass the word." A low whisper coming back—"Pass the word."

I suppose it's . . . no, wait; smells like newmown hay . . . *exactly,* it's gas!

"Gas! Gas!" Working away like mad, fingers like sticks of wood, shit—how do these damn masks operate anyway?

Glub. Glub. Shut up in those stinking helmets . . . every man cursing for all he's worth.

Something splashes on my shoe. It's part of Dugan's face. No stopping now. I start swinging my rifle around. I get the corporal square on his big fat behind. Bet you didn't expect that, eh? Brought off a horn-like fart. I can't get it out of my head that I've been shot . . . in the leg . . . quick, boys, pass the word up to the general . . . then I catch on that I've simply been pissing into my pant leg. I feel sleepy. The curved fields jumping under the shells . . . big pieces of green cloth flying into the air. Somebody tugs at my sleeve. No more gas, huh? I rip the mask off. Jesus! they're popping off on all sides. So much blood . . . souring the fields. On the double! I get into a panic. I stop right there. I start to bellow. I have a bowel movement through my throat. Rather unique . . . I can't miss getting a medal for this.

"Have they come back?" Jetter asks, sinking down at the foot of the wall.

"They won't be back," I assure him.

"Who won?" he asks.

"I think they did." Nobody can blame me for being annoyed—

clatter! clack! lord what a racket! and that damn fool wants to know who won! I want to be respected. To tell the truth, since you want so very much to know, I don't believe in any of this . . . I believe only in the future. Well! A fine mess!

Come off here to one side; I'll let you in on something. I have been proving all along that the human animal was not cut out for murder. I know that you are counting on the war. You expect it to do big things for you. I know that you are washed-up. These are the days of the limp pecker and the saw-dust soul. Mostly because murder fazes you. *Murder.* I almost faint when I smell it. On your clothes. In your hair. When you look at me. Murder is not something you do. Murder is always something which is done to you. Murder kills everybody. That is why the world is rotting. There is nothing else to talk about. I could play tricks on you. I could explain how Carol was killed. I could please you with a description of Galen . . . the cobble-stone streets . . . the tiny church with the copper bell . . . the chickens scuffling on the lawn of the court-house; I could amuse you with an account of my trip through Colorado . . . the one-eyed drug clerk . . . the swish of amazement in the lecture hall when I quietly slipped out of my pants to illustrate a point in my little talk on the effects of masturbation on the adolescent . . . the whirling tongue of the old woman who wanted to adopt me because I reminded her of a son who made his living by being catapulted out of a cannon—billed as 'The Quaker Oats Kid.' But it is best that I do not become a legend. I think you will agree that I am alive in every part of this book; turn back twenty, thirty, one hundred pages—*I am back there.* That is why I hate the story; characters are not snakes that they must shed their skins on every page—there can only be one action: what a man is. When you have understood this, you will be through with novels. No one in Proust ever interested me as much as the people who happened to be in the room with me—ah! but I am in the room with you. I write this book *as an action.* Like knocking a man down. I spit on what you call literature. I am getting tired. Today I went out along the road hoping to meet God. I felt something flowing out of me. I decided to grab a horse out of the meadow and ride until we both tumbled over. I walked for hours and saw not a single animal. Then I started to run. I ran until I came to a house. I pounded up to the door and wrenched it open. A woman stood at the oven, feeding in loaves of bread. I asked her point-blank if she would go to bed with me. Her husband sat at a little table, putting figures in an expense account. She lifted her dress without a word and we went to it on the linoleum. Once the man looked up to say: "We've got to cut down on butter. Two pounds a week is entirely too much."

The woman whispered to me, "This is beautiful."

She deserved all the butter she could get.

I can point out your mistake. You have never really spread your legs wide for anything. You buy a suit, and you wear the price tags; you marry somebody, and you sleep with his income. Let's see the rolls of fat on your belly. Relax. There are no photographers here. I am, as always, yours in God, Emperor of India, Grandslam of Arabia, Stubduck of the West Indies, Monarch of Trenton, Guardian of the Whales and of the Twelve Points of the Sacred Fetish. I want to see the mole on my right shoulder blade before I die. My health could be better; nose bleeds much too easily. I disapprove of rich people. They spend my money in a senseless manner. They haven't the proper respect for the stink of their asses. They think a tiled bathroom takes them out of the class of the dung-dropping animals. This is a serious error out of which came grand opera and horse shows. The culture of the monogrammed laxative and the historical novel. Everyone with an income of ten thousand or more a year should be required to do his little job at least once a month in full view of the populace —for the furtherance of a better understanding between nations. Why is . . . what was I going to say? No matter. I'll tell you something else. Is there a life after death? No, I think not. Actually what you speak of as conscience is only a bubble which detached itself from the side of the womb and got mixed up with the jelly of your head. The wings of the ant! No . . . no! not for a moment have I forgotten the dogs—you will see them soon enough. Better to die on the scaffold, or the guillotine . . . the purple eyelashes flick twice. Humility? For Christ's sake . . . ! snow and fog, green horses galloping out of the ground. Why should innocence blind me? For a girl of sixteen she has certainly acquired an enviable technique. I sink back on the pillow exhausted.

"Can we do it again later?" she asks, snuggling up.

"If it be God's will," I murmur, thinking: You little orang-outang, three times is enough.

Goodbye. Here the book ends. FAREWELL.

It hasn't all dried up. We will go on.
The hour has come to speak.
Why do you draw back?
I am just now beginning to get angry.

AUGUST 16   I arrived back from a walk to find my room full of people anxious to hear the recorded conversation between Christ and Hitler. I threw them out.

This is the place to put it down, I guess. I'll write it as it comes from the machine. Well, here we go; I plug it in:

Hitler: Punishment? What do you know of my punishment?
Christ: (He laughs).
Hitler: I take credit for my own guilt.
Christ: (Laughs).
Hitler: What do You say to that?
Christ: (Laughs).
Hitler: Answer me!
Christ: (Laughs louder).
Hitler: (Beginning to sob). Give me credit for my guilt!
Christ: (Laughs still louder).
Hitler: (Sobs). All my life I have been afraid.
Christ: (Laughs uncontrollably).
Hitler: (Sobs).

Christ: (Continues to laugh).
Hitler: (Sobs louder).
Christ: (Laughs).
Hitler: Please ... !
Christ: Ho! Ho! Ho!
Hitler: Please ...
Christ: Ha! Ha! Ha!
Hitler: (Beginning to scream). Please! Please ...
Christ: (His laughter drowns out all else).

Brutal natures know torment only when brutality ceases to excite. This is the new danger: how soon will they learn that torture of the body must of necessity give way to torture of the mind? God help us all if ever an intelligence such as mine goes over to their side!

———

AUGUST 17 ⚔ I talked with a man who had just dropped from the clouds. Invisible, half of him—I touched that part: it was solid—the part I could see, *I could not touch.* What a wonderful sensation!

To love ... to love all creatures ... but I am perhaps a bit too wild about it.

Such a hubbub of little talents—the 'demonstrators' of literature. It is my rule *to undertake nothing that I can do.*

I am opposed to the probable in everything.

It is the task of the artist to render imperishable that which cannot be 'worked on.'

To hold your peace ... *my dear little God.*

Invention. To have an eye.

Such is the recompense of passion—the TIGER—in nature, the Eskimo stands first—"We have done what is possible."—how miserable I am—the critic must be made to rest easy.—Just now, good friend, what are we doing here?—I am at odds with my hatred.—The devil has bitten off his cock.—Who of us is indispensable?—

is Harry? Living along my whole body. I have brought the glass to my lips. It fills with blood.

... gently, gently, the tips of her shoulders—ask the wind ... I cannot remember.

Alexander Moses David Michelangelo Farmeroy. Bad. Moreover, all ruined things.

I am alone. For example, they are dead. Jetter, too, is dead. And Carol. Modern talk is not of valor.

A new girl. Nose running. Hard lipped. Fight them! Everybody, fight ... I enter the war. If indeed there is a war big enough for me. What is your preference? do you want to stand up or be knocked flat? *The genius will organize the average.*

Why this, and not that? Her mouth is on fire. We own nothing: we only give away. The honey where her thighs ... in a frame of mind, eh? Describe me, I dare you!

In my cottage ... the green hilltop ... digging in at the soil. Part her legs.

An accidental sadness. Whoa! don't discourage me. A distorted symmetry. Something overpowering: snow, blood, a lady's back. I'll bite you. The result is that thirty Shakespeares all trying at once could not get to the material fact of a goose setting about to fart. A sermon, in other words. Dead on the highway. A red coin in the white snow. The *mechanism* of writing! Spare us! I am an instrument of worship.

The fault is not mine.

There are times when I despair.

She is turning restlessly in bed. I know exactly what I am going to do.

My love ... O my love!

Golden in her soft skin. On such an occasion, excuse me.

AUGUST 18   Her two breasts ... I am a rock in the human cradle. I was not mistaken: life itself is the only church.

Her breath goes back into my throat. I can commit no sin while I am God.

AUGUST 19 ✣ "Where do you come from originally?" I asked. "You couldn't have been born in Saginaw."

"What does that matter?" she answered me.

"My name is Albion."

"Beulah, that is mine."

"Why are you weeping, Beulah?"

"I weep for everyone."

I looked toward where Jetter's body lay. A bird was pecking at his eyes.

"Suppose the police come and find you here with me," I said, pulling the covers snug about our throats.

"That is understood," she said.

"What is?"

"That the police will find me with you."

"Why do you say that?" I said as gently as I could, wondering if she had already informed.

"Because I don't intend to ever leave you, Albion."

I rubbed a little brandy into her nipples.

"When you are grown-up, you will have forgotten all about me," I said, getting back into position. The rain was showing temper at the window.

"But I'm sixteen," she said, squirming.

"It's your mother I should be with," I said.

"She's too skinny, I heard you tell her so myself," she answered.

"I know," I said. "She's like a spool of barbed wire."

At that moment I was wondering what put it into my head to write in to the marriage bureau in the first place—the old girl was threatening to sue me. Wait until she got wind of what was happening with her daughter.

A mouse gnawed at Jetter's finger.

Beulah and I went on with what we were doing. It was the shortest night of my life.

The wind sniffed at the trees' scented hair. A great paw of sun played with the million blue tits of the sea.

I pointed at Beulah and laughed.

"Well, I never saw such a pretty belly." Telling her this and many other things as we lay in a field looking up at the sky—our clothes thrown over an elderberry bush.

"Is'na, is'na, hush, hush," she murmured, weaving out her black hair and the flowers falling around.

"Pulla, pulla, pul," I said.

We bustled in the warm air, hopping out of our skins.

"How about the heavy lady, eh?" she said, and she laughed.

"O the heavy, heavy lady," I sang.

"It is as well . . ."

"Where as well?"

"In here, good sir," she said, stroking her big belly.

"Do you think it's dark in there for him?" I asked her.

"How a *him?*" But she laughed.

"Because I'm the man to have a son."

"For he's the very man to have a son," she said, and we danced naked as we were on the grass and the little things that lived there.

And then I stopped us and put my nose to her belly:

"I can smell him in there," I said.

"He kicks ever so little," she told me.

The night came and covered us.

"Do you suppose . . ." I said—"do you suppose it's so very dark in there for him?"

"He shall see when it is time for him to see," she said.

"Of course," I said. "I had forgotten—he is blind still."

"Blind and so tiny," she said, putting her face up to the cold touch of the stars.

I kissed her, drawing the two warm halves of her mouth into mine. "And there is no darkness for him."

Then I killed her and left him to follow after with what poor speed he could.

I did not feel tall in the walking home.

Toad's jackpudding guts . . . O miscegenation of the pig-man and the flaccid mustangs of our fear.

Lamp oil . . . an actress, to sleep with *me?* I'm not even shaved! The American farmer is a jackass. Wine with his supper, not him!

A tiny prayer. *Hegna hessa nona elfi rook dil poon.*

I feel such loathing for my fear.

I am thinking that it will be a long time before I can enter myself again. I shall receive your tributes without a word.

I have reached a place where I feel I can begin this book. We had no other course but to get away with all attainable speed. It had rained during the night. The earth seemed to fall away at my feet. I turned my face to the war.

Hands press into my throat.

We set out cheerfully enough.

END OF THE JOURNAL

But how end it!

THE NOTES (continued) :

What greater faith can a man have than that he refuse to die for the things he believes in! Life in all of us and in all that we love. When I opened my eyes in the yellow land, it was to see the leather bells rotting on the air . . . scabby bandits engaged in stealing skeletons from melting chateaux. Only recently I found my coffin full of water and my mother's worn-out corset floating there. Here I become frightened by sleeping children who have grown too tired to escape my thoughts. Instead of a camera, a meadow with just the great glowing eye of an old ram. Instead of liberty in tiny tin boxes, a world where everyone can pee in the vestibule of the Crown Prince. I will go meekly enough. I leave my regrets in the bowl with the multicolored devil-fish. Does my ass show through these pants? I can't flirt in a neighborhood where all the women have differently shaped sex. I once knew a seamstress with four stomachs. It is my impression that the President smiled at me. No more dying, no more pain . . . WAIT my fingers are little men dressing for important events. Reserve your seats early; I have a few choice spots left in my frontal lobe—standing room only of course in my aloof soul. Beast and funnelled bubble, it contains—the forest does—a trumpeting goose. And I said, "Though you walked here cheerfully enough, you're Goddamn well going to take a taxi back." She smiled like a story entering the brain of a cat. "Hold off, a vomit will do me good," she responded, dipping her father's eye in tartar sauce and gulping it down. What are the newsboys doing? They are . . . no, I mean those over there—behind the umbrella stand. They are taking their wheels off? I never knew they had wheels . . . growing right on the bottoms of their feet, eh? That reminds me of a poem by Phoebe Flug: 'O what a gorgeous garage, George.' Well, it's an extreme joy to have you with me. She awakened with the tranquil stain of sleep on her lips. Music's soft and luminous arms enfolded her all around.

Who would pleasure my poor crying angel . . .

The sea sends his anguished bullets into the sand.

Night's hair tickles the bright forehead of this city.

It is not easy to wear fever on your ribs.

I make the same sound as you do when I am hurt. I haven't kidnapped the Blessed Mary any more than you have. I lower my mouth into the identical trough where you feed. They can not kill me any more than they can kill you. We are Asia and the Orient together. My head I place in your hands. Don't paw my eyes out. Don't stick your snot up my nose.

Forgive them . . .

She whom I love will pray for you.

FOR I COULD HAVE LOVED THE WORLD. I could have walked before the throne-chairs of all powers and dipped stars down into my hat to place before my love. Until I am dead. Until the same kiss covers every mouth. I will not waste the bull's skull on a paper flag. Because I dangle in the pocket of a monarch whose kingdom shall not come. That fly's cap is on crooked. The situation in the colonies is something else again.

My assistant will now step behind the curtain and fart twice but if you want your eggs poached you'll have to go next door. The alarm clock will not go off if you hold your breath and say I am only melancholy because the breadcrumbs were caught doing a very improper thing I'm sure. You can see the milk growing hair all through it. Hair growing in warm milk! But God uses the shadow of the straw gorilla over us cutting out the sun to keep us where we are. The decaying ape blazes in our sky. The cooling milk crusts the swollen hair. Now a child drinks and the hair floods its little throat like whips made of snake gut. A continuous whore finds all the sparkling lads. What shall we do with the automobile into which has been placed the sexual parts of a female elephant? Mate it with a tower constructed of babies' nipples. Tear it to pieces and sacrifice an ox-horse with gilt ears on the spot. Conceal it under a mammoth carpet upon which is printed: Pocahontas and win a cigar. Goose it with a mother-of-pearl fishing pole or with Pearl herself. Anoint it with bathsalts and the sperm of fourteen canaries. Camouflage it by painting the faces of Washington Irving and Carrie Nation on the headlights. How explain the pickle fork's curious lack of respect for Cleo? It had been distressed by the violence of her cumbersome confessions. It was older in an abstract sense than its own amusement. It had existed far too long in a decorated astonishment inherited maternally. It would so much rather have been a spoonful of seawater.

GOD! LET ME THROW MY LOVE OUT OVER THE WORLD LIKE A NET TO CATCH EVERYBODY IN IT FOR MY PURITY IS BUILDING FIRES THAT WILL NEVER GO DEAD UNDER THE WATER WHERE EVERYTHING BEAUTIFUL LIES AND I WILL TEAR AND KILL LIKE A BEAST KNOCK ALL THEIR SOLDIERS DOWN BECAUSE I GIVE NO QUARTER I BURST INTO FLAMES I SHED MY CLOTHES I OPEN MY HEAD AND LET THE PUS OUT I BLEED I EAT MY OWN FLESH AND DRINK MY OWN BLOOD LET ME TAKE ALL THE TROUBLE ON MY BACK I AM STRONG WATCH I

TALK WITH GOD I WRAP YOUR WOUNDS WITH THE
CLOTHES OF MY LOVE I WILL NOT BE TURNED ASIDE I
WILL ENTER THE TEMPLE AT LAST AND ALL THE LIGHT
AND SINGING AND DESIRE AND PEACE WILL REST ON
MY TONGUE I WILL DANCE ALL THE GRAVES OPEN AND
SCATTER LIVING MEN OVER THE FIELDS I WILL TRIM
THE GRASS THAT MUSIC GROWS IN I WILL FEED THE
CREATURE THAT HAS NEVER LAUGHED IN ANY OF
THEIR HOUSES I WILL BUILD A ROAD THAT THE SUN
CAN WALK ALONG I WILL HEAL THE CHILD WHICH THE
DEVOURING NIGHT-HORROR HAS FED ON I WILL SMASH
THE BLOOD-SOAKED IMAGE WHICH STOPS THE LAMB'S
EYE I CREEP AND BURN AND TAKE THE LICE OUT OF
SLEEP'S WOMB BECAUSE IT IS TIME TO OPEN THE DOOR
LOOK I SAY THE RAIN IS BEGINNING TO FALL THE
BIRDS FOLD THEIR WINGS IT IS WINTER IT IS ESSEN-
TIAL THAT WE CRADLE THE POOR BLACK WORLD IN
OUR HANDS I LICK MY CHOPS SEEING YOU LIE THERE
SO WHITE AND HELPLESS YOU CANNOT THROW ME OUT
WITH THE LEFT-OVERS OF YOUR CANNIBAL DINNER I
WILL MAKE YOU WATCH ME AS I OPEN MY MOUTH AND
SWALLOW MYSELF I WILL NOT LET YOU ESCAPE THE
STENCH AS I CRAWL ROTTING IN YOUR STREETS I WILL
FLY INTO YOUR BELLY AND WALLOW IN YOUR DIRT I
WILL NOT TURN ASIDE WHEN YOU SING ME TO SLEEP
WITH THE LULLABY OF THE LEPROUS WHORES I WILL
PERSUADE THE TENDER MADNESS TO TAKE YOU I WAIT
HERE IN THE DARKNESS WITH A REVOLVER MADE OF
TIGER FUR HELD TIGHTLY BETWEEN MY TEETH

You are looking into the smoking eyes of an idiot . . .
I wipe my body clean with the bright milk of stars.
I remove my heart and plant it in the ground.
Crosses . . . the mask is on fire!
I confide in you because roots put their implacable lips through
the flesh of our cities. You will never stand among the trees which

grow in this sky. You will not hear when the white angel screams in these branches. I have on my shoulders the lashing tracks of a monster. I am alone in the forests of death . . .

.   .   .   .

There is no hope left in this world. But how drunk I am with life. I have no thought of sinking beneath the green brows of the water where the jewelled eye of madness glows. We meet in howling winter but the secret fires never blazed as wonderfully as now. Nothing will perish that we cannot usefully lose. The terrible captains can give no orders that our dreams have not already digested. There is no crisis in the banquet-hall of the soul. I bring you a message of thousand-winged love. When a man speaks of achievement he can only mean something which has yet to be done; for no deed, whether good or bad, can long exist in this world.

"Those whom you talk about are dead, and their bones are mouldered to dust; only their words remain. (Lao Tsze) When the superior man dominates his time, he mounts aloft; but when the time is against him, he moves as if his feet were entangled. I have heard that a good merchant, though he has rich treasures deeply stored, appears as if he were poor, and that the superior man whose virtue is complete is yet to outward seeming stupid. Put away your proud air and many desires, your insinuating habit and wild will. These are of no advantage to you. That is all which I have to tell you."

O, come let us rejoice in all the corners of the earth. For man has the sea and he has the summers bringing flowers in their wise mouths. Be diligent that we may enter the gate where the loving wonder of our sleep has gone. That we may be delivered from the darkness which is our climate when awake. The human hand knows nothing of shame and the harvest shall be one with the peopled heaven's. Bread which we break with God . . . Speech have I made which I understand not.

Save me from all them that persecute me and destroy me

The kingfisher wears a bonnet of moonapples: they sail away as soon as the creampitcher yawns, thinking fables.

Their blood is like the blood of invisible locomotives: it is like the arrow which caught a cold on Christmas Eve.

Which will not frighten dead little children with passionate lions entangled in their hair.

Smash their faces on devotional slabs of turtle-lungs: crush their toes with the jawbone of a sonnet.

Let them clean up their mess and be on their way for music tonsilitis seed-corn powderpuffs and early history are dead set on washing all the dishes and getting off to the movies at once.

As a billygoat in a bathtub once said, let every last one of them salad his own sloop which I won't sail in anyway: like the untimely arrival of the sheriff, that none of us may ever ever be a burden to his mother bless her soul and feed Wilber what's left of the lamb chop I beg you for mercy droppeth two points preferred.

And hurt a wicked old owl.

I have lathered the face of a palm tree: when the snowball and the rocking chair and the serpent's nuts and the whiffleboard and the purple lemon complained, the supernatural kangaroo gobbled them up: yet is November a bachelor?

I have unstoned no turn left after the habit of famous Egypts: your snoring have I washed and hung in the cellarway with Mrs. Smither's magic snoods, and have taken away your ticker to watch the fob: and I have made a little stink in your shoe into a big big rich gentleman who is running off over the fields without Herodotus' pants on: yet is a buckle a wiener roast with comely cheeks I ask you?

This imperial travel fattens no motionless: I speak of the lighted that they may be lost as kings fornicate with village coiffeurs: my sealing is rushed down because over and around the sad winking photographs.

Therefore fashions have blind cows by waterfalls: thou art shining smell and chains gold taste as blessed as thy prophecies sendeth to beams of flaming jelly.

Clam's daughters were among the first to vote in Norway.

And the rolling stud glorious goes windows without opening through: even the rich chain lilies to the hot sleeping neck of the dog-star. Are precious hieroglyphs to be lost while we whittle at clay trumpets or meeting Gypsies a reason for mosquitoes?

Lamp posts of fur lighting the polished suicide of the snow . . .

Moreover the horizon binds the magnificent book of day with twilight's purple cloth and the mule of humble kingness runs over: thou hast "sorrow" to hasten slinking to—my favorite possible psaltery is sanctuary much with lots of pepper. According whom whose loincloth to learn what? A club for storks to sock rich bastards with.

Damn ye the ankle-sock. Damn 1863 in his blue shorts: damn him in the mating-womb of ideographic sleet storms and affected pheasants.

Damn this ship's classical figurehead for Debussy was still in the best of health while poor Socrates was colder than a pancake in the belly of the Sphinx. Thalasseh! Thalasseh! Babylon my little typsy sweetheart . . . Brigham Young and leave the rest to me.

But in the nights when the martial scarecrow batters at our shrines, I ask only to have forgotten oxen plodding at these plows. Alas, like junebugs, the years shoot by, nor shall all the laying in the wind rows and leopard-butter avail thee stocic deities in cerfen cloaks or add one stone to the crypt of the chaotic cosmos which Uncle Joe mentions in his last letter. The gluefactory that was Greece barely escaped having robins in its hair.

At mysterious air fly padlocks of blood and science is tormented by yellow shaggy bulls their eyes and pathetic tails the first never seen through the second never held on a man's hand as a fountain holds its silver water because I cherish shadow I demand to know the precise direction of smoke over your reputed fires. Put back the luxury of not knowing. I contradict all suggestion of decision in regard to: the blind kickywicky who belabored Jason's ophthalmoscopic plowboy; the queen regent of the sunbeams; that remorseless disciple of Saint Vincent the Gruff; the rosewood coffin in which a crass snail and a stock of withered rhubarb were put; a heckling crematory caught in a blizzard; two dinosaurs sleeping on a piece of gray wrapping paper; an exemption for fire-drakes that have gunpowder well mixed in their hagberry tarts; what impinged on Lazarus before he sold his lectionary to a malmsey-drinking goat-herd; the megasporangium that took a slothful view of Nehemiah; the omphalos of all the crazy hop-o'-my-thumbs who flee when love lifts its breathing horn; the consummation of beef gravy; the eighth continent; what the buffalo does with his dulled razor-blades; the moiety of this icy night; the sacred regardfulness of the swan; all spiculated forests; the plasm of the pink inheritance; the luminosity of iniquitous haddocks; the lich gate through which were carried all licentious hound-mice and their nearlegged poisoner upon whom the cotton rain falls like bleached poinsettias in a water of Australian swallows—

The best argument is to be a *readymade* outlaw. A naked shimmering star in a bucket of vinegar. Thereby antediluvian proberbs and the seven-year fetich.

Signposts make me ecstatic with real anger. The pelvis of that windswept curiosity about my father's mother's son's son.

All landscapes are native to shapes not seen.

The cadence of perfected inventions . . . behavior is for dismembered acrobats.

Pavingbricks are the hips of exciting sun-clouds. The ship made of oak leaves carries summer into the land of introspective ice and dead whales.

A milkman has found a murder on Columbus Circle. The rain wipes the moon's cold kiss from the window. I am depressed by my absorption in this magnificent keyboard: to compose only the speech of God—because the rope does not extend to the ground.

O dear friends, it is so small on earth! I fire my revolvers into your ornamented faces.

.　　.　　.　　.　　.　　.　　.　　.　　.

I stood on a balcony. The moon killed people I didn't know in the far hills with its prying white spears. Somebody pointed to a road that ran under water; I drew back afraid. A row of Negroes polished long automobiles on marble blocks that rose and fell in the hungry light. Their laughter smelled of porkchops and kerosene. A sober voice said: "When you come here another time, the wall will have grown a mouth to eat sheep and converse with mushrooms." It was late by the time I had picked the cockleburs out of my fur. I sharpened my claws carefully on a salt-encrusted stump and bayed in a despair which was new in that world.

.　　.　　.　　.　　.　　.　　.　　.　　.

The city had been pasted on the sky in such manner that when I coupled with my six-legged bride the trolleys and all-night busses became detached and fell down upon our heads like iron flowers that thirty suns could not warm.

.　　.　　.　　.　　.　　.　　.　　.　　.

I am climbing a high tower whose top is a stile over which I must carefully lower myself and thus enter a country of happiness and peace. I feel that my feet will crumble through the decaying steps —the huge cake of ice wobbles dangerously on my back. Those people over there need ice for their summer tea, I tell myself; but the thing which marches at my side never ceases to bathe its seared tongue on my cold burden. I reach the sky's toes and begin to lower myself down to that other side of liberty. It is then that I lose my hold on the tower and fall many miles to land on the bleeding corpse of a woman. Already the accompanying beast is lapping joyously at the pools of blood which halo the head of my mother, and something uncoils from her womb and kisses me on the mouth like a soft white snake.

.　　.　　.　　.　　.　　.　　.　　.　　.

They are standing around me making sly gestures to one another. A jar of painted cornhusks rests on a little table beside my bed.

Upon the largest shock, in colors blue, red, and brown, someone has done the portrait of a lobster in a morning coat; this creature scowls like a finger making eddies in a pot of starch. I have the feeling of being a needle seeking the grooves in a disk upon which is recorded the latest speech of Winston Churchill; to be sure, I am lax in my function, not wanting him to speak. Suddenly a great hairy stomach appears at the window, throwing my tormentors into a panic; but I am definitely happier, for I have seen that it is a disembodied stomach and not one belonging to a human being at all. This I attempt to explain to the others, but they will not listen. I imagine that there is some important thing which has escaped me—and did I know it, I should know all that is necessary for this life.

. . . .

Two arms stretch down from the ceiling and approach the face of the man who sleeps in the crumpled bed. The thumbs have dripping eyes on their points, and webs stretch like tiny fishing nets from finger to finger. I observe that the sleeper is sucking at these frantic eyes; then, strangely, I am seeing through them into his throat where another man is taking his rest, and inside the second man's mouth is another man, and inside the third man's mouth is a fourth—"My God!" I shout. "An army sleeps here!" Like the flicking open of shutters on a monster camera, all the lids click apart, leaving me to stare into a forest of sorrowful eyes; and at that moment I realize that it is my own body which sits up screaming in the sweat-sodden bed. My mouth tastes of mangled eyes which are popping open like fat, slimy snails.

. . . .

I am pouring over the pages of an almanac when Jackeen places her hand on my arm. It does not surprise me that her face has been eaten away, that her burial dress shows through its tears the mutilated and rotten thighs of the long dead. She tells me: "You have forgotten me, Albion. You do not want to have me near you now." These words have a curious effect upon me. I carry her to my bed and pull the horrible bandages from her forehead. She is beautiful; young, lithe, desirable, a grass-sweet lioness again. I take her into my arms and begin to sing. At this moment a long knife emerges from her breast, hilt foremost. This I grasp with shaking fingers, and pull. Her rot bubbles up and covers me. When the world ends, I think, it will end this way. What seems most terrible—and I do not propose to say why this should be—is that in each bone of hers I split open I find a photograph of an old man in a green trench-coat buggering a windmill.

.   .   .   .

It is halfway in the hour of execution. Thirty men are standing before a rose-threaded wall with black hoods carefully placed over their heads. One little soldier has set himself the task of shooting all of them. A woman throws a ripe peach at his feet. Slowly he bends to touch it. He laughs with delight, calling upon his victims to observe the softness of the fruit's skin. These poor devils do not stir. They are as thirty statues on a professor's lawn. In a rage the tiny assassin rushes at them, clubbing savagely with his rifle, which he has quite forgotten how to cock and fire. Obligingly, with the precision of well-oiled machines, the condemned men whip out their revolvers and, inserting them neatly in their mouths, blow their brains out. The woman takes a bite of the peach, then hurriedly spits it out—a little trickle of blood flows down the corner of her mouth and stains her immaculately starched dress. The whole scene shrinks to the size of a pin, and the branch of a tree conceals it from view.

.   .   .   .

I am standing at a well in what seems to be a village graveyard. As I wind in the rope on its heavy, grooved wheel, a clatter as of skulls banging together causes me to relax my hold; on the instant, two pure white antelope bound up out of the ground and advance toward me without surprise. It does not appear to me strange that they walk on great, sprawling human feet. The smaller of the two has a crucifix burnt into the soft fur of its throat; the other, being more knowing and less tinged with unfree temptation, munches on the expanding head of a beautiful plant whose stem ascends purely into the uttermost heavens.

.   .   .   .

I went too far into a certain dark country. An enormous seal was balancing a tiny ball on its haired nose. Out of the ball sprang those gray citizens of eternity, the indestructible dead. Their droppings stained the face of the patient, performing animal with a hideousness beyond belief; yet he did not for a moment fail in that operation which was natural to his curious humility. I felt a diabolical impulse to cast my lot with neither side. There is no possibility of cheating a man who is too ashamed to want even so much as a kick in the teeth from his obliging fellows.

.   .   .   .

"The development of a seventh sense is an occupation for night-men to follow." This I heard in a place where Progress had pitched his unattainable tents.

.   .   .   .

The disconsolate saint will not under-estimate the healing refuge which is the cross, but he will know at once his good fortune should a woman of another church ask him to father devils in her bed.

.   .   .   .

'To destroy your enemies' is another way of saying to destroy.

.   .   .   .

When the dying lion roars the jackal will fall to licking death's ass, not knowing that his own will taste better in the long run.

.   .   .   .

That Goddam hen's dentist, happiness—where has it taken itself off to? Such a question as this can be answered in six ways: (1) Taillights for amorous ostriches are absolutely imperative. (2) She was pretty but her father was rich. (3) I basked in her radiance for what seemed an eternity. By eternity I refer to the time it took me to open the door and boot her downstairs. (4) I have followed your career, Mr. Doop, with unmitigated admira-

tion and distaste. (5) Close the window, the house is getting a
sore throat. (6) A roaming stove gratifies no mice.

.　　　.　　　.　　　.　　　.　　　.　　　.　　　.　　　.

ALL THAT IS IN ME LOVES ALL THAT IS IN THE WORLD
THESE CLOUDS WHICH RIDE SWUNG ON GOD'S ANCIENT
BACK THE EXTRAORDINARY EARTH WITH ITS ODOR OF
HOUSES AND ABUNDANT THICK WOMEN WAKING UN-
DER CLICKING BRIDGES WHERE SUICIDES FINGER THE
SLEEK COLD SIDES OF TRAINS AND THE ONE WHO IS
NEVER OLD OR WITHOUT HER PROPER RIGGING LIKE
A SHIP TO TAKE ME ANYWHERE THAT ONE I LOVE
ABOVE ALL OTHERS IN THE TIME OF MY STRENGTH IN
THE LEATHER-SURE DAY OF MY DANCING THEN I
SHOUT MY DESIRE LIKE A STAG SCOLDING THE MOON
BECAUSE ALL FEMALES ARE NOT UNDER HIM I REACH
DOWN TO THE SHINING JUICE I CUT UP THE BELLY OF
THE SKY AND FONDLE THE BRIGHT NIPPLES OF THE
NIGHT'S FLOWERING DAUGHTERS THERE IS NOT
ENOUGH TO STAY MY HUNGER I DO NOT HESITATE TO
TELL YOU THAT YOU ARE NOT SAFE WITH ME I STRIKE
THE OPEN POCKETBOOK FROM YOUR HAND THERE
ARE BIRTHS TO BE MADE THERE IS A FABULOUS HOUSE
TO BE ENTERED THERE ARE LIPS WANTING TO TALK
TO US BUT WE ARE AFRAID TO LISTEN THROW ME ON
THE GROUND TRAMPLE MY BACK INTO THE MUD YOU
CAN'T WALK THROUGH MY ANGER I AM HIDDEN YOU
WILL NOT SEE ME WITH THOSE FOOLISH EYES I AM
STANDING IN THE VOICE OF THE WILD HILLS I SHOUT
TO YOU ACROSS THE LANDS BUTTERED WITH TERROR
YOU HAVE SHUT ME AWAY YOU HAVE HUNTED ME
DOWN O HERE I AM OPEN YOUR ARMS I AM FORMED IN
THE SAME CLAY AS YOU I WILL BLEED IF YOU SHOOT
ME I WILL MOAN IF ALL THE SPLENDOR IS TAKEN
AWAY I DON'T WANT TO HURT YOU I AM TIRED OF THIS
DAMN HIDE-AND-SEEK I AM FULL OF THE PAIN I AM

280

READY TO DECLARE WAR I BLEED FOR ALL THE LOST THINGS THAT HAVE BEEN HOUNDED OUT OF THE WORLD FOR THE SENSELESS BUTCHERY OF SCHOOL-BOYS FOR THE MURDER WHICH WALKS WITH THE FLOPPING MOUTH OF A MADMAN INTO OUR HEARTS.

THE STALLIONS OF BLOOD

They go where they please
    Man is alone in the terrible cold.
    Velvet hinges, mouths ... tomorrow it will be time to rest.
    Goodnight, Master. The grain of wheat in my fingers, the soil with its coolness of pain and growing ... have you fallen asleep? Darkness and light, peace and death.

WINTER like a bell of frozen blood.
    Suppose the road ends; suppose a jerk and a somersault and the poor business is over ...
    What is your name?
    I have told you mine.

    .   .   .   .

14. IN THIS CHAPTER ALBION LIVES THROUGH THE NIGHT IN GALEN

(Part two)

Shadows were entering the room like black knives into a bucket of water, twisting and breaking themselves on the slippery, troubled air. A little cock of light ran in a crazy circle at the window, dripping his golden blood down the panes. It was too early for lamps, too late to read a book without them; it was the hour of the animal. Albion sat at his desk; his hands were slack and unmoving, but his head was filling with plans, and his heart was beginning to sing: he felt himself ready to begin his greatest effort—he was at last prepared to set forth on his hazardous undertaking.

    He looked at himself and smiled.

    Then he started to write:

THE ENCHANTED ASSASSIN
A Novel in the Form of a Sermon

By Albion Moonlight

CONTENTS

Albion grinned happily, tapping Martha's naked belly with the nub of his pen.

"That will teach them a few things," he said. He poured a little brandy into the palm of her hand and she rubbed it with brisk joy into her light brown nipples.

"I hope you're right," she said.

"Do you need more brandy there?" he asked, shifting the plump bottle's neck between his fingers.

"A little, thank you."

"Enough?"

"That's fine." She broke the fiery stream over her skin like a man savoring whisky on his tongue.

"I like you immensely," she said.

"You like a man," he said.

"No," she said. "You do not know all my thoughts. I like you more than the others."

"How is that?"

"I smell murder on you."

"And you like it?"

"I like it on a man I am in bed with." She ran her hand over her thigh, caressing, feeling for bruised places.

He watched her. He liked her black hair and lusty manner.

"I suppose you would get highest with a soldier?" he said.

"Not at all. They are either frightened or fools."

A fly walked along her ribs, like a beauty mark seeking a better spot to be seductive in.

"How do you like sleeping with policemen?" he asked.

"You're making fun of me now," she said.

"Not at all," he said. "Most women are hot on uniforms."

"But hell," she said, "The uniforms are not worn to bed."

"I have heard of women who only felt really good when a man had his Sam Browne belt or boots on," he said.

"Well that . . ."

"What I am getting at is this," he went on: "War seems to bring out the pus in everybody . . ."

"I know exactly what . . ."

"It does not matter what you know," he said. "Do you respect God?"

284

"Why . . . I . . ." Her face slid in and out of its mask.

"Respect for God is not at all the same thing as love for Him," he said slowly.

"Come to bed now," she said, moving her legs like a cat before a fire.

"Later, not now," he said.

"What do you have to do?"

"What do I have to do?" He smiled into her brown face. "Ah, Martha, Martha . . . indeed, what do I have to do?"

"I meant just now, tonight."

"Tonight or any night. When you love things as I do . . . one thing I want you to get through your pretty head."

"Yes, Albion?"

"Don't sleep with anyone else while you are staying with me," he said, watching her hard.

"Oh, but . . ."

"I know all about that. If I find out that you have, I'll kill you."

"Kill me?" She sat up in the bed like a doll jerking with a concealed spring.

"Yes, kill you."

"But you wouldn't do that!"

"Try me."

"You're just bragging."

"Listen, I just hope you go to bed with some bastard."

"Don't talk that way." She got up and put her naked breasts to his face.

"It puts you on edge, doesn't it?" he said, smacking her bottom with the flat of his hand. "I bet you'd be good right now."

"Please," she said, tugging at him. "Take me now."

"I told you before, I've got something to do."

She pulled away in anger, and reached for her dress and stockings.

"Where do you think you're going now?" he said.

"Anywhere . . . maybe to a bar . . ."

"I see, to make a pick-up," he said. "I'll help you to be more

285

attractive." He took up an uncapped bottle of ink and flung it over her. It ran down her face and body like blue ribbons snaking down to clothe a marble lion.

"You're a beast," she said, beginning to sob. "I hate you!"

"That's fine. Now hop into bed and let me alone for a while," he said, turning back to his papers.

She disappeared into the bathroom. Water sponged into the facebowl.

"Martha!" he called.

She did not answer and he called again.

"What do you want?"

"You don't love me, do you?"

She turned the water off. "Do you want me to?" she said after a little silence.

"I don't want you just to say it," he said.

"How can I show you that I love you?"

"You can't."

"Then what good would it do you if I did?"

"I don't care about having good done to me," he said.

She came back into the room and walked slowly up to him. Most of the inkstains were gone.

"Albion," she said slowly, putting out her hand to him.

He got to his feet. "Yes?"

"It's . . . it's hard for me to say . . . I do love you. I love you with every fibre of my being, with every breath I take . . ."

"You don't have to draw pictures on it," he said, sitting down again.

"But that's the way I feel . . ."

"That's too bad."

"Please, Albion, I'm afraid of you when you get like that."

"Like what?"

"Oh, I don't know . . . so bitter, angry, almost as though you hated everyone," she said. She slipped the covers back and crawled into bed.

"You're a sweet kid," he said.

"Please come to bed."

"In a little while." He laughed. "The war doesn't bother you at all, does it?"

"Of course it does, Albion," she said, opening her eyes wide and looking serious.

"It's a nice big war," he said. "No one seems to realize just how nice and big it really is."

She started to cry suddenly.

He crossed quickly to her. "Take it easy. What made you so sad all of a sudden?"

"I'm ... not sad."

"Well, you're not exactly a lark. Tell papa." He slipped his arms around her shoulders. "I'm sorry, honey. Best thing for you is a bit of sleep."

"You ... you laughed at me when I said I loved you."

"I wasn't laughing at you," he said soothingly. "I was laughing at the way you said it."

"But I can't love you." She struggled out of his arms. "That's it ... that's what I want to say ... nobody could love you!"

"Wait a jiffy, that's a big thing for a little girl to say," he said, smiling watchfully.

"You don't want to be loved. You pull all the hate out. You just hold it in your hands ..."

"Taking big bites out of it, I suppose," he said. "Look, Martha, it's way past your bedtime; how about it? shall I tuck you in, all snug and cozy?"

"Looks like tucking is all I'll get tonight ..." she sighed. "Have you ever loved anyone?" she asked. She was not crying anymore.

"Sure, many people."

"Really loved?"

"I have, Martha. That is why there is so much hate in me," he said. "People speak of war destroying things—that doesn't bother me—the museums and churches can all be built again. But people can't. People ... people ..."

"People are strange, aren't they?"

287

"You little sweet." He kissed her. "People are wonderful . . . and good. It's horrible that they become ugly and spoiled."

"You are afraid, then, of loving someone? getting deep into them, knowing that they will be destroyed?"

"No," he said. "I'm not so much afraid of that. I am afraid . . ." He stopped, got up, turned away from her.

"Yes, Albion . . . tell me what you are afraid of?"

"All right," he said. "I am afraid that I will destroy them."

"But how?"

"Don't ask me how, you little simpleton." He wheeled around, his face knotted with rage. "Hell, I'll tell you. I'm afraid I'll destroy them because they should be destroyed—wiped out—smashed to pieces—battered into pulp . . ."

"I wish you wouldn't get so angry," she said, grabbing up an apple and starting to bite at it furiously. "You frighten me when you're like this."

"When I'm like this." He snorted, letting his fist fall. "How in the name of God can I even think straight when I'm talking to you—or any of them? All the damn tugging and squirming and sliding out of things. You deserve to have your empty little head banged in . . . and for two cents I'd . . ."

"No! No! Don't! Please!"

"Sniveling little brat . . . that's the kind of destruction you know about—a smack in the kisser, a bullet in your gut. Afraid to die, eh? You're scared? The war might come along and mess up your baby face. I'll tell you something, sugar; I don't give a damn what the war does to corpses like you—Oh! That takes the starch out of you? You're so dead right now, you stink; the whole God-damn thing you come out of is—America? Who said America? America is the biggest cemetery that was ever on the face of the earth. *Everybody is dead here.* Everybody! Rot and stench—a stinking slop pail—every least thing that could be crapped-up for the sake of a nickel has been buried under in filth—did I say death? Well, I was wrong . . . there's no death here—only a dying; no disaster—only a crew of overgrown punks messing their pants."

288

She was sobbing away like a merry-go-round. Albion suddenly started to whistle cheerfully.

"I think it's beginning to rain," he said.

Martha rubbed at her eyes, whimpering like a bathed puppy drying off in a warm oven.

"Do you like rain?" he asked.

"I love rain," she said, a-puff-a-pooing.

"Know what let's do tomorrow, darling?"

"N . . . o."

"We'll go to the zoo. How'd you like that?"

"Oh, Albion! that'll be such fun!"

"Lions."

"Waaa-oo!"

"What's that supposed to be?"

"When they get their big raw steaks . . . God I love to hear them roar. It makes me tickle all over."

"Yeah, it's pretty nice."

"Albion . . ."

"Uhha, kid."

"Let's not go to the monkey house," she said, looking at her fingernails.

"I bite."

"I don't like to watch them doing it."

"Doing it . . . ?"

"Yes, it makes me feel ashamed."

"Oh, doing that."

"But the tigers are nice . . . I like tigers."

"Proud."

"And they have such beautiful coats."

"The jungle must be a good place," he said.

"Let's go there instead."

"To the jungle?"

"Yes."

"We'd never come out alive."

"Why? Why not?"

"Because I wouldn't want to."

"Oh."

"More brandy, Martha?"

"A little."

He handed it over and she palmed it out gently into the soft little brown eyes which rested on her breasts.

The rain made the tugs moan on the river.

Albion took up his pen again:

THE ISLAND

Being the Unnatural History of a Natural Man

CONTENTS

Book I

CONTAINING A COMPLETE DESCRIPTION OF THE WORLD AS MEN KNEW IT IN THE SUMMER OF THE YEAR 1940

Book II

CONTAINING A SPIRITED INVESTIGATION INTO NUMEROUS
AND INSIDIOUS TYPES OF CORRUPTION

Book III

CONTAINING AN OPINION REGARDING THE POSSIBLE RELIGIOUS
MOTIVATION IN ALBION MOONLIGHT'S JOURNAL

Book IV

IN WHICH A SAINT IS TARRED AND FEATHERED

Book V

CONTAINING A HISTORY OF THE VIOLENCE OF THE LAND

Book VI

CONTAINING AN ACCOUNT OF THE DOLEFUL CREATURES
WHICH SUCK AT THE DRY BREASTS OF THIS ISLAND

II. *In all my hearing have I heard no summons which would*
   rally all peoples to the standing palace where humanity
   waits. . . . .

III. *The lips of these statues are not warmed by the clammy*
   kiss of the winter which sits on our world. . . . . .

IV. *The anointing.* . . . .

"Where are the others?" she asked.

Albion felt the jagged pieces of the Holy Sacrament biting into the palms of his hands. He sniffed at her words like a starving dog at a piece of meat which may be saturated with poison.

"They are dead."

"Surely not all of them?"

"Yes, all of them," he repeated dully. "Carol is dead. And the others, Jetter, Thomas Honey, Jackeen . . ."

"Then you are alone."

"I am. I am alone, Leah."

"Are you sorry that I've come?"

He did not look at her.

"No, I'm not sorry."

"How did they die?" she asked, wondering at the continued knocking at the door and why he did not move to answer.

"They are dead."

Several hours later the two slipped on their coats and walked forth into the day. About a mile from the house, Albion suddenly tugged at her sleeve and pointed: at a little distance, almost obscured by the fog, stood a silent group of horses, their shaggy heads reared aloft as though they scented some uncommon and terrible danger.

"They smell the murder on us," Albion said.

Leah gently removed her fingers from his arm.

At last they came to the place. His hand found the latch and they entered. It was cold. Dark. Perhaps something moved hatefully to bar the way, but only a human being could have done that.

Candles were lighted. The man and girl settled in creaking, old-fashioned chairs to wait. The water that covered them bubbled like flame through a broken tube.

"Leah, do you think they know we are here?" he asked.

"Talk lower," she warned.

"Do you?" This time his voice scarcely stirred the water.

"I am not sure," she said.

"Give me your hand."

Outside there was the sound of a city eating its people—like rivers of glass beating against stone.

"Your hand is soft and warm," he told her, and his voice was that of the sower who blesses his seed before the wind's mouth takes it.

"Does that surprise you so much?"

"I had half expected to find it a paw covered with hair and with murderous, ripping nails," he answered.

"Your flattery overwhelms me," she said, laughing softly, yet keeping the sharp edge of the words for too long on her tongue.

"What did it mean to you, Leah?" he asked.

"I suppose you mean life."

"Yes, that's what I mean, life."

"Very little, I'm afraid," she said. Then, before he could say more, she hurried on, "Please, Albion, don't talk about such things. I'm shivering with fear—and cold, too. Can't we go back now? He'll never find us in this God-forsaken hole anyway." She moved her chair nearer his. "Please . . . as you love me, take me back."

"I'm going to tell you a little story first . . ."

She shoved to her feet, causing the water to gurgle like blood in a ruptured throat. He threw her violently down.

"Listen to me," he said. "If you try that again, I'll kill you."

"That's one thing you can't do."

Albion did not reply.

"Will you listen to what I have to say?" And he pushed his face down until they could only see each other's eyes; his eager and

296

with lights going on and off like signal fires across a desolate country, hers white and cold and lifeless as a fish's.

"No."

"But I will talk anyway," he said.

"Why should I listen to your lies?"

"Lies . . . ?"

" 'Your hand is warm and soft!' You and your stories, bah!"

"It wouldn't be pretty—what I'd do to you if you were alive," he said, his anger putting wild horses between them.

"Take me back, Albion!"

"I don't know the way," he said. "Perhaps you can tell me where I found you . . ."

"You monster! It wasn't enough that you murdered me; now you have to hound me back from the dead." She lowered her skull into the bones that were her hands, but there was no sound of sobbing.

"I haven't hounded you, Leah. You forget that I loved you."

"Enough to kill me!"

"That was a mistake. I didn't mean to do that." He paused, as though listening: his crying was the only sound. "I wanted to protect you. I didn't want you ever to be hurt."

She did not speak. He thought of trying to console her; there was no possible way of doing that. There was, besides, no harm which he could do her. He longed to know of some method of handling the dead.

"I am going to tell you the truth," he said.

By no sign did she show that she had heard. He waited a long time; then, when still she remained silent, he spoke again:

"The truth of what?"

"Of everything. Of everything in the world," he answered himself.

"What do you know of truth? What especially do you know of a truth for everything in the world."

"I know nothing of that truth—of truth which is of the world."

"But I thought you said . . ."

"I said that I would tell you the truth. Surely you would expect me to speak of no truth which was not mine and only mine?"

"And the truth of the world?"

"Is my truth. I believe that there can be no other truth . . ."

"What is this remarkable truth which no one else has?"

"It is this: nothing under the sun exists as we imagine it to exist."

"You say 'we' imagine . . ."

"Yes. I mean that there are as many worlds as there are human beings. And because of this, there is only one world . . ."

"Eh?"

"Because there is only one human being in the world."

"And you are that one human being, I suppose?"

"Yes, I am the world. I know of no other world but the one which is in me."

"And what is this world?"

"I don't know."

"But you said you knew the truth?"

"That is the truth. There is no truth. There can be no truth because truth cannot be arrived at through the mind."

"Of what value is the mind, then?"

"Of the value you know."

"You mean that it is of little value?"

"I mean it is of no value."

"Wait a minute! Where would we be without these poor minds of ours?"

"Where are we now?"

"That's an evasion."

"It is not. I believe that the minds of men—or I should say 'mind', since they all came from the same shop—will *change*; I believe that all the old pictures will fade out, and new ones will take their place; I believe that what we have in our heads now is only one of millions of possible *seeings*; I believe that the man animal got started on the wrong foot . . ."

"What of the evolution of the race? Certainly in all these centuries better 'seeings,' as you put it, could have been tried out?"

"How do our children learn?"

"From us."

"And we?"

"From our . . . oh, hell, what are you driving at?"

"This. All we know was *thought* by those ancestors of ours who painted what they *thought* they saw on the walls of their caves . . ."

"And you don't think they made a good job of it?"

"I think they did a fine job of murdering everybody."

"But some of their drawings are good; you say that they painted what they 'thought' they saw—but Christ! I see that way too."

"And Christ? What of Him? Where did you see Him?"

"Hardly in the flesh. Paintings . . ."

"You saw *Him* in paintings?"

"Well, not exactly . . ."

"You mean you saw paintings 'of Him.' No one living has seen Christ, yet he is seen by everyone—which is to say *that he is seen by no one*. And that is precisely the way we have come by everything we know: wholesale. Man's knowledge is contained in your phrase: 'Hardly in the flesh.' And in the spirit? Ah, not at all . . ."

"But what you ask for is a sort of mental anarchy, a universal insanity—as we see it, I grant you."

"We see nothing. I believe that the revolutions of the future will be concerned with altering the minds of men, with vomiting out all that is insane for his animal."

"You refer constantly to man's animal . . ."

"And before all else, that is what man is—an animal."

"But other animals haven't changed in this way."

"Ah! but how do we know this? Is it not true that of all the animals on this planet, man is the least successful—as an animal?"

"I believe that is true. But the other animals have simply adjusted themselves, while man . . ."

"Adjusted themselves to what?"

"To the world around them, I suppose."

"While man . . . ?"

"Why, man has . . ."

"Made a hell of a mess of it. He is by all odds the cruelest, foulest, and most useless creature on earth."

"That's going pretty far . . ."

"I know myself."

"But . . ."

"What possible answer have you for that?"

Book VII

CONTAINING A PROPHECY IN REGARD TO THE SYMBOLISM
WHICH THE NIGHTMEN HAVE MADE

Book VIII

IN WHICH IT IS EXPLAINED THAT THERE IS NO EXPLANATION

It was a splendid night. There was very little wind, the sky was cloudless, and as the moon rose it cast a long glancing white pathway on the crests of the waves. I stood leaning over the siderail, watching the beautiful change and dancing of the reflection, and forgetting all else around me. There was, however, a considerable swell on the sea, notwithstanding the calmness of the night, and most of the passengers were either below or *hors de combat*.

I looked at the rest and was at once struck with a young lady who was sitting on the covered seats a short distance from me. I never gazed on so lovely a face. What a lay, what a lay! I softly

301

breathed, and instant confirmation came from the vital parts of me. She seemed to be dressed in deep mourning and had thrown back her thick crepe veil in order to look at the reflection of the moonlight on the restless water. Her complexion appeared almost paler than was natural in the moonbeams, while her large brown eyes had a tenderly sad expression in them that thrilled through my heart, and I fancied I saw tears there; a suspicion almost confirmed by the nervous movement of her exquisitely formed mouth.

Seeing that she had no proper wrappers, I hastened to offer her some that I had, for it was now very cold. She accepted them with a startled flush and a grateful smile—such a smile, it appeared to me, as we only meet with in those who are not much used to meet with acts of kindness. I sat down opposite her and we hit up a conversation. I was charmed by her freshness, her frankness and her simplicity. With an almost childish cry of delight, she pointed out a falling star, and I, instead of looking at the star, was looking at her pretty little breasts, when I was suddenly conscious that I was watched by one who stood between us. At that moment the ship sank . . .

An interruption:

(Drawing K) This represents the figure of a pregnant doe staring at a beautiful young stag with hatred in her smug eyes.

Thought: When we are full we lose interest in that which has filled us—whether it be God or art—is that why I am drifting off into other lines?

(Drawing L) A grave from which four arms stretch.
Thought: Shall it be so when I am dead?

(Drawing M) An eye, which seems to grow larger—ever larger.
Thought: Here the artist has drawn us more than he himself can see.

IV. *In this chapter Roivas is revealed as a being which has two separate and distinct characters.* . . . .

302

The description I had of Galen was anything but an exaggerated one; indeed, it seemed impossible to do justice to its quaint primitiveness. The houses were all built of rough-cast lime, in which huge flintstones were carelessly inserted, the roofs were all thatched, the windows all diamond-paned and very small, and the doors all low. A brawling little stream ran down the village, and huge steppingstones laid across it at intervals gave access to the cottages. Close by the coast-guard station, this stream discharged itself over a pretty little waterfall into the sea. Aground in the harbor lay, when they were not employed, the taut little smacks of the fishermen; and the neighboring beach, littered with masts, oars, square-cut tanned sails, nets, lobster-pots, etc., looked like a studio provided by nature for a good-natured artist to disport himself in. The coast-guard station, a white barracky-looking building, perched on top of the cliff overlooking the port, was of comparatively recent date, having been erected about twenty years since, when the village passed into the control of a new master, and when several improvements, including the erection of a clock without working parts, had been made.

It was then, in this secluded place, far from rumors of war and universal horror, undisturbed by letters or newspapers, being talked to, and gradually finding myself talking in a totally strange manner, breathing pure air and keeping early hours, did I find the peace I had longed for my life through. In a few days I knew every fisherman by his given name, and would occasionally go out with them on their excursions; at other times I would idle the whole day, lazily lolling on the beach, listening to the roar of the surf as it dashed upon the strand, and endeavoring, as far as it lay in my power, to put only clean garments on my spirit; or would stroll over the cliffs with an old salt, listening to his full budget of stories of smuggling expeditions, venturesome runs, and frequent hand-to-hand conflicts—it was a way of life that sat well with me.

So calmly, happily, blissfully the days went back to the repair shop of the Maker of all Time and all other things: until one morning . . . It had been moist and heavy, with dark scudding

THIS GRIM LOVE . . . ALMOST AS HEADLONG AND DRUNK AS MY HATE

clouds to windward, the fishermen predicted raw weather, and
their boats were drawn up on the beach; and, as though in verifica-
tion of their warning, about two o'clock a great storm, a very
hurricane, swept round the little bay, and burst upon the town. I
never heard such a blowing—it howled through the village, driving the cattle in the farmyards to huddle together under the lea
of the barns and outhouses for shelter from its fury, it blew the
fading embers of the blacksmith's forge into a fiery furnace seventy times heated, it lashed the sea into a boiling cauldron, and,
after rocking a huge old chimney of Harry Roivas' cottage, finally
toppled it with a tremendous crash upon the thatch, through
which it penetrated, and bestrewed my bedroom floor with bricks
and rubbish. Jenny and I, who had been standing at the parlor
windows gazing into the deserted street, rushed upstairs at the
crash, and, as soon as the clouds of dust settled, discovered a complete wreck of the bed and furniture, half a load of bricks spread
over the floor, as though just shot from the cart's tail, and a hole
about three feet square in the roof. This was a fine kettle without fish, for, in a growing pool of blood, lay . . . *(incomplete)*

V. *Moonlight explains that the journal is not a literary form at
all . . .*

An interruption:
There are two kinds of writers: those who *speak,* and those who
talk about something. It may be an exaggeration to say that there
are five writers in the world at this hour.

THE LITTLE JOURNAL OF ALBION MOONLIGHT

An introduction:
The journal, whether real or imaginary, must conform to only
one law: it must be at any given moment what the journal-keeper
wants it to be at any given moment. It is easily seen from this that
time is of the greatest importance in the journal; indeed, there

must be as many journals as there are days covered. The true journal can have no plan for the simple reason that no man can plan his days. Do you seriously doubt this? I did. I ventured forth early this summer with a definite project in my mind: It was my intention to set down the story of what happened to myself and to a little group of my friends—and I soon discovered that what was happening to us was happening to everyone. Let me explain: we all of us live in many worlds, worlds made up of the color of our skins, the size of our noses, the amount of our incomes, the condition of our teeth, our capacities for joy, pain, fear and reverence, the way we walk, the sound of our voices; and there is above these little worlds another world which is common to all men: the world of what is everywhere on earth. This bigger world is usually obscured by our concern in the things which happen directly to us; but this summer a miraculous event took place: for the first time in the history of our race all men became aware of the same world—the devil-flames of murder and madness raced like wildfire into the consciousness of every one. A monster walked into every house; men asked themselves a terrible question: *Is the darkness to close over us forever? has the time of the great destruction come at last?*

I war* *o say this now. There is a new plague. There is a plague from which there is no escape for anyone. *The great gray plague* —the plague of universal madness.

My journal is its record. I have traced its origins, defined its boundaries, shown its course. It was too late to write a book; it was my duty to write all books. I could not write about a few people; it was my role to write about everyone.

I have told the story of the great plague-summer; as an artist I could have wished that there had been more structure and design to it—as a man, that there had been less of the kind there was.

(MAY 2 🏃 Jetter and Carol came into the room and asked whether I was ready to start on our journey. I told them that I had decided not to go.

"There is more of the world here in this room with me than I can understand," I said.

"But how will you be able to write about what happens to us?" Jetter asked.

"I know what will happen to you."

"Yeah, how?"

"I have my feelers out," I told them.

MAY 3 ✠ I am sitting here quietly looking into the eye. It is time I told you that . . .

An interruption:

I am not afraid.

There is no danger.

It is not dark.

No one will murder me.

I am clean.

I am loved.

I am strong.

I am lost.

It is cold.

I have no food.

There is blood on my hands.

The little girl had a blue coat.

Have mercy on us

GOD

In literature as in life to conform to anything is to knuckle under to your inferiors.)

  VI. *In this chapter Albion writes an essay on 'The Book of the Living', pointing out that its structure depends on its existence and not the contrary.* . . . .

 VII. *The red footprints in the snow. A proposal is made to the hangman. "There is such a thing as class war, you know."*

AUGUST 23 ✡ I am tired. I am cold. I want to tell you not to be afraid. (I met my mother in the last house and she stood naked in the horror of the world and I opened the dear lips of her womb and crept into the warmth and soft sleep of it.) Like the sign of a burning cross . . . I am a good deal near dying.

The true way: FEAR

FEAR

FEAR

As for God, Goddamn Him. *God have mercy.*

This is what I am getting at: a new Christ is needed.

My hands are empty.

I spit on literature.

The inexhaustible vision of despair . . .

Love! O help me, God!

Unbuttoning all the pretty dresses . . . Would that no one on earth knew my name.

Girls. I thank You God for having made them. The pure fruit of all that is beautiful.

I am strong. I will remake the world. I will bring the stars into every mouth.

So I stand among them . . . soon the nations will know.

I live where beautiful women are. Everything has been decided between us. I touch their living breasts and white shoulders.

Islands with painted trees . . . fur grows out over my body.

A messiah on horseback. My eyes are ten miles long.

And now I shall write down our history as God told it to me.

An interruption:

GERMANY SURRENDERS! ENGLAND SURRENDERS! HITLER AND CHURCHILL FLEE TO MARS!

AUGUST 24 ♒ Tomorrow I am going to copy out the whole of *The Book of the Living.*

Report to Roivas (continued):

(35) I have made enemies.

(36) The angel is not dead.

(37) There is no such thing as super-realism. (The surrealists have managed to put on a pretty good vaudeville act for the middle-class; *but there isn't a religious man among them.*)

(38) Reality begins in the dream.

(39) Art must become anonymous.

(40) Reality must be explored—not explained or fought over.

(41) The great writer will take a heroic stand against literature: *by changing the nature of what is to be done,* he will be the first to do what the voice of dreaming does; he will heal the hurt where God's hand pressed too hard in His zeal to make us more than the animals.

(42) We must go into the silence where our own speech can be heard.

(43) Not to seek, but to accept; not to gain, but to lose; for what we cannot have is the only accessible thing in the world. The epic begins when a man leaves his house—not when he is throwing the boards of it together.

(44) The criminal does not search for a beautiful prison; he wants only a reason for his crime—the uglier and more horrible the better. We must *understand* our sense of guilt: the guilt itself is a disease of God for which we cannot be held accountable.

. . . I break off here in the report because someone is knocking at the door downstairs . . .

No one. No one there. But I found a smear of blood down the steps and somebody seemed to be moaning off in the night . . . *I am afraid that they will kill me.*

AUGUST 25 ⚜ I run my fingers over her throat. I feel the little bodies of words pushing out.

"Albion."

"Yes, Beth . . ."

"Do you really love me?"

"With all my heart."

The bitter voice of a foghorn speaks on the river.

"Albion."

"Huh?"

"What are you thinking of?"

308

"Nothing. Nothing much. I was only wondering how it should happen that those who are blind can dream exactly as we do."

"What do you mean?"

"I mean that dreaming they can see all the images which their eyes have not seen."

"That is curious."

"Curious? It's religion enough to make a hundred Christs."

‖‖‖

AUGUST 26 🜨 Tomorrow I shall be in Galen.

I feel the quiet strength of my skull.

One man sets a trap, another is snared; one man is damned, another is saved; one man kills his fellows, another himself; one man boasts in the temple, another weeps in his cell ... O may the neck of God feel this embracing noose! Aye, putting salt where the hurt is. Not that I am pure, but that I love purity; not that I am on fire, but that I love those whose souls feed the flames ... What profit it Thou to torture poor coots like me—nodding at the windows of this twilight Death. Prophetess of our night, make me clean; O terrible Mother, put my two burnt eyes in a terrorless face. Cold and dark and covering pain ... this cheating shadow ... sour jades of hell dirty my bed. Christ bless the minstrels of defeat. The snorting of humans caught in their own foul nets; the humming bodies locked together like stuck-dogs in the slums. I'll write my name in stars across your world. What is this beautiful covenant between us ... The hunter always has the face of the thing he tracks. O womb-chilled supplication. The whore's child is seated on my throne ... unceasingly ... *a laughing-stock* ... it's a bad messenger who has his head cut off. There can be no scaffolding for the dwelling I would build. I require nothing from you. Give me a double-malted and a Eucharist with cream cheese and jelly. I shall not awaken the world at all. I shall not lift up the eyes of these sick bastards. Without light, without HOPE ... ah, ah, *ah* I am the tower and the peace the midwet blooming god of hosts and the world is rusty-toothed and runnable an old bag of dead tricks swimming in a bog of pus so take her to bed, my lad, and make your own mythology I'm not speaking of course of Mary the mother of God and all points west I am yelling at the roof of me I don't know what I'm saying I'm only another quack I'm rapacious modest frugal celebrated droll audacious wicked sly worthless vigorous clever pitiless handsome ungainly gentle unreasonable sluggish determined reckless lasting serviceable unclean foul brittle ingenuous sick detestable hideous fertile gay sad massive irresistible weary ardent boundless real frantic miraculous callous insolent offensive delicate aristocratic spry extraordinary prodigious enormous meek barren unpolished wise taciturn matchless unruly empty extravagant dull corrupt chaste I am not guilty

THE GUILT IS GOD'S

Crenelate me, Jesus! An intonation from the grave. Do you feel jocund, brother? Ain't it offal? The pyrography of events. Tosspot. My sin-offering. What a gallimaufry of desires! Many were the dead. The bright sticky-still boys. Curse my unlucky talent. The biting blades of creation. Sit me in the sluggish mud. Let Alfa piss till Omega run dry. The howling of the emptied rabble. I am going to get in there sometime. Pretty dung of angels. My farewell to the maidens. God's daughter tosses under me. I always loved. Rutting up all the plump babes. What a rearing! O joyous jousting—a 2 dollar bill for your thoughts, my Lucy. No dallying. Sometimes a man wants more than any man ever got. Next, the horse's labyrinthine skull: fffug—shit on my divided ruin. I set out one day BLUG who violates whom? Joe Grace Tim. Like vomit. The night whereon you tell me not to enter. I was a little kid once. I didn't want to shove anything into anybody. It's fun to do it. But where does it get you? Love? It's nice to get into bed with any pretty anybody. If God made it to be all right who the hell are you (sweet sly little tail) to deny me? Give a man enough and he won't want to conquer any (there are two ways to spell it) countries. Jack-a-Lent, are we everyone. A malapropism altogether. Petrography of our miserable tombs. Have you seen Rhadamthus plain? I give you complete *bonus* for your misgivings. I defecate on your fee-faw-fums. Bed your giglet. The Boanerges! O oscillated despair. What shall be the ultimate hecatomb of our flabby race! The final, dreary menopause of our aims . . . This pyretic wish . . . Eat your rout-cake and be of grisly cheer. I am not a paraclete exactly. A punchinello. Am I to become the immunologist for all mankind . . . Don't show me your gonococcus! Carcinoma—O you've got one. I am religious (discordant, no?). What will your kamarupa be like? Overlook my gaucherie. Ormazd, protect us! (The automorphistic cataclysm.) Pansphygmograph, save us! Rejoice. Wild wives make for tame wedlock—without horns and horning. Ho! for the driving bone . . . she was not hurt, was never hurt, no, she never found it ill to lie under the going pump and the hot sweet holding push of me. Throw up the fire, get the bed wide with your moving—I'll be there soon, chick: when I've put the armies back to their heads. Proud full softfirm-assed bird—Lord God! I know the very thing to do to you. Give it to me before we get older. All this thick night . . . as I said before and as I say now, I want it where I find it and it's always good. Strong is the male for his lassie, strong to get and go to sleep. Not for me the woman who opens to all men like an idiot eating flies. I want to know what goes into love, not what has gone in and out of it. Pleasure is a lonely thing. The sun spins his golden top on the water. I go like a swearing ghost above these graves. O bonny love . . . Come blood and steel rain down on our houses. I call upon my proper schooling. The caressing heart. All carnivorous wombs. You won't buy peace in Paddy's Market. Yonder goes the ratting somniloquist. This mollescent filth *(ab uno disce omnes)*. O celestial razzle-dazzle. The fast cattle under guns . . . my alabaster ass . . . devirginated slim bitches (luxurious bowman) (great harts roam through heaven) (shifting mirrors) (go, my cuddlebug, soft tree without fruit) peek-a-boo (my vegetable hate) (A piece of tail—lest I find the ocean in my dream) *crux*

311

criticorum: genus irritabile vatum: to kalon: monumentum aere perennius (put me in the tomhouse). My melenemesis wound! The shrouded radiance . . . passive . . . humble . . . harnessed flesh

SYNCOPATED ecstasy
I DO NOT BELIEVE IN
DEATH
horror— I pr $41X^2$ will

||||||||||||||||||||||||||||||||||||||||||||||||||||||||||||||||||||||||||||||||||||||||||||||||||||||||||||||

AUGUST 27 ⚓ A savagely cold moon shines down on me as I move across the deep meadow which leads to the house of the Savior. I am no longer afraid. I shall not be lost ever again.

White slabs of living marble border my path. They gleam like teeth in the fat, sorrowful light. I think of the mocking headstones which mark the graves of the mad and the hunted.

This is what I have reached . . .

I hurry; stumbling and sobbing that all the pain will soon be done. The thick watermoon tosses on the curved horns of cloud.

Splintered throats of angels drip their wounded blood on the highroad where the stars walk.

The shine of the moon is fish.

Small eyes looking out of me. The rustle of my mouth in the shadow cast by this time . . .

I can see the house now. As I watch, jabbering like an idiot, all the lights go on, and in every window—glory to God!—the face of Christ looks out.

I am going to speak to Him.

He is smiling. He beckons.

I run ... with all the terror at my heels.

THE DOGS!

The dogs leave their places behind the great stones.

Horrible teeth tearing at my flesh. I taste my blood in their slavering mouths.

Dying I see the house of the Redeemer go dark.

Then ...

Now I seem to be standing aside. It is not my body on the ground there. I look at the mangled corpse of Albion Moonlight with indifferent pity.

It is not me they have killed.

Don't you understand! I have arisen not from the dead but from the *living*. It is my own face I see in the blazing windows of all the houses on earth.

There is no darkness anywhere. There are only sick little men who have turned away from the light.

God is seeing.

My eyes are watching you.

But I must tell you that what I have said is not true.

This is all a damn lie. The real truth is ...

What the hell do I care! Go bury your head in a pile of old bones. Get out of my way!

I am going to ... I am ... *What am I going to do?*

There is no way to end this book.

No way to begin